# 7 SYKOS

# 7 SYKOS

## MARSHEILA ROCKWELL
## AND JEFFREY J. MARIOTTE

HARPER

VOYAGER
IMPULSE

*An Imprint of HarperCollins Publishers*

EPub Edition JANUARY 2016 ISBN: 9780062434913

Print Edition ISBN: 9780062434920

10 9 8 7 6 5 4 3 2 1

*This book is dedicated to the ones we love.*

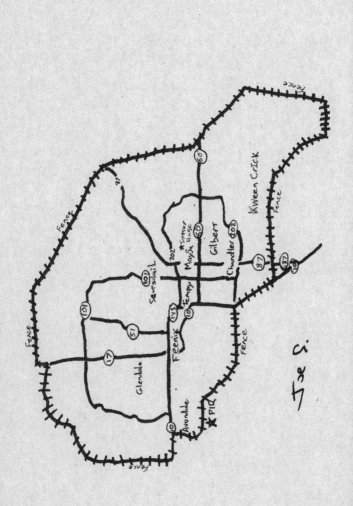

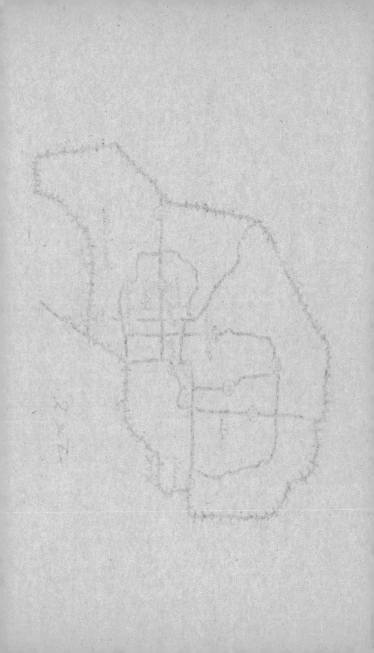

"The mind is its own place, and in itself
Can make a heav'n of hell, a hell of heav'n."

JOHN MILTON, *PARADISE LOST*

"We serial killers are your sons, we are
your husbands, we are everywhere."

TED BUNDY

"Every man has his passion; some
like whist, I prefer killing people."

RUDOLPH PLEIL

# PART I

# THE FENCE

PART 1

THE FENCE

**CHAPTER 1**

*132 hours*

The rig was state-of-the-art; Light's partner was not.

He would have expected it if Beverly Carson were an FNG—fucking new guy, or in this case, girl—but she was, in fact, an old-timer, and set in her ways. Light had been dispatched with her a couple of times before, when both their regular partners had been off on the same day for one reason or another. They had never gotten along, and each resented the other when they were forced together.

This one was a chest-pain call in central Tempe. The ambulance service covered the whole southeast quadrant of the Phoenix metro area, so Light and Bev had been dispatched after reporting back from a call in Chandler. The patient was female, sixty-two, and built like a bird. Light could have lifted two of her by himself. She presented conscious but complaining of sharp, excruciating chest pain, radiating to her back, neck, and jaw. She had fainted, which was when her daughter called 9-1-1, but she was awake and alert now. Her lung sounds were fine: clear and equal. The patient's mother had died of a heart attack in her fifties, and her husband had done the same just three years earlier. She was terrified of it happening to her.

"You're going to be fine, ma'am," Light told her. "Can you lie down on the stretcher, so I can check your abdomen?"

She shook her head with a vigor that surprised him. "It hurts when I lay down."

"It hurts now, right?"

"Gets worse, though. *Much* worse."

"What's your name, ma'am?" he asked. He already knew it, but wanted her to say it. He didn't think she had forgotten her own name, but some patients were reassured by the knowledge that they hadn't.

"Eugenia. Eugenia Kerr."

"I'm Hank Light, Mrs. Kerr," he said. "Don't worry, I'll take good care of you." He flashed the smile that had calmed the nerves of hundreds of patients.

Sometimes right before he killed them.

**B**ev had wanted to take her to a STEMI center. She insisted that the twelve-lead electrocardiogram showed evidence of a massive acute myocardial infarction, and her family history suggested the same. Light had to point out the subtle differences on the ECG pattern between an AMI and what she was showing—the concave ST segments, the PR depression in several of the leads.

"Besides," he argued, "the chest pain is worse when she's supine. It's pericarditis—probably with pericardial effusion, maybe tamponade. She could die if we don't get her into an ER, and there's one eleven minutes closer than the nearest STEMI center, so quit arguing and drive."

He had kept taking serial ECGs and transmitting them to the Tempe St. Luke's Emergency Department. The ED had confirmed Light's diagnosis, which had finally made Bev shut up. But Light could tell that his partner was still steaming, even after they had offloaded Mrs. Kerr, and she'd been whisked behind the double doors toward the OR. Bev stood in front of a snack machine just outside the waiting room, staring at the glass as if it held the answers to every question ever asked, her hands jammed into her uniform pockets.

"We should head back," Light said.

"Give me a few."

Light strolled back into the waiting room. Mrs. Kerr had still been conscious and lucid when they'd arrived; her life would be affected by her condition, and she might need open-heart surgery, if there was bleeding into the pericardium, as Light suspected. But she would likely live for years, and her quality of life would not be so degraded that she needed the special services

Light offered on appropriate occasions. He was a hell of a paramedic, and he saved lives all the time. But that was SOP for first responders. What he provided that most didn't was a quick, merciful end when it was called for. Others in his profession—throughout the medical community—were too often afraid of death. They didn't see it as the ultimate mercy.

Light knew better.

Everywhere he went, he encountered people who would be happier dead. Just that morning, he had passed a homeless old woman, sitting with her back propped against a traffic-signal post, a scrawny mutt tugging on the frayed rope that held him close. Somehow, she had scraped together enough coin to buy a marker—or she had shoplifted it—and she'd found a hunk of dirty cardboard, but her resourcefulness had not gone so far as to learn how to spell. He could see scabs on her face and neck as he drove by, and an angry purple scar on her shin. What purpose did she serve, to herself, that dog, or anyone else? How much better off would she be if she went to sleep for good rather than waking up in some desert wash or back alley and facing another day of breathing in exhaust fumes and getting melanoma from the bright desert sun?

Why would anyone want to go through life crippled, or suffering from dementia so bad, they couldn't remember their own name, or the faces of their loved ones? What joy could a blind and deaf person take from life? Who would truly rather live through the agonies of chemotherapy, or be kept alive by tubes and machines, than embrace the peace of eternal sleep?

Hank Light saw clearly where others did not. And he not only understood, but he was benevolent enough to do something about it.

He knew what they called people like him. *Angels of death.* They meant it as an epithet, but he wore it with pride. Death offered release from agony, and angels were here to help people. Angel of death, angel of mercy—the results mattered more than the vocabulary. There were no negative connotations to the title, as far as he was concerned.

The ER waiting room was packed. A young Hispanic couple sat on the floor, a blanket over the woman's chest as she nursed an infant. A heavy-set guy in a black-and-red plaid shirt and baggy shorts was leaning against a column as blood seeped out from beneath a ragged bandage just above his knee. Kids were sitting two and three to a chair, if they were skinny enough. Most of them, he guessed, were here because of the influenza epidemic sweeping the metro area. He saw a lot of red, puffy eyes and angry rashes on the cheeks, both precursor symptoms to the full-fledged onslaught. People sniffled and coughed, wheezed and hacked.

As he surveyed the scene, he heard a woman sitting alone—despite the crowd, the chairs on either side of her were empty, probably because of the rank miasma rising from her—muttering in a nonstop, nonsensical monotone. " . . . praise be to God and the merciful baby Jesus and the Holy Ghost, for the Great Tribulation is upon us, as described in the Book of Revelation, brought first by the crowned rider on the white horse. And Wormwood shall fall upon us and the land shall shudder and quake and the beast shall appear with the horns of a lamb and the voice of a dragon, and upon him shall be the mark . . ."

Light moved away, as repulsed by the stink of her as by her inane ramblings. She believed in another life after this one. Light had seen enough death to know that it wasn't a new beginning but an end to suffering, a release from pain, and a rest unlike any other, from which there would be no waking.

A different speaker caught his attention, this one a pale-skinned man, mid-forties maybe, with a bushy red beard and runaway eyebrows. He was talking to two younger women, who regarded him as if he were sharing the essential truth of the universe. " . . . the end of days," he was saying. "That meteor was a sign. A portent, if you will. And this bullshit 'flu' epidemic? When was the last time you saw a flu so virulent, one that spread as quickly as this one? I tell you . . ."

Light kept going, not interested in apocalyptic theories. The meteor the man had mentioned had broken up in the atmosphere above Phoenix. Meteors did that from time to time, around the world, but it had never spelled doomsday.

Hoping Bev had cooled down, he glanced toward the nook where the vending machines were hidden.

No such luck. Still roaming, Light found himself over by the glass double doors when an older man hurried in, wrinkled and worried, holding what must have been his wife by the arm. The left side of her face, from above the brow to mid-cheek, was bandaged, and the look on what Light could see of her was agonized. Her eyes were swollen almost closed, and her cheeks blazed a vibrant red. Curious, he trailed them to the admissions desk.

"Listen," the man said, before the sleepy clerk could even speak. "Rochelle was in here about twelve, thirteen hours ago. You folks stitched her up just fine, but now she's sick. She can't sleep, she's in a lot of pain, and she's got this bad flush on her cheeks. You think she could've been exposed to something here? Or maybe her stitches are infected?"

"What was she seen for earlier?" the clerk asked.

"Doorbell rang in the middle of the night," the man said. "Rochelle looked out that peephole, you know, and it was Margaret Blaine, the neighbor from across the hall. In her nightgown. Rochelle opened the door, and Margaret just lit into her."

"Lit into, in what way?"

"Scratching and clawing like a feral cat. I had to lay her out with a baseball bat just to get her off Rochelle. She's probably here somewhere, too, but we didn't stay around to see what became of her."

"I'll need your wife's name and date of birth," the clerk said. She shoved a pad across the counter toward the man. "Fill out the top part of this."

The man released Rochelle's arm and reached for the pad. The instant he did, Rochelle bolted. Her husband's spin toward her was almost in slow motion. His hand reached out and closed on empty air, his eyes went wide, his mouth dropped open.

But she had already pounced on a young, pregnant woman, sitting next to what must have been the baby's father, their joined hands resting on the substantial bulge of her stomach. When Rochelle landed, those hands flew apart, the young lady's pinned beneath Rochelle's weight.

Before the father-to-be could react, Rochelle had shaped her hands into claws and started digging into the mother's face. A fingernail snagged the corner of her left eye and ripped down, opening a gash. Both father and mother screamed as blood streamed down her cheek. Hissing like a steaming teapot, Rochelle jammed her nails into the tear she had made and pulled, as if intending to tug off the side of the young lady's face.

Finally, the father gained his feet and acted, punching Rochelle hard enough to dislocate her jaw. The older woman hit the floor. Her stitches had torn open, and blood splashed the tiles around her, from her wound as well as from her hands and the young mother's ruined face. Light saw a couple of pudgy security guards finally hustling toward the scene—one wiping chocolate from his fingers onto his uniform pants—and figured they would put Rochelle in cuffs, and that would be the end of it.

He was wrong.

It was only the beginning.

The room erupted in a howling riot of unbridled carnage.

The bearded man who had been lecturing about the end of days was on the floor, one of the young women subjected to his diatribe beside him, bashing his skull again and again on the tiles.

The nursing mother clawed at the soft spot on her baby's scalp as its father tried to hold her back, but then she turned on him, and the infant fell to the floor, its cries unheeded.

The guy with the injured leg had caught up to Rochelle's husband and was smashing the old man's head against the edge of the counter over and over. The older man was already dead, but the big guy didn't stop until skin and skull were cracked, and brain matter tinged with blood leaked out. Then he sat cross-legged on the floor with the man in his lap and started scooping out brains with his bare hands, shoveling them into his mouth and growling at anyone who ventured near.

Light was fascinated by the tableau playing out before him. Some of those doing the attacking, like Rochelle and the big man eating her husband's brains, had clearly suffered recent injuries. Others had not, but he couldn't tell, through the frantic motion and showers of blood, who might have been showing symptoms of the flu, or of any other illness, before chaos broke out.

He wasn't sure he quite cared at this point.

*Where is Bev?* he wondered. He didn't have to like her to know that if things got too hairy, it wouldn't hurt to have her at his back.

He started toward the vending machines, but before he had made it three steps, a woman who had seemed to be sleeping—or dead—sprang from her chair and lunged at him. Light tried to stiff-arm her, but despite her small stature, her strength was ferocious. Her arms were a whirlwind of motion, her hands like claws, and as she snapped and snarled, spittle flew from her mouth, wetting Light's face. He got some in his mouth, and spat.

Then someone else was on him, attacking from behind. A strong hand grabbed his shoulders, and an arm snaked around his neck. Already off-balance from the first attacker, he went down on one knee. The one behind him—a man in his fifties, Light judged when he saw the guy, with wire-rimmed glasses, short hair, and the mild look of a clergyman or an accountant—released his shoulder and ripped at his face, opening a wound there. The man was wounded himself, and blood from his forehead dripped into Light's cut as he tried to dig deeper into Light's flesh.

As if encouraged or enraged by the sight of blood, the woman came at him again. She raked her nails across his cheek, taking skin with them. She wasn't working in concert with the man, Light was sure. They both seemed to want the same thing—judging by the guy he'd seen earlier, Light's brains—but their attacks were not coordinated. It was as if each was un-aware of the other's presence.

He hoped he could use that to his advantage.

Light pushed to his feet and stomped down on the man's insole, putting all of his strength into it. He felt bones give under his boot, and the man's grip loosened. Light spun, grabbed the man's shirt, and swung him around into the woman. They both fell to the ground and discovered the squalling baby, whom they immediately began fighting over. Light backed away and resumed his search for his partner, a little more urgently this time.

Heading for the vending machines again, he saw the woman who had been praying and ranting about the Great Tribulation. She lay on the floor, glassy-eyed, blood seeping from several head wounds. She wasn't dead; her breathing was ragged, her extremities twitching. Not dead yet, but soon, and mercifully so. Light brushed back his bangs and glanced at the waiting room's cameras, ensured that none would show her on the floor, and knelt beside her. When he closed his hands over her mouth and pinched her nose shut, awareness returned to her eyes. But only for a few moments; and then she was blessedly still.

When Light rose again, Bev was emerging from the nook. "Light, we've to get out of here!" she cried.

"Just been waiting on you," he answered calmly. He stepped over the corpse on the floor and headed toward his partner.

She was a solidly built woman, five-nine or -ten, two hundred pounds easy. She outweighed Light by at least twenty-five, probably more. He was on the lean side, for an EMT, but with the upper-body strength necessary to do the job.

He hoped she could fight. He had a feeling he'd find out.

But before he could reach her, a teenage boy jumped onto her back. He was wiry—all limbs—attacking with such ferocity that Bev couldn't shake him. The boy got a grip on the right side of her mouth, then buried a finger in her left eye. Gelatin-like aqueous and vitreous humors mixed with blood slicked Bev's cheek, and her wail was audible even over the rest of the din.

That was enough for Light. More than. He darted out the front door and into the nighttime darkness. The chaos outside was even worse than what he'd just left. He heard sirens approaching, helicopter blades chopping the air, but they were too late. Safely inside the rig, it occurred to him that whatever virus was racing through the Valley of the Sun, it was no flu. He cranked the motor, and the rumble of the Mercedes Sprinter TraumaHawk's V-6 brought him comfort. As he pulled away from the hospital, he saw people blocking the drive. His headlights showed their flushed cheeks and puffy eyes and the hungry way they looked at him, and he stepped on the gas.

He barely felt the impacts as the Sprinter mowed them down.

# CHAPTER 2

*96 hours*

Breakfast for Fallon O'Meara was a slice of whole-wheat toast with almond butter and some plain Greek yogurt with blueberries and wheat germ stirred in, accompanied by a small glass of orange juice and a mug of a dark-roast coffee. Sometimes she added a poached egg or a slice of cantaloupe, but not on this morning. Running late because Mark had silenced the alarm and left her sleeping, she was acutely aware of every passing minute. She'd been pulling twelve- or thirteen-hour days lately, which was why Mark's impulse had been not to wake her. But she was working so much because there was so much to do—research, administrative work, HR tasks, all of it on her back—so getting to the lab late meant staying that much later in the evening. Not that she really minded; at least at the lab she felt needed.

Jason would be three in six weeks, which meant it had been three years since Mark had worked outside the home. He did okay doing silk-screening out of the garage—enough to pay for the diaper service and other assorted child-oriented expenses—but she resented his lack of ambition sometimes. She had tried to encourage him to put Jason in day care and go back to work, at least a couple of days a week, but he had been steadfast in his insistence that he wanted to be with Jason every day until the boy started kindergarten. Fallon admired his dedication, but she thought he had forgotten a thing or two about keeping a regular work schedule. Like the part about its being regular. Income wasn't a huge issue, though more was always nice. But she worried that he was leaving adulthood behind; as Jason gradually matured, Mark slowly regressed, and the two would meet in the middle.

The kitchen was particularly chaotic this morning. On the countertop flat-screen, morning news talking heads wore their serious faces as they discussed the worsening flu epidemic. "Authorities," one said, "are advising people to stay out of the Valley altogether, if possible. If you can't, they're asking you to keep out of this area. Take a look at your screen, now."

Fallon glanced toward it. The well-coiffed anchor was pointing toward a zone marked in bright red on a map, stretching from Mesa to Avondale, Deer Valley to the north and Chandler to the south. *So yeah*, she thought, *pretty much the whole Valley*. At least home and the lab were both outside it.

The anchor said something else, but Fallon couldn't hear it. Mark and Jason were playing some sort of game that involved stuffing Cheerios into their mouths, then making funny faces at each other. Mark bugged out his eyes and raised his eyebrows what seemed like half-way up his forehead—that expanse exaggerated by all the hair he'd lost in the last couple of years, which he claimed was a sign of virility—and Jason laughed so hard that Cheerios blew out onto the table, and she worried he'd fall out of his booster seat.

And no doubt choke to death on more Cheerios.

Of course, that was always the direction her thoughts went. Fallon was the analytical one whose mental path inevitably veered toward the most disastrous possible outcome. If Mark ever worried, about *anything*, she didn't see it.

She multitasked her way through the meal, spooning in yogurt and munching on toast while checking messages and texts on her phone, glancing at the TV screen now and again, and trying to look like she saw the boys' game as something more than medical bills in the making. It was difficult, though, since her preferred hospital for Jason was Phoenix Children's, and that was almost smack-dab in the middle of the "danger zone."

*Stop obsessing*, she mentally chastised herself. *He's going to be fine.*

She turned back to her phone. Among the usual

work-oriented semi-crises, she had two urgent "Call me!" texts from Gloria Upjohn. She soaked in the kitchen's decibel level for a few seconds, then decided she would call Gloria from the car. When she was finished with her breakfast, she stacked her dishes in the sink, where Mark might or might not deal with them during the course of the day, and went upstairs to the master bath for final prep.

Five minutes later, she returned to the kitchen, purse and briefcase in hand. Mark and Jason had switched to peekaboo, hiding their faces behind cloth napkins. "I'm going," she said. Jason laughed uproariously. Not at her, at Mark. "I'm going now," she said, louder.

Mark turned to her. "Kiss," he said.

She leaned forward, kissed him. He broke it off before she was ready and swiveled his head back toward their son, mumbling something that she guessed was a wish for her to have a good day. That wish seemed unlikely to be granted.

She didn't know then just how bad the day would be.

" . . . flu epidemic continues to spread. Medical researchers from the Centers for Disease Control are in the Valley to study the strain, in hopes of determining its origin and hopefully arriving at a vaccine. Meanwhile, Valley hospitals report record—"

Fallon punched the radio's POWER button because she heard Gloria pick up her phone.

"Hello?"

"Hi, Gloria."

"Fallon! Thank God."

Fallon didn't like the sound of that. "What is it?"

"I saw him. Elliott."

Fallon had to fight to keep her Volvo in the lane. Offhandedly, she noticed that traffic was heavy, with lots of military and law-enforcement vehicles heading toward Phoenix. But she was focused on her call—on Elliott—and paid them scant attention. "Where?"

"Downtown. I had an early meeting at the Hyatt Regency. He was eating breakfast in the café there. The Terrace Café, I think it's called."

"With who?"

"Alone. His back was to me most of the time, but I'm sure it was him."

Fallon pictured the back of her partner's head. He grew his hair long in back—long for him, though not quite to the length at which he could wrap a rubber band around it and call it a ponytail. It curled, though, and the most distinctive curl was right at the center of his head, in back. Fallon had always wanted to yank on it. Gloria had only worked at the lab for six months, in its early days, when they were still struggling to find funding. But Elliott hadn't changed much, physically, over the last few years. If Gloria thought she'd seen him, she probably had.

"I'm surprised he's still in the state," Fallon said. "Much less in town."

"Maybe he can't get out. Flights are still—"

"Yes, right." Air travel out of Phoenix had been curtailed a couple of days ago, in hopes of limiting the spread of the flu virus. People could still choose to fly into the city, but not many did.

"Anyway, I thought you should know."

"Thanks, Gloria. I don't have time to check it out right now, but I will as soon as I can. I appreciate the call."

"Of course. I know you've been looking for him."

She paused there, as if hoping to be filled in on why Fallon was looking for him. That wasn't happening, though. Fallon was not telling Gloria, whom she considered a good friend. She wasn't telling *anyone*.

After all, what could she say? "He stole our only prototype of MEIADD—Miniature Encephalographic Imaging/Analysis/Dampening Device—which we spent years developing so that we could identify and possibly treat psychopathy in people, and I *have* to get it back?" That would mean admitting that MEIADD even existed in the first place, which she didn't want to do yet . . . especially not until they came up with a less clunky acronym. They pronounced it "May-add," but even lab personnel sometimes struggled with it.

Anyway, it wasn't really theirs. Once they had provided proof of concept, government grants had begun to roll in. That R&D money had sped the process up considerably, but the catch was that the government had a claim to the final product and the associated research. That didn't mean they couldn't eventually develop alternate versions for civilian use, but for now, she and Elliott were only MEIADD's keepers, not its owners.

Or rather, Elliott was its keeper, since he had absconded with the prototype. And the key that activated it. Sure, she could make a new one, but that would take time she couldn't spare.

Instead of letting that all out in a rush, Fallon wished her friend a good day—aware even as she said it how vague it was, how much like Mark's parting comment—and ended the call. She was almost at the lab, anyway. From her home in Maricopa, it was only a twenty-minute drive in the worst of traffic. She turned the radio on again, expecting more flu news.

Instead, the news anchors were talking about Kim Kardashian's butt, a viral video of a cat drinking milk from a bottle, a self-driving car, and a baby born with two front teeth. She switched to another local news station and found mostly the same sort of thing. No mention of the flu, for what seemed like the first time in days.

Had the outbreak ended? During the time she'd been on the phone with Gloria? That was impossible.

*Something* had changed, though.

She didn't have time to figure it out. The gates of the Maricopa Neuroscience complex were dead ahead. Fallon slowed for the electronic verification, and the gates parted for her, swinging inward. As soon as she was through, they would swing shut quickly and without pause—nobody piggybacked into this place.

They didn't want any surprises.

And yet that's exactly what she found. The parking lot—usually almost empty at this time of day—contained three Maricopa County Sheriff's Office SUVs, two black Escalades with heavily tinted windows, and a pair of sand-colored military Humvees. They were all bunched up near the main entrance to the lab and office structure, parking-space lines ignored.

Fallon parked—inside the lines, unlike her surprise visitors—draped her ID lanyard around her neck, grabbed her purse and briefcase, and stormed toward the building. It was two stories, a stucco adobe-look pseudo-Santa Fe style structure with a flat roof and vigas sticking out just below it. She waved her keycard at the reader, and the doors opened with an audible electronic thump.

The lobby was full of uniforms. Sheriff's officers, military officers and a couple of grunts, and four men and a woman in crisp, dark business suits. The men wore ties. Two of them had sunglasses on.

The oldest of the suits came toward her, one hand extended and the other holding a leather wallet. The woman followed close behind.

"Dr. O'Meara?" he said. He was in his forties, maybe, with some grey just beginning to fleck his thick, dark hair. He looked solid under his suit. Something that might have been mistaken for a smile touched his lips, then was gone. "I'm Special Agent Guzman." He flipped the wallet open long enough for her to catch a glimpse of an FBI badge, spread-winged eagle on top.

Fallon glanced at the woman, who stood behind Guzman's elbow, silent and without expression. There to catch Fallon if she fainted, maybe, or to Tase her if she tried to run.

"Yes, I'm Dr. O'Meara. What can I do for you?"

"We need you to come with us."

"Come where?"

"With us."

"That's all you're giving me?"

"We need you to come with us, Doctor."

"Am I under arrest?"

"No, ma'am."

"What if I decline your invitation?"

"I'm afraid that's not an option."

Fallon shrugged, then turned to the reception desk. Nora sat behind it, a helpless expression on her face. "I'm sorry," the receptionist mouthed. Fallon just shook her head to indicate it wasn't the other woman's fault. "Nora, please let everybody know what's happened. Apparently, I'll be late to work today."

## CHAPTER 3

*96 hours*

**F**allon sat in the backseat of Guzman's Escalade. The woman, who had eventually introduced herself as Special Agent Barksdale, sat beside her. In the front passenger seat was an agent who had not been introduced, one of the men who wore his sunglasses inside. *And probably at night, too,* she thought.

The other vehicles either led or followed, a mysterious convoy about which Barksdale and Guzman would answer no questions. Nor would they entertain any about where the convoy was going, or why. When Fallon asked Barksdale what she'd had for breakfast, hoping to discern some semblance of humanity, Barksdale's response was, "Coffee. Black. Strong."

"Probably why you're such a chatterbox," Fallon said.

Barksdale said nothing.

The ride wasn't long. They drove to the Gila River Memorial Airport, where, instead of entering a terminal, they headed directly onto the tarmac and stopped beside a helicopter, its blades turning lazily and flashing at they caught the morning sun. Guzman killed the engine, got out of the SUV, and opened Fallon's door.

She eyed the chopper. "You're kidding, right?"

"No, ma'am," he said.

"If you've done any research on me at all, you know I hate flying."

"Yes, ma'am."

"But you're going to make me get in that thing?"

"Yes, ma'am."

"They serve peanuts? Drinks?"

Guzman's flat expression didn't change.

"So it's just like flying commercial," Fallon said. "You're coming, too?"

"Yes, ma'am."

"Sit close," Fallon said. "If we crash, I'm landing on you."

This time, Guzman's smile was genuine and went all the way to the eyes, but it didn't stay much longer than the last. "Yes, ma'am."

**T**he military and law enforcement personnel stayed behind, but all the suits clambered aboard with Fallon. The flight was mercifully brief. They flew over South

Mountain, then up the next valley, following the path of what was still called the Gila River even though most of the year it was nothing more than a dry trench. Green saguaro dotted the hills, like ranks of soldiers marching across rock-strewn battlefields. As they neared civilization, the helicopter began to descend. Fallon was close to vomiting the whole time, from the motion and the uncertainty, even fear. And she was pissed. Guzman was unfailingly polite, the rest impassive, and nobody would tell her what this was all about. She tried her best not to show how she felt but worried that her trembling hands gave her away.

She wondered if they'd finally talk if she started throwing up.

As they dropped, she looked out the window at what seemed to be their destination. "PIR? Is there a race today?"

"No, ma'am," Guzman said. Somehow, he could speak loud enough to be heard over the propeller racket without sounding like he had raised his voice.

She wasn't going to learn anything from him, she decided. She hoped that the Phoenix International Raceway would be their last stop and not just a place to get into more cars.

She looked again. The first time, she had glimpsed something about the outline of the enormous raceway that wasn't familiar, that seemed wrong. It hadn't registered in that moment, through her relief that they were landing, her queasiness, and her anxiety. But then it sank in, and she focused this time just outside the raceway's high northern wall, where the grandstands were.

The Salt River flowed into the Gila just east of there, and the riverbed was deeper and wider. A high bridge arched across it, connecting the raceway to the southern stretches of Avondale and from there to the sprawling suburban/urban mass that was the Greater Phoenix Metropolitan Area. What didn't fit was all the activity on the north side of the bridge. Dropping ever lower, it became clear as her angle of view changed. Somebody—no, not somebody, *soldiers*—were building a massive fence, probably twenty feet high and stretching as far as she could see to the east and west. Beyond that was another fence, just as tall, and a third stood on the far side of that one. There was never any traffic out here except on race days. A handful of pickup trucks and banged-up cars were gathered on the outside of the fence, their occupants standing around talking. One of them kept gesturing angrily toward the barrier. Fallon wished she could hear what he was saying, but she thought she had a pretty good idea.

Then the chopper sank below the grandstands, settling to the ground with a couple of *thumps* that made her stomach lurch. They were in the center of the track, next to the small, fenced enclosure around the scoring tower.

Fallon turned to Guzman, who had indeed flown in the seat next to hers. "What are we—oh, never mind."

"Yes, ma'am," Guzman said. He was, she observed, beginning to enjoy this a little too much.

The door opened, and she unbuckled. Barksdale went out first, motioning for Fallon to follow. A couple of soldiers stood outside to help her down. At first, she was unsteady on her feet, despite the flight's brevity, but it only took a few moments to trust her balance, then she eyed her surroundings.

Soldiers were everywhere.

She had been to NASCAR races here a couple of times. Not that she was particularly interested, but Mark enjoyed them, and she had accompanied him twice before Jason was born. After that, she was content to let other friends go with him, people more tolerant of the noise and the crowds.

Even on the busiest race day, the place had never looked like this.

All over the track, and inside it, military vehicles were either parked or moving. Some of them were the familiar Humvees, but others were bigger, armored, and bristling with big guns or rocket launchers, and still others were oddly shaped trucks of various sizes. Soldiers, alone or in groups, moved here or there with what seemed to be serious intent. She saw people wearing familiar, colorful Hazmat suits, and others wearing similar getups but in military camouflage, gas masks hanging at their necks. A cluster of young men worked on some sort of structure, putting up the framework as she watched. Buses and trucks drove in from the outside, and more soldiers piled out, gathering to await their marching orders, she supposed. The grandstands were nearly empty, with just a few people sitting and watching the buzz of activity.

Fallon felt Guzman's presence at her left shoulder. "Well, we're here," she said. "What now?"

"You'll find out soon, Doctor," he replied before launching into one of his longest sentences yet. "I'll need any mobile devices you're carrying, and anything capable of storing data. Phone, iPod, flash drive, anything like that."

"You're joking," she snapped. Annoyed to indignant in no time flat.

"No, ma'am. You'll be entering a secure area."

"What if I say no?"

"I'm afraid that's not an option."

She hated the idea of handing over her property—it felt like surrendering her rights as a citizen. And she hated Guzman's "not an option" answer even more. But she had to admit her curiosity was piqued by all the fuss, almost enough to outweigh her growing anger. Reluctantly, she handed Guzman her smart phone. "That's all?" he asked.

"Well, my brain stores data, but you're not getting that. Everything else is at home or in the lab. Which you didn't let me get into."

"All right," Guzman said, seemingly willing to take her at her word. He pocketed the phone.

"I'll get it back when I leave here?"

"You'll get it back," he said. She noted that he had dropped the dependent clause but decided it wasn't worth fighting over. "General Robbins is waiting to meet you."

He gave a brisk nod and turned away. Before she could say anything, the suits formed a phalanx around her. Hot sun pressed down on the track and was thrown back up again, but after a couple of minutes, they were in one of the luxury suites overlooking turn two. She had heard about these suites but had never been in one. Maybe the races would have been bearable from inside those. The chill of powerful air-conditioning worked through her, making her back and shoulders twitch. Here, too, there were uniformed military personnel, along with more people in suits and ties, and some in shorts and T-shirts, more appropriate for the weather outside. Everybody wore ID badges, either clipped to their clothing or on lanyards, like hers. She noticed now that even the FBI suits who had escorted her inside had conjured them from somewhere and put them on.

Most people glanced at them and went back to what they were doing, but one soldier, tall and seemingly bald under his cap, strode toward them purposefully. He wore camouflage fatigues, like the other soldiers she'd seen, but he walked with an air of command, and when he came close, Fallon saw three stars mounted on a patch on his chest. Above his right breast were the words U.S. ARMY, and above the left, the name ROBBINS.

"Dr. O'Meara, I presume," he said, grinning like he had just made an original joke. "I'm Carter Robbins. Thank you so much for joining us."

He put his hand out, and she shook it, tentatively. His grip was firm enough to hurt. "Didn't seem like I had much choice, General."

"Carter, please, Doctor. We're a little too busy here to stand on ceremony."

"Busy doing what?" Fallon asked. "Building a military blockade of a major American city? Because that's what it looks like to me."

The general's head swiveled on his muscular neck, taking in the scene. "Let's go someplace quieter and have a chat. There's some folks here anxious to meet you."

"Me?"

He waved her toward a corridor. "This way. We've got a conference room all set up."

People wanting to meet her, and a conference room in a racetrack grandstand. She had figured this wasn't a spur-of-the-moment idea since all those people had been waiting for her at the lab this morning, and the helicopter had been ready to go. But it was starting to feel like a party to which everyone had been invited except her, only she was the guest of honor. Couldn't somebody have called and mentioned something?

In the hallway, the noise from the reception area was muted, and the lights, hidden behind textured glass, were dimmer. Recessed spotlights shone down on autographed photographs of drivers, some so famous even she had heard of them.

"There anything you need?" Robbins asked. "Coffee, tea, pastry?"

"Some water would be good, I guess."

"It's already in there." He stopped before a door, mostly frosted glass with some highly polished, reddish wood around it, cutting across at an angle on the hinge side, and a tall, brushed-steel pull bar. "Here we are," Robbins said. He paused with his hand on the door. "You're the woman of the hour, Doctor. I know it's all a little strange, but everything will be explained soon."

"Explanations would be wonderful, General."

"Carter," he corrected.

She didn't intend to be that familiar with him until she knew what was going on, and maybe not even then. Politeness dictated that she reciprocate, but to hell with that. As far as she was concerned, he could call her "Doctor" all day long.

He hesitated another moment, as if in expectation of the correction that wasn't coming, then pulled the door open and held it for her.

"Ladies and gentlemen," he announced as she entered, like he was a herald and she some sort of royalty. "Dr. Fallon O'Meara."

# CHAPTER 4

*95 hours*

Inside the room, a bevy of somber people sat around an enormous, highly polished, wooden conference table. Huge windows facing the track had been curtained off, the individual seats removed, and the table occupied the space where catering would normally have been set up. Some of those in attendance wore military uniforms, others civilian clothes. They were mostly male and mostly white, but not entirely either. General Robbins indicated a chair next to his head-of-the-table position. A legal pad and a pen had been neatly placed there, and a glass of ice water sweated beside them. Fallon stood behind the chair as Robbins hurried through the introductions. Names flew in and out of her head instantaneously; the overwhelming message she got was of government-agency titles and acronyms. She met the Assistant Secretaries of Defense for Health Affairs, for Homeland Defense and Americas' Security Affairs, and for Public Affairs, along with representatives of the National Center for Medical Intelligence and the CDC, DHS, FEMA, NSA, and FBI. The only person in the room she already knew was Jack Thurman, a DOJ official she had met through her government contracts. He was seated next to Special Agent in Charge Soledad Ramirez, who ran the Phoenix FBI office, and whom Fallon had at least heard of. She hoped she wouldn't have to learn the other names—that she'd sit here for a while, maybe answer some questions, then get to leave.

An empty whiteboard stood at the far end of the room. Fallon saw faded spots on the wall where pictures had hung, and in one corner, she spotted a stack of racing posters mounted on heavy board. Robbins, or whoever was in charge, had tried mightily to erase the vestiges of racetrack from the space but hadn't entirely succeeded in making it look like a high-level government conference room.

She wondered what was important enough to require such a serious environment and all the fuss to bring her into it.

"Please, Doctor," Robbins said when the introductions were finished. "Sit."

He moved to do so himself, so she pulled her wheeled chair back, parked herself in it, and rolled to the table.

"First of all, Dr. O'Meara, we apologize for the somewhat abrupt, unannounced nature of our invitation today. We've brought you here to ask you—" Robbins began.

She cut him off. "I'm not answering anything until *I* get some answers, General Robbins. What is all this about? What's with the big fences being built outside the raceway? Why are all these important people sitting around a table in Arizona?"

"In due time," Robbins said.

"No. Now, or I'm going back to work."

"This is a very sensitive matter," one of the various assistant SecDefs said. She had already lost track of which was which. "Highly classified. I don't think—"

"Look," Thurman interrupted. "If what we believe to be true really is, she'll need to know anyway. And even if it's not, I'm sure Dr. O'Meara will prove invaluable. Let's fill her in to the extent that we can, so she'll have some context for our questions and be able to provide more meaningful answers."

"What we discuss in here can't leave this room," Robbins warned.

"Fine," Fallon said.

"We'll have you sign a statement to that effect."

"Understood."

"Very well. Would you do the honors, Mr. Thurman?"

"Sure," Thurman said. "Fallon, you've heard about the flu epidemic in the Valley, right?"

"Of course."

"It's not the flu."

*No shit,* Fallon thought. She bit her lower lip to keep herself from saying it, and nodded. Clearly, though, her face showed what she thought of the rather obvious statement. To his credit, Thurman didn't seem embarrassed in the slightest.

"Yes. The thing is, we know that for certain now. What we don't know is what it *is*. It doesn't act like any viral infection known to medical science. We don't know if it's man-made, or what."

Kyle Billings, the NSA man, leaned forward.

"For our part," he said, "we're operating under the assumption that it's an act of terror, and we're responding appropriately. We're jamming all communications—every phone call, text, tweet, or e-mail, into or out of the Valley. We're screening every second of every video-surveillance recording we can get our hands on. As far as we're concerned, that's all SIGINT, and potentially valuable."

"Sig-what?"

"Signals intelligence," the man said.

"Ah."

"It could be terrorism, or it could be just a natural phenomenon," the woman from the CDC said. "The last Ebola outbreak in Africa started because a little boy played in a tree that had bats in it. Sometimes the most seemingly inconsequential acts can cause serious outbreaks. We have a few theories, but we haven't been able to pin down the origin of this one, though we're working on it day and night."

"Yet that would still only answer the *why*," Thurman said. "And it's not clear it even does that yet." Billings looked like he was about to respond, but Thurman cut him off. "As I noted, though, we are trying to determine the *what*—and that's what Dr. O'Meara really needs to focus on right now."

Fallon considered nodding, but she wasn't sure there was enough information to agree—or disagree—with anything at the moment.

One of the group's other women—one of the few African-Americans—spoke up. She was a representative from FEMA, Fallon recalled. Her voice was like aural honey. "Agent Thurman is right. Whatever the cause, Doctor—and it's important to find that out—our immediate concern is the effect. It's not a flu, but it *is* an epidemic. And it doesn't just make people ill. It makes them incredibly, uncontrollably violent."

She paused a moment, letting that sink in. Fallon had no response. "I know how this sounds," the woman continued. "But it's all documented. People infected with what we're calling the 'Crazy 8s virus' attack the uninfected. They try to bash open their skulls, so they can—don't laugh—eat their brains."

Despite the admonition, Fallon couldn't help but let out an involuntary bark of laughter, though she pulled it back before she broke down entirely. "Sorry," she managed. If she'd been upset about being dragged here before, now she was bordering on enraged. *This nonsense is why I'm locked in a room with all these people?*

And yet, no one else was laughing.

"Obviously, anyone whose brain is even partially consumed dies, from the cranial trauma. But those who are attacked without having their head opened up and their brains dug out become infected almost immediately—within a few hours, at most, and more often minutes or seconds. Because of this, we're theorizing that the virus is a blood- or fluid-borne contagion. And it is *incredibly* contagious. Maybe in the 99-percent range. Virtually everyone exposed to it contracts it."

"Why Crazy 8s?" Fallon asked. Other, more complex questions swirled in her thoughts, but she had to tease them out one by one to know how to even approach them, and finding out why they'd chosen to name a deadly virus after a child's card game seemed like a good place to start.

Robbins answered that one. "Because of a military preparedness plan that seems to fit this situation," he said. "CONPLAN 8888."

"Which is?"

"You'll see soon enough."

"You said—I'm sorry, I've forgotten your name."

"Virginia Johnstone," the CDC woman said.

"Virginia, you said that 'virtually' everyone exposed comes down with it. That means there are exceptions?"

"That's right," Robbins said. "*One* exception that we know of, to be precise. That's why you're here."

"I don't understand."

Robbins pushed his chair back from the table. "Let's take a walk," he said.

Pens and water glasses were placed on the polished wood, and the other people around the table stood up. Fallon did the same. "To where?"

"To the media center," Robbins said.

"Because?"

"You'll see."

**T**en minutes later, they were all seated at small desks in the media center. A wall of windows provided a bird's-eye view of the track. Mounted on the other walls were TV monitors, dark at the moment. The carpet was considerably less plush than in the grandstand suites, scarred by cigarette burns and stained by years of spilled drinks and dirty shoes.

When they were all settled, General Robbins said, "Roll it," to somebody in a control room, out of view. The screens flickered to life, and images began to appear. They showed surveillance video from various sources. Most had time-and-date stamps. Some offered strictly indoors views and others outside, some both. She saw the interior of a Circle K store, a sidewalk, a freeway, a mall, the inside of a bank. Fallon counted twelve different feeds, making it hard to focus on any one of them.

Almost at the same time—they had obviously been carefully cued up—people appeared on each screen. Then other people came into frame—these bloody, in most cases, their clothing torn and soiled. Without hesitation, they charged the other people, attacking with nails and teeth and fists. Fallon tried to pay attention to one screen, where the video had been shot from high above a bank of gas pumps. A car had pulled next to a pump, and the driver was gassing up his SUV when he was set upon by a woman with bloodstained cheeks and chin. Little remained of her light green shirt, and blood spattered her bust and bra. He fought back, even spraying gasoline at his attacker, but in the end her strength was too much. The driver was trying to clamber back into the driver's seat when she caught his neck and shoulders and hurled him to the pavement. He almost regained his feet, but she straddled him, grabbing his head in both hands and smashing it repeatedly on the pavement.

Fallon thought she could tell the moment he died, when he quit struggling and his eyes went blank. Blood spread beneath his head, a dark pool in the black-and-white footage. The woman kept at it until his skull was sufficiently pulped, then rolled him over and tore into it with both hands. Fallon had to look away, or lose what little breakfast she'd eaten.

A glance around the room told her that similar scenes were playing out on all the other monitors. The overwhelming impression was of a world gone mad with bloodlust. Fallon—who had once sat alone in a room for four hours with a man who had murdered his parents, his grandparents, and his three siblings, then had gone on to end the lives of fourteen more human beings, all women, with a knife, slicing off the tongue of each one and laying it carefully across her crotch—had never been so frightened in her life.

Robbins noticed that she was looking at the floor. "That's enough!" he called. "Cut it! All but eight, and freeze that."

The monitors went blank, except for one. A hand touched her shoulder, and she jumped. "I'm sorry, Fallon," Jack Thurman said. "I wanted to warn you, but they thought you should see it cold, like the rest of us did. In real time, some of us."

"It's . . . it's awful," she said. "Is it Flakka? Something like that?" Use of the synthetic drug was spreading around the country fast, and it had been known to make people paranoid, violent, and seemingly insane.

"It's far too widespread for that," Thurman said. "And it's incredibly infectious. You can't go nuts by being attacked by somebody using something like bath salts or gravel or some other new 'insanity drug.'"

Of course not, Fallon knew. She had blurted it out, an immediate gut response, without thinking it through. The whole situation—the government people, the chopper ride, the fence around the Valley—was all too bizarre, like a dream that seems to make sense until you wake up and realize it was disjointed chaos. It was getting in the way of rational thought. "They're . . . they're *zombies*."

"We don't use that word around here," Robbins corrected. "We call them 'Infecteds.' In the movies, zombies are reanimated corpses, but the Infecteds aren't dead. They're just, well, *changed*. We don't know yet, obviously, but it could be that with treatment, they can be changed back."

"They present very few outward symptoms," the woman from the CDC added. "Flushed, mottled cheeks. Puffy, bloodshot eyes. And an insatiable desire to consume human brains."

"And the savagery needed to kill people to get them," Robbins said.

"You said it's really contagious?" Fallon asked.

"More so than any virus we've ever seen," the woman said.

Fallon sat for a moment, trying to digest what she was seeing and hearing. There had been mention of a plan. Surely this whole setup was prelude to something. "What's going to happen?"

"We're going to nuke the place," Robbins replied.

"You can't just drop nuclear bombs on a major American city!"

"Watch me."

"There might be another answer," Thurman said, cutting off Fallon's retort. "Which is where you come in."

"This is all pretty far outside my area of expertise," Fallon said. Anyone's *expertise*.

"Not necessarily." Thurman crossed to the one monitor that still held a frozen image. On the screen, a short-haired, wiry guy in the uniform of a paramedic was looking almost right toward the camera. Blood had splashed his face, and his eyes looked a little mad. "See this guy?"

"Yes . . ."

"His name is Light. Hank Light."

"So?"

"We think he's immune. We've looked at hundreds of hours of video, collected eyewitness accounts, intercepted phone calls and texts by the score. This is the only person we've seen or heard about who's been exposed but not infected."

"Okay, that is intriguing. Still, not my field. You want to find out why he's immune? You need a geneticist, not a neuroscientist."

"We have a whole team of geneticists, studying every chromosome the guy's got. We're examining his blood, his urine, his skin and hair and teeth. That's not why we brought you here."

"What, then?" she asked.

"We think he's immune, Fallon. And we need his help. But he's not exactly cooperating."

"You're the guys with the guns," she said, not sure where he was going with this. "I'm a scientist, not a . . . I don't even know. Some kind of enforcer. Where do I fit in?"

"Actually," Thurman said, smiling slightly, "we think you're the perfect person to deal with him."

*Alice in Wonderland must have felt this way at that tea party,* she thought. None of this made any sense. "Why me?"

"Because we think he's a psychopath. And that's right up your alley."

**CHAPTER 5**

*95 hours*

**B**ooker Eisenstadt—"Book" to everyone he worked with at the NSA, whether he liked it or not—hugged the thick files he carried to his chest like they were armor against whatever he was about to face. He was a data analyst, and he guessed he probably looked the part, with his thick glasses and hair that Einstein might have envied. And he was damned good at what he did but still not the kind of essential personnel who normally got invited to attend meetings with three-star generals and higher-ups from other assorted alphabet agencies.

Well, "invited" probably wasn't the right word. More like "ordered." The kind of order whose refusal was usually met with the barrel of a gun.

Which in itself was surreal. He worked with computers—numbers, information, patterns. Gun-toting soldiers and nuke-dropping generals were *way* out of his purview.

Science, however, was not, and that's what he tried to focus on as he took a deep breath and entered the ersatz conference room.

There were only three people waiting for him when he stepped inside, which was something of a relief. General Robbins, Jack Thurman—to whom Book's services were temporarily "on loan"—and a slim, auburn-haired woman in a dress suit. She seemed outwardly calm, as though tête-à-têtes with people who could order surgical missile strikes were a common occurrence for her. But her eyes were constantly moving, from the men seated across from her, to the door, to a laptop on the conference table that was paused at the beginning of the Hank Light video, and finally to him.

She reminded him of a quiescent volcano, and while he would normally have considered her pretty, if a little too stressed-out for his tastes—maybe not surprising, given the circumstances—the wildness he sensed just beneath the surface gave him pause.

"Dr. O'Meara, this is Book Eisenstadt, our resident whiz kid," General Robbins said, as all three of them rose from their seats.

"Book?" she asked, raising an eyebrow at him.

"Booker, actually, but you know how it is with nicknames," he replied, sticking out his hand.

"Like gum on shoes," she said with a rueful twist

of her lips as she shook his hand. "And you can call me Fallon," she added, earning her a side eye from the general. In that instant, Book decided he liked her, highstrung and restless or not.

He gestured toward the laptop.

"They show you that yet?"

She shook her head. "I guess they were waiting for you."

"Well, I'm here now, so let's get started."

As the others sat, Book set his stack of files on the table and leaned over to push PLAY.

The video had been queued up right to the point where Light was being attacked in St. Luke's ER by two of the Infecteds, a man and a woman. He stomped on the man's foot and swung him into the woman, then moved on as the two began to claw at each other over something she couldn't see.

The angle switched as Light moved out of view of the camera, and this time it was his reflection in an array of glass windows they watched as Light knelt beside a woman on the floor. She was bleeding from several head wounds and looked half-dead already. After a quick glance to ensure he wasn't in direct view of the camera, Light covered her mouth and pinched her nose. The woman jerked involuntarily, as though trying to fight for that last breath he was stealing, but after a moment, she lay still, and Light was on his feet again, his reflection moving away from the windows and out of view.

Book stopped the video.

"So you think he's a psychopath because he ended some poor woman's suffering?" Fallon's tone was skeptical. "Is that all you've got?"

"Not by a long shot," Book answered.

He pulled out a sheaf of papers and handed them over to the doctor.

"Light's work history. He's had half a dozen EMT jobs and one as an orderly. You'll notice that at each, there were at least eight to ten unexplained deaths. All patients Light had access to, either in the ambulance or the hospital. All people who were seriously injured or extremely ill. Some were definitely terminal cases, but there were others doctors believed might have recovered if not for Light.

"He always left before anyone could start putting the pattern together, but it's right there once you have his complete employment records."

"Angels of death are hard cases to prove," Fallon said as she leafed through the file. "Their victims are already on death's door, and determining if someone gave them a shove over the threshold is no easy thing."

"There's more," Thurman said. "When he was picked up at the quarantine blockade, he was too calm, too collected. Other people who made it that far were screaming, terrified, begging to be let through. Not him."

Fallon shrugged. "He's a first responder. It's his job to stay cool in a crisis."

General Robbins spoke up. "Not like this. I've seen soldiers in war zones with gunfire and mortars going off all around them who've stayed steady and taken their targets down without batting an eye, but he made them look like scared little girls." At Fallon's frown, he held up his hands, palms out. "Sorry. Point is, he wasn't just cool. He was *ice-cold*. Until he realized my men had noticed, then he tried to fake being frightened, but they weren't buying it. They're trained to spot liars. That's why they held on to him."

Fallon's frown deepened, turning the worry lines on her forehead into rolling hills.

"Show me."

Book hurried to comply, typing at lightning speed on the laptop's keyboard and bringing up footage from cameras at the security checkpoints along the blockade.

The video showed an ambulance rolling up to the gate. There was blood all over the grille, a broken headlight, and the fender was dented. Stuck to the grille was a hank of hair. As one of the soldiers flagged the vehicle to a stop, another approached and peeled the hair off. It was attached to what could only be part of a human scalp.

Light climbed out of the cab as a third soldier covered him with a machine gun. Fallon started in her seat as his voice came from the laptop speakers.

"You have to let me out of here. I just came from St. Luke's. Everyone has gone crazy there, attacking each other—I barely made it to my rig. Then they were all over the parking lot, in the streets, coming at me like some kind of mob. I had no choice but to drive through them."

He sounded convincing to Book, but Fallon's lips quirked, and she leaned closer to the screen.

"Can you back it up and zoom in on his face?"

Book did as she requested, wondering what it was she'd seen. He didn't have to wait long.

"See his eyes? He looks right at the soldier the whole time, never glancing away."

"So?"

"So, when people are remembering details, they tend to look up and to the right. When they're making stuff up or embellishing, they look to the left. Well," she amended quickly, "right-handed people. It's the opposite for lefties. But his don't move in either direction. That usually means the liar's aware of the tell and trying to compensate for it.

"Of course," she added, sitting back, "you can't base an assessment of truthfulness on eye movement alone. But he also didn't use a contraction there, where most people would have. That can be another tell, being overly precise when lying."

She looked at Book.

"Anything else?"

He nodded, hit a few more keys, and called up the footage from the ambulance's dash cam.

They watched as the vehicle pulled out of the bay, the scene much as Light had described—people attacking each other in the parking lot, swarming around a cab, a group converging on the front of the ambulance. As Light jerked the wheel to one side to get past them, the video caught another ambulance crashing through the ER doors, the back opening up as an EMT fled from a woman with bloody fingers, trailing an IV bag.

Light made it past the mob, hands and arms slapping against the windshield, leaving red streaks. Once he was clear of the press, the vehicle lurched forward, narrowly missing another cab as Light hit the gas.

Out on the street, there were fewer people, and most of them seemed to be running. The ambulance shot through an intersection as cars careened into each other, Infected passengers and drivers turning their interiors into mobile charnel houses.

As Light plowed down a stretch of road, a woman could be seen kneeling beside the body of a child. She stood, headlights illuminating the hopeful expression on her face as she tried to wave him down to get help for her boy.

The ambulance lurched again. Instead of slowing, Light had hit the gas. He ran the woman down without hesitation, the video taking in the moment—too late—when her hope turned to terror. Then her face disappeared beneath the hood, and the video shook for a moment as the ambulance's wheels bumped over the two bodies, and Light raced on.

Book hit PAUSE and looked at Fallon.

"Okay," she said, clearly shaken by what she'd seen. "He could be a psychopath, but that's not something that can be determined by watching videos. And while that's obviously interesting to me, in an academic sense, I'm still not sure what it has to do with—with whatever it is you're doing here?"

Thurman brushed a hand through his short, blond hair. "We have a theory," he began. "The Crazy 8s virus, as we've described, is incredibly contagious. Light was right there in the middle of it all, in contact with Infected blood and fluids, but he didn't catch it. He seems to be immune, and so far, he's the only person we know of who is. We've been investigating different physiological aspects to see what exactly in him gives him that immunity, but have been drawing a blank. Then I remembered your work on psychopathic brain structure. If he's immune because of that—if somehow, that structure is resistant to a virus that strikes at the brain and causes its victims to want to ingest other, unaffected brains—we need to know. Which means we need to find out if other psychopaths share that immunity."

Fallon took a moment to consider the question. A heretofore unknown virus that homed in on grey matter? Could brain structure confer immunity to that?

It was possible, she thought, if the virus targeted a specific region. In psychopaths, the limbic system was often underdeveloped, experiencing less blood flow and less neural activity than a "normal" brain. A virus that attacked the areas of the brain that were typically impaired in psychopaths might not be able to gain a foothold.

And now her professional curiosity was engaged; even if the fate of the Valley—and maybe the world—wasn't at stake, she wanted to know more.

"Can I talk to him?"

Robbins smiled.

"Thought you'd never ask."

## CHAPTER 6

*94 hours*

**A** green jeep that looked like something from the set of *M\*A\*S\*H* took Fallon and Robbins out across the track and pulled up in front of the infield garage. Thurman and Book had stayed behind, though Book had provided her with an iPad that contained the video clips and all of his files on Light. Of course, it wasn't connected to the Internet, and even if it had been, it wouldn't have mattered since the only people in the Phoenix metropolitan area who were able to access the web were back in the room she'd just left. She already knew she wouldn't be able to take it away from the track, for the same reason they'd confiscated her phone.

"He's in there?" she asked, a little surprised. The

low-lying building was just a long collection of bays for cars to lounge in until the race began. Sure, they had electricity, but that was about it. From what she'd read, Gitmo had better accommodations.

Then again, the Crazy 8s virus made 9/11 look like a road-rage incident, so she imagined prisoner comfort was not high on the government's priorities list at the moment.

She wondered if they were even *taking* prisoners.

"For now," Robbins answered. "Until you tell us if he is what we think he is."

Of course, Fallon was almost a hundred percent sure he was just that: a psychopath. But . . . if he really was immune to the virus that had taken out one of the largest urban centers in America in a matter of days, he wouldn't just be an angel of death. He'd be the country's savior.

First things first, though.

"I want to talk to him alone."

Robbins frowned, but he nodded. "'Alone' is a relative term. The place is wired. Someone's always watching him."

Fallon didn't know if that was an observation or a threat. She supposed it didn't really matter, either way. "Noted."

One of the bays had been repurposed into a holding area, and Light was inside, in a barred, freestanding cell that Fallon was able to walk around as she made her observations.

He wore handcuffs and ankle bracelets, both connected to a chain around his waist. There was a chair in the cage, which had been bolted to the floor; Light had been sitting, but he stood when she entered the bay.

Polite, probably charming one-on-one. That would help explain how he was able to go from job to job without raising eyebrows—a silver tongue was a classic hallmark of psychopathy.

He watched her curiously as she walked around the cage, not making notes on the tablet, just taking him in. He turned his head to track her progress as she went around behind him, not giving her the satisfaction of moving his body to follow but obviously uncomfortable with her being out of his sight. She stopped directly behind him, just out of his peripheral vision unless he really strained his neck, which she knew he wouldn't do.

She waited. If he spoke first, he'd be giving up a measure of control, however slight, and that would tell her much about him.

His not speaking would tell her even more.

Fallon watched as a single bead of sweat rolled down from his blond hair, down his ear, hanging from the lobe like a crystal on a chandelier before crashing down to the bloody collar of the EMT uniform he still wore. And that told her something, too.

She resumed her stroll, tapping at the screen of the iPad as though she were taking notes now, but more interested in his response to her assessing him than in recording it for posterity. Besides, Robbins said the place was wired, which meant he was watching her watch Light. Plenty of time to review the video later.

When she stood in front of him again, she cocked her head to one side.

"Why'd you kill her?"

Light looked surprised, then puzzled, which might not actually have been feigned. She hadn't been very specific, after all.

"The woman in the ER at St. Luke's. She was dead already. If not from her wounds, then when those brain-eating crazies got done with the bodies that could move and started in on the ones that couldn't. What did you gain? Compared to what you could have lost, taking those few extra seconds to kill her instead of fleeing?"

She knew, of course. He gained the knowledge that it was *his* choice when the woman died, not nature's or some Infected's, or even that of some doctor or insurance company. Or the woman's herself.

*His* decision to allow her those last moments, or to steal them away. Him, the only god who could answer or ignore her prayers as the light faded from her eyes.

Ultimate control over another person's fate. There was no headier ambrosia for the psychopath.

"I don't know what you're talking about."

"No? Maybe this will refresh your memory."

She tapped a few icons on the screen for real this time and brought up the video of Light kneeling next to the woman in the ER. She turned the tablet so he could see the screen, let it run once, then played it again, watching his reaction.

He couldn't keep his eyes off it. If anything, he paid more attention the second time than the first. She wondered if he was becoming aroused. Many serial killers used murder as a substitute for sex, often because they lacked the capacity to achieve satisfaction any other way.

She made as if to play it a third time, watching his eyes follow her finger. His fingers flexed unconsciously at his sides, and he swallowed.

*Definitely* aroused.

Instead of playing the video again, she turned the iPad back around and gave him a quick, tight smile when his eyes flew up to meet hers. Letting him know she'd seen and knew his secret. Anger flashed in his blue eyes for an instant, then he had control of himself again.

"I want a lawyer."

"Lawyer's not going to do you any good. You're not walking away from this one, and now that they've discovered your little predilection for playing God, your life is going to be under a microscope all the way back to the womb. It won't be long before they pin a half a dozen or more murders on you. And, since you're fairly new to the Grand Canyon State, you may not know that we're big on capital punishment here. Can't imagine you're going to like it too much when the roles are reversed, and you're the one lying there, helpless, with the moment of your death being determined by someone else's whim."

Light smiled, an expression that didn't reach his eyes.

"I don't think I stuttered."

Fallon shrugged. "Suit yourself. But you have to know you'll be better off if you cooperate."

"I . . ."

Fallon kept talking. "You can't think they'd have hauled you out here and trussed you up like Hannibal Lecter just because of some woman in an ER."

" . . . want . . ." Light enunciated the words carefully, every syllable sharp enough to slice a throat.

"Or even a dozen women in a dozen ERs."

" . . . a . . ."

"You have something they want. If I were you, I'd be thinking about how to capitalize on that."

Fallon thought she detected the briefest hesitation before Light finished up, the cold smile never leaving his face.

" . . . lawyer."

She shrugged again.

"Suit yourself," she repeated, turning away, hiding a smile of her own as she did.

She'd planted the seed. It wouldn't be long before it sprouted and bore fruit.

# CHAPTER 7

*94 hours*

**F**allon found General Robbins waiting outside, the old jeep backed just far enough into one of the open garage bays to provide shade for him and his driver. The engine was running. At her approach, the driver got out and opened a door for her. Robbins waited in the backseat, one greying eyebrow arched in anticipation. "Well?"

"He wants a lawyer."

Robbins let out a laugh. "He's a little late. Due process went out the window about three days ago." Addressing the driver, he added, "Let's go, Jerry."

The driver gave a sharp nod and stepped on the gas. The vehicle lurched from the bay and out into bright sunlight. "Why the antique?" Fallon asked.

"The jeep? She's been with me a long time."

"Since the Spanish-American War, from the looks of it." Fallon couldn't bring herself to speak of the thing using the feminine pronoun.

Robbins laughed again, then fell silent. Fallon gave him several seconds, to see if he would volunteer any more information about the vehicle. Or anything else. When he didn't, she brought up something that had been nagging at her. "You mentioned earlier that the virus was called 'Crazy 8s' because of some plan?"

"CONPLAN 8888," he said quickly.

"Which is what?"

"You'll laugh."

"Trust me, General. I'm not finding much of anything funny today."

"No, I suppose not. CONPLAN stands for 'Concept Plan.' You probably know how we military types love our acronyms."

"I've heard."

"Trust *me*, you don't want to know the full title. But the part that comes after the quadruple-eight is 'Counter-Zombie Dominance Operations.'"

"General, I don't know who you think—"

"I'm serious, Doctor. That's the name. It's a contingency plan to preserve non-zombie humans from threats posed by a zombie horde. I think that's verbatim, or close to it. You can look it up, it's unclassified."

Fallon stared at him, trying to see if there was a twinkle in his eye or the hint of a smile around his lips.

There wasn't.

"You think I'm full of it," he said. The jeep had pulled to a stop beside the grandstand with the converted suites above, but Robbins made no move to get out. Jerry sat behind the wheel, trying hard to pretend he wasn't listening.

*I think you're as crazy as your plan's name.* "Something like that."

"The basic thrust is that we needed a plan to respond to some sort of invasion or other unrest. The goals were to protect the civilian population by maintaining a defensive perimeter, conduct combat operations to eradicate the threat, and help civilian authorities restore order. Starting to sound familiar?"

"The first part, yes. I just can't quite see the top Pentagon brass sitting around talking about zombies."

"Look at it this way. If they put together a plan that named a particular enemy force—Iraqis, Russians, whoever—and that plan leaked to the public, there would be an outcry that we were making secret war plans against whatever country we put in the document. And leaks happen. A lot. By using zombies, we aren't creating any expectation of combat operations against any given population."

Fallon thought it over. "I guess that makes sense."

"Of course, at the time, nobody knew the first time we implemented the plan, it would be against real— well, you know. Infecteds."

"I'm sure they didn't."

"But it's a good plan. What we're doing here will help people, Dr. O'Meara. It really will."

"Let's hope," Fallon said.

Robbins touched his door, and Jerry sprang into action. He opened both doors, and Fallon and Robbins climbed out. "Stay close," Robbins said as he passed the driver.

"Yes, sir."

The general led her back up to the conference room. Some of the people had changed positions at the table, but the cast remained the same. Fallon's chair was unoccupied, so she took it again, and Robbins resumed his place at the table's head. "Dr. O'Meara has had a brief conversation with the subject," he said. With a wry smile, he added, "Man wants a lawyer."

"What do you think?" Ramirez asked. "Is he a psychopath?"

Fallon wanted to be tread carefully. She still wasn't certain what the agenda here was, or if different players had different ones in mind. Making casual statements that she couldn't back up seemed as ill-advised here as it would be in a courtroom. "I can't make that determination after just a few minutes," she said. "He presents as one, yes. Depending upon how informal a definition you want to use, he probably is. But psychopathy is a spectrum, not an either-or. I couldn't say whether he is clinically psychopathic without a more extensive examination. And I don't think he's inclined to allow that."

"Do you need his cooperation?" Robbins asked. "Can't you study him anyway? What if we sedated him?"

"That would make it harder, not easier," Fallon replied. "It's important to engage a subject in a dialogue. And sedation might dampen some of the brain activity I'd be watching for. If he were sufficiently restrained, maybe . . ."

"We can restrain the hell out of him," Ramirez said. She appeared almost gleeful at the prospect.

Fallon took a deep breath, buying herself a few moments to consider. She was no squishy civil libertarian. She believed in the law, in the fundamental fairness of the American system of justice. But she was also a scientist whose work brought her into proximity with the fruits of that system, so she knew it was far from perfect.

And performing medical procedures on people against their will, even ones that weren't physically invasive, felt not too far removed from the human experimentation that the Nazis did. The United States had a Constitution that theoretically prohibited such practices, in sense if not in precise language. There was much the framers couldn't have anticipated, including machines that could scan people's brains and determine the extent of their pathologies, but it wouldn't take a huge leap of logic to know what they'd have thought.

She glanced around the table, at the expectant faces looking back at her, awaiting a response. What was happening in Phoenix was unprecedented in human history, and if left unchecked, could bring about global catastrophe. Ebola was a summer cold by comparison.

If she could do something—anything—to help avert that, didn't she *have* to try?

Besides, she was kind of fond of Phoenix—though she would be less so as summer dragged on—and she didn't want the Valley nuked. The fact that Elliott Jameson was presumably somewhere inside the quarantine zone was an argument in favor of mass destruction, except he had their only functioning prototype with him.

"All right," she said. "I'll do a full workup. I'll warn you, there is no guarantee that his brain structure will show any abnormalities. The psychopathic brain, as a general rule, has pronounced differences from yours and mine, but that's not true in every case."

*Well, not mine, anyway,* she thought but couldn't say.

A test run of the MEIADD prototype on herself and Elliott had shown surprising results, particularly in her case: Her brain structure mirrored the "typical" psychopathic brain in almost every respect. That discovery had been life-changing; ever since, she'd been using the prototype on herself, and her relationship with Jason, at least, had never been better. Not even Elliott knew.

She didn't want to think about what these government stooges would do with that information.

"Not everyone we think of as a psychopath has that structure," she continued. "The more pronounced it is, though, the more an individual is likely to lean in that direction. It's an indicator, from which we can make certain generalizations, but it's important to remember that those generalizations are not true at all times for all people."

"What are the other factors?" one of the assistant SecDefs asked. She had long since forgotten which was which.

"It's nature and nurture," Fallon explained. She didn't want to go into full-on lecture mode, but there was a limit to how concise she could be and still hit the main points. "Someone with a textbook psychopathic brain structure who's raised in a loving household, with no personal experience with violence, who has a circle of supportive friends—maybe a successful romantic relationship, children, grandchildren down the line—might live a long and happy life without ever experiencing what we would think of as psychopathic tendencies. None of the various triggers would have been pulled.

"On the other hand, someone *without* the brain markers that I study, but who's raised by parents who beat and abuse him, who confuse his gender identity and ignore his education—this person might never learn empathy. He might drop out of school at sixteen, find himself unemployable, drift into crime, become a con artist and a user, sexually and socially disconnected. Before too long, he might have racked up a significant body count. You would certainly categorize him as a psychopath, even if his brain showed only a few of the markers we look for. Brain structure is a piece of it, but it's not the only piece."

"What we need to know," Robbins said, "is whether Hank Light is one, and if so, why? Is it his brain structure? Something else? What differentiates him from other people that would make him immune? We've got other experts investigating different avenues, but so far, the idea that his immunity might be related to some abnormal brain structure is the best lead we have. And since we don't have the luxury of time, all this research has to be done concurrently. So while those other tests are being conducted, we want you to learn what you can, within your specialty."

Fallon had resigned herself. "Wrap him up, and I'll get him into my lab and see what I can find out."

"He can't leave the compound," the Department of Homeland Security man said. Burt Ehlers, she thought his name was. Something like that. Name tags would have been nice.

"Then I can't—"

"We'll bring a lab to you," he said. "Give us a list of what you need. We'll get what we can from your lab, and what we can't take out, we'll acquire."

"New?" she asked.

"Of course. I don't need to remind you, Doctor, that we're dealing with a national emergency here. The cost of some lab equipment is nothing compared to the cost of the economic disaster we're facing. Not to mention the human factor." The way he said it, Fallon got the impression humans were no more than an afterthought.

"No, sir," she said. "No, I think I've grasped that

pretty well. Can I get some of my people brought over?"

The general fielded that one. "Out of the question," he said. "I'm sorry, Doctor. If you need trained personnel, we'll provide them from the military community."

"Fine." In that case, she might ask for a few extras. The pad was still on the table in front of her. She drew it closer and began to write.

## CHAPTER 8

*91 hours*

**E**hlers had taken her list and gone off someplace to make it all happen. The meeting was adjourned, at least for the moment, and Fallon sat in a grandstand seat, sun beating down on her, thinking about the last time she had been here. The incessant roar of the cars competing with the din of the crowd must have shaken the angels in heaven. Here in the grandstand, the smells of burning rubber, sunscreen, and beer battled for all-out supremacy. A day at the track was an exercise in extreme overstimulation, causing Fallon to want to spend the next day in dark, quiet isolation. Maybe the next *week*.

"There you are."

She twisted in her seat to see Jack Thurman coming

down the steps toward her. He had taken off the blazer he'd been wearing inside and rolled up his shirtsleeves. He wore his usual easy smile, and it was only when he got closer that she could see the weariness in his blue eyes. He looked like he'd been chewing on his lips, too. "How are you, Jack?"

"Been better." A glance toward the fence separating the raceway from the Valley told her why.

"I know what you mean."

"Pretty impressive bunch of people here," Thurman said. "And on the ground. Do you have any idea how hard it is to fence in an entire valley of this size in a few days? The logistics involved?"

"Hadn't really thought about it. Hard, I imagine."

"And then some. If the place hadn't already been descending into chaos, it would have caused a panic. As it was, the Valley's inhabitants barely noticed."

"A great relief to them, I'm sure."

Thurman ignored the comment. "Fallon? Who would you say—within a radius of a hundred miles or so—would most closely fit your 'classic' psychopath mold, based on your studies? Brain structure and any other genetic criteria included?"

*Besides me?* she thought. Again, it was not something she dared voice out loud. Beyond that, she had to consider for a long moment. "I guess Randy Wayne Warga," she said finally. "Randall, officially."

"Why him?"

"He's probably committed at least a dozen murders. He's down at the Arizona State Prison Complex, in Florence. He was convicted on thirteen charges of second-degree homicide and sexual assault, but I'm sure he's done more than that. He's a sexual sadist of the first order, and I suspect he's been raping and killing for years."

"Warga?" He spelled it out.

"Right."

Thurman raised his left hand in the air. Immediately, Fallon heard boots hurrying down the concrete steps and turned to see two police officers coming toward them, in full tactical gear. When they were close enough, Thurman said, "Randall Wayne Warga. ASPC-Florence, Central Unit."

"Got it, sir," one of the officers said. They about-faced and rushed toward an exit.

"What was that all about?" Fallon asked when they were gone.

"If it is his psychopathy that makes Light immune," Thurman said, "we need to know if it's true of other psychopaths, too. Which means we need . . . test subjects."

"Lab rats."

"That works, too. Look, Fallon, if we had months or years, we could test on animals, rats or chimps or whatever. We could do a careful, appropriate sequence of tests, working up toward humans, who we'd expose little by little, under controlled conditions. Hell, you'd know more about how that works than me. But we don't have that much time. We have days. Hours. We're at the 'quick and dirty' stage. We need to know what we need to know, the fastest way possible."

Fallon mulled for a few moments, fighting back sudden anger that threatened to boil over into rage. "But you know Light's immune because you saw it on the video. Incontrovertible proof that he was in close contact with Infecteds, traded bodily fluids with them."

"Right."

"So if you bring in psychopaths from outside the quarantine zone, how will you . . . Oh, no. No. Jack. With real zombies? Infecteds, whatever."

"It's the only way to be certain, Fallon. And we *have* to know."

"But—but, what about *their* rights? Jack, they've done bad things, but they're still human beings. Throwing them to the wolves like that—that's just not right. What about cruel and unusual punishment? What about the Constitution? How can you countenance—"

"I assure you, Dr. O'Meara," came another voice. "We're all supporters of the Constitution." Ehlers was coming up the stairs toward them. "At DHS, we defend it every day. We defend the freedom it promises. But there are a million and a half people in the city of Phoenix, and more than four million in the entire metro area. As infectious, as dangerous, as Crazy 8s is, if it were allowed to spread beyond the Valley, the whole country would be at risk. The whole world. It's possible, of course, that it's already out there—that someone got on an airplane to Atlanta or Tokyo or Paris symptom-free but then spread the virus. We might be too late. But we can't proceed on that assumption. We have to believe there's still something we can do, and we have to do it."

"I suppose," Fallon said, hardly mollified. "But, still . . ."

"Sometimes the rights of a few have to be infringed upon to guarantee the rights of the many," Ehlers said.

"And in this case, the few are known killers," Thurman offered. "Society isn't losing much if they fail the test."

*Society might not be,* Fallon thought. *But what about us? What do we lose, when we turn other human beings into unwitting test subjects?*

Before she could frame another objection, Thurman and Ehlers excused themselves and walked off. Fallon was almost alone, except for the minder she'd been assigned, Specialist Timothy Briggs. The young soldier was sitting fifteen rows behind her, well out of sight and hearing. She rose from her seat and walked up, past him, high enough to see over the wall to where the quarantine line was still being hardened with razor wire.

As she watched the soldiers at work, she wondered how much of the rage simmering inside her was due to righteous, patriotic fervor, and how much to that trait in her that she didn't like to acknowledge. According to the scans—repeated several times, to rule out testing errors—she was potentially as psychopathic as Warga, if not more so. Under the unexpected stress of the day, had that tendency pushed to the fore? And how could she possibly tell?

They could ask her to study Light and Warga and whoever else they brought around, give them the information they needed to do whatever had to be done, she decided. She'd do it, but she would also scrutinize herself as closely as she could.

And *that* information, she would keep to herself.

# CHAPTER 9

*89 hours*

**S**he wasn't sure how long she'd been standing there, watching the Valley of the Sun being systematically cut off from the rest of the word, but when someone politely cleared their throat behind her, Fallon suddenly realized her cheeks were hot, and sweat was running down the back of her neck.

She turned to see Book.

"Yes?"

He blinked, seemingly taken aback at her tone. She realized how curt she must sound and decided she didn't care. She'd protested their plans for Warga, but the truth was that her constitutional rights were being violated just as surely as his would be. What was this if not unlawful seizure? Virtual imprisonment, since she couldn't leave, couldn't talk to anyone she knew. Couldn't talk to her *family*.

She had every reason to be short-tempered.

"I thought you might want to know that I can try to get a message to your family, to let them know you're okay. If you want."

The sudden anger passed as swiftly as it had come, and Fallon forced a chagrined smile. It came out as more of a grimace and sat uneasily on her lips for a moment before going the way of her earlier ire. She could tell he was smart but hadn't realized he was a mind reader. Still, what he was offering wasn't what she wanted.

"I can't talk to them myself?"

Book was starting to sweat, and she realized he probably spent most of his time in air-conditioned rooms on the East Coast—even this relatively mild ninety-degree weather was probably too much for him. She gestured for him to walk back down to the shaded seats, following on his heels. The analyst spoke as he went.

"No, sorry. The Powers That Be are afraid you'll try to warn them away, since they're outside the quarantine zone, and that kind of thing can cause a panic. Besides, they—the PTB—are trying to keep a lid on the whole thing. Well, to the extent that they can, anyway." He'd reached the shade now, and moved aside for her to sit first.

As she took her seat, he continued.

"Nobody can fly or drive in or out of the city now—

it's completely cut off. The barrier in this area follows the rivers west, then north to the I-10. East of here, it basically follows the same alignment as the proposed South Mountain Freeway—down around the south side of the mountain, tying into Pecos Road, and from there to the southern stretch of the 10. Not sure about it from there, in either direction.

"All communications in and out are also being jammed. For the moment, the press is cooperating—well, that and the fact that we've isolated those who've shown up here, which is beginning to piss them off royally. There will come a time when somebody breaks the embargo, and then shit's *really* going to hit the fan. But the longer we can keep the blades feces-free, the more time we have to come up with a solution. I'm sure you'll agree that doing that without *also* dealing with a panicked populace or international condemnation is the best way to go."

She wanted to argue with him, but she couldn't.

"Well, then, I guess just tell them I'm okay, but some stuff has come up at work, and I won't be home for a few days." She thought of them at the table that morning, how they'd barely noticed her leaving, and wondered if they'd even care. "And . . . tell my son I love him."

Book nodded.

"Will do." He was about to say something else when Briggs approached, taking the stairs two at a time.

"Sorry to interrupt, ma'am," he said diffidently, nodding to Book, "but they're ready for you now."

Fallon frowned, confused.

"Who? And ready for what?"

"They're back from Florence, ma'am. With your test subject."

**B**y the time she'd made it down from the grandstand to the trailer where Book's Powers That Be awaited, they were already setting Warga up in a nearby modular building Fallon was certain hadn't been there when she'd arrived.

She watched with the others as soldiers ushered the convict in through a door to the middle of the building, which was essentially just one big, square room with cameras at every corner. Fallon saw another door on the opposite side of the building, but the soldiers ignored it as one of them undid Warga's shackles, the others covering him with their rifles. Then they slowly backed out of the room, leaving the man to rub first his wrists, then his eyes.

"We sedated him for the chopper ride back," Robbins told her. That explained how they'd gotten him here so quickly. But it also meant they'd effectively tied one hand behind his back before sending him to the slaughter. Then she remembered the dozen-plus women he had killed and violated, both pre- and postmortem, and could conjure little sympathy.

Still, even he had rights. But before she could point out how this was yet another abuse of those rights, the other door opened and three people stumbled in.

No.

Three *Infecteds*.

Two men and a woman, they all bore superficial wounds on face and arms, as well as the hallmark puffy eyes and red cheeks.

Fallon watched in fascinated horror as they paused inside the doorway, then their heads all swiveled toward Warga, like dogs picking up a scent.

*Rabid dogs,* Fallon thought as they charged. "Really? What if they kill him?"

Robbins gestured toward the rafters. Four soldiers crouched there, aiming rifles down toward the Infecteds. "Sharpshooters," he said. "They won't let him get really hurt."

Warga was a big man—there wasn't much to do in prison but work out, after all. But he was groggy from whatever they'd given him for the flight and utterly unprepared for what was coming. Still, you didn't survive long in a place like Florence without being able to adapt quickly, especially when someone was attacking you. As the first Infected reached him, Warga set himself, ducked his shoulders, and let the man's momentum carry him harmlessly up and over.

The man landed with a grunt of pain, but Warga had no time to follow up because the other two Infecteds were there. The woman growled like a vicious beast as she clawed at his eyes with long, manicured nails; Fallon could see light reflecting off the polish. As Warga brought one beefy arm up to protect his face, the second man launched himself at the convict's throat, jaws wide, like something out of a horror movie where the vampires were actually scary.

Warga met the man's mouth with his fist, and blood and teeth flew, but the Infected was undeterred. He latched onto Warga's hand, sinking what remained of his teeth deep. Warga swore, but instead of trying to pull away, he drove his fist deeper, twisting as he went. The Infected held his ground, reaching vainly for Warga's head even as his own was slowly being forced into an alignment not meant for anyone who wasn't spewing Latin and vomiting pea soup.

"Damn," Fallon heard someone mutter. "It's like the thing's on PCP or something."

"Shouldn't those sharpshooters do something?" Fallon asked.

"They will if they have to," Thurman said. "Warga's not in serious trouble yet."

"Looks serious as hell to me."

Then there was an audible snap, and the Infected suddenly went limp, his weight pulling Warga off-balance before the convict could shake himself free. The woman took advantage of his distraction, darting around his blocking arm to dig the nails of one hand into his cheek, right below his left eye.

Warga howled, trying to pull away, just as the Infected behind him, who'd finally regained his feet, leapt on his back, grabbing onto both ears as though they were reins and Warga some bucking bronc.

The convict spun, a chunk of flesh torn from his cheek as he tore free of the woman's grasp and slammed his would-be rider into her. The three went down in a heap of limbs and blood.

The two Infecteds were on Warga in an instant, ripping at his hair and tearing at his face. It was all he could so to bring his arms up to try to defend himself.

Then the man reclaimed his hold on Warga's ears and started slamming the convict's head into the floor, over and over again.

"That's enough," Robbins said, as drops of blood flew from Warga's battered scalp. "Take them out."

Fallon couldn't tear her gaze away from the violence in front of her, wondering, as she so often did lately, if it were scientific curiosity or bloodthirstiness that held her so enthralled.

Two shots rang out, and the two Infecteds' heads exploded in a shower of pink and grey rain.

Soldiers—in full biohazard gear this time—entered the space again. They let Warga be, lying in a bloody, gasping heap in the center of the carnage. After several long moments, he levered himself up into a sitting position, found the nearest camera, and gave them all the bird.

As the soldiers secured him and prepared to transport him for treatment and observation in another insta-building, Fallon turned to the others.

"Well," Robbins said, "we should know in about twelve hours whether he's immune or not."

"And what will that prove?" Fallon asked. "We still won't know for certain if it's being a psychopath that grants immunity to the virus."

"No," the general agreed. "But it's a damned good argument, don't you think?"

"Close enough for government work?" she quipped sarcastically.

Robbins showed her something that might have been a grin but probably wasn't.

"Basically," he said. "Under the circumstances, that's got to be good enough."

# CHAPTER 10

*82 hours*

The sun was sinking low in the sky by the time the trucks rolled into the infield. Soldiers had been busy throughout the hot afternoon setting up a lab to Fallon's specs, running pipe for water and sewage and massive trunk lines for power. Her power needs, she had told Robbins, would be enormous. When the trucks halted around the big, roll-up loading doors, more soldiers appeared from somewhere and began the unloading process. She hadn't expected to get everything on her wish list, but when she saw the huge Siemens MRI scanner come off a truck— brand-new, from the looks of it—she couldn't suppress a little thrill. It was newer than hers, top-of-the-line. She'd been longing for one for months, but the grant money wouldn't stretch that far.

"You really like this stuff," Soledad Ramirez said. Fallon started. She had come up from behind while Fallon watched the bustle of activity, oblivious to extraneous sounds. "Sorry," she said.

"It's okay. I guess I was . . . distracted."

"Watching instruments and cartons of software and accessories hauled off trucks. That's what made me think you love it. You're not just into the gadgets, you're into what they can do."

"You're right, I do love it. I can't help it."

"Nothing to help," Ramirez said. "It's good to see someone who loves her work."

"My husband might think I love it a little too much." *And him, not enough.*

"Lot of spouses feel that way about their sweethearts' jobs. Mine did. He told me I had to choose." She shook her head, a wry smile flitting across her face. "Sometimes I miss him."

Fallon laughed, though it struck too close to home to really be funny. "There's so much good work being done in neuroscience these days," she said. "Work on resilience, mindfulness, PTSD, neuro-immune interaction. We're right on the cusp of making real progress against Parkinson's, Alzheimer's, MS. But me?" She shrugged. "I work with psychos. Go figure."

"Somebody's got to. I guess."

"When I was in school, I thought only creepy old guys with beards and thick glasses would specialize in that kind of thing. Guys who were maybe halfway nuts themselves. Then I had a class in psychopathy, and I was hooked. Dr. Shepherd had been inside prisons all over the country, interviewing murderers, compiling case histories and statistics, building profiles of people who were otherwise ignored by society. Convicted, locked up, and forgotten. They fascinated me. I used to sit in his office late into the night—he gave me a key—and pore through his files." Fallon chuckled. "Some people have sports, some have porn. I had psychopaths."

"I know what you mean," Ramirez said. "It's more than a job. It's a calling. Same for me."

*Not necessarily a calling when you actually have those tendencies,* Fallon thought. "That's a good way to look at it."

"If we lose Phoenix, though . . . I don't know. I've never heard of a SAC whose home city was melted into glass. Pretty sure that ends a career with the Bureau."

"Would they really do that? Drop a nuclear bomb on an American city?"

"There's no choice, Fallon. If we can't come up with a cure, a vaccine, something . . . we can't let that get out into the world. We just can't."

Before Fallon could reply, Briggs approached. He had sweat running from beneath his short brown hair and an apologetic look on his face. "Seems like I'm always interrupting, ma'am. Can you come inside and show them where to place your equipment?"

"Yes, of course." She met Ramirez's gaze for a moment. "Sorry. Duty calls."

"I get it," Ramirez said. "Go. Do your stuff. Save the world."

"But no pressure, right?"

Ramirez laughed out loud, and said, "Right. No pressure at all."

**H**elping the soldiers position the instrumentation just right, watching it be plugged in and powered on, Fallon felt young and optimistic again, as she had when she and Elliott had struck out on their own in the first place. They had both walked away from lucrative private-sector positions, because they believed they had a sound concept and the knowledge to make it real. The world didn't know it yet, but they'd been right. Their work was important and would yield real benefits to society.

All she had to do was find Elliott, get the prototype back, and survive the epidemic.

*No problem.*

They had collected her desktop computer and her backed-up files, because she'd said she couldn't accomplish anything without the data stored there. She was still denied Internet access, but she would soon have an intranet, so she could access whatever she needed from the desk they'd provided. Given that she'd always had an impression of government as a huge, lumbering beast bound by red tape and weighted down by regulation, she was astonished at how quickly they had pulled everything together. It hardly seemed possible that she had only arrived at PIR this morning, and already she had a functional lab that was, in many ways, superior to her own. It even smelled new.

General Robbins had checked in, as had Burt Ehlers of DHS. Both tried to impress upon her the importance of her work to the overall effort. She was willing to stipulate to that. The big problem was that she wasn't entirely certain what her work would comprise. Somehow, she was supposed to determine what—if anything—in the psychopathic brain structure would render psychopaths immune to the Crazy 8s virus. That part of the theory was sound—recent research had determined that the central nervous system was directly linked to the peripheral immune system through the action of meningeal lymphatic vessels, so it was possible that brain structure or chemistry could confer immunity, under certain conditions. The geniuses on tap would try to come up with a way to use that knowledge to effect a treatment or a preventive vaccine, or both. But how did you turn brain structure into a pill, or an aerosol mist that could be sprayed on the city from helicopters? And if you could alter brain structure that way, how could you do it without turning the recipients into psychopaths?

She was still puzzling over that when Jack Thurman showed up. "Everything to your satisfaction?" he asked.

"It's great, Jack." She swiveled her chair to face him and waved a hand as if to indicate what she was enthused over, but there was too much—it was all around her, and so she let her hand float down to her lap. "It's a fantastic setup, but I'm not sure exactly what I'm going to do with it all." As she explained her concerns, he sat wearily in a chair still enveloped in plastic shrink-wrap.

"You just worry about your end of it, Fallon," he said when she was finished. "We're all specialists here. Except me and Carter, and maybe Book. You have your niche, and the folks who need to figure out a way to pharmaceuticalize—is that a word?—your research will do that."

"We're not going to be able to go in there and give every victim an injection of something."

"No, of course not. But we have people working on delivery, too. And we're not even sure about the psychopath angle yet, so we're working other, different angles at the same time. When I say we're got some of the nation's best minds on this, I'm not exaggerating. And you're included in that company."

Fallon felt her face flushing and hoped it wasn't visible. Jack had a long career in law enforcement behind him, though. He noticed things. No way he couldn't see her cheeks turning red, even if he was too much of a gentleman to mention it.

Well, let him notice. So she blushed when she was complimented, at least to some degree. So what? She hadn't had much experience with it at home lately, or with being noticed at all, for that matter.

"I . . . appreciate that, Jack. I just want to be sure I can hold up my end."

"I have no doubts. Neither do Carter and the others.

I advocated bringing you in, Fallon. I know it's a pain in the ass. I'm sorry about the way it happened and about taking you away from your family and your regular work. But it really couldn't be more important. And there's nobody in the field who's better qualified than you. I assure you, your qualifications were thoroughly vetted before the decision was made. You're here because we all think you can contribute to the success of the mission. It we didn't, you'd be back in your lab, oblivious. Probably happier, too."

Fallon considered. Happier? If ignorance was truly bliss, maybe. She had been brought here clumsily, abruptly, without being consulted. The thought of it still made her angry. But the stakes were such that she had to set aside selfish considerations. She was an American. She was a human being. She was a mother. Those facts required her to take action, if she could, against a scourge that could threaten both Americans and all humanity. Including her own son.

"No, I'm—and if you tell Robbins this, I'll deny it to my dying day—I'm glad you brought me in, Jack. Sure, it's inconvenient. And I might not feel this way if it lasts very long. But I don't do what I do just because I'm fascinated by dark and twisty minds. I do it because I think understanding these things is good for society. If I really want to help people, I can't just hide in the lab for the rest of my life. I have to be where I can do something concrete."

"I'm glad you feel that way." Thurman bit back a yawn. "Hope sleep isn't important to you."

"Not as long as there's plenty of coffee."

"Coffee we have although I won't vouch for its quality."

Fallon smiled. "Do you have any guess as to how long we'll be here?"

"Not long, really. Carter's concerned about the virus escaping the quarantine zone. We've got about"—he glanced at his watch—"eighty-two more hours before the bombers come in. Ninety-six-hour countdown started at six this morning."

That rocked Fallon. Less than four days until Phoenix was obliterated by nuclear weapons. The bombs dropped on Hiroshima and Nagasaki were primitive by comparison, but they were still horrible enough to convince the world to do everything possible to avoid ever using them again. Now the United States would not only be the first country to have used atomic bombs, but also the second—and on its own citizens. The world seemed to darken around the edges, and for a moment, she was afraid she was about to faint.

"How can anything be done that fast?" she asked, her voice tight. "Much less finding a cure, manufacturing a vaccine, delivering it . . . ?"

"We don't have to do it all. If we're on track for a cure, Robbins will hold off. But we have to have made good progress. As for doing things fast?" He indicated their surroundings with a nod. "Did this lab exist earlier today?"

"Touché."

"Carter Robbins is not an evil man, Fallon." Thurman rose from his chair and paced while he talked. Fallon could see how tired he was, but also how agitated. She wondered how long it would be until she felt the same way. "He's a worried one, and I don't blame him. For the first few days, the city wasn't sealed off. Once we realized the magnitude of the problem, we tracked down people who had flown out of Sky Harbor and tested them. Couldn't find anyone who had been infected. You might have heard about the private plane that crashed in Colorado, after flying out of Phoenix. We tested those folks, the survivors and the deceased. Trace amounts of the virus's biomarkers, but nothing dangerous. We've tried to trace people who left the area by bus or train, too. But that still leaves everybody who drove out, or through, who we don't know about. We have to assume it's already out there in the world."

"Then what's the point of the quarantine? Isn't the horse already out of the barn?"

He stopped pacing and squeezed his lips together until they went white and nearly disappeared, then answered. "It's still concentrated in the Valley. We don't know yet if an incidental contact with an infected person will spread it the same way it has in Phoenix, but we know what it's doing here. Containment is never a permanent solution to something like this. The longer we try to keep them in, the harder some folks will try to get out. The clock's ticking. Getting Carter to wait another eighty-one hours and change was a struggle, and it's hard to argue with his reasoning."

"I hope we can come up with a better plan, then. I

hate the idea of nuking the Valley, especially if it might already be too late."

"So do we all, Fallon," Thurman said. "So do we all." He started for the door, then stopped and looked at his watch again. "All hands meeting in twenty, in the usual conference room. Have Specialist Briggs drive you over in about fifteen minutes."

Then he was gone, leaving her alone with her instrumentation and her racing mind. She would have to wait awhile before firing up all her equipment. She couldn't risk using it until she had tested it, ensuring its functionality and noting baseline measurements. This attitude—*it's a crisis, time is of the essence, so let's have another meeting*—was more what she expected from a bunch of government bureaucrats.

She wondered how long it would be until she was part of the problem.

**CHAPTER 11**

*81 hours*

**B**ook stood at the end of the room, using a laptop to project a PowerPoint presentation onto a blank wall. He was wearing faded jeans and a white shirt with the sleeves rolled up over his wiry forearms. He knew the underarms were dark with sweat, and his mop of curly hair was all over the place, but he didn't care. He'd been working hard, and if these people had wanted a fashion model, they'd have picked another analyst. He'd at least sworn off pocket protectors back in grad school, so they should count themselves lucky for that.

The first slide was a map of the Valley of the Sun, with rough, semiconcentric circles in different colors emanating from an area toward the right side. "I've been trying to map the spread of the contagion," he said. "It's difficult, because until people realized there was a problem, nobody was monitoring it. But I built some algorithms to backtrack from what we do know, and I think this is pretty close."

He stood beside the projection and tapped the spot in the middle of the rings, but he caught himself before he spoke, and turned to the room.

"Dr. Johnstone," he said, addressing the representative from the Centers for Disease Control. "You've said that the virus doesn't resemble anything known to modern medical science, correct?"

"That's right," she said. She steepled her fingers together, her elbows on the table. "It's not just a new strain of something we've already encountered. It is, as far as we can tell, an entirely new beast. That's very unusual, as you might expect."

"I might have an explanation for that," Book said, turning back to the map. He put his finger on the same spot at the center of the colored circles, and held it there. "According to my calculations, the virus started right here. It's a spot in the city of Mesa."

"Why there? What's significant about that spot?" General Robbins demanded.

"You remember the meteor that broke apart over Phoenix a few days ago?" Book asked.

"Of course."

"This," Book said, torn between an impulse toward theatrical suspense and his own pragmatic nature, "is where the biggest fragment landed. Same spot. Now, maybe that's a coincidence, but I don't think so."

One of the assistant SecDefs rose halfway from his chair, his palms flat against the table. Rosy blotches marked his face. "You're talking about pan . . . something," he said. "That's just a theory!"

"Panspermia," Book agreed. "The interplanetary or interstellar transfer of organic matter. And as of now, it's far more than a theory. I believe it's the only explanation for what we're up against."

Before him, he saw several unbelieving faces. "Some people think that life on Earth came about through the mechanism of panspermia," he said. "Traces of organic matter, caught in comets, meteors, in space dust and debris, could survive almost indefinitely in some cases, making the long trip from star to star in a state of suspended animation. Upon finally landing somewhere, though, if that somewhere is conducive to that matter, it essentially wakes up. Comes to life. There could be pockets of life throughout the universe, all spread the same way."

"That's a little far-fetched," the SecDef said. The red spots on his cheeks were beginning to fade.

"More than a disease that turns people into zombies?" Fallon muttered. Book kept his smile to himself before countering the SecDef in his own way.

"No more so than any other theory," Book said. "Including the one that says God rolled some clay between his hands to make a ball, then used a pinch more to create Adam and Eve. Regardless, the fact is we have a pandemic of unknown origin, and it emanates from the exact same spot where the biggest piece of material from outer space landed right before the virus began to spread. Sometimes two and two doesn't make four, but there had better be a pretty compelling explanation for why it doesn't. I can't quite conceive of any other explanation for this."

"Wouldn't the virus have come from different spots around the area?" the woman from FEMA asked. "That meteor broke apart, and fragments landed all over the place."

"Maybe it was concentrated at the meteor's core," Book said. "And the landing shattered the core enough to let it out. I'm not saying my theory is necessarily a hundred percent solid. There are still a lot of unknowns. I'm just saying that at this moment, it's the best I've got."

"If it's true," Johnstone said, "then we have to get our hands on that meteor fragment. We've been trying to study the virus from the sample population we've picked up, but in those cases, it's already been genetically corrupted by its victims. It's proving incredibly hard to isolate. If we can get some pure, undiluted samples, we can make a lot more progress."

"That's going to be tough to do," Soledad Ramirez observed. "That big chunk landed in the City of Mesa Basin. Law enforcement got out there as fast as they could, but by the time they reached the site of impact, it was gone. We don't know who took it, or how, or why. There were smaller bits all over the county, some of which were grabbed by souvenir seekers. Arizona State asked for samples for it to study, and got some.

But those were collected by private individuals, most of whom don't have sterile collecting equipment or experience with such things, so we'd have to consider them potentially contaminated. Anyway, ASU is inside the quarantine zone, so those samples are effectively as out of reach as the missing core."

"If someone took it from the basin," Ehlers asked, "wouldn't that also be contaminated?"

"We think that piece was almost three feet in diameter," Book replied. "If that's the case, then the surface might be, but there could be enough material beneath the surface that hasn't been exposed. I agree with Dr. Johnstone; getting our hands on the core is our best bet."

"If that is the origin of the virus," Fallon asked, "that means we'd have to confiscate every bit of the meteor, no matter how small, right? If there's no way to know for sure how much of it contained traces of whatever bacteria caused the outbreak, we can't leave any of it out there. Dust from the meteor breaking apart might have fallen someplace, with trace organic matter inside."

"If we can come up with a treatment," Dr. Johnstone said, "then such extreme measures might not be necessary."

Thurman cleared his throat, and the others quieted down to listen. "Here's the problem, as I see it. We don't know where that big fragment went. We could find it, with a little time. Except that we can't go into the zone without risking infection. We've never seen anything so virulent. So how can we get in to look for it?"

"Exactly," Book agreed. "The spread of violence matches the spread of the virus, almost to a T. And it's getting worse every minute. Even if we could get a team in there, the chance of them getting out again is pretty slim."

"You're right, Book," Ramirez said. "Law enforcement inside the zone is already overwhelmed. Where they're still alive, they're sheltering in place, trying to defend themselves. There's no such thing as control anymore; there's only survival—if you're lucky enough."

"You have helicopters," Fallon pointed out.

"Sure, we could send choppers in," one of the other service secretaries said. "But they can't land. We can't let anybody drop down into the city. They'd be infected, or torn apart. Even with hazmat gear, until we really know what we're dealing with and how it's transmitted, we can't guarantee anyone's safety. And hazmat gear doesn't keep an Infected from bashing in your skull. We need boots on the ground in there, but the situation doesn't allow it."

"I might have a way," General Robbins put in.

Book waited, expecting him to recommend immediate bombing runs. Instead, Robbins surprised him. "I've got some Stryker NBCRVs on hand. For you civilians, that's a Nuclear, Biological, and Chemical Reconnaissance Vehicle. It can go into an area where there are potential radiation or biological or chemical hazards. It's got every kind of sensor and scrubber you can think of. It'll carry a four-man crew—all with personal protective gear on, as well—and they'll be able to collect samples from the inside, without ever opening the hatches. The samples are stored in secure vials, and they can be brought back here to study."

"It's not ideal," Dr. Johnstone said. "But it could work."

The assistant SecDef turned to him. "Use volunteers, Carter," he said. "Real ones. And be sure they know what they're getting into."

"To the extent that I do, anyway," Robbins said. "Yes, sir."

**D**riving Fallon back to the lab, Specialist Briggs hemmed and hawed until Fallon insisted that he come out with it. "I, uhh . . . I'm gonna have to turn you over to someone else for a while," he said.

"You mean some other soldier will be watching my every move in case I turn out to be a terrorist or something?"

"That's not exactly the task I've been assigned, ma'am."

"I'm just giving you a hard time, Specialist. Why are you dumping me?"

"I'm trained as an assistant surveyor, ma'am. That's one of the MOSs aboard a Stryker NBCRV."

"MOS?" she repeated.

"Military occupational specialty."

"So you're going to go in the quarantine zone and survey, or whatever?"

"That's right, ma'am."

"It's dangerous in there."

"I know."

"But less scary than minding me?"

"Not less scary. More important, though. I don't think you're up to any trouble. I want to be where I'm needed."

"I know the feeling," Fallon said. "Best of luck in there, Specialist. Come back to me in one piece."

"I'll try my best."

"I know you will."

He brought the vehicle—not much more than a glorified golf cart, painted in a camo design—to a halt by the door. The lab building set up for her also contained her living quarters—a bedroom, a bathroom with a functional toilet, sink, and shower, and a tiny kitchen area. She'd spend a little more time getting to know the new instrumentation setup, then call it a night. She felt like maybe she should hug Briggs before he left on what was surely a very risky duty. But taking risks was part of a soldier's job, wasn't it? And he probably had somebody to hug who meant much more to him.

Although whoever that was likely didn't know where he was, or where he was going, given the nature of the assignment. She could use a hug herself—especially one from Jason, whose little arms held on so gloriously tight.

She wondered if she would ever get another one,

or even see her son again. She'd been trying to keep worst-case scenarios out of her head, but even the best-case ones looked pretty bad. Given what she knew so far, she put the odds of human survival at somewhere south of fifty-fifty. Maybe twenty-eighty, if she was feeling optimistic.

And she didn't see much grounds for optimism. As she climbed out of the cart, she leaned over, put a hand on Briggs's shoulder, and squeezed.

"You be safe out there," she said, hoping it didn't sound as cold in his ears as it did in hers.

## CHAPTER 12

*70 hours*

**F**allon had only intended to spend an hour or two at most familiarizing herself with all the new equipment, but a scientific appreciation for the state-of-the-art machines and their sheer power compared to anything in her old lab—coupled with a decidedly less scientific love of new gadgets—got the better of her, and before she knew it, midnight had come and gone.

A long, uncontrollable stretch and a yawn that popped her jaw convinced her that it was time for some shut-eye. After all, the instruments would all still be there in the morning, and she'd be spending pretty much all her time with them soon enough.

She got up from her chair, rubbing the small of her back and making a mental note to ask someone to requisition a lumbar roll. Then she crossed over to the door that led to her quarters and was just reaching to flip the lights off when the lab's outer door opened.

Thurman walked in, glancing quickly around the lab until he located her.

"Sorry, I saw the lights were still on and figured you'd want to hear the news."

Fallon's fatigue evaporated in an instant.

What news? Had Briggs been hurt? Had the virus escaped quarantine?

Had something happened to her son?

Thurman shook his head at her barrage of questions.

"No, sorry, nothing like that," he said apologetically. "I should have phrased it better. No, Book spoke to me about some of your concerns, so I did a little arm-twisting, and they're going to let you call home."

Fallon liked his use of the word "they," as if he weren't one of them, when he so obviously was. A small cog in the behemoth Military-Industrial Complex, to be sure, but a part of it all the same. Then again, she'd gladly taken government funds for her own research, so she was probably an even smaller cog herself. And yet none of that mattered.

*They're going to let me speak to my son.*

Well, no, not at this hour. She'd be surprised if Mark even answered the phone—she was the one who always handled late-night calls because they were always for her.

"When?" she asked, hoping Thurman would say that was up to her.

"Now," he replied, crushing that hope in the same offhand way a chain smoker stubs out one cigarette before reaching for another. "And it'll be monitored. If you say anything that can be construed as an attempt to let your family know what's going on here or to warn them to flee, the call will be cut off, and you won't be allowed to make another one."

Fallon nodded, trying not to let her disappointment show.

"I understand."

Thurman produced a satellite phone and handed it to her. Fallon quickly punched in her home number and held the phone to her ear, listening to it ring.

And ring, and ring.

Mark didn't believe in answering machines or voice mail—he only had a cell phone because she insisted on it, in case he was ever somewhere with Jason and needed help in a hurry, but even then, he left the thing off half the time. She was up to forty-two rings and counting when Thurman cleared his throat. Fallon held a finger up, not looking at him, not wanting him to see the mix of desperation and mounting fury on her face. She'd give it fifty rings, and then she knew she'd have to give him the phone back. She wouldn't have a choice.

*Come on, Mark. Answer the damned phone!*

On forty-nine, a groggy voice sounded in her ear.

"Hello?"

*Thank God.*

"Mark, it's me."

"Yeah?"

Her lips thinned of their own accord. "I just wanted to let you know I'm okay."

"I didn't have any reason to think you weren't," he replied, his voice tinged with confusion and annoyance. She couldn't argue with that—she often worked late and seldom bothered to call.

"I know, I just . . ." She trailed off, knowing she was treading dangerously close to the line, and whoever was listening in could end the call at any moment. "Is Jason up?"

"What? No, of course not, Fallon." A pause and the sound of fabric shifting. "It's almost two in the morning. What's wrong with you?"

If he'd said it with any true concern, she might have told him everything right then and there, national security be damned. But instead he was irritated, and he made no effort to hide it. And knowing that she would have been just as pissed—if not more so—had their roles been reversed did nothing to alleviate the sudden sharp pain in her chest that made it momentarily hard to breathe.

*They don't need me. They never did.*

"Nothing. Just tired, I guess. Sorry for calling so late; I lost track of time," she said when she could speak again, fighting to keep her tone even. "Anyway, I'm not going to be home for a few days—big deadline at the lab."

"Yeah, I know. Some guy from your office called earlier to say the same thing."

"Right." She'd forgotten that. "Sorry. I just wanted to remind you to tell Jason I love him."

"I will. You know I always do," he said. *Even when you don't say it.* The unspoken words echoed loudly in her head.

"I know. Thank you."

Thurman cleared his throat; she needed to wrap it up.

"Okay, I have to go. Just . . . promise me you'll keep Jason safe?"

She never heard his answer; the call cut off like it had been severed with a guillotine. She handed the phone back to Thurman, who was frowning.

"That was pushing it, Fallon. Any more of that, they won't let you call home again."

"It doesn't matter," she said, shrugging to mask her sorrow. "I said all I needed to."

And so, she thought, had Mark.

Her cot could have been prison issue—a thin mattress over a metal frame, with a lumpy pillow and a scratchy blanket that she suspected was a wool blend. Not usually a smart choice for summer in Phoenix, but the instruments in the lab had to be kept cool, so the air-conditioning was set in the sixties, and Fallon found herself wishing for a few more of the rough coverings as she tossed and turned through what remained of the wee hours.

She was up before six, the sounds of the camp around her filtering into her consciousness through the metal walls, like the fabled Taos Hum on steroids. She hadn't bothered to change her clothes before falling into bed—hadn't even considered whether or not anyone had thought to provide her with any.

There was no closet in her living quarters, but there was a military footlocker at the base of her bed. She opened it and was pleasantly surprised to discover the extra sets of clothing she kept at the lab for nights when she wound up sleeping there, folded far more neatly than she would have done. There were even a few new pieces, in the same sizes and styles as the rest. Book's doing, she imagined—he seemed like one of the few people here who really saw her as a person and not just a walking psychopath detector.

She grabbed the set on top, a pair of sturdy khakis and a light blue button-down shirt, along with a no-frills white bra and panties. Then she straightened and headed for the bathroom.

As she expected after finding her clothes in the footlocker, her toiletries had also been transported from the old lab and were arranged neatly on the shelves above the toilet, along with some towels and a few rolls of toilet paper. One-ply, she was sure.

Fallon quickly stripped off her sweat-stained clothes and stepped into the shower stall. The water was immediately hot—it didn't really come in any other flavor in Phoenix, at least not until September or so. She stood under it for a few moments, allowing the pressurized stream to pound against the muscles in her back. Then she washed with soap from a handy dispenser, shampooed and conditioned with the vaguely rose-scented products from the two other dispensers, turned the water off, and stepped out to dry. The whole process had taken five minutes, if that.

A few more minutes to dry off, brush her teeth, comb her hair, dress, and apply the tiniest bit of eyeliner so she looked like she'd gotten six hours of sleep instead of three. Judging the reflection in the mirror to be adequate, she headed for the kitchenette, where an automatic coffeemaker had already been preprogrammed to start brewing at five-thirty. She loved coffee, the darker the better—especially when she was operating on amounts of sleep that could as easily be calculated in minutes as hours. An obscure Austrian study had shown a strong link between a fondness for bitter tastes—coffee was the example used—and what they called "malevolent personality traits." Those traits included narcissism, sadism, and taking pleasure in manipulating and hurting others. Your garden-variety psychopath, in other words. After a big cup of Army-issue java, Fallon finally felt like she might be ready to face the day.

She headed back to the bedroom to make up her bunk out of habit and stopped when she saw the framed picture sitting on the metal side table. Her knees went suddenly weak, and she sank down onto the bed, looking at the photo.

It was the picture she kept on her desk at her lab.

One of the few of her and Jason, from when he was just learning to walk. They'd been at some park, the three of them, having a picnic. Mark had been trying to get Jason to walk to him, and Fallon had managed to get a few shots of their little guy taking a single step before falling back on his diapered behind. They'd given up, deciding he just wasn't ready yet, and focused on getting their lunch ready.

Fallon had been so intent on taking things out of the picnic basket and arranging them just so on their clichéd little red-and-white checked blanket that she hadn't noticed when Jason had used the big wicker container to pull himself up. But some mother's instinct had made her look up just as he let go and took one step toward her, and then another, and another. She'd held her arms out to him, tears sparkling in her eyes, the delighted smile on her face reflected perfectly on his.

Mark had snapped the picture just as Jason had held his arms up for her to catch him. The twin smiles, the fingers—one set long and slender and the other kissably pudgy—reaching out but not quite touching, the milestone moment caught forever on a digital canvas, just before Jason had lost his balance and toppled toward her, laughing and trusting as she caught him up in a fierce hug.

It was one of the only times she could remember being truly happy.

Fallon blinked, swallowed, then abruptly stood and finished making the bed. She deserved more of those moments. So did Jason—that's why she'd been using the prototype on herself—and she resolved to do everything within her power to make sure he got them. That they both did.

Determination squaring her jaw, she turned smartly from the bed and the photograph and headed toward the lab.

Time to make it happen.

## CHAPTER 13

*69 hours*

**T**his time when she entered the lab, the lights were already on, and there were two armed guards—one by the door to her quarters and one by the door leading outside. Fallon wasn't sure if they were a result of her near-lapse on the phone last night, or if she would have woken to find them babysitting her regardless of how circumspect she'd been. She supposed it didn't really matter; they were here now. So she might as well put them to good use.

"You," she said to the soldier by the far door. "What's your name?"

"Davidson, ma'am."

"Davidson. Can you poke your head outside and ask your counterpart on the other side of the door to have Hank Light brought here? I need to run his scans." Davidson looked a little nonplussed, as if being ordered about by a civilian was something he wasn't entirely used to. Which was going to have to change in a big hurry if he was going to be assigned to watch her. She was shorthanded, and no one got to just stand around in *her* lab, gun or no gun. "Oh, and make sure he's cuffed with zip ties—nothing metal. I'm going to need to do an MRI, and I'm sure none of us wants him loose for that."

"Yes, ma'am," he said, likely responding more to her assumption of authority than to any orders he might have been issued to put himself at her disposal while on guard duty. Fallon didn't much care why he listened; she was just glad he did.

As he stuck his head out the door and conversed in low tones with someone Fallon couldn't see, she turned to the other guard.

"And you?"

"Ma'am?" This one was older than Davidson, probably no green recruit. Though she doubted anyone who was truly that inexperienced would get called in for the task of cordoning off a major U.S. city. She was pretty sure there was no—what had Briggs called it? MOS?—for that particular task.

And it wasn't as if even the high-ranking officers would have seen action quite like this before. Coupled with the fact that the military was all-volunteer now, and maybe green was as good as it got.

"What's your name?"

"Romero, ma'am."

"Okay, Romero, I don't know if they're going to send guards over with Light or if they're going to expect you and Davidson to pull double duty, watching him *and* me, but if it comes down to it, and you have to choose one of us to shoot? Just make sure it's him."

Romero was no scarlet-clad bearskin-wearing British guard; he actually cracked a smile.

"I'll take it under advisement, ma'am," he said, and Fallon nodded. That was probably the best she was likely to get. She'd take it.

As she waited for Light to be brought over from the infield garages, or wherever Robbins might have him stowed now, she got the MRI scanner up and running. She'd fired it up last night, just to make sure she could handle it on her own since it was a much newer machine than the one in her old lab, and the help Robbins had promised her had thus far failed to materialize.

Not that she needed them. She wasn't generally the one who ran the tests—that fell to one of many research assistants—but she prided herself on being able to use every piece of equipment under her roof, and if someone was out sick or on vacation, she didn't hesitate to step in. Elliott had often joked she was a one-woman lab, and only needed the rest of them for more grant money—the bigger the lab, the bigger the check. But considering what Elliott had done with the fruits of the research that money had paid for, she sometimes wished she really *had* been doing all the work alone. At least then she wouldn't have to worry about a renegade partner running around doing God knew what with their only prototype.

Satisfied that she'd be able to get Light's scans even without any help, Fallon sat back in the chair on the other side of the RF-shielded window, marveling at how quickly the Army had managed to put together the MRI room. Magnetic Resonance Imaging units not only employed a strong magnetic field but also a specific radio frequency that transmitted the images to the computer on her side of the window. An MRI enclosure had to be constructed so that not only was there no magnetic material inside the room, but also so that no outside radio signals could get in to interfere with the signal from the unit. Fallon knew it usually involved copper and plastic and concrete, though she didn't see how they could have used concrete this time around, since it wouldn't have had enough time to cure.

But whatever they'd used, she had to assume it was up to specs. All she really knew was that she had a state-of-the-art fMRI machine at her disposal, and she sure as hell wasn't complaining.

Well, not about *that*, anyway.

The door opened, and Light entered, followed by another armed soldier, who nudged the former EMT along with the barrel of his M4, and not gently.

Fallon spun her chair all the way around so she was facing them.

"Good morning, Mr. Light, and congratulations."

His eyes narrowed suspiciously.

"For what?"

Fallon smiled.

"You get to be my first guinea pig."

Light scoffed, and Fallon raised her eyebrows, then shrugged.

"Or lab rat, if you prefer. Either way, you're about to get strapped down and shoved into a metal tube, so I can take pictures of your brain. I hope you're not claustrophobic." Her smile widened a bit at the thought. She knew she should be playing the dispassionate scientist, but she didn't like Light, and she felt no particular urge to hide the fact. Every time she looked at him, she saw the woman and child he'd run down with that ambulance, and her own face, and Jason's, superimposed over theirs.

"I suppose I don't have any say in the matter," he said dryly, clearly amused.

*No more than your victims had,* Fallon thought, but didn't say. Light was a psychopath and a master manipulator. She'd already given him too much ammunition by letting him see her distaste; that had been a mistake. She didn't intend to compound it.

"Not really, no," she said, and the guard behind him jabbed him in the back with his rifle for emphasis, eliciting a pained *oof.*

"Look at it this way, Light," she added. "It'll be good practice for the next time you're strapped down."

"What are you talking about?" he asked, suddenly wary.

Fallon smiled again, and despite her best intentions, she couldn't keep just a trace of smugness out of it.

"Well, isn't it obvious? When they give you the needle."

**T**he hard part was that Light had to keep his head still for the scan. Most psychopaths she had worked with were volunteers, willing to cooperate because they had been promised privileges of some kind at whatever maximum-security prison they'd been sentenced to. Light was no volunteer, and he let Fallon know it by pretending to comply, then jerking his head around at key moments, spoiling the scans. She was eating up data storage space on nothing.

After his third such stunt, Fallon brought him out and spoke to Romero, where Light could hear them. "I was told that the prisoner could be more . . . *comprehensively* restrained, if need be. Can you handle that?"

"I can truss him up like a Thanksgiving turkey, Doctor. That what you want?"

"That would probably do. As long as you can get his head into some kind of nonmetallic brace that'll hold it absolutely motionless."

Unfortunately, his hands had to remain free. Because this was a functional MRI, he would have a series of tasks to perform, which would require use of a device he could hold but not lift to where he could see it or do anything else with it.

"It wouldn't hurt," she added, "if you left him that

way for several hours after I'm finished, too. Just in case."

"In case of what?" Light wanted to know.

"Just . . . in case."

His voice took on a menacing tone. Psychopaths could be charmers, but they could also be bluntly threatening. Sometimes in the same sentence. "You really don't want to do that. You already told me I have something you—or they—want. You tie me up, you're not going to get it."

Fallon decided that honesty was the way to approach him—as long as that honesty met threat with threat. "Well, here's the thing, Light. I won't actually know if you *do* have it until I run these scans. Maybe then you'll be in a position to bargain. Right now, you're not. I don't necessarily want to strap you down like a mummy, but I will. In fact, I'll leave you wrapped up for forty-eight hours straight and not lose a minute's sleep over it. Is that what you want? To be lashed to a cot for two days and nights, lying in your own waste, without food or water?"

"You can't—"

"The hell I can't," she interrupted. "You haven't forgotten the most basic fact of your life already, have you? You have no rights. None. I can do whatever I want with you. If I want to put a bullet in your skull and leave you in the desert for carrion eaters, I can."

The start of a smile snaked across his lips. "You couldn't kill anyone."

"Maybe, maybe not," she said. "Whether I'd pull

the trigger is irrelevant. There are plenty of soldiers here with plenty of experience killing people. And nobody here would shed a tear for you."

"Just say the word, Doctor," Romero said. "I'd be happy to do the deed."

Light's smile faded. His eyes were wide, fixed. No doubt thinking, trying to find some other angle to play. But he was strapped prone on a high platform, and two armed soldiers were standing just far enough away to shoot him before he could reach them.

She could see the moment resignation set in. His eyelids closed the slightest bit, his jaw relaxed. "Okay, I'll play your game. This time. What do you need me to do, again?"

She repeated the instructions she had given him the first time . . . and the second. First he would see a high-resolution video of a peaceful scene—prairie grasses undulating in a gentle breeze. That would not only help with any sense of claustrophobia but would focus his eyes on the screen, where she needed them. After a couple of minutes, the testing would start. First he'd view a variety of images and catalogue them according to how immoral the scenes they showed were, then he'd try to memorize a long list of words—the ones he could remember would tell Fallon a lot about him. But the cameras recording eye movement and the fMRI scanners measuring blood flow to the different parts of his brain would tell her so much more.

When he indicated that he understood, Fallon and the soldiers left the MRI room for the fourth time, moving into the control room so they could see and hear everything Light did. The door to the MRI room locked with a loud *thunk* that reminded most psychopaths she'd scanned of prison doors. So far, Light had never spent time in prison.

That, she was sure, would soon change.

The guards left with Light, and Fallon made some observations while the scan was in progress, but comprehensive analysis would have to wait until high-powered computers had crunched the data from the thousands of images the machine had amassed. While she perused what she could, her mind raced down different avenues, working toward a destination of its own design.

Finally, she left the computers to do their thing. She wanted to check in on Randy Wayne Warga. By now, if he was going to show signs of infection, they should have manifested. Davidson escorted her to the building where the murderer was held—not the garage where she'd first observed Light, but yet another of the new buildings popping up in the infield like weeds after a monsoon. He had a bunk and combination sink and toilet, and that was all. There were other cells, too, on either side of him. They were empty, but there were others farther down she couldn't see into; she imagined that Light was now residing in one of those, but didn't care enough to ask.

Warga was dressed in prison orange, but in spite of

that sartorial disadvantage, he was a good-looking man. His blue eyes were clear and bright, his jaw was square, his brown hair cut short and as neatly finger-combed as he could manage in here, with no mirror. He had a muscular build, broad-shouldered and deep-chested. His prison tats had been kept to a minimum—a snake coiled out from under his collar and wrapped partway around his neck, and he had a series of eleven black dots on his right temple that Fallon didn't want to speculate about. Those looks, she knew, were part of how he earned the trust of his victims . . . right before he brutalized them, raped them, and strangled the life from them with his powerful hands. She took a good look, focusing particularly on his cheeks and eyes, but saw no signs of illness. His hand was still bandaged, but the scratches and bruises he'd received fighting the Infected seemed to be healing quickly.

"Didn't get enough yesterday, Doc? I can take my shirt off, you want to see more? Hell, why stop there?"

"I'm not here to admire you, Randy."

"You always say that. But you always come back for more."

"Scientific curiosity," Fallon said. "About your twisted brain, not your physique or any imagined sexual prowess."

"You'd have to have a pretty wild imagination," he said. "Or you'd sell me short."

"I doubt that."

"Live and learn."

"I intend to. But not about that."

"What, then? I can tell by lookin' at you, you ain't getting enough at home."

That stung, but she kept her expression flat. Having plenty of experience with psychopaths, she ignored most of what they said—in her line of work, it was crucial. Sure, maybe he could tell, but more likely he was just fishing.

She wasn't biting.

"I'm doing just fine. Thanks for your concern."

"You know I've always thought you were a looker, Doc. I'd give you a good pounding."

"Pass," Fallon said. "I just wanted to see if you're infected yet."

"With what?"

"You don't remember being attacked by three people who wanted to eat your brain yesterday?"

Warga chuckled. "I just figured that was another of your crazy tests. You're always showin' up, wantin' to probe something or other. About the only thing you ain't done is hook electrodes up to my junk."

"Anyway, you appear to be fine."

"Damn straight. Better than fine."

Fallon turned her back on him and headed for the door. He wouldn't quit—never had, in her experience. She had learned that a summary dismissal was the best way to deal with him.

Halfway back to her lab, she could still hear him shouting after her, rattling off a series of suggestions so lewd she would have blushed if she hadn't spent time with him before.

"That one's got quite a mouth on him," Davidson said.

"He lives for sex. His idea of it, anyway, which is different from most people's."

"Different how?"

"Ever heard about the mating habits of praying mantises?"

"The bugs? Can't say I have."

"During copulation, or right after, the female typically bites the head off the male. Warga's a little like that, only he can't finish unless he's got his hands around the woman's throat. If he climaxes while she's dying, that's fine with him, but he likes it better if she's already dead."

Davidson stopped in his tracks and stared at her. "Really? That guy you just talked to does that?"

"Whenever he can."

"Doctor, you sure know some strange characters."

"That I do, Davidson. That I do."

# CHAPTER 14

*68 hours*

Fallon and Davidson were almost back to the lab when she heard someone call her name. She turned and saw Special Agent in Charge Ramirez walking toward her across the track. Heat radiated from the pavement in waves, making the agent's approach resemble some kind of apparition.

"A moment, Fallon?" she asked when she was near enough. The glance she shot Davidson wasn't hard to interpret.

"I'll be close by, Doctor, if you need me."

"Thanks, Davidson," Fallon said. "What is it, Soledad?"

Soledad matched Fallon's stride as they continued toward the lab. "You saw Mr. Warga?"

"That's right."

"What's your take?"

"Well, he's obviously not infected."

"And you're sure he's a psychopath?"

"Textbook. I've scanned him a couple of times, once with a standard MRI, once with a functional."

"What does that show you?" Ramirez asked, curious.

"The most notable aspect of a classic psychopathic brain is a significant lack of grey matter in the paralimbic region. That's the orbitofrontal cortex, the amygdala, the posterior cingulate cortex. The fMRI shows reduced blood flow in that region, too. It's like it's atrophied down to almost nothing."

"Which results in what?"

"I assume you want the capsule version and not the Neuroscience 101 lecture?"

"Capsule is fine."

"The paralimbic system regulates things like impulse control, empathy, emotional learning, motivation. The amygdala is particularly affected in these brains—that's the center of perceiving and processing emotions."

"So somebody with a damaged amygdala—"

Fallon didn't wait for the rest of the question. "Might never feel emotions the way most people do. In psychopaths, emotional response tends to be flat. They don't understand—can't even grasp—why the rest of us feel things. To them, emotions are useful tools only in that knowing what they are, what our emotional responses might be, allows them to manipulate us. But they're not feeling them in the same way. They're much more basic. What's love? Sex. What's fear? Kill or be killed."

"So basically what you're saying is that all men are psychopaths."

Fallon glanced at her, looking for a hint of a smile, a twinkle in the eye. Didn't see it. "I guess that depends on your experience with men." Elliott's face flashed through her mind, and she chased it away. "Whatever it is, magnify by a factor of a thousand, and you get somebody like Warga. He's shaped like a human being, but that's about the only area of commonality."

They reached the lab. The guard outside, whose name Fallon still hadn't caught, opened the door and waved her and Ramirez through. The agent looked around and gave a low whistle. "Nice setup."

"They did good," Fallon admitted.

"You scanned Light earlier this morning, right?"

"Yes."

"And?"

Fallon's gaze was drawn to the bank of computers near her desk. "Data's processing," she said. "Initial scans, though, indicated that his paralimbic cortex was nearly as lacking as Warga's."

"So he has a psychopathic brain structure."

"Pending further analysis, I would say yes. He does."

Ramirez eyed a rolling office chair that Fallon had pushed up against a wall. "Mind if I sit?"

"Go for it." Fallon pulled her own desk chair back, swiveled it to face the SAC, and lowered herself into it. "What's up?"

Ramirez waved a nail-bitten hand in the general direction of downtown Phoenix. "My city's being destroyed from the inside out. I've put a lot of sweat and blood and time into protecting it, and now I feel . . . so helpless. Like I can't do anything but stand back and watch it happen. I hate that."

"I'm sure."

"I want answers. I want action. I'm tired of waiting. I want to *do* something."

"I know how you feel, Soledad. But even if we determine with absolute certainty that psychopaths are immune, it'll take time to figure out why. More time to turn that knowledge into something like a vaccine. Months. Years, maybe."

"There won't be anything left in there in months or years. We have days, at best."

"Before the nukes."

It wasn't really a question, but Ramirez answered anyway. "Right." She put her hands behind her back, stretched. "Before this—your research. You've been working on technology that could detect psychopathic brain structure and maybe do something to dial back psychopathic impulses."

Fallon didn't answer. Only a few people in the federal government were supposed to know the details of her research. Soledad Ramirez wasn't one of them.

The agent went on. "Could you maybe reverse the process? *Make* psychopaths?"

"For study subjects?"

"Well, for starters. Wouldn't more subjects make the research go faster?"

Fallon wasn't surprised by the SAC's lack of ethics—she figured you didn't reach a high position in the FBI without a certain degree of larceny in your soul. But it bothered her that the woman seemed to know so much about her work, and she said so.

"We were all briefed on you before they brought you in," Ramirez said. "Special Agent Barksdale is one of mine, and I wasn't going to send her to collect you without knowing what she was in for."

Which meant Thurman had briefed them, since he was the only one here—that she knew of—who was aware of what the lab's research was all about. She'd thought she could trust him. He'd bear watching from here on out.

Of course, she had to admit these were exceptional circumstances. If people like Light had surrendered their human rights, having her professional secrets revealed to a group of people trying to defend the human race probably wasn't so bad.

Still, there was a limit to how much she would spill. She didn't want to admit that there was a working prototype—or, more importantly, that she didn't know where it was.

"We never even considered that possibility. It's really outside the realm of our work," she said. "We're still trying to figure out what makes them tick, and with luck, how to beef up the damaged portions of the brain, to help with self-control and the processing of emotions. Reversing course would be a big jump—not something that could be done quickly."

"So you couldn't just turn the population of Phoenix into psychopaths long enough to stop the spread of the disease?"

"I can't imagine that would be possible, let alone ethical. And it might cause more problems than it solved."

"I had to ask."

"Of course," Fallon said. She hadn't been entirely honest. There might be a way to do what Ramirez had suggested, at least on a small scale. She'd have to have the prototype, of course, and some time to work with it, but she didn't think creating psychopaths was *impossible*. Still, it wasn't the avenue her thoughts had begun to travel down.

"I do have the beginnings of an idea, maybe," she said. "It's not fully formed—not even enough to articulate. But I promise, if and when I work out the details, I'll bring it to you. Okay?"

"Whatever you come up with, Fallon, I'll look at with an open mind."

"That's all I can ask."

The agent excused herself, and Fallon started in on Light's fMRI scans.

As she'd thought, he showed the classic structure. His orbitofrontal cortex was underdeveloped, his amygdala dysfunctional—his whole paralimbic system was a mess. That in itself didn't turn someone into a serial killer, but it was a good start. Nature went so far, then nurture took over. Early life experience wrought epigenetic changes, which could push someone who had poor impulse control and an inadequate emotional regulatory system over the edge. Add in an introduction to violent behavior somewhere along the way, and it became almost impossible to expect a normally functioning human being. Someone would have to map Light's genome, but she already suspected that many of the genetic traits common to psychopaths would show up.

So far—on paper, anyway—Hank Light was a pure psychopath.

A commotion outside tore her attention away from her data. Had Light escaped, or Warga? Had the fence been breached? Fallon couldn't think of any possibilities that weren't bad. Davidson still hadn't come inside, even though Ramirez had been gone for a little while. She and Romero exchanged glances, then simultaneously started toward the door.

She stepped outside. Davidson and some others were running toward the main gate. Her gaze followed their path, and she saw what was causing the fuss. A Stryker was rolling in through the gate. When they'd left, they were painted in olive drab, but this one looked like it had been attacked by graffiti artists—it was splashed liberally with what appeared to be gallons of red paint, and plastered with . . . well, *what*, she couldn't tell from here.

She hadn't taken very many steps toward it when she realized that the paint was actually blood, and the rest were parts.

Fallon looked beyond the carnage-encrusted Stryker, but she couldn't see the other tactical vehicles anywhere.

The Stryker slowed to a stop, but soldiers on the ground frantically motioned to the driver to keep going. The vehicle stuttered, as if the driver was unsure, but then it started rolling again. The soldiers directed it into one of the new infield buildings that looked like a big garage. The sliding door was thrown open, and the Stryker moved inside. Fallon heard sounds she couldn't identify. She started toward the garage, along with Romero and most of the troops who were outside. By the time she reached it, doors banged shut, and locks were thrown.

She saw Davidson standing outside the garage, and stopped beside him. Following his gaze, she looked into the brightly lit space. The Stryker sat inside what looked like a giant terrarium. "What is that?"

"Quarantine chamber," Davidson said.

"A quarantine chamber big enough for a tank?"

"It's not a tank, it's a Stryker NBCRV."

"I wasn't being literal."

"'Course not, sorry."

The vehicle's hatches opened, and soldiers emerged. The last one out was Specialist Briggs. He looked thirty years older than when he'd left. He was too far away for Fallon to be certain, but she thought his eyes looked shadowed. Haunted.

By now, General Robbins and a couple of assistant SecDefs had shown up, along with Ehlers, Thurman, and some of the other top dogs. Book was there, too, but he hung back from the rest, spying her and navigating through the throng to stand beside her, where he seemed to feel more comfortable. Fallon nodded at him before returning her attention to the bigwigs.

They congregated close to the glass—or Plexiglas, she couldn't be sure—and gathered around what she realized now was a microphone. A squeal of feedback, quickly cut off, told her that the inside of the glass was miked, too. The soldiers stood on the other side from the brass, ready to make their report. But before Briggs could speak, Robbins's voice boomed out, carrying over the murmuring crowd and the all-but-abandoned track.

"Where the hell are the other Strykers?"

Silence descended as Briggs answered.

"Gone, sir."

"What was that, Specialist?"

"They're gone, sir," Briggs repeated, louder this time, though Fallon was sure everyone had heard him just fine before. "Destroyed, their crews dead.

"We're the only survivors."

## CHAPTER 15

*67 hours*

**B**ook wasn't sure if it was his own gasp he heard, Fallon's, or a collective shocked intake of breath from the entire crowd. Then everyone seemed to start talking at once.

"Did you hear? *No survivors . . .*"

" . . . is that even possible? Those things are armored up the ass . . ."

" . . . can take out a Stryker, what good is a fence going . . ."

"Ten-*HUT!*"

Book wasn't sure which officer had barked the command—it would have been beneath Robbins—but suddenly, every soldier, inside quarantine and out, was standing with heels together, chests out, heads high, and mouths closed.

Into that silence, the general spoke.

"Give me your report, Specialist."

Book was close enough that he could see Briggs nod, but not so close he could see the other man's eyes or make out his expressions. As the soldier began relating his tale in a voice just this side of the grave, Book found that he was glad.

"Yes, sir. Things were pretty quiet once we went outside the wire. Sergeant Kenton was in the lead Stryker, relaying intel back to us. There wasn't much movement in the residential areas, but we could feel people watching from behind shutters and curtains. Not so different from being on a convoy in the sandbox, really, except we didn't have to worry about getting fu—sorry, sir, I mean, we didn't have to worry about encountering any IEDs.

"Didn't start to get hairy until we were on the highway, heading into downtown. There were cars pulled off onto the shoulder, sitting in the divide, just stopped in the middle of the lanes, but we were able to navigate around them. Or through them.

"Then we got to the tunnel."

Book wasn't from Phoenix; he had no idea what the significance of Briggs's statement was, but he saw Fallon wince, and even some of the local soldiers around him shifted uncomfortably. He understood enough about combat strategy to realize it was a chokepoint, and that screamed ambush. Years of playing MMORPGs in his downtime were good for something, it seemed.

But he didn't understand why a place that would

be an obvious spot for an ambush in a real war would be one in a battle against violent individuals with a penchant for grey matter. It wasn't as if the Infecteds could act in any coordinated fashion. Moreover, he still couldn't understand why they would even bother with a heavily armed vehicle if there was easier prey in the vicinity. And there *had* to be easier prey, downtown in a major metropolitan center.

"Some of us suggested going around, but Sarge wanted to go straight through. Didn't want to waste time looking for another route. So we put the headlights on, slowed down, and started through, his vehicle taking point, mine bringing up the rear.

"The east side of the tunnel was still open, but as we went in, it was clogged with more and more cars. Sarge's Stryker was able to push the smaller vehicles out of the way, but it was slow going.

"And then we ran into people."

Briggs's voice had grown quieter as he spoke, and it was almost comical to see the soldiers still standing at attention straining forward to hear. Book thought he could probably topple them like dominoes without too much effort, but figured the brass would frown on that. Still, he couldn't hide a small smile at the incongruous thought, which earned him an odd look from Fallon.

*Great, now she's going to think I'm a psycho, too.*

His fledgling grin died in infancy, and he looked back toward the garage quickly.

"They were all grouped together between some

stopped cars, standing over something. Someone. We weren't supposed to stop, but they were blocking the way, and Sarge figured someone was hurt, maybe couldn't be moved. So he ordered a halt and sent Haskins and Phelps out. Phelps had taken some nursing classes before joining up, so Sarge thought he'd be the best one to assess the situation."

Even at this distance, Book could see the greenish cast to the specialist's skin, the horrified look on his face.

"They had their guns ready, but . . . they thought they were dealing with ordinary people—hurt, scared, maybe, but on our side. We all did."

"Idiots," Fallon murmured under her breath. Book shot her a glance; she was shaking her head and frowning the way people watching a horror movie often did, her face awash in a mixture of frustration and dread.

"They got about five feet away and could finally see what the crowd was looking at. Phelps described it to the rest of us, whispering over the com—several children sitting around a woman's body. The car closest to them had the driver's door open, and the windshield was starred and bloody on the inside where someone—Phelps thought the woman—had cracked her head open when the car rear-ended the one in front of it.

"He said it looked like the kids had pulled her out of the car and sat down to make a picnic out of her brain. They'd picked her brainpan clean. When he said that, Haskins turned around and threw up.

"And that's when the rest of them took notice."

Not even military discipline could keep the crowd from moving forward, hanging on Briggs's every word. Book moved with them, Fallon beside him, one of the soldiers who had been assigned to watch her—Romero, if he remembered correctly—on her other side.

"They swarmed Haskins and Phelps before either one of them could get off a shot. We could hear them shouting and screaming over the com. Sarge was blasting into them with the M2, but it was too late. Phelps and Haskins were . . . just . . . gone."

"What do you mean, 'gone,' soldier?"

It was the first time General Robbins had spoken since Briggs had started his story. Book couldn't see the general's face, but he thought the man's voice sounded gruffer than usual.

Book didn't really think Briggs's word choice needed elaboration—it was pretty obvious the two soldiers had died horribly—but when he saw the specialist, who'd been on the verge of tears, straighten and collect himself, the analyst understood what Robbins was doing. Bringing the soldier out of the memory, back to the present. Back from the edge of hysteria. His respect for the general rose a notch.

"Sorry, sir. Um, they died, sir. Were killed by . . . the Infecteds. Torn apart.

"Sarge ordered a retreat, but he was in the lead. By the time the rest of us could reverse course, the Infecteds had left Haskins and Phelps behind and started toward their vehicle. Sarge was able to take out some of them with his fifty-cal, but most of them just wouldn't go down, and they made it to the Stryker and started climbing on it.

"I don't know how they figured out how to get in—maybe it was just like a big metal skull to them, and they just kept at it 'til they cracked it open. But somehow they got the rear hatch open and got inside. Sarge was in there, and Cooper. We heard gunfire, screams. One loud report that I think was . . . was Cooper offing himself. Then we just heard grunts, and growls, and . . . slurping noises."

Book glanced at the gore on the Stryker and gave silent thanks that he hadn't yet eaten.

"But Sarge had the last laugh," Briggs was saying. "I guess he managed to pull the pin on a grenade before they got him, because all of a sudden there was this roaring sound over the com, and we could feel the ground shake as we hightailed it out of there. Corporal McCann was in the second Stryker—now the last one—and he got eyes on Sarge's vehicle. What was left of it was up against the side of the tunnel, wheels still turning even though it couldn't go anywhere. The top hatch was blown off, and the rest was smoke and flames and body parts.

"Corporal Healy was in charge now, and she ordered us to take the first exit when we got out of the tunnel and take surface streets the rest of the way. And no more stopping, no matter what."

Briggs looked up then—he'd been staring at the

floor for most of the tale except when Robbins spoke to him directly.

"We got through downtown, though we kept having to detour where the cars were jammed too close. And we kept running into Infecteds, more and more the farther east we got. Healy ordered us to flatten anyone—any*thing*—that got in the way, and we did." He shuddered then, and Book had a sudden flash of the video footage of Light running down that woman and her child in the street. "I mean, we *thought* they were Infecteds, but . . . they looked just like us, really, so we couldn't always be sure."

"Did anyone think to bring a psychiatrist when they set this place up?" Fallon asked suddenly, jarring Book out of the memory. He looked over at her.

"What do you mean?"

"A psychiatrist. Briggs and the other survivors are going to need one—probably half the people listening, too. But especially the soldiers. Living through that kind of trauma, when they're all so young? You'd be surprised at what effects early-childhood trauma has on people. And even later in life, protracted, traumatic stress—such as combat—can cause a similar impact. It doesn't even have to cause PTSD to affect their brain structure."

Fallon didn't say it, but he knew her specialty was psychopathic brains, so he had to assume the changes she was talking about weren't for the better.

"I don't know," he replied. "I can look into it."

"Do," she said. "And soon."

She turned back toward Briggs, and Book did the same. The specialist was still talking.

" . . . though she'd ordered us not to stop, sometimes we had to. Stop, back up, go around. One of those times, Healy's Stryker got stuck, wedged in between a couple of semis we were trying to get past. Before she could get it unstuck, Infecteds on the other side of the big rigs attacked.

"Healy ordered her crew out, sent them to the next Stryker in line, told them—us—to get the hell out of there. She stayed behind, taking a page out of Sarge's book and lobbing grenades out in front of her Stryker, into the mob of Infecteds. When she ran out of those, she used the top-mounted MK-19. When they got too close for that, she used her M4. And, finally, when they were on top of her, she ate her sidearm. But she gave the rest of us time to get away.

"She saved us," he said, suddenly earnest as he looked at General Robbins. "She was a hero."

"And she'll get a hero's recognition, son. You all will."

Briggs nodded, seemingly reassured by the general's surprisingly gentle tone. Then the specialist took a deep breath and continued his horror story.

"That left us with no one who knew the area and me in charge. GPS said we were more than halfway to the meteor site, with no easy way to get there from where we were. I had to make a decision."

Briggs stopped, took another deep breath.

"I decided to push on. So when Gordon's Stryker

got overrun with his crew and the rest of Healy's inside, those deaths were all on me."

Book hoped Robbins would disagree and disabuse the specialist of his shame, but the general said nothing. And so Briggs continued, his guilt unabated.

"There was nothing else I could do at that point. The closer we got, the more Infecteds we encountered, and we had just the one Stryker left—damaged when a grenade bounced the wrong way—and virtually no ammo. I ordered the retreat. We barely made it back here. As you can see."

"You did the right thing, Specialist," General Robbins said, but from where Book stood, Briggs didn't look convinced. He nodded anyway, and returned the general's salute smartly, ever the dutiful soldier. But Book watched him after Robbins turned and barked at everyone to return to their duties, and the young man's head fell, and his shoulders drooped, as if telling his tale had snuffed out whatever spark had gotten him back to the PIR. Book suddenly wondered how many guns were still in the Stryker, and if any of them still had bullets. He fervently hoped not.

As the crowd dispersed in response to Robbins's order, Fallon pushed her way upstream, toward the general and the rest of the head honchos, and Book followed in her wake.

" . . . theory's useless if we don't have a way to test it. I don't see what other option we have, except to move up the timetable," Robbins was saying. He and the others started walking back toward the grandstands, arguing heatedly among themselves, but Fallon hurried and grabbed Thurman and Ramirez before they could follow.

"What is it, Fallon?" Thurman asked, somewhat brusquely, eyeing the departing group, clearly anxious to join them.

"Never mind them," Fallon said, pitching her voice low. "Briggs and the others couldn't get to the meteor, but maybe there's someone else who can."

"What are you talking about?" Ramirez asked. Fallon had her attention, and Thurman's now, too.

Fallon smiled, her expression inexplicably giving Book a chill.

"I have an idea . . ."

# CHAPTER 16

*63 hours*

**T**hurman hadn't loved her idea, but Ramirez had been
all for it, and the two women had finally prevailed on
the DOJ official to put the plan in motion. The first
hurdle had been cleared.

The next hurdle was getting Light and Warga to
agree. Fallon didn't particularly relish having to negotiate with either one of them, but she knew Light
would be the more aggressive of the two since he was
arguably smarter and already knew they wanted something from him.

So she'd start with Warga.

It was past noon when she and Davidson entered
the modular building Fallon had come to think of as
the Prison Block. She had no idea why the thing had

so many cells—she'd asked Book, and he told her there were twelve—but she was glad it would be able to house all of her psychos once they got here.

Her stomach grumbled, and she realized she hadn't eaten anything today. And that gave her an idea. She turned to the guard stationed inside the door.

"Have you given the prisoners lunch yet?"

The young man, his face a prairie dog town of acne, looked at Davidson uncertainly.

"Don't look at me, Private!" he barked, much to his credit. "I'm not the one who asked you a question."

"Yes, sir!" the private answered, so green and flustered that he forgot that, as a corporal—she was pretty sure that's what the two stripes on Davidson's shoulder meant, anyway—her new handler wasn't an officer; he worked for a living. The young man looked back at Fallon, his face flushing. "No, ma'am. Sorry, ma'am. It hasn't been delivered yet."

Fallon nodded, accepting his apology. It wasn't like she wasn't used to blatant sexism in the scientific field; the military was only marginally worse.

"Good. When do you expect it?"

"It's already an hour late, so any minute now, ma—"

Just then, the door opened, letting in a blast of oven-hot air and a young man carrying two boxes.

"Lunch?" Fallon asked him, and this one, apparently a little more experienced than the pimply-faced guard, nodded and yes ma'amed her. "I'll take them, then."

She didn't begrudge him his look over at Davidson,

and neither did the corporal, seemingly, because his reply was considerably quieter this time.

"Do as the doctor says, Private."

"Yes, Corporal."

The private dutifully handed the boxes over to Fallon, saluted Davidson, did an about-face, and headed back out into the heat. Fallon handed the top box to the other private and opened the bottom one. It contained a paper-wrapped sandwich, a bag of potato chips, an apple, a cookie, and a carton of milk. Far better fare than most prisons served.

"This is perfect," she said. She looked at the private. "You can take that one to Light. I'll take this one to Warga."

"Yes, ma'am."

"Oh, and can you get me a chair while you're at it?"

"Yes, ma'am."

As he scurried off to do her bidding, Davidson looked at her.

"Should I even ask?"

"Only if you really want to know the answer."

He grimaced.

"That's a 'no,' then."

"Exactly."

The private returned fairly quickly with a folding chair, which he handed to Davidson.

"Okay, Corporal," Fallon said. "Let's go. But stay out of sight. This won't work as well if Warga thinks we're not alone."

"Guess you should carry this, then," he replied, handing her the chair.

She walked down the hallway toward Warga's cell, Davidson several feet behind her. The sound of the air-conditioning was louder here than in any of the other newly erected buildings—Fallon figured the Army might not have spent quite as much money or effort on insulating it, considering the people it housed.

When she reached Warga, she greeted the murderer cordially.

"Hello, Randy," she said as she unfolded the chair and set it down, facing toward the bars. Then she sat on it, the box on her lap.

"Couldn't stop thinkin' about me, huh, Doc?" He leered at her from his bunk.

Fallon ignored him, taking the top off the box and setting it on the floor beside her, making sure she tilted the bottom up as she did, so that Warga could see the contents.

"Hey! Is that my lunch?"

She pretended not to hear as she started unwrapping the sandwich noisily. It was just peanut butter and jelly—grape, which she hated—but her mouth started watering anyway. She really needed to stop skipping breakfast.

She lifted the sandwich to her mouth, took a bite, chewed and swallowed, all while Warga looked on hungrily.

"I'm sorry, Randy, what was that?"

"Bitch. What the hell kind of game are you playing now?"

Fallon feigned surprise.

"No game, Randy. Just a reminder."

His eyes narrowed. He'd gotten up from the bed and crossed over to the bars, his hands grasping two of them tightly. He was probably imagining they were her neck.

"A reminder of *what*?"

Fallon took another bite before answering, then set the sandwich down on its wrapper and grabbed the milk. Opening it, she took two long gulps, then wiped her mouth with the back of her hand. She placed the empty carton back in the box, stood, and walked toward Warga. Out of the corner of her eye, she saw Davidson tense, but she ignored him. When she was just beyond Warga's reach, she stopped and crouched, placing the box on the floor.

"That the creature comforts you enjoy so much come at a price."

The veins in his hands stood out as he clutched the bars, and his face almost matched his prison jumpsuit. Fallon thought she could even hear his teeth grinding, but that was probably just wishful thinking.

"Yeah? And what price is that?"

She gave him a friendly smile. "Let's talk about the comforts first, shall we?"

"You mean like my lunch?"

She shrugged.

"Well, sure. Food," she said, nudging the lunch box

with her toe, "water, sunlight. A bed. All things you have access to now that could easily be taken away from you. But I was thinking bigger. Like, say, temporary freedom."

*That* caught him off guard.

"Say what?"

"Freedom. No more cell, here *or* back in Florence."

He frowned suspiciously.

"How temporary?"

Fallon shrugged again.

"Depends on you, really. How soon you do what you need to do, how well you do it. Might not even be temporary, if you're successful."

"And what is it I need to do, exactly?" he asked. His hands were still on the bars, but they'd relaxed enough that she could see the bandage on the right one. He'd almost gone for the shiny lure. She just needed to wiggle it a little more, and he'd bite.

"Remember those three people who attacked you in the other building?"

Warga rubbed the spot on his cheek where one of them had torn away a small chunk of flesh, held together now by two butterfly bandages.

"People? You mean *things*. That you *let* attack me."

Fallon held up a hand. "That was *not* my idea. But it did help us gain some valuable information."

She was close enough she could see the slight widening of his eyes at the word "valuable."

*Wiggle, wiggle,* she thought.

"Such as?"

"Well, Randy, it appears that you and people like you—you know, murderers, rapists, and other flavors of psychopath—are immune to whatever it is that's turning people into those things you fought. So you're being offered the rare opportunity to serve your country in exchange for all those creature comforts you love so much."

"What, like, in *Armageddon*? So I won't have to pay taxes anymore?"

"That can probably be arranged."

"And what's the catch? They had to become astronauts and go out into space and most of them didn't make it back. Is it going to be like that?"

Fallon hid a smile as she starting reeling in her catch.

"Something like that, yeah. You'll go in with a team of . . . like-minded individuals . . . and retrieve the source of the virus—a meteor, or part of it, anyway—which we'll then be able to use to formulate a vaccine."

It wasn't that simple, of course, but details would only confuse the issue. Especially since they hadn't all been hammered out yet.

"So we'll be heroes."

"Yes, I suppose you will."

"Chicks dig heroes."

Fallon stopped herself from rolling her eyes in disgust, but just barely.

"Some of them." The ones with death wishes, if Warga was their idea of a hero.

He smiled, a predatory smirk that Fallon wanted to claw off his face.

"Okay, Doc. Sign me up. When do I leave?"

"Tomorrow, probably." She used the side of her foot to shove the box of food across the floor, where it fetched up against the bars. "In the meantime, enjoy your lunch."

**L**ight had finished his lunch by the time Fallon and her shadow made it down to his cell, on the opposite side of the corridor from Warga's, the last one in the row.

"Hello, Clarice," he said when she walked into view.

Fallon almost chuckled at that. "Hello, Light," she said instead. "Turns out you won the lottery—you do, in fact, have the brain structure of a psychopath. Not that there was really even any doubt."

"*That's* what I have that the feds want? It's not my stunning good looks or off-the-charts IQ?"

"'Fraid not."

"So, what—they want me to turn me into some kind of covert assassin?"

Fallon did laugh this time.

"You watch too much TV. No, they want you to go back into Phoenix—"

"*Back* in there? You're crazier than I am!"

"—with a team of other psychopaths and recover some fragments of a meteor that fell on the east side. It's the source of the virus that's causing everyone to go crazy and bash each other's heads open. A virus that your brain structure apparently makes you immune to."

"That is the stupidest thing I've ever heard."

"And yet, it's the offer I'm making, so trust that it's real."

"And what if I refuse?"

"Stay here and rot. Hope this place isn't overrun by Infecteds in the meantime, or that someone remembers to move you when they decide to drop the nukes." She nodded toward the box on his cell floor, empty now except for the trash. "Though judging by how late that was, I wouldn't get your hopes up."

"Nukes?"

Fallon nodded.

"That's the only other option. You bring the meteor back so we can make a vaccine, or they're going to turn the Valley of the Sun into a parking lot."

"Not much of a bargaining position, Doc."

"Never said it would be."

"When?"

"Tomorrow, most likely."

He pretended to think it over. It wasn't like he had much of a choice.

"Okay, I'll do it. On one condition."

Fallon blinked.

"Okay, I'll bite. What condition?"

"Since it's likely to be my last meal, I want steak tonight."

Fallon cast a glance over at Davidson, who nodded.

"I can probably make that happen. How do you want it?"

Light smiled, showing perfect teeth.

"Bloody, of course."

# CHAPTER 17

*57 hours*

The helicopter kicked up dust and grit that stung Fallon's cheeks and nearly blotted out the track lights filling the infield with artificial daylight. She squinted and looked away, but too late; her left eye felt like a pebble had lodged in it. Or a boulder. She blinked, hoping she'd tear up and wash it clean in a hurry. Meeting a psychopath while looking like you'd been crying was never a good idea. They thrived on human weakness and exploited it at every opportunity. The "something in my eye" routine—even when true—wouldn't fly.

"This is Antonetti," Thurman announced. He was standing still, feet spread apart, spine rigid. If the mini-haboob bothered him at all, he didn't show it. "You've met him, right?"

Fallon nodded. "I know Gino. The warden at Menard let us take a mobile MRI scanner in and study some of the inmates. Paolo was the one we really wanted, but Warden McCall insisted that we scan some others, too, or it would look like Paolo was getting preferential treatment of some kind. Gino was one of the extras."

"Shame we couldn't get Paolo."

"That would've been . . . difficult."

"To say the least."

Eleven years earlier, Gino Antonetti and his cousin, Paolo Pittarelli, had terrorized two southern Illinois counties, killing fourteen people over a six-week period. Paolo—six years older than Gino, an ex-Marine with a long record of violence—had an old, grey Nissan Sentra that looked like ten thousand other cars on the road. He had taken out the rear seats and cut a hole through the back of the trunk, then a smaller one from the trunk to the outside. Gino had been nineteen, skinny, and when he lay on the floor, upper torso through the hole into the trunk, he could aim a sniper rifle through the smaller hole. Paolo threw a dark blanket over him, once he was in position, so even if someone glanced into the car, they wouldn't see Gino.

Paolo parked at different places—a highway rest stop, a couple of mall parking lots, a rise overlooking residential streets, across the road from gas stations with convenience stores—and Gino shot at whoever caught his attention. Only one shot in any given location, and during the inevitable chaos that followed a hit, Paolo drove away. If no one was hit, sometimes nobody even noticed that a shot had been fired at all. Still, they took off, casually, no more than five miles per hour over the speed limit. Playing it safe.

Finally, a convenience-store clerk spotted the car and reported it, and three days after that, a police officer on patrol saw it on the road. By the time Paolo stopped the Sentra, there were eight law-enforcement vehicles behind it. He drew a .38 and bolted from behind the wheel, firing, trying to make a run for it. He took three bullets, shattering his pelvis and punching a hole in his gut. He survived, but physically was never quite the same.

Gino had stayed in the car until the police surrounded it and showed his hands when they commanded. He'd said that it had all been Paolo's idea—some half-formed notion of teaching people that life was cheap, or precious, maybe both at once—but Gino hadn't needed much convincing, and he never showed an instant's remorse. The scans had shown a severely underdeveloped limbic system. Based on his brain structure and a violent, impoverished upbringing, Fallon was sure he would have shown homicidal tendencies sooner or later, even without Paolo's help. But although Gino had done the shooting, she'd asked for Paolo to be brought in. Despite a limp and some lingering abdominal issues, he was in reasonable health, and his brain was considerably more classically psychopathic than his cousin's. When Book had inquired on her behalf, though, he'd learned that Paolo had been killed by a couple of prison guards after a ruckus in the yard. With no living relatives besides Gino, his personal effects had been sent along, to be given to Gino when he arrived.

As the blades slowed and the prop wash settled back to the ground, Thurman stepped forward. Fallon kept pace, blinking and rubbing at her eye. No relief yet.

Then the copter's door opened, and there was Gino Antonetti, looking older than Fallon remembered— then again, she no doubt looked that way to him—but otherwise the same. Still skinny; obviously weight training hadn't been as appealing to him as it was to many inmates. His hair was black and wavy, his face jowly, hangdog. He always looked sad; even when he smiled, it came across as phony and made him seem more pathetic still. His hands were cuffed behind him, and a burly soldier held on to his arm until another soldier rolled steps up to the helicopter's door. Which, Fallon figured, was probably a hatch or a point of egress or something, in military speak. To her, a door was a door.

Antonetti paused before stepping out of the chopper. His eyes darted this way and that, as if scanning for threats. Maybe he had been locked up so long that big, open spaces scared him. Then his gaze touched upon Fallon and stopped. That smile—still as convincing as a salesman's handshake—appeared. "Hey, Doctor," he said. "Nobody told me you'd be here."

"Did they tell you anything?" she asked.

"Not much. Said I was taking a trip. Put me on

an airplane, then on this whirlybird, and here I am. Ahhh . . . where, exactly?"

"Arizona, Gino. Outside Phoenix."

"This is what the desert looks like? I thought there'd be camels, you know. Sand dunes."

"Not in this desert."

"I never been west of Kansas City, what do I know?"

"I'm sorry about your cousin, Gino."

His face softened, and his shoulders slumped. "Yeah, so am I."

She wasn't surprised by his reaction; Paolo had been the dominant partner in their murderous relationship, and Antonetti had looked up to him. Even psychopaths could have what passed for human attachments.

Like a mother and her child, for instance.

"Were you there?" she asked. "When it . . . ?"

"They kept us pretty separate."

A soldier stepped out of the helicopter, carrying a clear plastic bag. "They sent Paolo's things," Fallon said. The soldier handed it to her, and she held it up, peering inside. "Looks like a wallet, some keys. Dog tags. A couple of other things. The gum's probably a little stale."

"All I care about's the tags," Antonetti said.

"I'll see that you get them."

The soldier gripping his arm gave a tug, and Antonetti stumbled down the steps. "Move it."

"Easy with him!" Fallon said.

"He's just a murdering scumbag," the soldier snapped.

"He's *our* murdering scumbag," Thurman said. "And we need him in one piece."

The soldier dropped his hand from Antonetti and stood up straighter, as if Thurman's words carried more authority than hers did. Which was true, she supposed, but she'd never seen this soldier before, that she knew of, and she didn't think he knew her. He had probably accompanied Antonetti all the way from Illinois.

Antonetti's head swiveled as he looked from Fallon to Thurman and back again. "What's going on?" he asked. "Why am I here?"

"You're here because I had you brought here," Fallon said. "As for why, that's going to wait until the others get here. I've already explained it more times than I care to."

"What others?"

"You'll see, Gino. Just be patient."

"Doc, I been in prison for more than a decade. Maximum security. Sometimes in solitary. If there's one thing I'm good at, it's patience."

Lily June Ogden and Caspar Willetts Pybus arrived on the same chopper, less than an hour after Antonetti. They'd both been incarcerated in Kansas.

Pybus had been held at the United States Penitentiary, Leavenworth. He'd been sentenced there when it was still a maximum-security federal prison. By the time it was downgraded to medium security, he was pushing fifty, and during his eight years there, he'd never been a disciplinary problem, so he was allowed to stay. He'd been older going in than a lot of inmates were coming out, if they got out at all.

Lily was serving her sentence at the Topeka Correctional Facility, the state's only women's prison. She was twenty and looked younger, but there had never been any question about trying her as an adult.

This time, Ramirez accompanied Fallon to the helipad, with Davidson following right behind. And this time, she knew not to stand so close.

"He's a psychopath?" Ramirez asked, as Pybus stepped down from the helicopter's belly. "Doesn't look like much."

Fallon understood her question. Caspar Pybus came across as mild-mannered. He might have been an accountant, or maybe a classics professor at some private university. Wire-rimmed glasses perched on his nose, constantly in danger of falling off. With his neatly trimmed hair turning grey at the temples and a mustache always trimmed precisely at the corners of his mouth, he even looked prim in prison orange.

"Neither did John Wayne Gacy," Fallon said. "Looks have nothing to do with psychopathy. Caspar killed four women. He'd meet them at gigs—he played guitar and sang with a cover band at country-western bars—invite them to his home, and then imprison them for a few weeks in a basement room. After he killed the first one, he cut her up and cooked as much as he could, and later made a point of serving pieces of his most recent victim to each new one. Again, after locking them up for a couple of weeks. They never did find out if he raped them or what because it's hard to run a rape kit on a pot roast."

Ramirez shuddered.

"I know," Fallon said. "So, yeah, psychopath of the highest order. You should see his limbic system."

"That's okay, thanks. Aren't African-American serial killers relatively rare?"

"People think that because in movies and TV shows, they usually see white ones," Fallon replied. She was surprised Ramirez didn't know, but the fact was that most FBI agents didn't spend a lot of time chasing serial killers. "Actually, the ratio of minorities to whites among serial killers is basically proportionate to their representation in the overall population. It's an equal-opportunity aberration."

Lily came off next. Pybus had been allowed to disembark by himself, but Lily had a soldier holding each arm. She was short, curvy without being heavy, and looked surprisingly fresh-faced. Fallon had seen pictures of her during trial and knew she could come across as the girl next door. But she'd also seen photos of Lily from before her arrest, when she did the full-on Goth thing; hair like spilled ink, enough eyeliner to drive up Max Factor's stock prices—or Hot Topic's, more likely. On the top of her left breast—kept discreetly concealed in the courtroom—she had a tattoo that said "Born Dead" in Gothic lettering.

"You're not thinking of sending *her* into the zone?" Ramirez asked. "What'd Lily do, skip school?"

"She'll only answer to Lilith, since that's what she was called in the press after her arrest," Fallon said. "She persuaded five different men to kill for her. That's what she was convicted of, anyway. She claims there were seventeen victims, but the prosecution couldn't get enough evidence to make a case for the other twelve. She also claims she did some of the killing herself—including that of the aunt and uncle who raised her, and, she says, took turns molesting her and farming her out to their friends. But she didn't tell anybody that until after she'd been convicted of conspiring to kill, and she never made a formal confession. She told me when I scanned her, but I wasn't an agent of the court. I told her warden, but it was hearsay and not admissible in court."

"So nobody really knows if she's killed or not."

"Not for sure, no. Didn't stop Charles Manson from spending the rest of his life in prison. He encouraged murder, conspired to murder, but there's no evidence that he did any of the killing himself."

"Sounds like you really establish a rapport with some of these crazies."

"I'm not there to judge them, and they know it. They also trust that what they tell me won't get back to the prison population."

"What about Lily's—Lilith's—non-confession confession?"

"In that case, I guess if the warden was careless or

corrupt, it might have come back around to bite both of us on the ass. But if there were innocent men doing time for murders she blamed on them, I wanted someone to know it."

"Makes sense."

The helicopter blades had stopped spinning, and the dust was settling, so Fallon and SAC Ramirez stepped forward to greet the prisoners. Pybus gave a courtly bow, and Lilith flipped Fallon the bird. "You tried to fuck me over," she said.

"Corrupt, or careless?" Ramirez whispered.

"Dr. O'Meara?" Pybus scoffed. "Impossible. Her ethics are beyond reproach."

"She reproached me right up the ass with a two-by-four," Lily—no, Lilith; if that's what the girl answered to, Fallon wanted to think of her that way—said to him, but her next words, full of a little too much hurt, were directed at Fallon. "I trusted you."

"Look, Lilith, you're right. You trusted me, and I threw you under the bus. I couldn't bear the thought of someone wasting away in prison because you fingered him for a killing you did. I'm sorry."

Lilith barked a loud "Hah!" Her breath smelled like stale tobacco smoke, and maybe pot. "Don't sweat it," she added. "Got me some new respect on the block, and they ain't gonna try me again, so whatever the fuck, right?"

"Sure," Fallon replied. "Whatever. Anyway, we're going to make you comfortable—within reason, anyway—for a while. We're waiting for one more to arrive."

"One more what?" Pybus asked. His voice was deep and pleasant. She had never heard him sing, but had no doubt that it would sound wonderful.

"One more psychopath, Caspar," Fallon said.

Lilith laughed again. "Had to be either that or human sacrifice, right?"

"Or both," Pybus added.

*You don't know how right you are,* Fallon thought. Instead of saying it out loud, she directed the guards toward the Prison Block, where those reasonably comfortable accommodations awaited.

"One more," Ramirez said after they were out of hearing. Her tone was unsettled.

Fallon knew what she was getting at. They'd been over the plan a dozen times, at least, and that was always a sticking point. They both thought an odd number of psychopaths was a better idea than an even number— there might be times, inside the quarantine zone, when they'd have to vote on a course of action, and they'd need a tiebreaker. Fallon had identified seven likely subjects, but it turned out that one was in the hospital after having been shanked by a cellmate, and his chances of pulling through weren't looking good. So her final list consisted of six. They could send five in, but it was going to be dangerous in there, and five hardly seemed like enough even if they were all seasoned killers.

Before Fallon could answer, the sound of another helicopter cut through the desert night. In another minute, its lights came into view as it dropped toward the PIR. "Joe Sansome," Fallon said.

"He's the one who decapitated all those women?"

Fallon nodded. "Seven of them. Each one a green-eyed blonde with an overbite. They reminded him of the girl who broke his heart in high school."

"Some guys just can't handle rejection, I guess."

"Apparently not. The weird thing is, he completely lost track of her after high school. Her name was Becky something. Anyway, one day he's standing in a supermarket checkout line in west Texas, buying some soft drinks and candy. He looks up and sees her."

"Becky?"

"Becky. She's just coming in the store. She doesn't see him, but he can tell it's her a mile away. He goes out and sits in his stolen car. The candy bars melt. Finally, she comes out. He follows her home, stalks her for a week. To work, to the gym, shopping, back home again. Trying to work up the nerve to cut off the one head he'd been after, metaphorically, all along. Instead, he realizes he can't do it, so he calls the police, and says, 'I think you're looking for me. I cut off some girls' heads.'"

While they talked, the helicopter lowered to the earth. Prop wash smacked the ground and threw up a cloud. By the time it subsided, Sansome had been walked off the chopper. He was enormous: a walking, talking, semiliterate refrigerator crate with a wide, flat face—a physical trait often linked to aggressive behavior in men. Fallon had always thought there was a strange, simple sweetness to him . . . if someone whose hobby was cutting off heads could be sweet.

She was tired of talking to psychos, and he not only had chains around his wrists connected to more around his belly and his ankles, but he was gagged with what looked like a bondage getup. She waved his escorts toward the Prison Block, and a soldier stepped up to show them the way.

"No conversation?" Ramirez asked.

"Sansome's not much for talking."

"One more question? I know it's late."

"Sure."

"What'd he do with the heads?"

Fallon managed a weary smile. "Bowling-ball bags."

"Bowling balls?"

"When he turned himself in, local law enforcement searched the stolen car. In the trunk they found eight bowling-ball bags. One was empty."

Soledad chuckled, a dry laugh without much humor in it. "You're tired," she said. "Me, too. We should turn in. Tomorrow, we can bring your psychos up to speed. I still wish we had an odd number, but we'll just make do."

"Yeah, Soledad? About that . . ."

"Yeah?"

Fallon's mouth opened, but then she saw a jeep barreling toward them, Jerry at the wheel. Book sat next to him, Thurman and General Robbins in the back. "Here comes the brass."

Jerry pulled the jeep up beside them just as the helicopter's propellers picked up speed. Everyone was quiet for a few moments until the bird had lifted off, and the racket had died down.

"Looks like we missed the party," Book said.

"Everybody's over at the Prison Block," Fallon said. "I'm sure they'll be rocking the night away."

Robbins laughed. "Prison Block? Good name for it. Better than 'temporary confinement facility.'"

"Head over, sir?" Jerry asked.

"I'm in no hurry to see them," Robbins replied.

"If you have a minute?" Fallon said.

"Sure, Dr. O'Meara. What's on your mind?"

"I was just about to tell Special Agent in Charge Ramirez, but as long as you're here, it probably makes more sense to tell you all at once."

"Tell us what, Fallon?" Thurman asked.

"You know we wanted to get seven . . . umm, *volunteers* here, right? In case there are disagreements between them during the mission."

"Six will do," Ramirez said.

"Better than none," Book added. "At least there's a chance to avoid the nukes."

Robbins scowled at the back of Book's head. "Go on, Doctor."

"Well, there is one more person available to us with the correct brain structure. Someone who's also immune to the virus."

"There is?" Thurman asked.

"Who is it?" Robbins demanded.

"No, Fallon," Book said, looking alarmed. "Don't do—"

Fallon swallowed hard, interrupted.

"Me."

*53 hours*

# CHAPTER 18

"**W**hat?" Ramirez and Thurman asked at the same time. Robbins frowned, and Book looked like he might be ill.

"Me," Fallon repeated, louder now and more confidently. Her secret—well, one of them—was out now, and there was no turning back, only forging ahead. Time to own it. "I've done the scans, multiple times. They were supposed to be part of the control group—a normal baseline to compare abnormal brain structures against. Turns out my 'normal' . . . isn't so much."

"But you haven't killed anyone," Thurman protested. "They ran a thorough background check on you and everyone else in your lab before funding your grant. Something like that would have popped, for sure."

"Having a brain structure common to psychopaths doesn't automatically make you one. Just like having a genetic predisposition to a particular disease doesn't mean you're ever going to get it. Biology isn't destiny. And psychopaths aren't born; they're made—typically by genetics coupled with childhood trauma and abuse. But I didn't grow up surrounded by or subjected to violence. I had a loving, two-parent home where the worst thing that ever happened to me was not getting that Red Ryder BB gun I wanted for Christmas. In short, I have the nature but never had the nurture."

It was the textbook explanation for why some people with dysfunctional or damaged limbic systems became cold-blooded serial killers, and others never did. It was also Fallon's mantra when she was lying in bed at night, and sleep wouldn't come.

"Luckily," she continued, "I don't need to have had any of the awful experiences so common to psychopaths in order to be immune to the virus. I just needed to win the brain lottery."

"Not sure I'd call that winning," Ramirez muttered.

Fallon ignored the comment, pressing on with her hard sell. She didn't want anyone dwelling on the negatives or giving Robbins a reason to nix the idea. Not only did putting her on Team Psycho solve the odd-number problem, but it meant that she could get inside the containment zone, and after some late-night soul-searching, she'd decided that was something she really needed to do.

The route she and Ramirez had worked out—assuming there were no Infected-inspired detours—

would take them right through downtown Phoenix, where Elliott had last been seen. If he was still there—and if she could find him—then maybe she could get the prototype back. She could build another easily enough, provided she could get more funding. That wasn't the issue.

Time was.

She had been using it on herself for months. She had worried that Jason was slipping away from her—or she from him—and even more worried that she didn't care all that much. So she decided to try tamping down her psychopathic nature with the MEIADD. The effects were only temporary, though the more she'd used it, the longer they lasted, and she suspected there might be a cumulative benefit if she kept it up. At any rate, she had become a better, more caring mother, and Jason had seemed to respond in kind. She wasn't about to give that up now.

And who knew what Elliott might do with the prototype? Sell it to the highest bidder? She had staked her career—and now her personal life—on developing the technology. It was all she had, outside of her family, and without it, she might lose both

She had to get into the city, and this looked like her only path. Not just for her own benefit, though that was paramount, but for Phoenix's, too. And maybe it was the so-called "warrior gene" in her expressing itself, but if she had nothing left to lose—if she couldn't retrieve the MEIADD—then going down swinging in defense of the human race definitely had some appeal.

"It makes sense," Fallon insisted, focusing her argument on Robbins since he was the one who would have the ultimate say-so on whether she'd be able to join the others. "I'm the one who developed the plan with Ramirez, and I live here. I know the proposed route, and how to get around if the way is blocked. I know what to expect—I've seen the videos. Aside from Light, I'm the only one who does, and you really don't want *him* leading the team, do you?"

"I don't want *any* of them leading it. I don't even want there to be a team that needs to be led," the general replied.

"But if there's a chance—" Ramirez began, and Robbins cut her short with a wave of his hand.

"We've had the argument, Soledad; you and the good doctor already won. We'll give the psychos some time to try to find this meteor of yours and bring it back. Despite what you may think, I'm not particularly eager to nuke one of the biggest cities in the country. But I'm not afraid to give the order if I have to."

"Let me go with them, and there will be less likelihood of that," Fallon urged quietly.

"She's right," Thurman said suddenly, surprising them all. "We can't trust any of them to do what we're asking once they're not bound and gagged. Fallon knows them, she knows the area, she knows the job. If she's really immune, there's no better choice to lead them."

"I am," Fallon replied. "I can show you the scans if you don't believe me. Or you can just ask Book."

Everyone looked at the analyst, who reddened under their scrutiny.

"It's true," he said grudgingly, his eyes never leaving Fallon's. She could see how much it pained him to say it—of all of them, he was the one who knew the most about her, since he'd had access to all her files, personal and otherwise. He knew what she was, and what she'd be leaving behind. "I've seen them. Her brain is just as messed up as theirs are, so if we're right about psychopathic brain structure conferring immunity—and I believe we are—then she's immune, too."

*Thank you,* she mouthed. Book looked away without replying, swallowing hard.

"Well, Dr. O'Meara," Robbins said, "I guess you've got yourself a new job—Top Psycho." To her surprise, he reached out to shake her hand. "Good luck."

"I'm gonna need it."

**T**he six psychos were lined up in front of her, decked out in their orange jumpsuits and chains. All they needed were blindfolds and cigarettes, and they'd be ready for the firing squad. An option they might prefer to the one Fallon was about to give them.

There was no place in the Prison Block where she could address them all at once, so she'd asked for them to be brought to the same building where Warga had fought the Infecteds. No one had bothered to clean up the blood yet, so the soldiers guarding the prisoners were all wearing biohazard gear. The silent, gun-toting astronauts standing behind each psycho just made the scene that much more surreal, and Fallon had to fight the urge to laugh at the absurdity of it all—a space-borne virus that turned people into violent, brain-eating, not-dead zombies, being essentially kidnapped by the government and hustled off to a secret lab, relying on these six people to save the world.

Well, seven.

"Eyes front, Randy," Fallon said sharply to Warga, who'd been trying surreptitiously to catch glimpses of Lilith. Fallon had had the girl placed at one end of the lineup and Warga at the other, precisely for this reason. Light was next to her, cutting her off from the others. Fallon figured he was a safe bet—Lilith wasn't currently at death's door, so the patient-smothering EMT would have little interest in her.

Warga did as he was told—he'd been in prison long enough that his first instinct was to obey an order, and only afterward to check to see who'd given it.

"I'm sure you're all wondering why you were brought here. What you're about to hear will seem unbelievable to some of you, like something out a science fiction or horror movie, but I assure you, it's all very true, unfortunately."

Fallon looked at Light, whom she'd been told had enjoyed his ultra-rare steak immensely.

"Hank, you want to tell them what you experienced in the emergency room?"

Though the psychos had no reason to trust each other, they had even less to trust her—she was the only one in the room who didn't have a guy in a hazmat suit pointing a gun at her head, after all. The "us vs. them" arrangement—which Fallon had specifically asked for—would make them more inclined to believe one of their own. At least, she hoped so. Because, while she didn't technically need any of them to agree to the mission, things would go so much more smoothly if they all did.

Light—who, as she'd expected, couldn't help but preen a little at being singled out like her second—replied with a confident smile. "Sure thing, Doctor."

He looked at the men to his left, ignoring Lilith. Interesting.

"I'm an EMT when I'm not in shackles and a jumpsuit. Long story short—a meteor broke up over Phoenix a week ago, parts falling all over the city. Some kind of insanity virus hit a few days later—people going crazy, attacking each other, breaking skulls open and scooping out their brains, just like in some lame B horror movie. Except it's real, and the government has quarantined the whole valley."

"Bullshit," Lilith said, her voice shading into pouting petulance. She did *not* like being ignored, especially by a fairly good-looking man. "There's no way the government could do that. And who are you to *her*, anyway? The rest of us are killers—you're a dogooder."

Light laughed, finally deigning to glance to his right.

"Not exactly, sweetheart. See, I'm what you call an

angel of death—I kill my patients with love." He drew the last word out lasciviously, earning chuckles from some of the male psychos.

"That's enough, Light," Fallon broke in. She looked at the others. "Technically, you're all psychopaths, whether you've killed anyone or not—you all have an abnormal brain structure. That's why you're here. Because Light's telling you the truth. Not only has the entire Phoenix metro area been completely cut off from the rest of civilization, but if the largest remaining piece of the meteor can't be found in time, they're going to nuke the entire Valley."

"Told you," Light muttered.

"Pray tell. Dr. O'Meara—what do our brain structures have to do with the meteor?" Pybus asked, diffident and courteous. Fallon found herself feeling grateful for the man. It was so hard to remember that of all her team of misfits, his crimes were the most inhuman and grotesque. "Since I assume you wouldn't be talking about them in the same breath if they weren't related."

"You're exactly right, Caspar. They *are* related. The virus caused by the meteor targets the brain. People with psychopathic brain structures are immune to it. They're the only ones who can go into the quarantine area to retrieve what's left of the meteor, so the scientists back here can come up with a cure and hopefully prevent the annihilation of 4 million people, give or take."

"By which you mean *we're* the only ones who can do it."

"That's correct, Caspar."

"And if we should choose to be . . . less than altruistic?"

Light snorted.

"Then they'll stick us back in our cells here and forget we exist when the time comes to evacuate. Isn't that right, Doc?"

Fallon ignored the EMT, still talking to Caspar, and through him, to the others.

"That virus has caused thousands of deaths so far, and it's going to cause millions more if you—if *we*—don't stop it."

"We?" Caspar asked. "You're coming with us?"

"Yes."

"But aren't you going to get infected right away? What's the use of that?"

"I won't be infected."

"So what?" Warga asked, "You'll be all gussied up in one of those hazmat suits? What a waste, hiding that body in one of those things."

"I won't be infected," she said, ignoring Warga, "because I have the same brain structure that you do."

There was silence for a moment as that sank in, until finally Pybus put it together. "You mean all this time you've been studying us, Doctor, it's been to learn more about yourself?"

"Bull*shit*," Lilith repeated at the same time, her voice angry where Pybus's had been only intensely curious. "No way *you've* ever killed anyone!"

"Volunteering to be my first?"

That shut her up and cut off any arguments the others might have made.

"Yes, I share your same brain structure, though I've never actually acted on the impulses you seem to delight in. So I'll be going in with you. Risking the same things you are. More, because I actually have a life *not* behind bars to come back to."

"We can still refuse," Lilith said. She was definitely pouting.

Fallon nodded.

"Of course you can. But if you don't—if you agree to help me—you'll be helping yourselves, as well."

"How?"

"Whoever makes it back with the part of the meteor we need—and some of us, realistically, might not—will naturally be granted some concessions for their role in saving humanity. That's kind of how the hero thing works."

She could see the word worming itself into their thoughts. No matter how evil their actions, no one ever really thought of themselves as the villain in a story, and these six were no exception. Whether striking back at abusers, helping the heaven-bound along, or acting out some other twisted mission that only made sense in their own warped brains, each one of the people in front of her already thought they were heroes. They wouldn't be able to resist letting the rest of the world know it, too.

"Kinda like the sound of that," Gino said softly. There was a chorus of agreement, then Pybus looked at each of the other five psychos, then at Fallon, the seventh.

"All right, Doctor," he said. "It looks like you've got your team."

**O**nce they'd all agreed, Book, a medic, and another soldier who'd been waiting in the observation area entered the room. They were wearing the same astronaut getups as the soldiers, and both Book and the medic carried a case. The medic's bore a white circle with a red cross inside it, but Book's was a metal briefcase with a biometric lock.

"What's this?" Light asked. It was Book who answered.

"We're going to outfit you all with GPS implants that will allow us to follow your progress."

"You mean so you can keep track of your assets," Pybus said.

Book shrugged.

"However you want to look at it. You're not going in without them." His voice was hard, and he was looking back at Pybus, returning the other man's stare, measure for measure. Still, Fallon was pretty sure his words were aimed at her.

"I'll go first," she announced, walking over to the medic. "Show you how easy it is; that you don't have any reason to be scared."

"I ain't scared," Sansome bristled, and there were similar mutters from the others.

Fallon flashed a conciliatory smile, which she knew would come across as patronizing. "Okay. Nervous, then. Nothing to be ashamed of. Lots of people have issues with being cut into."

*Like your victims,* she thought, but didn't say. No point in antagonizing them any more than she had to in order to get them to do what she wanted.

Fallon stood in front of the medic, but her eyes were on Book. He hadn't mentioned this to her—had barely spoken to her since she'd revealed the truth about her own psychopathic brain to the Powers That Be. She was sure it had been his idea, though. He'd have sold it easily enough—the Army would, as Caspar had said, want to keep track of its assets.

The medic handed his case to the soldier, who held his arms out like a chest-high human desk. Opening it, he pulled out a syringe.

"A little lidocaine and some epinephrine, to keep it from bleeding," he said, using one hand to pinch some skin together at her left temple while he injected her with the other. "Might sting."

In point of fact, it burned like hell, but she schooled her features to show no pain or emotion. Nothing the others could view as a weakness.

*I've been doing the same thing with Mark for a long time. Feeling one thing, showing another.*

He pulled out a small red sharps container and deposited the used syringe in it, then grabbed a scalpel out of a small leather case. She steeled herself not to flinch when he sliced into the side of her face. Then it was Book's turn.

The analyst—who was obviously quite a bit more than that—pulled out a tiny electronic device that looked a little like a metal spider and moved forward. She felt some pressure at her temple, then Book was stepping back, and the medic moved in again, this time with a needle and thread. A couple of stitches and she was done, a little bloody, but no worse for wear.

"See?" she said, turning toward the others. "What'd I tell you? Nothing to it." She nodded at Light. "You're up next."

As the medic was working on Light, she turned to Book.

"What the hell are these things?" she asked in a low voice. "How can they act as a camera or a radio without tapping into the optic or auditory nerves?"

Book shrugged.

"I honestly couldn't tell you—it's above my clearance level. I only found out about them a few days ago. Apparently, there had been discussion about implanting them in the soldiers who took the Strykers in, but the brass ultimately decided against it. I probably would have wound up monitoring the feeds, so I'm glad they did."

He moved over to implant another of his impossible bugs into Light's head, then came back to stand by her side. In the brief time she'd been here, she had started to think he took a special interest in her. They were both smart, data-driven, and out of place here among the military and law enforcement types. There were other scientists on the premises, she knew, but so far, she hadn't had any interactions with them.

Maybe he was drawn to her. She couldn't say that she felt the same way—but she couldn't honestly say that she didn't. She'd been impressed with him thus far, but that could just as easily be the simple respect due a fellow professional as it could be anything more. Employees at the lab sometimes gave her a hard time for coming off as emotionally clueless, and she had to admit that was often accurate. Trying to puzzle it out now would serve no purpose, though; instead, she quizzed him on the device in her temple, which was starting to throb now that the lidocaine was wearing off.

"Yours is special," Book said. "It has a camera and two-way communications capability."

"So you'll be able to see what I see, hear what I hear?"

He nodded. "That's right. I'll be in what they call the tactical operations center, the TOC, where I can follow your route via GPS. And talk to you, but only you. You're the only one here who's not expendable."

"But . . . all the time?"

He chuckled.

"It's not like a cop with a bodycam. You can turn it off when you want to, like if you're using the bathroom. And, of course, if you close your eyes, nothing will be transmitted. Same if you were to plug your ears. Just assume that it's on unless you signal to turn it off."

"How do we turn them off?"

"Click your heels together three times, and—"

"I'm serious," she said, trying not to smile.

"Blink in Morse code. O-F-F when you want to turn it off and O-N when you want to turn it back on. I can override it if I see that you're in trouble, but I'd only do that in an emergency. I'm not some kind of perv."

"Of course you're not. But . . . Morse code? Seriously?"

"Long, long, long. Pause. Short, short, long, short. Pause. Then repeat the last one. To turn it back on, it's long, long, long. Pause. Long, short. Pause."

"Great. I hope I can remember that."

"You can always ask me."

He'd been taking care of the other psychos intermittently during their conversation, and now he moved away to give Lilith her implant. She was the last one.

When he came back, Fallon looked at him.

"You didn't have to do this, you know."

"I didn't—" he began, but she shook her head.

"I work with psychopaths, remember? I'm trained to spot a lie a mile off. I know it was your idea. I just wanted to say thank you."

"You don't have to thank me. Just come back in one piece. Jason's counting on it, whether you believe that or not." His face was so serious, so earnest, Fallon had to wonder if he'd lost his own mother as a child.

"I'll do my best," she promised, and meant it.

Then she turned back to the psychos, all metaphorically locked and loaded.

"You'll be taken back to your cells, where I've been told you'll have a change of clothes waiting, and some food. Get changed, cleaned up, eat, sleep a little. We're leaving before daybreak."

None of them replied. The implants made it all real, and no one had the heart for wisecracks.

As she watched them file out—orange, white, orange, white—she wondered how many of them were actually going to make it back to enjoy that hero status, and how many were going to be honored posthumously, if at all.

She said as much to Book, who gave her a look she couldn't read.

"One," he said. "At least one."

"You promised."

# PART II

# THE ZONE

## CHAPTER 19

*48 hours*

The sun would be up in less than an hour. Forty-eight hours left on the clock. A little less.

Although the area around the gate appeared clear of Infecteds, heading into the quarantine zone—"the zone," as they'd started calling it during their abbreviated planning sessions—under cover of darkness seemed like the best idea. Fallon drove the camo-painted passenger van they'd been given, on the theory that it would attract less attention than the tactical vehicles had. Lilith had called shotgun, and nobody challenged her for it. Sansome sat behind Fallon, with Light beside him. Pybus, Warga, and Antonetti rode in the back. They all wore camouflage uniforms, sans rank insignia, provided by the Army. Fallon's was a little too big, Sansome's way too small, and Lilith absolutely swam in hers. Antonetti had insisted on wearing his cousin's dog tags, and Fallon had finally relented, but otherwise none of them carried identification of any kind.

Once Fallon's presence on the mission had been agreed to, preparations had been so brisk, she'd hardly had time to get nervous. She had managed to squeeze in a twenty-minute catnap, and although she didn't like the idea of setting off on a task like this with so little sleep, she knew the nuclear clock was ticking.

Now, though, driving through Avondale toward the interstate, reality was sinking in. Her gut churned, and her arms and legs trembled. She gripped the wheel tightly, hoping no one would pick up on her terror. Psychopaths were like wild animals that way; when they sensed fear, it spurred them to attack.

"Pretty empty here," Light observed.

"People were told to stay inside if they could," Fallon said, fighting to keep her voice neutral. She sniffed the air, redolent of manure and smoke from distant fires. "This is a rural area anyway, so chances of infection are less than in more congested neighborhoods. These people are probably hunkered down, waiting for some kind of solution."

"Or they're already dead," Lilith added. "Brain-meat for the mob." She sounded almost gleeful at the idea.

"Wonder when we'll see some," Sansome said. His voice was unexpectedly high-pitched for such a big man, and he spoke so softly he was often hard to hear.

"Some what?" Warga asked. "Infecteds? Soon, I hope."

"With luck, we'll find our meteor fragments and get out without seeing any," Fallon said. A Circle K store caught her eye; its front windows had been shattered, and one display fixture jutted halfway outside. Only one car sat in the parking lot, and fire had reduced it to scorched steel and burned rubber. She had to look away, couldn't bear thinking about what had happened there. "We're not here to fight the Infecteds, we're here to collect some rocks and scram."

"Where's the fun in that?" Antonetti asked in a near whine.

"We're not here for fun, either," Fallon countered. "Let's just do the job and get home."

"Easy for you to say, Doc," Warga put in. "Your home's not a ten-by-ten cell."

"I told you that you'd be compensated for your trouble, Randy. That ten-by-ten cell is open for negotiation if we pull this off."

"Yeah, negotiation. Which means I could just as easily be tossed right back in. Or stuck someplace worse."

"I also told you I couldn't make any specific promises in advance. I don't control the criminal justice system. I was told that there would be a variety of options for you, upon successful completion of the mission. Those options include early release, parole, more comfortable living situations, financial rewards, and more. You'll be heroes, after all—just about anything's on the table. But it'll be decided on a case-by-case basis when we get back with the meteor."

"In other words," Light said, "we're all fucked. We'll get back, some shitbird colonel will shake our hands, then it's prison for all of us. I don't know about you guys, but I only agreed to this to stay *out* of a cell."

"But you gave your word," Pybus said. "We all did. Do you mean to back out on it now?"

"Fuck that, old man," Light replied. "Maybe the rest of you don't mind being sheep, but this wolf's gotta howl."

"Caspar's right," Sansome said. "We all promised Dr. O'Meara. And those other people. We need everybody."

"What are you gonna do about it, Dumbo? Kill me? Then you still won't have me, but you will have another murder rap."

"Don't you call me that!" Sansome's hurt sounded genuine. Fallon supposed a guy his size had probably been compared to elephants on a fairly regular basis.

"What, 'Dumbo'? It fits, doesn't it, Dumbo?"

"Children," Fallon warned. Her voice was steadier now, anger lending it steel. "Don't make me stop this car."

That drew a laugh from Lilith, at least. The others gave no sign of having even heard her.

"See here, Mr. Light," Pybus said. "We all have to work together. Starting out by insulting one another is not helpful."

"I'm not insulting poor Dumbo. I just call it like I see it."

"Why don't you keep out of it, Pybus?" Antonetti said. "Pie-bus! That's a hell of a name, isn't it? Mr. Pie-bus! There's no pie on this bus, Dumbo!"

In the rearview, Fallon saw Sansome turn toward Antonetti. At first she thought he was going to actually hit the other man. Instead, he drove a massive fist into the back of his seat, right in front of Antonetti. The thump of his fist was loud, even over the din of voices, and everyone went silent for an instant.

"That's it!" Fallon cried. She yanked the wheel right, pulled onto the shoulder, and killed the engine. They had passed out of the open landscape and into a residential area, with small, single-family homes spaced well apart. "Listen, all of you! I'm not going to—"

The words were barely out of her mouth when Light grabbed the door handle and yanked. The door slid back, and he jumped out. He hit the ground running.

"Hank!" Fallon cried.

"I'll get him," Sansome said. With surprising speed, he vaulted from the van. Warga, nearest the door in the back row, slid out and followed suit.

Fallon shoved her own door open, remembering at the last instant to pocket the keys. *That didn't take long to fall apart,* she thought. "Stay put!" she told the others. *Like that'll work.* She slammed her door and ran into a home's front yard. In the dim, predawn light, she could barely make out Sansome's mass, heading around the side of the house. Light was already lost in the gloom.

Racing toward them, she heard another van door

open and close. Lilith, then; the two in back would have gone out the open side door. Fallon couldn't look back to see which direction they were going—not falling on her face in the dark took most of her attention. She'd have to count on Book to locate them if they spread out.

Then from up ahead came the crash of bodies colliding, and with it grunts and moans and an expletive or three.

Lilith charged past her, oversized uniform catching air and sounding like faraway thunder as she ran. By the time Fallon caught up to her in the unfenced backyard, out of breath, Light and Sansome were circling each other warily. Warga and Lilith watched from the side.

"Kill him, Hank!" Lilith shouted. "Murder that big motherfucker!"

"Lilith!" Fallon tried to snap the word, but it got tangled in an exhalation and barely slid out of her mouth.

She took a deep breath and tried to speak again. "Hank, what the hell was that about? You can't just take off like that."

"You're the one who wanted to bring me back into the zone," Light said. "I never asked to come. But I figure as long as I'm here, there are probably plenty of folks around who could use my special services. I don't give a damn about chunks of space rock, and none of these other psychos should, either. You don't think I'm ever going back across that line, do you? Back into military custody? Fuck that noise."

Theoretically, Fallon was in charge of this mission, but if it came down to physical combat, any of them could probably kill her. Only by establishing herself as an authority figure who commanded respect and obedience was she likely to pull it off. There had been a lot of discussion about letting a bunch of psychopaths have guns, and in the end, Robbins and the others had agreed that because they were being sent into what was clearly dangerous territory, they needed to be able to defend themselves. The guns were locked up in the back of the van, and she had the only key, on the ring with the ignition key.

If Sansome and Light really got into it, she wouldn't be able to pry them apart. Maybe with a gun, she could fire a couple of shots in the air, get their attention that way. But that might also attract the attention of those she'd rather avoid.

The thought had barely crossed her mind when Light made his move. He lowered his head and rushed Sansome, throwing punches at the big man's jaw. Sansome seemed to shrug off the blows; he was bringing his hands together, reaching for Light's head. "I'll bring him back," Sansome said.

"In how many pieces?" Warga asked. He craned his neck to look at Fallon, as if trying to gauge her response to his joke, but then he froze, staring past her. "Hey, Doc."

She turned to see what had caught his eye, half-worried that Antonetti and Pybus were hoofing it the other way.

But it wasn't Pybus and Antonetti. Past the corner of the house, she saw headlights weaving unsteadily toward them, coming from the direction of the interstate.

"Can the Infected drive?" Fallon asked.

"Not that I've seen," Light said. His battle with Sansome already seemed to be forgotten. They were all watching the car pulling ever closer to the van where the last two psychos still presumably sat, unarmed.

"Come on!" Fallon shouted. She made it sound like an order.

When nobody obeyed, she couldn't claim to be surprised. She took off at a run, pawing the keys from her pocket. If whoever was in that car had been infected, her people would need weapons. They were immune to the virus, but not to some Infected bashing their skulls in to get to their deliciously uninfected brains.

But her nerves betrayed her. The back door was locked, and she only managed to get a key in and turn it after several fumbled attempts. The strongbox holding the weapons was a different story. Its lock was smaller, and the box sat on the floor of the van's cargo area. Her body blocked the glow of the streetlamps outside, and the third row of seats shaded it from the van's interior lights. She finally got the key in, but it wouldn't budge. By the time she realized she'd shoved it in upside down, the key was stuck. When she finally yanked it out, the car had come to a stuttering halt beside the van.

The box remained locked. She stepped away from

it, peering into the car. Two people—kids, it looked like, teenagers. Boy at the wheel, girl beside him with a Culver's fast-food bag on her lap. They could have been siblings. The boy lowered his window and leaned out, arm on the door, hand hanging down. Fallon didn't see anything violent in his behavior, or the girl's. "Are you okay?" she asked.

"I . . . uhh, I don't think so. We don't. Me and Chelle. We need help." After that first pause, the words fell out of him in a rush, as if he wasn't sure he'd live until the end of his sentence.

Fallon took a step closer, moving to the side so her shadow didn't fall on him. Then she saw it: His cheeks were flushed, practically glowing, and his eyes looked vaguely bloodshot.

Infecteds. Not over the cliff yet, but standing on the edge, with the dirt crumbling beneath his feet. She risked getting a little closer so she could see Chelle. The girl was in the dark, but Fallon was pretty sure she was just as rosy. The bag in her lap looked like it had been around for quite a while.

"I'm afraid we can't help you," she said.

"We can't find a doctor anywhere," Chelle said pleadingly.

"We're really sick," the boy added.

*You don't know* how *sick*, Fallon thought. Instead of saying it, she backed away, easing toward the van's cargo area and the box of guns. She realized for the first time that Sansome and Light had stopped fighting and had come back to the van with Lilith and Warga.

That brought her some small comfort. *Safety in numbers, or something like that.*

"I wish we could help," she said. She could hardly force the words out. "We don't know anybody around here. No clue where a doctor would be. You should just . . . keep driving. Keep driving."

She made it to the van's back door. This time, she knew where the lock was and how the key fit, and she got it in effortlessly. The key turned, the box opened, and Fallon drew a handgun from the shadowed inside. It was a Glock 19, nine-mil, seventeen-round standard magazine. Thurman had briefed her on the weaponry, quizzed her until she remembered. She'd been told that all the guns would be loaded, and there would be extra ammo in the box and more stashed elsewhere in the van. She hoped the part about being loaded was true.

Holding the gun at her side, using her leg to hide it from the kids in the car, she stepped back around the van's rear door. "Really, there's nothing we can do for you."

Bloody tears were filling the boy's eyes, streaking his flushed cheeks. "You don't have, like, a first-aid kit or nothing?"

She did, but nothing in it could help them. "You're beyond that," she said. "I'm sorry. Truly. You have to move on, now."

The boy just sat there, arm against the outside of his car door, tears painting their crimson courses down his face.

Fallon turned, just enough to let him see the gun in her hand.

"Okay, fuck it," the boy said. He jammed the car into gear. "And fuck *you*. All of you."

He stomped on the gas pedal, and the car rocketed down the road. Toward PIR, where they would be turned away again—if they reached it at all. Depending on how far gone they were, he might lose control of the vehicle before then.

Fallon felt something sitting in the pit of her stomach like a ten-pound weight and recognized it as despair. This was a hopeless task. Two young teens, not even at the most infected stage, had practically terrified her. And she had been ready to respond with violence, even though she'd never been violent in her life.

"That was intense, Fallon."

Light stood at her right shoulder. She hadn't even heard him approach. "Yeah."

"You did the right thing. Nothing you could do for them."

"I know."

"Me, maybe. I might have been able to help."

"Your kind of help they don't need."

He shrugged. "Who's to say? Better than what's in store for them."

"I'm surprised you came back."

"I might be a psychopath, by some definitions," Light said. "And you might not believe it, but I got into the profession I did to help people. My . . . extracurricular activities come from the same place."

"So you have a, what, a well of compassion deep inside you that makes you kill people?"

"People who aren't going to live anyway. Who are suffering needlessly."

"According to you."

"I'm the only one I have to go by," he said. He looked almost solemn, and for a moment, Fallon could believe that he believed what he was saying.

But he was also a psychopath, a practiced liar who lived to manipulate other people's emotions, perhaps because he experienced so few of his own.

Maybe she could do a little manipulating, herself. "I'm sorry, Hank," she said. "I didn't mean to question your sincerity. Let's get back on the road, okay?"

He didn't smile, but she thought there was an instant's twitching of his eyes that might have been all he allowed himself. "Yeah, okay" he said. "Space rocks, here we come."

## CHAPTER 20

*46 hours*

**E**veryone was quiet for a change. The van roared past a hotel and what was probably the Culver's Chelle's bag had come from. Fallon supposed any pensiveness had to do with actually meeting human beings who would, in a short while, hardly qualify as that anymore. It added weight to their mission, somehow. They had to stop the virus from spreading any farther, for all those—in the city, and around the globe—who were not yet infected.

The eastbound interstate on-ramp came up almost immediately after the fast-food place. Fallon stepped on the gas as she climbed it, before it occurred to her that although she would ordinarily do that, this was no ordinary time. She wouldn't have to match the speed of vehicles doing sixty to seventy miles an hour—for all she knew, the roadway would be jammed with cars, and she would instead smash into something that wasn't moving at all.

Briggs had said they'd been able to make it to the tunnel, so presumably there was a pathway at least big enough for a Stryker to fit through. Book had shown her aerial images of the route, but she'd had a hard time translating the tiny objects in the photos to anything from real life. She slowed to a crawl, not knowing how hard it might be to thread the needle.

"You drive like my aunt," Lilith complained. "*After* she was dead. Alive, she drove like a NASCAR champion compared to you."

"This is all uncharted territory," Fallon replied. "If the road's clear, we'll speed up."

The road wasn't clear, but it wasn't as bad as it might have been. Although a few abandoned cars, SUVs, and trucks dotted the pavement, there was plenty of room to go around them. Fallon gave the van a little more gas as she wove in and out of the strangely silent, unmoving traffic. It felt like a moment frozen in time; one that could thaw at any moment, returning to normal life, to sound and motion, to vehicles full of impatient drivers, and angry ones, and even the occasional courteous one. The freeway would fill, engines would growl, exhaust would float above the pavement with that too-familiar odor, as irritating to throat and lungs as a scratchy wool blanket to tender flesh.

None of that happened, and she shook her head to

rid it of the idea that it might. She hadn't left her home planet, but she was in a different world now, with different rules. The only thing she could safely expect was the unexpected.

After about a mile, the abandoned vehicles grew sparser, and Fallon picked up more speed. She drove this stretch of I-10 on a fairly regular basis and thought she knew it well enough to risk traveling a little faster. The deadline—*and isn't that word more appropriate than ever?*—they faced was never far from her thoughts.

The sun lifted above the horizon as the van approached 99th Avenue, with its nearly mile-long exit ramp to 91st Avenue. Driving straight into the sunrise, Fallon was almost blinded.

So even though she heard the rumble of an oncoming truck, she couldn't see it. Hearing the big truck's approach but being unable to spot it, she pulled to the right, knowing that she could take the off-ramp if she needed to.

And when the truck hurtled off that ramp—coming up the wrong way—she was directly in its path. Lilith screamed. Still half-blind, Fallon saw a huge, dark shape bearing down on them. She jerked the wheel to the left but too late.

The truck clipped the van's front passenger-side corner, sending it into an uncontrolled spin.

The van shuddered, slid sideways, threatened to roll. The squeal and stink of hot rubber filled it. A Buick left partly in two lanes loomed large, and the van narrowly missed it as it continued to spin on locked wheels toward the edge of the road.

Standing on the brake didn't help. Fallon watched the guardrail grow ever nearer, panic welling up inside her. It was a long drop from here; they could survive the collision and still be killed by the fall.

Lilith was still screaming, joined by someone in the back—Antonetti, Fallon thought, or maybe Pybus. It took all the strength she had not to join them. The van skidded, perhaps slowing just a bit, but still too fast, too fast—

—and then they struck the guardrail.

Fallon felt it give . . .

. . . but not break.

The van came to an uneasy rest, perched on the edge of the overpass like a diver with her toes over the end of the board. "Everybody out!" she shouted, afraid its weight might still snap the rail. "Now!"

She couldn't open her door; it was wedged against the guardrail. She had to wait for Lilith to get out, and the girl was moving slowly. As she pushed open the door, Lilith glanced back at Fallon. Blood streamed from her nose, and she looked like she would have a pretty good bruise on her forehead. She'd hit the dash, or her window, or both, Fallon guessed.

*I wonder if I look any better.*

She took a quick self-inventory: ribs aching from where the seat belt had cut into her, panic ebbing but leaving her drained, otherwise undamaged.

Not everyone was so lucky. When she had both feet firmly on the pavement, she saw that while there were no life-threatening injuries, no visibly broken bones, everyone was shaken up, and there would be plenty of sore muscles. Sansome's nose was bleeding, too, but he seemed unaware of the fact until Pybus pointed it out.

Fallon braved a peek over the guardrail, to see what they'd been saved from. Instead of an empty street below, though, there was a group of people, thirty or forty of them.

No, not people.

*Infecteds.*

She couldn't afford to think of them as human. They were looking up at her, and at the same time starting up the ramp. From here, she could see visible wounds on some. One dragged a broken leg, bone jutting out through flesh and torn work pants. But they were all on the move, almost as a single body. Probably why that truck had come up the wrong way—the driver had seen the size of the mob and panicked.

"We're going to have company," she said. "Let's get ready."

"You mean guns?" Pybus asked, with a fearful quaver in his voice.

"Yes, Caspar. I'm going to trust you all with guns. Call me crazy. On second thought—"

She broke off her own sentence. Something about the general quiet had been nagging at her, and she had just realized, with a jolt of fear, what it was.

The truck's engine noise had stopped.

It hadn't faded away into the distance. It had just stopped, sometime while the van had been spinning, or immediately afterward.

The morning sunlight reflected off the nondescript silver trailer. The truck had traveled a short distance up the freeway before stopping dead.

The driver's side door flew open and a man climbed unsteadily from the cab. As he made his lurching way toward Fallon, she could see that he was at the same stage of infection as the teenagers had been—same red face and eyes, same ability to drive and talk and control the urge for grey matter, but for who knew how much longer?

"*¿Qué coño ha pasado aquí?*" the man asked with a heavy Mexican accent. "What kind of idiot parks in the middle of the road? You damaged my boss's truck; you're going to have to pay."

Except, of course, she'd been on the shoulder, and he'd been coming the wrong way up the ramp. His cognitive function seemed further deteriorated than the teenagers' had been. Fallon imagined he was on the precipice between human and Infected. And there was nothing she could do to keep him from falling.

She was trying to figure out how to placate him while signaling to the others to get ready to take him out when there was a huge *boom* from inside the truck trailer. The doors shuddered once, then burst open, and people spilled from the back.

Again, several had suffered what looked like pretty serious injuries, but that didn't seem to slow them down. This group was closer than the ones below, and with the sun beaming at them, she could make out the redness of their faces, like bad sunburns. Their eyes were so red, she wouldn't have been surprised to see blood leaking from them. There were six of them, different ages, all Hispanic, but wearing different types of clothing. One kid wore low-hanging pants, a long T-shirt, and chains around his neck; a man had on a business suit that looked like he'd been dragged behind a truck in it; a silver-haired woman wore only a housecoat and sandals with two mismatched socks. They hadn't been together before, but they were now, with only their infection in common.

Correction. As the last one cleared the back of the trailer, Fallon saw the piles of bloody corpses and body parts left behind. Señor Road Rage was a coyote—probably en route from some East Valley drop house—and his cargo had two things in common. First, they'd all paid money to be smuggled over the border. Second, none of them cared about that anymore. All they wanted was brains.

As if privy to Fallon's thoughts, they suddenly rushed toward her and her team, trampling the hapless coyote in the process.

Fallon lunged for the gun locker. The truck's impact had wedged the rear doors shut, though—and, she saw now, bent one rear wheel almost parallel to the ground; this van was toast. At least she still had her pistol. She drew it from her waistband and fired twice, over the heads of the oncoming Infecteds. Warning shots.

They didn't slow. Before she could shoot again, Antonetti snatched the weapon from her hand. "If you're not gonna use it right, give it to someone who will," he said. "Any time you shoot, make it count."

She was angry but intrigued. This was the first time she had seen him show any initiative. He'd been willing to go with the flow, do whatever the others wanted, without argument. Completely passive, until now.

He aimed the gun, lower than she had, and squeezed the trigger twice in rapid succession. The older woman staggered back as both bullets found their mark, center mass, but she kept coming. Bloody flowers bloomed on her housecoat. The six were almost on them now, snarling and snapping, the old woman in the lead. She seemed to have Lilith—closest to the truck, having given the van a wide berth after jumping out—in her sights. Antonetti fired again, and again the woman lost half a step. The bullet tore her housecoat, right between her breasts. She didn't go down. One more shot tore through her forehead and blew out the back, taking chunks of brains and skull with it, and she finally fell, just feet from Lilith.

Fallon had seen before, on video and with Warga, how hard it was to stop an Infected. But this one—an elderly woman—had taken four rounds before she went down.

And there were five more behind her.

Light snatched up a chunk of the van's fender, torn almost all the way off by the collision, and turned to face the Infecteds with it. Warga wrenched off the exhaust pipe, though it must have burned his already-damaged hands. Lilith scampered back to relative safety behind

Fallon and Antonetti. He still had Fallon's gun, but she hadn't originally thought to grab ammunition for it, and figured it must be getting low. Pybus had picked up some good-sized rocks from around the guardrail and held them in his hands, as if weighing them before deciding which to throw first. Sansome, unarmed, stepped forward to meet the charge.

The next to reach them was the healthiest-looking of them all. In his twenties, Fallon guessed, his torn T-shirt revealing a solid build, toned and muscular. He came with hands outstretched, his mouth opening and closing, spittle flying from it like rain. Sansome moved into his path, a fleshy wall. The man stopped abruptly, and Sansome grabbed him by his right shoulder and left rib cage. Without apparent effort, he lifted the man from the ground—his feet kicking wildly at the air— and hurled him over the guardrail. The man let out a cry as he fell, but it was cut short with a sickening *thump.*

She barely had time to take it all in when everything started happening at once. The Infecteds reached the psychopaths, with no weapons other than their own hands and their nearly unstoppable, raging hunger. Light slashed with his steel shard, Antonetti fired at their heads. Pybus hurled his rocks, then scooped up more. Warga swung his pipe like a major-league ball-player aiming for the fences. One of the Infecteds got his hands on Fallon's head, digging his nails into her left cheek, but Warga took him out with a well-aimed swing of the exhaust pipe.

The Infecteds had momentum on their side, and rage-induced strength. But they were disorganized, without strategic thinking, and in less than a minute, they had all fallen to the psychos, their heads bashed in or sliced open, brains destroyed. Fallon, Light, and Warga had been clawed, scratched—Light had a bloody gash across his neck—but not mortally wounded.

*Seven against six*, Fallon thought. *And we just barely beat them.*

She was looking at the bodies, trying to replay it all in her head, when a shout from Pybus made her look up.

The other Infecteds had reached the top of the ramp and were coming their way.

At the same moment, she realized that she didn't know where Sansome was. Seven against six had been tough—against thirty or more, they'd need all hands, and then some.

The shattering of the van's rear window glass gave her an answer. The big man had gone back in through the open door and retrieved the lockbox with the weapons in it. He shoved it out through the broken window. It landed on a corner, and the steel buckled.

Light reached it first. Straining, he hoisted it waist high and dropped it against the pavement again. This time it burst open, spilling guns into the street, along with some hand grenades and other implements of destruction. Light took up an M249 light machine gun with a two-hundred-round ammo box. Antonetti and Warga went for M240Ls, only slightly heavier but firing a bigger round. Lilith grabbed an M4. Antonetti still had Fallon's Glock, so she chose another one.

Pybus and Sansome, she noted, didn't take guns. Instead, Pybus picked up the length of pipe that Warga had abandoned. Sansome waited, his hands still empty.

Antonetti opened fire first. Only he and Warga had ever used guns in their killings, Fallon remembered. Maybe Lilith—her aunt and uncle had been killed with their own shotgun—but there was still some question about who had done that. Fallon had thought the Infecteds were still too far away, and maybe they were for her pistol, but not for the machine guns. Antonetti fired in short bursts, raking across the oncoming mob.

As if he had set off a chain reaction, Warga and Light started shooting, too. Fallon let them get a little closer, then she joined in. Her aim was lousy. Studying psychopaths had put her in touch with enough law enforcement personnel that she had been invited to shooting ranges a few times, but she'd never taken to it, never mastered the skill. The mob was thick enough, though, that she was pretty sure she was hitting something.

Somewhat to her surprise, she didn't feel bad about it. Those were people. Infected, yes, but still, despite her earlier resolution not to think about it, they were living human beings. But this was truly a case of kill or be killed. They wouldn't negotiate, wouldn't stop to chat. If they could reach her, they would do everything they could to kill her and eat her brains for breakfast.

She fired until the magazine was empty, then dropped the gun and picked up another. Time enough to reload later, she hoped.

After a few minutes, the gunfire tapered off to a couple of random bursts, then nothing. Fallon's ears rang, and she tasted bitter smoke. Her hands and arms were sore—from the gun's recoil, she guessed, though some of it could also be from the truck's initial impact. Some of the Infecteds were still twitching, but all were down; the threat had been eliminated. It had been, all in all, easier than she'd expected.

Lilith, Pybus, and Sansome hadn't fired a shot. The latter two hadn't in their murders, either. Sansome had used his powerful hands and a bow saw. Pybus had rendered his victims unconscious with roofies, strangled them with clothesline, and cut them up with a chainsaw, then used an electric carving knife to prepare them for the table.

But Light had never used a gun, either, and Warga just once, when one of his victims had pulled it on him. He'd taken it away from her and shot her six times, in a fit of rage. Those two were looking at the devastation they had wrought with their high-powered weapons and grinning like little boys who'd just won favors at a birthday party. What was it about them that made them take so eagerly to a different method of killing? Or about the others that kept them from it?

And her? She hadn't minded shooting—*killing*, she corrected— either, although she had never killed anyone or shot at a living thing before. *Kill or be killed,* she reminded herself. But it wasn't just that. It couldn't be.

Not for the first time, she wondered just what the hell she had gotten herself into. And how she would ever keep her promise to Book and get herself out.

**CHAPTER 21**

*46 hours*

**B**ook sat staring at a video screen and wished he'd been allowed to give all the psychopaths cameras, because with just Fallon's view, it was sometimes hard to tell exactly what was going on. Which, right now, was utter carnage. This had been a deadly free-for-all, one that even Fallon had played a part in. The bowling ball guy—Sansome—had thrown one of the people from the truck right over the guardrail, for Pete's sake!

He wasn't naive, though. He knew some of the Infecteds—maybe a lot of them—would die before the mission was complete. He just wanted to minimize the number of those deaths that were needless.

"You okay, Fallon?"

She didn't speak, but opened and closed her eyes in a staccato pattern.

F-I-N-E.

Looked like she hadn't needed his primer on Morse code, after all.

"The road is clear up ahead. Any of the cars look drivable?"

Fallon relayed the question, making it sound like it was hers alone. Book realized that the others weren't yet aware that she could communicate with him. Playing her cards close to the vest until they'd do her the most good. Smart.

Most psychopaths were.

He shook the thought away, dismissing it as unfair. Having a deficient limbic system didn't make her a psychopath any more than having asthma made him Darth Vader. Though he *had* just watched her firing into a crowd of people with no apparent hesitation . . .

"The van's out of commission," Light replied, "and I don't see any handy keys sticking out of any ignitions."

"I can hotwire one," Sansome volunteered. "I've stolen a buncha cars."

"The passenger cars are all too small for seven of us and our gear. There's a pickup—no, it's got three flat tires. An SUV with the hood open . . . and the battery gone. Dammit! Looks like scavengers have already been through here."

"We might be able to get something running," Light said, but Fallon shook her head.

"I don't want to spend that much time up here."

Whatever else Fallon might have said was lost in the sound of the door behind Book swinging open and two people barging in. He turned away from the monitor showing the psycho feeds to find Thurman and Ramirez there.

"Can I help you?"

"How're they doing?" Ramirez asked, honing in on the psychos' monitor. Thurman glanced at it, but most of his attention was focused on the other monitors in Book's array, showing video footage from drones flying over the city as well as from various traffic cams and other cameras he'd been able to tap into to get an idea of what was going on inside the quarantine zone. Nothing good, that was for sure.

"Just had their first encounter with a large group of Infecteds," Book reported dutifully, choosing to leave out any details that weren't specifically requested. He had a feeling that the less the top dogs knew about how Fallon was achieving her mission goals, the better.

"Any losses?" Thurman this time, finally taking an interest. He looked at the screen as he asked, answering his own question, but Book replied anyway, keeping his tone carefully neutral.

"Not so far, no."

"Thank God," Thurman muttered. "If they lose anyone before they reach the point Robbins's men made it to, I'll never hear the end of it."

"Because *that's* the important thing," Ramirez said, rolling her eyes and echoing Book's own thoughts on the matter. She looked at him. "How's she holding up?"

The implant didn't measure vitals, but he could guess at things like pulse rate and respiration based on what he could see and hear.

"Scared, but less so the farther they go, and doing a good job of hiding it. She's getting her feet under her." *Or embracing her psycho side.* But he wasn't going to say that to present company. He wished he hadn't thought it himself.

"Good," the agent said, her tone pleased. "This whole mission hinges on her ability to control the others and get them to do what needs to be done. I'm not sure it would have had a chance of succeeding if she hadn't been immune herself and volunteered to go along. Lucky break, that."

"Yeah, lucky," Book echoed, thinking the exact opposite.

"What are these ones doing?" Thurman asked, pointing to a separate monitor, divided into nine screens, showing feeds from various cameras around the city. The one that caught Thurman's eye displayed an aerial shot from a hovering drone. Book checked the coordinates—the drone was in Tempe, near the ASU campus. He hit a few keys, and the screen showing the psychos and the one showing drone footage switched places. Once he had the Tempe feed in front of him, he tapped a few more keys, and the drone zoomed in on the scene Thurman had pointed out.

The Infecteds here weren't some wandering mass, all traveling in a similar direction because a noise or a movement had caught their collective blood-red eye. It looked like they were testing the door of each business they passed, pulling and pushing, trying to get inside. As Book and his two guests watched, the Infecteds found one that was unlocked. Some of the Infecteds peeled off the larger group and went inside, while the rest continued on to the next business.

"What are they doing?" Thurman asked suspiciously.

"Let's find out," Book said. Not all the feeds were in real time since he wasn't a robot and couldn't keep track of everything happening on every monitor at once. Plus, Fallon and her group had taken up most of his attention since they'd entered the quarantine zone. Knowing that they—*she*—would, Book had put some of the other feeds on a time delay so he wouldn't miss anything. The Tempe feed was one of them.

He sped up the video until it showed the Infecteds coming back out through the same door they'd entered. Their faces and mouths were covered in blood. Clearly, there had been somebody inside, and the Infecteds had known it.

"That's . . . not good," he said.

"What does it mean?" Ramirez asked.

"I don't know," Book answered worriedly. "They're getting smarter? Less raging hunger, more patience and planning?"

"That's not good," Thurman repeated—unironically, as far as Book could tell. Perhaps he hadn't heard Book say it the first time. More likely, he just hadn't been listening. "I need to let Robbins and the others know about this."

"And I need to tell Fallon," Book said, switching the feeds out again as Thurman started for the door, Ramirez on his heels. "Fallon—" he began, trying to raise her on the two-way, only to be interrupted by a blaring Klaxon.

"What now?" Thurman exclaimed as he hurried out, followed by Ramirez.

Book switched feeds again, this time cycling through cameras placed around the perimeter of the raceway, looking for a breach. Expecting to find one, with a mob of Infecteds streaming through it. But there was nothing.

Still, the siren screamed. Book began cycling through camera feeds inside the base. It didn't take him long to find the reason for the alarm.

Briggs and the soldiers with him were still in quarantine, and it was a good thing, since the other soldiers had all apparently succumbed to the virus and were now attacking the poor specialist with tooth, nail, fist, and foot.

Book had never really thought of Timothy as a warrior—he was a nerd, like Book, wearing an Army uniform to pay for the education he'd received, and when that debt was cleared, he'd be swinging through the concrete jungle, wearing a white collar and a spotted loincloth. But Briggs was every inch the soldier now, using martial arts moves Book had only ever seen in movies, driving the heel of his palm into one of the Infecteds' noses, smashing his foot into another's temple, the culmination of a truly impressive roundhouse kick.

With the first two Infecteds down, Briggs turned to face the third, a big guy everyone called "Andre," for reasons that escaped Book.

Briggs started off throwing punches at Andre's midsection, with no obvious effect.

"Come on, man," Book muttered. "You know that won't work!"

Briggs apparently came to the same conclusion, just as Andre backhanded him, sending him sprawling. Briggs scrambled to get up, but Andre was on top of him before he could gain his feet. The second Infected was up again now, too, and heading for the fray. The first was still down, not moving. Book figured Briggs's palm strike must have driven bone or cartilage or something up into that one's brain, killing it. Still, it was two-and-a-half on one, and the odds were definitely not in Timothy's favor.

Until a small door in the back of the room opened and two soldiers in biohazard gear stepped in. Book didn't know what kind of ammo they were using, but one shot to Andre and the other Infected's heads, and Briggs was covered in a pink and grey spray. Bruised, bloodied, covered in brain matter, but still alive.

So then why was he looking up at the camera—looking straight at Book—with such an expression of anguish?

And then Book realized. The others had become Infected. Briggs hadn't. Whether by virtue of genetics, upbringing, and/or the traumas of a constant war footing, he was immune.

Timothy Briggs was a psychopath.

## CHAPTER 22

*43 hours*

**"H**ow about the truck that coyote was driving?" Fallon asked after a few moments of contemplating their complete lack of other options. The driver still lay where he had fallen. His throat had been crushed and his spine snapped just below the neck, but his brain hadn't been destroyed, and he was still twitching, fingers tapping on the pavement.

"It's full of corpses," Antonetti said.

"Oh, that's right," she said. Then she stopped herself, remembering who—and what—her traveling companions were. "Is that a problem?"

"Not for me."

"Anybody?" she asked.

"Can I ride in the front?" Lilith asked. "It's pretty gross."

"And you call yourself a psycho?" Warga scoffed.

Lilith flipped him off, and he just laughed.

"I'll check it out," Light offered.

Fallon didn't trust him for a minute, but she nodded her approval, and he crossed to the truck. He climbed into the cab, then popped the hood and poked around in there, and finally crawled underneath. He came out after a couple of minutes, dusting off his back and shoulders as best he could.

"Nobody's going anywhere in that," he said when he had rejoined the others. "Gas tank's ruptured. He must've gotten here on fumes."

"Just perfect," she said, frustration getting the better of her. Not only couldn't they drive the truck, but now it blocked the pathway they had driven through. They weren't getting back out on this freeway unless somebody came along with a bulldozer or a tow truck.

"Everybody gather as much gear as you can carry," Fallon ordered. "Weapons, ammo, food, water— especially water. We're going to take a little hike."

"Ughh, I hate walking," Lilith complained.

"It's good for you," Warga told her. "Makes your legs strong and firms your ass."

"That how you like 'em?" Lilith asked.

Fallon cut in before he could answer. "Randy! Don't even answer that. Keep your mind on the mission, not on her."

"No problem, Doc," he said, grinning. "I like my trim a little older, anyway."

"Trim. Classy guy." It was Book's voice, coming

in her right ear—but not. Near her ear, anyway, as if he were standing behind her, with his head over her shoulder.

"You might need to send over the Army's sexual-harassment guidelines," Fallon replied softly. A snort of laughter let her know that Book had heard.

"Talking to yourself?" Light asked. "Voices in your head? Early warning sign of a psychotic break, Fallon."

"My psychotic break was when I volunteered to come in here with you people. Come on, load up and let's go."

Fallon clipped three canteens of water onto her belt, two on her left side and one on her right. She stuffed some meals, ready-to-eat—what Book had called MREs—into the cargo pockets of her fatigue pants and hoped they could find more appetizing food en route. Ammunition for the Glock and an M4 went into other pockets. The rifle had a strap, so she slung it over her shoulder and tucked the Glock into her waistband. All around her, the others were performing similar tasks.

Sansome and Pybus stood off to one side, watching the rest. "What are you taking, Joe? Fallon asked. "Caspar?"

"I don't like guns," Sansome said.

"I've never even held one," Pybus put in.

"Why the hell's he here, Doc?" Warga asked. "He's old, and he's never killed anybody."

"I didn't say I hadn't killed," Pybus corrected. "Just not with guns."

"It's not that hard," Antonetti said. "You point the end that shoots at somebody, and you pull the trigger."

"Do me a favor," Fallon said. "Both of you, at least take a rifle, and one of these pistols. The Glocks, like I'm carrying, don't weigh that much, but they pack a good punch. You might be glad you did."

Sansome stepped forward, took an M4 from the box, and a Glock 19. Then he stood back and watched Pybus do the same. "I'll carry them," Pybus said. "But I don't have to like them."

"No, you don't," Fallon agreed. "I don't like them either. But the life you save might be mine."

Before they left the van, Fallon checked her team. Lilith was the only one not carrying water. When Fallon pointed this out, the girl said, "I hate water. There'll be Coke machines, right?"

"You need *water*, Lilith." Fallon felt like she had moved a dozen years or so into the future, like Lilith was Jason and she was being Stern Mom, telling him what to do.

Lilith gave her a rebellious look—Fallon half expected to hear the line her petulant four-year-old nephew lived by: "You're not the boss of me!"—but then the girl went back into the van, emerging moments later with two canteens, which she attached to her belt. Fallon hoped they were full, but there was a limit to how hard she could ride any of them. Like her, they were more or less volunteers. Any of them could have refused to come. Granted, what awaited them if they had wouldn't have been much of a life. But they were here now, risking their necks for the common good, and that bought them a little slack.

When they were all similarly burdened, Fallon led them toward the long ramp to 91st Avenue. Sansome walked beside her, unbuttoning his camouflage shirt as he did. Beneath it was the same light brown T-shirt they all wore. His broad, clean-shaven face was filmed with sweat. "I'm hot," he announced.

"It's early yet. It'll get hotter."

"Where we going?"

"To look for a ride."

"Like hitchhiking?"

"Like something we can commandeer."

"Is that another word for stealing?"

"More or less," Fallon admitted. She shrugged. "We have a job to do. Getting it done is more important than following laws that don't apply anymore."

"How far away is Glendale, Doctor?" Pybus asked, drawing even with her and Sansome.

"I don't know, exactly." She waved her hand in what she thought was a northwesterly direction. "That way, a few miles."

"Will we pass it?"

"We're going the opposite way, Caspar. Mesa is due east. Why?"

"Marty Robbins was born there."

"Who?"

"Marty Robbins. One of the most successful country musicians in history, with several crossover hits on the pop charts. 'El Paso' was his signature song, but he had hits with 'Big Iron,' 'A White Sport Coat and a Pink Carnation,' and—"

"Sorry, Caspar. I'm not getting the connection."

"When I visit a place where one of the legends was born, I like to pay my respects, that's all."

"Maybe after this is all over, but not now."

"He drove in NASCAR races, too. That's what made me remember because we were at the track. He was partial to Dodge Chargers, and—"

"Dude!" Lilith cried. "She just legit told you to shut up, and you're still all fuckin' blah blah blahdi blah."

"I did not," Fallon objected. "But Caspar?"

"Yes?"

"Please shut up."

By the time they reached 91st Avenue, Fallon was sweating, too, though not as profusely as Sansome. She'd been right; the day was warming quickly. Heat shimmered off the blacktop, offering no respite. Once the summer monsoon started, the days would start out muggier but would cool as storms blew through. During a monsoon storm, the temperature could drop twenty or thirty degrees in a matter of minutes, and hail could fall even in hundred-degree weather. People had died of hypothermia during summer thunderstorms, despite Arizona's baking desert heat.

*One more thing to worry about,* Fallon thought. Was there anything inside the zone—including her companions—that didn't want to kill her?

"What now, Doc?" Warga asked.

Fallon halted, looked around, getting her bearings. At the bottom of the ramp stood a Legacy Suites Extended Stay hotel. All of the windows on the ground floor were smashed in, as were some of those above. A few vehicles were scattered in the parking lot, but Antonetti had checked them and found no keys. Staying near the building for too long made Fallon nervous. No telling who was in there. Or what.

She pointed southeast, across 91st from the hotel. "There's a residential neighborhood," she said. "We'll have better luck finding wheels there."

"Sure," Light agreed. "Pick a house with a good-sized truck parked in the drive, go inside, kill everybody, and take the keys. Easy-peasy."

"I think we can do it with a little less drama."

"You say 'drama,' I say 'excitement.' This is starting to be fun, Fallon. You don't want to take that away from us, do you?"

"Fun? Killing people?"

"They're Infecteds, not people."

"They're still people. They're sick, that's all. Maybe they can get better."

"I have a feeling that once you've started subsisting on human brains, you're pretty much beyond redemption. You think people are going back to Applebee's and Chipotle after that?"

"That's not our call to make, Hank. We get the meteor back to the scientists. They take it from there."

"You have an awful lot of confidence in science."

"I *am* a scientist . . ."

"Yeah, but ever think maybe that's how we got here? Not you, maybe, but someone else. Maybe it wasn't the meteor at all. Maybe it was some kind of scientific experiment gone haywire. Or maybe the virus trapped inside the meteor was intentionally put there by alien scientists. Science has its uses, but blind faith in it is dangerous."

*The whole world is dangerous,* Fallon thought. She didn't say it, though. Instead, she just started across the street, and the others followed.

Getting involved in philosophical discussion with psychopaths, she was learning, was not her idea of a good time.

The flip side was that she wasn't sure what her idea of a good time *was.* She went to work, she went home. Mark had usually started dinner before she got there—sometimes hours before. She ate with Mark and Jason, unless the boy was already in bed, but most nights, whatever had been happening during the workday still occupied at least half of her mind. She often stayed up working after Mark went to sleep; unhurried lovemaking was a distant memory that sometimes felt more like a half-remembered dream. Even on weekends and their rare vacations, she was glued to a phone, tablet, or laptop much of the time. You couldn't start a business, a lab, without being devoted to it, she had argued. Once it was on a sound financial footing, she would be able to take time away from it. It wouldn't be long, she'd told Mark. Certainly while Jason was still young. She didn't want to miss that.

But she *had* been missing it, day in and day out. Jason was growing up, and milestones were happening without her all the time.

If she got back—*when* she got back—things would change. She would make sure of that.

And finding the MEIADD would help a lot.

**"Y**ou doing okay, Fallon?"

She still wasn't used to Book's voice suddenly sounding in her head like that. Normally, when someone talked to you, they were near you, or you were on a device like a telephone or Skyping or something. This disembodied-voice thing was just odd.

"I guess. I'd be better if we had wheels."

"I think you're right about the chances being better there in the neighborhood."

"You heard that?"

"Like I said before, assume I'm always watching and listening. It's not really always me—sometimes even my Herculean bladder control is bested, after all. But it's mostly me, and we're monitoring you most of the time."

"You must be bored to death."

"Far from it. It's almost like I'm there. Only without the part where I can turn into an Infected or be eaten by one."

"When you put it that way," she said, "you want to trade places?"

"Not in a million years. I'll check in again later. Be safe, Fallon."

"That's the idea, Book, thanks."

The residential streets were still, empty. Spooky.

Lights burned inside some houses, but not many. Through one window Fallon saw the distinctive flickering glow of a TV screen, but when Lilith peeked inside, she said there was nobody around. At other houses, windows were broken, doors wide open, and sometimes bloody streaks on the sidewalks or spatter staining the walls. In one front yard, a ceramic donkey pulling a flower-laden cart was surrounded by nine corpses with shattered skulls. Animals—dogs, maybe coyotes—had been at them, too.

"Stinks around here," Lilith said.

"Doesn't bother me," Warga replied.

"Yeah, but you're a sick fuck."

"Just your type, baby," he said. She flipped him off, and the conversation died again.

The odor was sickly sweet, but also reminiscent of turned earth with something sour buried beneath it. Fallon realized that although it was more potent here, more immediate, she had been smelling it ever since they had crossed 91$^{st}$ Avenue.

Perhaps there were people in some of these houses, huddled together for safety, barricaded in, bristling with weapons, petrified with fear. But in others— probably most—there was only death.

Light, Warga, and Antonetti took turns going into houses with appropriately sized vehicles parked outside, searching for keys. Sometimes, Lilith accompanied them, sometimes not. Pybus and Sansome stayed close to Fallon. On two occasions, they found keys, but in the first case the truck's engine wouldn't turn over, and in the other, the key belonged to a vehicle that was nowhere in sight.

Sansome still insisted that he could hotwire one. Fallon was hesitant. She wanted something they could rely on in an emergency, not something that might slow them down if they needed to move out in a hurry. "We'll keep looking for a while," she said. She was leading them ever eastward, so although progress was slow, it was at least in the right direction.

Then they ran out of neighborhood. Across some cultivated fields was a huge building, a warehouse or some kind of office complex, Fallon guessed. *Dead end.* But then she noticed a line of trucks parked outside. "Where there are that many trucks, there have to be keys," she said. "Come on."

She was glad to get away from those haunted streets. Fresh air wafted over the fallow field, and she breathed it in, held it. Just a couple of days without vehicles on the roads, without industry, and the air already smelled cleaner than she could remember—the stench of death notwithstanding. Lilith and Antonetti grumbled about having to walk in the dirt, but when the rest followed without complaint, they joined in, not wanting to be left behind.

They had almost reached the tall, black steel fence around the building when the first shots came.

## CHAPTER 23

*41 hours*

The first round went wide, way off to the right, kicking up dirt a little ahead of their position. The next was more on target, but high, whizzing over their heads. Fallon threw herself down. Remnants of whatever crop had been tilled here poked at her, but she figured a bullet would hurt more.

Most of her psychos had done the same, but when she looked back, she saw that Sansome was lowering himself slowly, and Lilith stayed on her feet until Warga shoved her, then flung an arm across her back to keep her down.

Fallon eased her rifle from her shoulder—not that easy to do while pressing herself flat against the earth. Antonetti and Light were already returning fire. The first shots had come from a darkened loading dock, but there were several of those, and she hadn't seen a muzzle flash to tell her which one.

Then another thought struck her. "Stop shooting!" she shouted. She could barely hear herself over the din. The firing continued. Remembering what she'd heard in a hundred movies and TV shows, she tried it another way. "Cease fire!"

Antonetti heard her and stopped. "Hank!" Fallon cried, louder than before. "Hold your fire!"

He looked at her, his meaning clear.

*Why?*

"Have you ever heard of an Infected using a gun? That's got to be a person."

"I don't give a rat's ass," Light said. "He shot at us."

"He probably thinks *we're* Infecteds. Just hold off for a minute."

Light shrugged but lowered his weapon. Fallon risked rising up on her elbows so she could project better. "You, in the dock! We're not Infecteds! I'm guessing you're not, either!"

Nobody answered for long enough to make her wonder if they'd killed him, then: "How do I know you're not?" It was a man's voice. Gruff, but anxiety or adrenaline lent it a slight quaver.

"Same way I know about you!" Fallon replied. "Infecteds don't use guns, and they don't speak!"

Another pause came. "Let me see you!"

"Okay!" Fallon called. She started to get her knee under her.

"Doc, don't!" Warga said. "It's a trap!"

She'd spent her whole life studying other humans, though. "I don't think so," she said. She rose to her feet and started toward the fence.

"What are you doing, Fallon?" Book asked. "Be careful."

"Trust me, Book," she said softly.

"I do, but . . . watch yourself."

"I thought that was your job."

Nobody shot her. She kept going, until she was right up against it. She wrapped her fists around two vertical bars—as much to still their trembling as anything else—and showed her face between them. "Look," she said. "No flush. No bloodshot eyes. I'm healthy. We all are."

Only silence came from the darkness of the empty dock. A sign told her that the place was a distribution center for QuikTrip convenience stores. Finally, the man spoke again. "You look okay."

"I'm telling you, we are. All of us." She debated how much to tell him, ultimately deciding on *not much*. "We're immune. We're trying to put an end to the virus, but we need to get to Mesa."

"Immune? Nobody's immune."

"Look at us," she said, releasing the bars so she could gesture toward herself and the others. "We're in uniform. We're here officially. We just need wheels. You have the keys to those trucks?"

"You know how to drive an eighteen-wheeler?"

"I don't, no. But someone on my crew probably does."

"You don't have the training, you're not likely to even make it to the road."

*How hard could it be?* Fallon wondered. Then she looked at the trucks, thought about the way they barreled down the interstates. *Probably pretty hard.* "I'll ask if anybody knows how."

Turning her back on the unseen gunman was frightening, but she hoped it would demonstrate trust and earn the same in return. "Guys!" she called. "Anybody have experience driving big rigs?"

Her question was met with a chorus of negatives. She turned back to the dock. "Okay, I guess I was wrong. Can you drive one?"

"Hell, yeah. Been paid to do it for the last nine years. Almost a million miles under my belt."

"Then maybe you could . . . ?"

Silence stretched out between them, taut as a rubber band. Finally, he said. "I got all kinds of food in here. Water, sodas, medical supplies. Candy. Everything I need."

"Are you alone in there?"

"Last day or so, yeah. Since the last couple of guys got ate."

"Do you want to stay that way? All by yourself in that huge space, shooting at anyone who comes near? What happens when you run out of ammunition? What happens if there are more Infecteds than you can shoot?"

"Figured I'd burn that bridge when I come to it."

"I think you mean 'cross,'" Fallon corrected. "Just

the same, we're here to try to do something about it. Not just to hole up someplace. To fix it. All we need is a ride."

"To Mesa?"

"That's right. And maybe back again, with some cargo."

Again, the unseen man was quiet. Considering, Fallon hoped.

After a while, he said, "Yeah, okay, I guess. You really think you have a chance? To fix it?"

"We wouldn't be here if we didn't."

"I'll give you a lift to Mesa, then. Don't know that I'll hang around while you do whatever you got to do there. I'm pretty comfortable in here."

"For now."

"Yeah, for now. But now might be all I got, right? All anybody's got."

"The sooner we get to Mesa . . .'"

"Yeah, I hear you." Finally, the man stepped out of the shadows and onto the end of the dock. He held his rifle in his left hand, vertically, so it wouldn't be seen as a threat. "Tell your people not to shoot me."

"They won't," Fallon said, hoping they really wouldn't.

The man waved to his right. "I'll get one of these rigs started," he said. "Meet me at that gate."

He disappeared back into the shadows, presumably to get a key. Fallon returned to her team. They were up from the dirt, now—Lilith and Sansome standing, the rest sitting down. Pybus was taking a long drink from his canteen. "We have a ride," Fallon said. "All the way to Mesa. I'll ride in the cab, to keep an eye on him. The rest of you will have to ride in the truck's trailer."

"Is there water in the truck?" Pybus asked.

"I don't know what's in it. Maybe."

"I sure hope so."

"We'll find out when you get in," Fallon said. She heard the growl of a truck engine turning over, startling in the quiet of the day. "Come on, we're supposed to meet him at the gate."

"Better than sitting out here in the sun," Antonetti said as he got to his feet. "Gonna be a hot one."

"No shit," Lilith said. "It's Arizona in the summer."

"Not summer yet," Sansome countered. "A few more weeks."

"We'll probably all die of heatstroke," the girl said.

"Not if we get in the truck," Fallon reminded her. "Let's go."

They waited beside a sign that said DRIVER'S PLEASE SIGN IN BEFORE DOCKING. While Fallon shuddered at the grammar, Light and Sansome forced the gate open, so when the truck approached, it could pass right through. The cab was white, the trailer mostly red and white, with a row of soda cans pained on it in alternating colors. The driver looked mixed, too, dark-complexioned and dark-haired. White, with maybe some Native American or Hispanic, probably some African-American, too. *The new face of America,* Fallon thought. *If it lasts out the month.*

He stopped, climbed down, and opened the trailer. Cartons were shrink-wrapped on wooden pallets, some of the boxes bearing familiar brand names. Nuts, chips, candy, aspirin, motor oil, and more; at least the psychos wouldn't go hungry back there.

When they were in, the driver closed the doors. He latched the back but didn't lock it. He was a little shorter than Fallon, somewhat bowlegged, with a gut that was starting to overlap his belt. His skin was weathered, making him look older than he probably was, and the grey showing in his bushy beard added to that effect. He wore a uniform shirt with a name tag, jeans, work boots. "I'm Fallon," she said, extending a hand. It was a relief to come across an actual human in the zone even if he had tried to shoot her. This close, she realized that although his warehouse had most of what he needed, it apparently lacked a shower. She wasn't sure when she'd get her next one, though, so she couldn't be too judgmental.

"Everybody calls me Bull," he said, taking her hand for a quick shake.

"Bull? Why?"

"I think because I'm stubborn. I like to get my way." His face broke into a smile. "Also 'cause I'm so full of bullshit." He let out a wheezing laugh and climbed back into his cab. "Better get in," he said. "This load's got to be on time."

Fallon rushed around to the other side, climbed up onto the step, opened the door, and hoisted herself in. She had never thought about how much work it took just to get into one of these. This cab was strictly utilitarian, she saw, made only for driving around the area, not for long hauls. His rifle was leaned up against his door, out of her reach. She did the same with hers.

Bull eased it into gear, and the truck gave a lurch, then started forward. "Freeway okay?"

"Whatever's fastest," she answered.

"Where in Mesa?"

"You just get us there. Take the 60."

"You got it," Bull said. "Hold on tight."

He entered the interstate at 83rd Avenue, and the going was relatively clear. Talking over the bellow of the engine was more a matter of shouted phrases than actual conversation, but that was okay with Fallon. Bull didn't know much about what had happened, just that a lot of people had gone nuts, turned on each other. He and a few other employees had taken refuge in the distribution center. During the night, one of them had stepped outside for fresh air and Infecteds—Bull called them *Eaters*—had caught him, then come in through a door he'd left open. They had killed Bull's other two companions before Bull killed them. He had, he said, dumped all the bodies into an empty trailer parked at one of the docks and locked it up tight.

"You got lucky!" Fallon shouted over the racket.

"Luck, hell!" Bull replied. "I'm good with a gun!"

"You missed us!"

"I wanted to give you a chance to prove yourselves! Thought you might be alive!"

*Alive?* Fallon thought. That word was taking on new

meaning, here in the zone. Or else losing its meaning altogether. She wasn't sure which, or if it mattered.

**W**here the freeway was relatively clear, the truck tooled along at a good clip. Fallon almost started to relax for the first time since entering the zone. The city flashing by the windows was so still, she had to fight against complacency. Birds perched on signs mounted above the freeway. Tendrils of smoke spiraled into the sky from various points. A coyote ambled down the center of the road, barely deigning to glance up as the truck rumbled past.

But every now and then, the highway was clogged, and they had to exit and find open surface streets. On those, she saw things that reminded her of why they had come. The fires throwing up smoke were probably buildings burning out of control because emergency services were nonexistent within the zone. Occasionally, looking at city streets from her elevated position in the cab, she saw an Infected, or a pair of them, and sometimes more, wandering around.

Did the fact that they weren't feasting on brains mean the healthy population had been effectively wiped out? If that was the case, could they just wait until all the Infecteds starved for lack of uninfected brains?

No, she decided. The likelihood that Infecteds would escape the zone was simply too strong— proactive steps needed to be taken. Maybe the people left here were just hiding out, waiting for the cavalry.

They might have a long wait because the cavalry were Fallon and six fellow psychos, their trusty mounts were a single QT truck, and their chances of success were about a million to one.

The closer they got to downtown Phoenix, the more Infecteds she spotted on the streets. And when she saw that they were approaching the Deck Park Tunnel, she tensed up. That was where Briggs and the others had been ambushed.

That was probably the wrong word for it, though. She doubted that a deliberate trap had been laid. More likely, they had just happened across a large group of Infecteds who reacted to their presence. Still, as the truck slowed down at the tunnel's entrance, she said, "Bull, keep your eyes open in here. There were reports of a lot of Infecteds in the tunnel."

"You watch for them, Fallon," he replied. "I got my hands full with the obstacle course." Abandoned vehicles were thick on the ground here, made more so by remnants of the Stryker, and he eased the truck along slowly—too slowly for her tastes—threading a narrow path. She hoped they could make it all the way through; getting stuck inside the tunnel could spell the end of their mission. No one would ride to this cavalry's rescue.

"You okay, Fallon?" Book's voice, in her ear. She blinked an affirmative. "Stay sharp in there," he added. "We haven't been able to see inside."

"I will," Fallon said softly. Bull shot her a confused look but didn't pursue it.

Reminding herself to breathe, Fallon scanned the tunnel as best she could. Soon, the Stryker wreckage came into view. It leaned up against the tunnel wall, wheels out, as Briggs had described. Beyond it, parts of the tunnel's roof had caved in, making their path through even more difficult.

She did not, however, see any Infecteds. They had probably vacated when their food supply ran out. At the thought of their food supply literally running out of the tunnel, she allowed herself a brief smile.

Very brief.

She grew slightly more comfortable when sunlight from the far end began to filter in. The way forward was clear, and Bull gave the truck a little more gas. In another couple of minutes, the truck exited the tunnel, into the clear morning, and she blew out the breath she'd been holding.

Then she saw the flames.

After the tunnel there was a slight uphill climb. About halfway up the grade, the road was entirely blocked by cars. Several of them were sideways, perpendicular to the roadway—not abandoned, but deliberately placed. All of them were ablaze, sending up thick clouds of black smoke. And Infecteds were gathered around them, seemingly waiting for whichever fly happened into their web.

*Maybe I was too quick to dismiss the idea of an ambush,* she thought.

"Bull . . ."

"I see 'em. Hold on to your britches."

Sudden acceleration pushed Fallon back against her seat. Bull worked through the gears, gaining as much speed as he could in the space available. He was going to ram them, to drive his however-many-tons of not-flaming metal into those other tons of flaming metal. She wished she could have talked to Jason the other night, instead of just Mark, because she was realizing that it might have been her last chance.

Bull either didn't think so, or he didn't care. He started to laugh, his amusement growing as they neared the conflagration. When the truck plowed through several Infecteds, then through the blazing cars, he threw his head back, screaming laughter to the skies. On the other side he hit more Infecteds. She was afraid he would laugh them right off the road in blind hysteria.

Half a mile later, he was still laughing. With his head back, beard raised off his neck, she saw a long scrape there that she hadn't noticed before. It wasn't fresh, but it looked like it had been a deep one. "When did you get that, Bull?" she asked. "When you fought the Eaters?"

Overcome by his paroxysms of laughter, he couldn't speak, but he managed a nod.

She was starting to ask for more details when she heard a gunshot from behind them, in the trailer. "Bull! Pull over!" she shouted. She thought they'd put enough distance between themselves and the ambush to risk it.

He kept laughing, his face turning deeper and

deeper red. "Bull!" Did men *ever* listen to women? She was beginning to have doubts. She punched his thigh, hard. "Stop the truck!"

The punch got his attention. "Huh?"

"Stop the truck!" Fallon repeated. "I need to get in the trailer!"

Bull was slow to respond, but the message sank in. He moved his foot. The air brakes squealed, and the truck ground to a halt.

Fallon was out the door before it had stopped rolling. She ran around to the back, worked the latch, and threw open the door. "What the hell was that?" she demanded.

"It's my fault," Lilith announced, with what sounded like pride. "They were fighting over me."

"Who . . . ?" As Fallon's eyes adapted to the darkness of the trailer, she knew at least part of the story. Warga sat on the floor, his back against one of the pallets. His injured right hand was pressed against his left collarbone, and blood seeped between his fingers. His skin was pale, his expression pained. Higher up, a hole in the trailer wall let in a narrow beam of light. "Fuck! What is the matter with you people? Randy, who shot you?"

Warga didn't answer, and the pained expression on his face didn't budge. Fallon looked at Lilith, who spoke up again. "It was Gino! He shot Randy."

"Gino?"

"Yeah, I did." Antonetti admitted. "He wouldn't shut up about Lilith. He was saying the nastiest things."

"Dude!" Lilith said. "You killed, like, fourteen people or whatever, and you get all whacked out if someone mentions my tits?"

"It was a lot more than that," Antonetti argued.

"It was," Pybus confirmed. "Randy was way out of line."

"Randy's an idiot," Fallon said. "But shooting him's out of line, too."

"I didn't kill him," Antonetti said. "I could have. It was just a nine, through-and-through. Didn't hit anything vital."

"Thank God for small favors."

"Hurts like a motherfucker, though," Warga said between gritted teeth.

"Serves you right," Antonetti said.

"Go to hell—"

"We kind of need *all* of us," Fallon said. "Undamaged would have been nice."

She heard the truck's engine shut off, Bull jumping down from the cab, and his door slamming. He was coming their way, and in a hurry from the sound of it.

But when he came around the corner, he wasn't Bull anymore. Not completely.

His face, already red from laughing, was even redder, almost glowing. His eyes were bloodshot. His mouth hung open, saliva glistening at the corners. In his left hand he held his keys; his right arm was extended, hand open as if to grab the first person who came in range.

"He's infected!" Pybus shouted.

He was right. Fallon took a step back, grabbed for her Glock. Light, Antonetti, and Sansome were faster, though. Light and Sansome were using their long guns. Rounds stitched up Bull's torso, driving him back, then pulverizing his skull. As he fell backward, the keys flew from his hand, over the barrier and down to the road far below.

"They heard that," Pybus said.

"Who?" Fallon asked, before his meaning sank in.

Pybus looked behind her. She spun around.

The Infecteds from the roadblock—those Bull hadn't run over—were coming their way. She wasn't sure how many. A little less than forty, she gauged.

She wasn't sure she'd be able to get the truck started, didn't know if there was another key, but she had to try. She ran around toward the cab, then stopped in her tracks.

Another group was coming from that direction. A bigger group, more than fifty Infecteds, she thought.

They were pinned between a hundred of them. "Guys?" she called, racing for the cab and the two rifles inside. "You might want to grab your guns. Somebody wants to have us for brunch."

# CHAPTER 24

*39 hours*

**"S**tart shooting, try to maintain a buffer, and head south!" Fallon shouted, suiting word to deed as she took aim and fired at some of the Infecteds approaching from the roadblock. Light fired at the other group, and the rest of the psychos needed no further urging, opening up on the two swarming mobs with abandon.

Well, most of them, anyway. Lilith still had her M4, but as far as Fallon could tell, the girl had yet to pull the trigger. Her claims of multiple murders by her own hand seemed less and less credible the farther the psychos went into the city. A few more encounters like this, and Lilith might even start recanting. Fallon was pleased to see that Pybus and Sansome both fired their weapons, though—although Pybus wearing a silly grin the whole time was slightly unnerving.

*Still not as bad as a hundred Infecteds looking to swallow you whole.*

The suppressing fire kept a gap between them and the Infecteds until the two groups of brain hunters converged by the QT truck. Seeing an opportunity, Light stopped firing and grabbed a grenade from his belt. He pulled the pin and lobbed it toward the Infecteds. It hit the pavement, bounced twice, and rolled under the truck.

*Great,* Fallon thought, *he couldn't even land it in the middle of a mob of—*

Then it exploded, a clap of metallic thunder in an echoing valley, reverberating off the cars, the buildings, the road. The explosion flipped the truck and ignited its gas tank, creating a smoky conflagration worthy of any Michael Bay movie. Bits of metal, rubber, and flaming upholstery rained down like some dark parody of a child's snow globe. Some of the Infecteds were torn apart in the blast; others, crushed by the truck. Still others were on fire—walking, wailing torches tearing at their own skin and hair. None of them were paying attention to the psychos.

Which meant it was time to exercise the better part of valor.

Fallon looked at the others. They'd stopped firing once the grenade went off and, to a person, were just standing there, seemingly mesmerized by the flames.

That lasted until the chain reaction started. First,

the nearest vehicle—a sedan—burst into flames, then the next several in line, working all the way down to join the fiery wrecks at the roadblock by the entrance to the tunnel. The next to explode was one of those, followed by one closer to the psychos, by the QT truck. The explosions hopscotched around, probably depending on how much fuel was in their tanks, or how dried out their interiors were, or something. The heat caused its own whirlwind effect, hurling metal shards and more all around them.

"Hey!" Fallon barked at them. "You need an invitation? *Run!*"

**A**fter a few blocks—including some judicious twists and turns—with no sign of being followed, Fallon called for a stop. Though some of the psychos were in decent-to-good shape and managed the run without effort, others were lab rats and bookworms, more likely to participate in Netflix marathons than real ones. She herself was out of breath and struggling not to show it. And Warga, paler than ever, was still bleeding from his gunshot wound, though now that they'd stopped, Light examined him and looked at Fallon, frowning.

"Can you bandage him up?"

Light looked around, spotted a car with a headless body half-in and half-out of the passenger seat. He walked over to the vehicle and divested the corpse of what was left of a long, bohemian skirt.

"Didn't know you were into that sort of thing," Warga said with a weak grin as Light returned with the cloth, which he ripped into long strips.

"I'm not," the EMT replied shortly. "Dying is kind of a turn-on, but I've got no use for them once they're dead. Now shut the fuck up and let me do my work, or I'll just let you bleed to death. Mox nix to me."

Warga wisely closed his mouth and allowed Light to wrap up his shoulder and chest. When he was done, Warga looked like a cross between a peacock and a mummy, from the waist up. Which pleased Lilith to no end, judging by the girl's snort of laughter when Light stepped back to examine his handiwork.

"It'll do for now," Light announced, "but he's going to need stitches at some point."

"That's why we're headed this way," Fallon said, secretly grateful for the opening. The psychos had been too busy running to ask why they were going south instead of east, and she had no intention of revealing her true purpose in selecting the Hyatt Regency as their destination. When they'd come off the freeway, she had recognized where they were—just blocks from where Elliott had last been seen. But the less the psychos knew about him and the prototype, the better. "We're going to the Hyatt. I've been there before, and had to avail myself of their medical supplies, so I know where they're kept. And the hotel has a restaurant, so there should be food. Maybe even a shuttle we can borrow."

Light's lips twisted at her words—possibly due to

her euphemistic use of the word "borrow"—but he didn't argue. Instead, he gave her a short, mocking bow and gestured down 7th Street with a flourish.

"After you, O Fearless Leader."

Lilith giggled at that, too, and Fallon wondered idly whether the girl might be in shock. Light could probably tell, but Fallon was in no hurry to bring it up if it kept Lilith quiet.

Fallon took the lead, Light following, then Warga, Lilith, Sansome, Antonetti, and Caspar Pybus bringing up the rear. As they walked down the center of the street, Fallon was struck by the eerie quiet. It was as if they were traveling through some ancient ravine, inhabited only by dust and wind and ghosts. Nothing moved, save the occasional bit of trash sent sailing in a sudden gust. Downtown Phoenix, which was never silent and still, was now quieter than a tomb.

Fitting, she supposed, since that's essentially what it was.

It wasn't entirely silent, though. Fallon could hear something up ahead, an arrhythmic slapping against the pavement. She held her hand up in a fist—something she'd seen in action movies but never knew the exact meaning of—to get the others to stop so she could listen more closely. Apparently, they all watched the same movies because they halted in their tracks, like birds sensing unseen danger.

Except this danger was no snake or raptor. Those were footsteps, not the beat of wings or the slithering of scales. And since they were the only humans dumb enough to be wandering the streets right now, the footsteps could only belong to one other group.

Infecteds.

Fallon cast about quickly for a place to hide. She didn't want to confront any more Infecteds while they were still so close to the freeway—who knew how far the noise might carry in this echoing urban canyon? Nor did she want to face two-to-one odds—or worse— and from the sound of the approaching feet, that was a conservative estimate.

She spied a storefront with an open glass door. Some kind of art gallery.

"This way!" she hissed, heading for it herself, not bothering to see if they followed. If they didn't, they'd be dead, and Fallon wouldn't lift a finger to help. With as many Infecteds as were about to spill out onto 7th from a side street, anything short of tossing a dozen more of Light's grenades—which she was pretty sure he didn't have—would be suicide. And despite depictions on popular television, that was hardly most psychopaths' preferred endgame.

She reached the door and swung it open, grateful that it was unlocked and careful to grab the bells hanging from it before they could make any noise. Warga came in next, followed by Light, then Lilith. Sansome and Antonetti tried to crowd through at the same time until Sansome elbowed the smaller man in the face. As Antonetti clutched at his bleeding nose, Sansome smiled and strolled into the gallery. Antonetti followed sullenly, and Pybus was the last one in.

"They were just coming around the corner—at least ten that I could count, with more behind," he whispered as he passed her. Fallon nodded, carefully closed the door, and let go of the bells. Then she turned to look for a place to hide.

Like most galleries, there were paintings on the walls, but this one also had sculptures on thick rectangular stands, glass cases displaying jewelry, and trifold dividers adorned with black-and-white photos in plain black frames.

The others were already hiding. Lilith and Antonetti had both crouched behind sculpture stands, skinny enough to be completely hidden by them. Sansome was behind a divider—Fallon could see his foot sticking out. Light, Warga, and Pybus were nowhere to be seen.

Hoping they hadn't found a back door and taken off, Fallon hurried over to another trifold, this one with black, white, and red photos. As she got closer, she saw that the pictures were not, in fact, partially colorized; the red was on the outside of the glass.

Blood, long dried.

Rounding the near end of the divider, she saw two corpses on the floor, strips of bloody scalp littering the tiles beside them, their heads broken open, their brains long gone. The photos here were mostly red, their subjects obscured by blood and bits of flesh and bone.

Fallon pushed one of the fractured skulls aside with her foot so that she could get behind the divider. From here, she could see Caspar behind one of the glass cases.

He nodded to her, then carefully raised his head to peer through the case toward the front of the gallery.

Fallon couldn't see what Pybus saw, but she knew someone who could.

"What's he seeing, Book?" she whispered.

"Infecteds, thirty, maybe a few more. Headed north on 7th Street. I don't think they'll bother you, though. They've already been through this stretch once."

Fallon frowned. "What does that mean?"

"I wanted to wait to make sure it wasn't an isolated thing, but right before the alarm went off—"

"What alarm?"

"In a minute. Right before, we saw groups of Infecteds in Tempe doing what was basically a house-by-house search for . . . survivors. Only not to rescue them."

Fallon felt ice form in her gut. If the Infecteds were displaying group intelligence—a herd mentality—then their mission had just become that much more dangerous.

And their odds of surviving—not all that high to begin with—had decreased considerably.

"I hoped it was an anomaly, but I saw it over and over again in different parts of the city, though it's definitely more prominent the farther east you go."

*Wonderful.*

"They're gone now. Made a right at the corner. You're good to go to that hotel." A pause. "You're a little off course, you know."

"Warga's hurt," she whispered. She turned to face a

wall, fully aware that she was showing her back to six convicted killers. "We need—"

"I know, Fallon. He might be milking it a little, though."

"I can't take that chance." She didn't like lying to Book, but she found it easy enough to do. That was one of the traits she shared with psychopathic killers. She preferred to tell the truth when she could, but when she needed a lie, it was right there.

"Anyway," he said, giving no indication of whether he believed her, "it looks like it's safe to get back on the road."

Fallon looked over at Pybus questioningly. "How's it look out there?"

Pybus opened the door, looked outside, then came back in and nodded. "Coast is clear," he said in a low voice.

Fallon moved out from behind the trifold divider.

"Then let's get to the Hyatt and get Warga patched up."

"And get something to eat," Lilith added as she stood and stretched. Antonetti was watching her, so the girl took her time, raising her arms over her head languorously and sticking her chest out. "I'm hungry," she said, winking at Antonetti, who blushed and looked away.

Fallon thought of Elliott and the prototype.

"We're all hungry for something," she murmured, but she was pretty sure Book was the only one who heard.

The Hyatt Regency was on 2$^{nd}$ Street, between Monroe and Adams. Fallon led her team down 7$^{th}$ until they passed the University of Arizona's College of Medicine, a satellite campus to the main one down in Tucson. "What about that place?" Warga asked. "Got to be better medical supplies there than in some hotel."

She couldn't stand the thought of being so close to Elliott—to the prototype—and not making it all the way. "We can't go there," she said. She paused, not sure what came next.

"Too many Infecteds," Book said.

It took a moment to understand his meaning, but when it became clear, she said, "Infecteds went to medical facilities when they started getting sick, or were attacked and injured. Right, Hank?"

"That's where I first saw them," Light agreed. "In the ER."

"That place might be crawling with them," Fallon said. "The hotel is safer."

"Whatever the fuck," Warga said. "Let's just go."

They went. They made a right on Monroe, traveling past Heritage Square, the Convention Center, and St. Mary's Basilica. Though Fallon wasn't religious, she felt an almost primal urge to run to the sanctuary of the church. The bodies spilling out the doors and onto the sidewalk were enough to convince her she was better off trusting in more secular means of salvation.

Once at the hotel, they found that the automatic doors wouldn't work, and metal security gates had been drawn across every entrance. Someone inside had had the presence of mind to close the place off, but whether they themselves were now dead, alive, or otherwise was anyone's guess.

"Now what?" Light asked.

Fallon surveyed the doors. There had to be a way in. Bend the metal, break the glass? No . . .

*Break the wood.*

"Joe. The valet window. The cover is just wood. You can break through it, can't you?"

Sansome looked where she indicated, a small window in a curved section of wall.

"Yeah, I can break it, but what good is that going to do? I can't fit through it."

"You can't, but Lilith can." Fallon turned to the girl. "Once you climb through, you can open the door to the valet station for us. There's a door on the other side that opens up into the lobby. We get in without damaging their defenses or creating a path the Infecteds can follow."

Lilith actually looked impressed.

"Okay, I'm game."

It only took Sansome two blows to crack the wooden cover enough to tear it off. He boosted Lilith through the small opening, and a moment later, the door to the valet station swung wide.

"I feel like I should be getting a tip," the girl said, as Fallon and the others entered.

"I'll give you a tip," Warga replied, leering.

"And I'll blow it off," Lilith replied with a sweet

smile, hefting the M4 Fallon had returned to her once she was inside the station.

"Come on," Fallon said, stepping between them. "I don't have time to referee or give a lecture on hostile work environments. Besides," she added, looking at Warga, "don't you have enough gunshot wounds for the time being? Lock the door and let's get into the lobby and find those medical supplies."

"And real food," Lilith said.

"Yes, Lily. And food."

She'd been walking into the lobby as she spoke, the others following close behind. Pybus had just entered the lobby when there was a sound of several chambers being racked. A group of men appeared from behind the wall that hid the elevator banks, and others popped up from behind the check-in counter. They all had guns pointed straight at the psychos.

"Welcome to the Hyatt," said a man whose uniform— a dark, formal suit, just this side of a tuxedo— instantly identified him as the hotel restaurant's maitre d'. He had his tie knotted tightly at his throat and a Beretta nine-millimeter pistol aimed at Fallon's head. "You can either turn around and leave the way you came, or we will make sure that you do *not* enjoy your stay. At all."

## CHAPTER 25

*38 hours*

**T**he psychos all pointed their own guns at the hotel staff before Fallon could stop them.

"Whoa, easy there! Let's everyone just calm down a bit," she said, employing her most authoritative yet conciliatory tone. Which sort of made her sound like she did when she was trying to reason with her toddler. "We're not sick. We just need to get our man patched up, maybe get some food and rest awhile, then we'll be on our way. No need for more violence, especially among fellow humans."

The maitre d' looked suspicious, but another of the men—who Fallon thought she recognized as the guy who'd bandaged her hand up after the last time she'd stayed here, when she'd gotten mad about something she could no longer remember and smashed her fist through a glass table—lowered his weapon.

"She's right, Quinn. What are we going to do, anyway? Have a shoot-out in the lobby? Like that's not going to bring those . . . *things* running?"

"Shut up, Parker," the maitre d' snapped. "How'd they even get in? How do we know they didn't just leave the front doors wide open for . . . *them*?"

"Because no one can get through the front doors?"

The maitre d'—Quinn—just glared.

"Look," Fallon said hurriedly, sensing the need to bolster a potential ally before he turned on them, too, "we came through the valet window. And we locked the outside door behind us. The Infecteds aren't smart enough to climb in through a broken window." Though after what Book had told her about their going building to building looking for survivors, she wasn't entirely sure about that. But she sure as hell wasn't going to share those doubts with Quinn and crew.

"They're hurt and hungry, Quinn," Parker pressed. "I'm sure they're not here to rob us at gunpoint. Are you . . . ?"

"Fallon. And, no, we're not." She put her own gun away and motioned for the others to do the same. It was grudging, grumbling, and slow—pretty much par for the course with this group—but they all eventually did as she'd asked. "There. See? We're not dangerous. We're just tired of running." Well, half of that was true, anyway.

"Come on, Mr. Quinn." It wasn't Parker this time,

but another of the hotel staff, a short-haired woman Fallon had initially mistaken for a man. Her name tag read KARENA. She lowered her weapon, and the other staffers followed suit until only Quinn was left, his pistol still pointed at Fallon's head.

She saw him swallow, saw sweat beading at his temple. He was this group's de facto leader and didn't want to—probably couldn't afford to—appear weak in front of them. He needed to feel like this was his idea, not like he'd been bullied into it.

"It's up to you, of course. We can go back out the way we came in, try to find somewhere else nearby that has medical supplies and food to spare, maybe a place to rest up for a few hours." Fallon kept her voice as even and calm as possible though she could feel the other psychos tensing around her. They were used to taking what they wanted, usually by force. Fallon planned on getting what she wanted, too, just with a more subtle weapon than a gun. "We didn't mean to step on anyone's toes. You're in charge here. Whatever decision you make, we'll abide by it."

Quinn's lips twisted in a fleeting smile, there and gone again in swift seconds, but still long enough to give Fallon a glimpse of gloating. His chest puffed out like some sort of gaudy bird in the middle of a mating dance. He lowered his gun. Fallon hid a smile of her own. She had him.

"I suppose we can afford to let you stay for a few hours," Quinn said, reveling in his role of magnanimous monarch demonstrating his *noblesse oblige*.

"Thank you," Fallon said simply, knowing a longer response would only give him time to think and maybe figure out he'd just been manipulated.

Quinn nodded. "We keep the first-aid supplies in the manager's office." He pulled a set of keys out of his pocket and tossed it to Parker. "He'll take you back."

Fallon motioned for Light and Warga to follow Parker. Being an EMT, Light would be better able to use what was in the kit to get Randy patched up. Though Fallon was pretty sure the hotel wouldn't have any lidocaine on hand, so whatever he did to Warga, it was going to hurt.

She was also pretty sure Warga would be the only one who'd be upset by that fact.

"The rest of you can head to the ballroom," Quinn was saying. "We have it set up as a cafeteria—Networks is too exposed to have people eating in there even though it's a pain to shuttle food back and forth from there to the ballroom. People can come and go as they like, eating whenever they want." His tone made Fallon think he took a lot of pride in his own restaurant—which must be the revolving Stratosphere-like Compass upstairs since he was dressed far too formally for Networks, a run-of-the-mill bar and grill—and he considered the idea of people's people being allowed to sit wherever they wanted whenever they were hungry a personal affront. "But you have to check out with one of the staff members there so we can keep track of what you're eating and how much. No one is allowed to take too much. We can't exactly call and have more food delivered."

*Rationing by any other name,* Fallon thought. Still, it made sense. Even a hotel with multiple restaurants could only feed its guests for so long before the food started to run out. Fallon didn't want to be around when that happened.

She turned to the others. "Go ahead and get something to eat. I'm going to talk to Quinn, see if I can't get us some new transportation."

Pybus nodded and led the others toward the ballroom, following yet another hotel employee. Fallon was beginning to wonder if the place even had any guests—it was almost summer in Phoenix, after all; hardly a vacationer's paradise. She dismissed the trivial thought as she watched the other staffers dispersing, going back to whatever jobs they still had to do here when they weren't pretending to be armed guards.

Fallon blinked the Morse code for "off"—she didn't want anyone to see what came next—and looked at Quinn. "Is there someplace we can talk privately?"

A bushy eyebrow rose, and he gestured over to the check-in counter.

Once there, Fallon lowered her voice, which made it easier for her to sound helpless.

"Please. The others I'm traveling with don't know this is why I convinced them to come to this hotel instead of trying another one, but my husband checked in here a few days before people started going crazy. We've been having a rough time lately, and he wanted a trial separation. But with all that's happening, those troubles seem small and petty, and I just want to be back in his arms, safe, like I used to be." She wondered briefly whether, if she had been talking about her actual husband, this would still be true? She didn't dwell on it, though; the answer might not be pretty. "Can you tell me if he's still here? His name is Elliott Jameson, and I really need to find him. Please."

Quinn frowned.

"Look, Mrs. Jameson, I'd love to help you. Truly, I would. But I can't give out that kind of information."

Fallon let her eyes fill with crocodile tears. *The only kind most psychopaths could shed,* she thought, then quickly rerouted that errant train.

"Please, Mr. Quinn. Those—those things *ate* our son, right in front of me, and there was nothing I could do to save him. Elliott's all I have left now." That last sentence rang with more truth than Fallon would like to admit.

"All right. I'm not supposed to do this, but I suppose unique times call for unique decisions." He turned to Karena, standing behind the counter. "Karena, please check for Mr. Jameson."

She typed for a minute or so, then looked up from the screen. "I'm sorry," she said. "There's no record of anyone with that name checking in within the last month."

"Are you sure it was the Hyatt, Mrs. Jameson?" Quinn asked with a frown. "There are several other hotels in the vicinity." *And you'd rather we had barged into any of them,* Fallon thought.

"Yes, I'm sure it was this one," Fallon said, frowning herself. "Maybe he checked in under a different name? He's tall"—she indicated a spot above her head—"wears a little ponytail, and has a scar on his neck and jaw that make his beard grow unevenly there."

Quinn's eyes widened just slightly—he recognized the description. Now to see if he'd tell her where Jameson was.

"Yes, that sounds familiar," Karena said. "I believe he checked in under the name Ed Johnson."

Quinn's eyebrow rose again, as if waiting for Fallon to explain why her husband would need an alias, but she had no desire to enlighten him. When she didn't, he looked at Karena again. "Give Mrs. Jameson a key, please," he said. To Fallon, he added, "I'd rather call up there, but the entire telephone system has been out for a couple of days. And I'm sorry, but I can't spare anyone to go up with you. The next visitors might be less friendly than you."

"He's up on sixteen," Karena said. She swiped a blank keycard, wrote the room number on it, and handed it over to Fallon. "Good luck with your reunion, Mrs. Jameson."

"Thank you so much," Fallon said gratefully, taking the proffered card. "I can't wait to see him." *And blow the bastard's hands off for daring to steal from me,* she thought.

For once, she didn't even care how much like the others she sounded.

The manager's office wasn't large, but it was sumptuously appointed, with lots of leather and gleaming brass and highly polished wood. On the desk were a computer keyboard and monitor, various piles of paperwork, a half-buried hardcover book on management theory, and a nameplate identifying the manager as Annette Kwon. Light didn't bother to ask what had happened to her. A built-in shelving unit across from the desk, behind a rich leather-and-brass couch, held more such books, along with family photographs, awards plaques from the Hyatt organization, and a white-and-red case that Parker removed and handed to Light.

"I hope you know what you're doing," Parker said. "We have a nurse practitioner on call, but she fell off the radar a couple of days ago, and we haven't been able to get any medical professionals in since then."

"I'm an EMT," Light said. "Don't worry, I can stitch him up in no time. You mind if he sits on the couch?"

Parker's eyes involuntarily narrowed, and he bit his lower lip. He would obviously prefer that Warga's patching up be done somewhere else. Maybe he hoped to inherit the office . . . and the job title. Light could read people as well as Annette Kwon could presumably read books—or at least purchase them and line them up on shelves. Having noted Parker's dismay, he was determined to spill some blood on that pricey leather couch.

"I think—"

"I've got to do it right now," Light said, cutting off any potential argument. "He's lost a lot of blood."

"All right," Parker said, resignation apparent in his tone. "Go ahead."

"Thanks," Light said. "Sit, Randy."

Warga sat. Light put one knee on the couch, his other foot on the floor, and made a big show of inspecting Warga's wounds. In-and-out, like Antonetti had claimed, with no major arteries impacted, no bones hit. External tissue damage, obviously, and some muscle impairment was likely—Warga wouldn't be lifting that arm above his head for a long time if ever.

"This might hurt," Light said. He pulled Warga forward a little and stuck his index finger into the exit wound, rubbing it to get some blood flowing, then pressed the sexual predator back against the leather. He didn't like Warga, even a little—rapists were the worst, as far as he was concerned, and if he could chemically castrate the man while patching his wounds, he would.

They had to work together, for the time being. And he *was* a healer, or at least one who wanted to end suffering. But maybe once the mission was done, he could save the lives of countless other people by taking Warga's. It was an idea, anyway. Something to look forward to.

"You got a shot of something strong?" Warga asked Parker. "Pretty sure there's no local anesthesia in that kit."

"No," Light said quickly. "Ignore him, Mr. Parker.

You've got to have your head on straight out there, Randy. You hit the sauce and it could get us all killed." He found a needle and thread in the kit. It would be a quick sewing job, just enough to close the wounds and protect them from infection.

And it would hurt like hell.

"I need something," Warga whined.

"I'll tell you some jokes, take your mind off the pain."

"Is that like stepping on my foot to help me forget that my hand hurts?"

"How many dead hookers does it take to change a light bulb?"

Warga's face brightened a little at the thought image, and Light jabbed the needle through his flesh. "I don't know—nnnnh! That hurts—how many?"

"Must be more than four," Light replied. "Because it's still dark as a motherfucker in my basement."

Warga burst out laughing, yanking his shoulder from Light's grip. Light grabbed him and muscled him back against the couch, hard. "Hold still, dammit!"

"That's a good one," Warga said. He winced as the needle broke skin again. "What else you got?"

"Why did the French hooker retire at sixty?" Light asked.

Light pulled thread through the opening, and readied the needle for the next insertion. "Because you can't . . ."

## CHAPTER 26

*38 hours*

**T**he elevator doors chimed open on the sixteenth floor. Elliott's room was at the end of the hall. As Fallon walked down the strangely silent corridor, she felt like there were eyes pressed against every peephole. The skin on the back of her neck began to crawl, and she couldn't suppress a shiver.

As she neared her destination, she saw an old room-service tray sitting outside the door. It had obviously been there since the world turned upside down, and whoever was responsible for returning the trays to the restaurant kitchen found more important things to do with their time—like trying to survive. Though flies buzzed thickly around it—a sound almost worse than the carpeted quiet of a few moments ago—Fallon could still see the small empty bottles of Merlot, and the hamburger buns with the middles torn out and eaten, the crusty shell discarded. Elliott's favorite drink, and his habitual meal. She hadn't been a hundred percent sure Ed Johnson was in fact Elliott Jameson, but now she was certain beyond a shadow of a doubt.

Fallon didn't bother knocking, just used the keycard to open the door, which, fortunately, was not chained on the other side. As it swung open, two things caught Fallon's attention.

First, a curvy Latina woman in a tight dress and heels, one of which was splattered with blood. Second, a chair in the middle of the floor, its legs cracked and splintered in places. On the floor around it were lengths of rope, duct tape, and a pair of pliers, jaws caked with something black and flaky.

There was no sign of the prototype or Elliott, but Fallon had a pretty good idea of what had happened to him when he had been here.

He'd been tortured.

*Dammit,* she thought. *The bitch beat me to it.*

**P**arker led Light and the stitched and rebandaged Warga to the "cafeteria." Light got a BLT and nibbled around its edges, but he was increasingly ill at ease. He didn't like the way those hotel employees stared at him and the others. They weren't infected, but they looked hungry just the same. Or fearful. Under these circumstances, there wasn't much difference between the two.

Sitting around waiting for Fallon was stupid, he decided. What she had told them was bullshit. She'd been gone way too long. Meanwhile, Infecteds owned the streets, preying on defenseless human beings.

Those humans needed an angel, and he was it. Angel on the hunt. Prey turning on predator. The idea of it made him grin.

"What's funny?" Pybus asked.

The old man's eyes were brown and moist and reflected the overhead lights. A poet would have had a field day with them. To Light, they just looked like candles that needed to be snuffed. "I'm going for a walk," he said. "Check the perimeter."

"Dr. O'Meara said to wait here."

"Well, she's not here, is she? Who knows if she's even coming back? I want to see what's out there."

"Go for it, Hank," Warga urged. His voice was weak; undergoing Light's ministrations had been hard on him. "If any Infecteds spot you, make sure they chase you away from us."

Light ignored him. That was, he had learned, the best way to deal with Warga. He always wanted to get under your skin—and in the case of anything female, under their panties.

"Back in a while," Light said. Sansome raised an objection, too, but Light hurried out before the big man could even finish his sentence.

The street was quiet. The whole Valley seemed to be, for that matter. Light had expected hordes of rampaging brain-eaters, like the ones he had mowed over at the hospital. Sure, they'd encountered groups of them here and there, but in the usually bustling downtown area, nothing seemed to be moving at all. He had thought that by now, there might also be pockets of human resistance—like the people in the hotel, but more assertive, taking to the streets to defend their right to intact craniums. *This is Arizona, after all; we have more guns per person than almost any other state. If they were illegals instead of brain-eaters, people would be out here in force.*

He wandered down 2nd Street, and as he crossed Adams, he spotted a trio of Infecteds coming his way. They were scanning storefronts, looking in windows the way hungry diners studied restaurant menus before going inside. They didn't see him, so he dashed across the street and took refuge in an alley midway down the block. A Dumpster and some shipping cartons shielded him from view; though if they came down the alley—or if they could somehow sniff out living humans—they might still find him. They would also find destruction from the barrel of his M249.

A couple of minutes later, they passed the alley with barely a glance inside and continued down 2nd. He gave them some time to get past, then moved cautiously to the alley's end and peeked around the corner. The Infecteds had moved on at a reasonable clip. Checking their back trail seemed beyond their mental capabilities, but Light took no chances; he followed, but quietly, taking advantage of recessed doorways, newspaper boxes, and any other cover he could find.

The light rail ran down Washington, and there was a train parked at the station. From the corner, Light couldn't see anyone on it. The Infecteds noticed it, too, and diverted their course, crossing the usually busy street diagonally, a move that might have gotten them run over if the city had been functioning normally.

They climbed up into the train, looked around, and left again. Empty, then? Light waited until they were down the next block, then raced across the street on the same path they'd used. He hoisted himself up into the car.

Not empty, after all. There were plenty of people inside, but they were all dead. He couldn't count how many because some had been torn to pieces, body parts strewn on seats and on the floor among the whole corpses there. Mostly whole, anyway, except for skulls cracked open and brains removed. The stench was ghastly; these people had died in the last few days, their clothes still reeked of the piss and shit of their final evacuations and the blood from the wounds that had killed them. Flies were thick on the corpses, an undulating, buzzing black blanket.

Light had seen enough gore in his life that it seldom bothered him. This scene made his gut clench, though, his blood run cold, despite a vague stirring of arousal. His killings were merciful, meant to deliver people from pain and hopelessness. But maybe he was a psychopath, like O'Meara claimed. Maybe he was fooling himself about the nature of his actions, and he really did belong in a cage.

He looked up and saw that the Infecteds had re-versed course. They were coming back his way. He ducked so they couldn't see him from ground level and moved inside the car just far enough that if they looked at the doorway, they wouldn't spot him. His left foot brushed up against an arm that had been ripped off just above the elbow, with stringy muscle and flesh hang-ing out. He glanced at it, dispassionately, his momen-tary doubts forgotten. Touching a severed arm would bother some people, but not him. Hank Light was stronger than that. Better.

He lifted his head above the window's edge, just enough to keep track of the Infecteds. They were wan-dering down Washington, back across 2nd, toward Cen-tral. He waited, immersed in the stink of violent death, flies crawling on his skin and buzzing around his face, until the Infecteds were almost out of sight. Then he jumped down from the train and darted toward the corner. By the time he reached it, they were almost to the corner of 1st Street. They crossed it and kept going. When they reached Central, Light hurried to 1st, across it, and down the next block.

He made it to Central just in time to watch them go into Duck and Decanter, in the One North Cen-tral Tower. He'd been there before; it was a small, up-scale food and gift market and eatery, tile-floored and trendy, with huge windows all around. Light went to a window and stood, mostly blocked from view by a section of wall, and watched.

The Infecteds were two men who had probably

been in their mid-twenties before Crazy 8s got them, and an older woman, sixtyish, with silver hair and deep lines in her face. All three had the rosy cheeks and red eyes symptomatic of the virus, and their cheeks and lips and chins were bloodstained, symptomatic of creatures that fed on human beings. Their clothes were filthy and torn, as one would expect of those who walked the streets and survived through violence. The market appeared empty, but the Infecteds spotted a door, back past the refrigerator cases and the soda dispenser. They tried the door handle, but it didn't open.

Light expected them to give up and started to duck back behind the wall. Instead, one of the men picked up a chair and started slamming it against the door. The chair was wood, and it splintered before the door budged. The Infected tossed it aside, then he and the female hoisted one of the tables. It had a steel center post with short crosspieces at the bottom, for stability. Together, they rammed the door with that end.

The fourth time, the jamb gave way, and the door swung open. Light could hear screaming from inside. He ran around the exterior, to a window that offered a better view. Behind the door was a storage area containing steel shelves stocked with drink cups, napkins, cartons of foodstuffs and merchandise.

Two people had been holed up in there for days, from the looks of them. One was a young woman, blond and pretty despite being unkempt, and the other was a man in his forties, unshaven and greasy-haired. They both wore shirts bearing the Duck and Decanter logo. Employees, Light guessed, who had taken refuge early on and stayed inside, probably subsisting on stored food and beverages. He guessed there was probably an employee bathroom back there.

They both tried to fight off the Infecteds, the girl with a carving knife and the man with a length of steel pipe that looked like part of the shelving. But the Infecteds were not dissuaded. The knife struck home a couple of times, and the woman was battered with the steel bar. They kept going, though, ignoring their wounds. When the girl saw that her knife was doing her no good, she hurled it aside and tried to run deeper into the back room, screaming so loud Light could hear her. In her panic, she collided with one of the shelving units, and the delay allowed one of the Infecteds to catch her long hair. He yanked her backward and got his hands around her throat, then drove her down to her knees, and farther. When she was face down on the hard floor, he started bashing her skull against it, keeping up a steady, rhythmic pace. Light saw when the blood started to flow, and when her resistance was gone, he knew she was dead.

The other man joined the woman, attacking the older man in the Duck and Decanter shirt. He swung his bar for all he was worth, but finally the woman batted it out of his hand. With that out of the way, she surged forward, biting and clawing. The man stepped in on the guy's side, cutting off his only avenue of escape. The guy punched and kicked, but those were no more effective than the bar had been. If the Infecteds were hurt at all, they didn't show it. When the woman got in close enough, she dug her teeth deep into his throat and tore. Blood geysered forth, and the guy's knees went weak. They let him fall to the floor, then the woman picked up his metal bar and started jabbing the end of it into his skull.

Light stood there, watching, unnoticed, while they exposed the brains of their victims, then scooped them out with their hands and ate them. They shared, two brains between three Infecteds. Watching the greyish folds dangling from between bloody teeth was disturbing, even to Light, but he pushed from his mind the idea that either the victims or the Infecteds had ever been human and was able to watch with the dispassionate interest with which he'd view a TV show about life on the veldt. A lion eating a zebra was pretty much the same thing.

The Infecteds were efficient machines. They had done away with the niceties society imposed upon them and focused on their own needs. There was no communication between them that he had heard, but they knew they were safer together than alone. They didn't bother trying to sweet-talk their prey, but took what they wanted by force.

It wasn't for him, of course. His calling was to end human suffering or to limit it as much as possible. But he didn't see a lot of difference between a psychopath like Sansome or Warga and these once-human creatures. Fallon said he was a psychopath, and he supposed he was, in a clinical sense. He knew most people would think of his services as murder, so he was careful to provide them only when he could be sure it was safe. He didn't experience emotions the way other people did, but he thought his way was better. Safer.

Anyway, considering how he was brought up, who could expect him to live up to society's definition of normal? His mother had died giving birth to his sister Juliet, leaving both kids to be raised by their physically abusive, drunken wretch of a father. The old man had farmed out a lot of that work to a succession of short-term girlfriends who shared his general temperament and weaknesses. Light's first time helping someone out of misery had come when he was fifteen and Juliet twelve. The old man and his current piece, Constance, had been fighting. Somehow, Juliet had found herself dragged into it, and when it turned physical, she'd been knocked down the stairs—by whom, Light never found out. He had been downstairs, and when he heard the commotion, he raced to her side. Her neck was broken, and her eyes pleaded for release. By the time their father and Constance got downstairs, Light had set Juliet free with a pillow. He lied to the paramedics when they arrived, and he decided then that he would someday join their ranks.

He also decided he would do what he could to help those beyond the reach of medical intervention. The next time came soon after, when Constance passed out with a lit cigarette between her fingers. She woke up when the cheap sofa burst into flames, but she'd spilled so much gin on her blouse that she couldn't escape the blaze.

She was so badly burned that no one bothered to look for another cause of death. Like suffocation. But her pained mewling had been infuriating.

Warga and the rest were psychos, sure, but he was no cold-blooded killer like them. He rendered the only aid that could ease the pain of the unfortunates he encountered. He was a caregiver, really. Instead of a prison cell, he deserved a medal.

Maybe he'd get one, when this mission had been accomplished. If he bothered to stick around for it.

# CHAPTER 27

*38 hours*

"**W**here's Elliott? What have you done to him?" Fallon demanded, stepping into the room.

"*No hablo Inglés,*" the Latina replied, gesturing help-lessly with her left hand. Her right hand was behind an open case on the room's desk. Fallon couldn't see the contents from where she stood, but she imagined it included more torture implements.

"Bullshit. Elliott doesn't speak Spanish, so if you were trying to question him, it would have had to have been in English. Try again, sweetheart." As she spoke, Fallon pulled out her gun and started to raise it, but the other woman was faster, snatching a gun of her own out of the case and leveling it at Fallon's head.

"Put your gun on the floor and kick it over here.

Sweetheart," the Latina said, her accent heavy, her r's rolling like marbles across tile. Even so, her sarcasm came through loud and clear.

Fallon briefly considered refusing. If she gave up her weapon, there was nothing to stop the woman from killing her outright. She wasn't so sure of her aim up close and personal like this, though. It was one thing shooting into a crowd of Infected—they were the proverbial fish in a barrel. Even for a definitional psychopath, it was an entirely different proposition to shoot at someone who you *knew* was human and who could shoot back at any second. She wondered how many people would still hunt for sport if the animals also had weapons. Not a lot, she imagined.

*Even psychopaths prefer their victims to be helpless.*

Fallon slowly bent to place the gun on the floor as instructed, her eyes never leaving the other woman. Once she'd released it, she straightened and used her foot to shove the weapon halfheartedly across the floor toward the Latina. It made it about two feet before friction from the carpet slowed it to a stop, in between the two women but closer to Fallon. The Latina frowned in annoyance.

"What do you know about Jameson? Why are you here looking for him?"

Fallon decided to use the same lie here as she had downstairs. After all, it had worked once. Maybe it would again.

"Elliott's my husband. We've been separated, but our son was killed by one of those brain-eating . . .

*things,* and now he's all I have left. And I want him back."

"What is the word you used? Ah, yes—'bullshit.' Jameson was not married. We did a thorough check on him."

That was interesting. Apparently the Mexican version of Jessica Rabbit was not working alone.

"So why are you really here? Jealous lover? He owes you money? Perhaps you are *la policía?*"

Fallon laughed bitterly.

"I'd like to think a cop wouldn't be so easily disarmed, wouldn't you?" She knew the woman would pump her for information—maybe even torture Fallon like she had Elliott—and then kill her. Keeping the conversation going until she could get her own information and find a way out of this little predicament seemed like a good idea.

As did honesty.

"He's my partner. He stole from me, and I want a piece of his hide."

Well, partial honesty.

"It seems your Elliott is good at that. But what, exactly, did he take from you? Money? Or something else?"

Fallon knew the Latina was fishing, and the fact that she was focusing on "something else" gave her a pretty good idea what the other woman was hoping to catch.

She didn't have the prototype. Which meant Jameson couldn't be dead, because he was the only one who knew where it was.

"Tell me what you did with him, and I'll tell you what he stole," Fallon countered. If the woman couldn't—or wouldn't—tell her where Jameson was, there was no reason to keep playing her game.

"Wrong answer," the Latina said with a hard smile. And then she pulled the trigger.

The Infecteds had finished their deli meal and were on the move again. Light hung back but kept an eye on them, torn between being riveted by how they fed their terrible hunger and wanting to put an end to them. If he had known about the people hiding in the back room at the market in time to save them, he would have opened fire. Next time, he would be ready.

It didn't take long for the next time to come around. The Infecteds were walking past a UPS delivery truck parked beside a curb. They seemed to hardly notice the truck, but then one of them stopped and climbed up onto the front bumper. He put his hands against the glass and peered through.

Although Light couldn't see any communication taking place, the other two moved toward the rear of the truck. The first one got down from the bumper and went to the curbside door. He tried it but couldn't get in. A concrete garbage bin with a removable steel top stood on the sidewalk nearby; the Infected hurried to it, snatched off the top, and returned to the truck. A few blows with the steel broke through the window, and the monster dropped his tool and reached through, opening the door from the inside.

Light readied the machine gun. If there were human beings in that truck, he would open fire before they were hurt.

Then everything happened so fast, it caught him off guard. The back doors flew open, and four people sprang out. One wore UPS brown. The Infecteds were ready, though. They caught two of the people—both women—immediately. The UPS driver made it a couple of steps, then tripped on the curb, and before he could get up, the Infected who had broken the window was on him. The fourth human, another man, sprinted away down the middle of the street.

Light opened up with the M249. He squeezed the trigger and held it down, firing an extended hail of steel-tipped rounds. The weapon had a serious recoil, but his targets weren't far away, and he was able to maintain his aim well enough. The Infected wrestling with the UPS driver went down first, his arms flailing at the air until the bullets penetrated his skull. The other two fell more easily, first the other male, then the female, both of them jerking spasmodically as the heavy rounds tore into them. Brass clinked around Light's boots, and the air filled with the biting scent of gun smoke.

When he was sure the Infecteds were finished, Light walked closer to their victims. He was too late for the first two, it turned out. The UPS driver still lived, but there were tooth marks on his face, where his cheek had been bitten into, and his neck showed multiple claw marks. He was alive but infected. Unless he had a psychopathic brain, he would become one of them.

And he was in incredible pain. He couldn't speak, could only make pathetic, squeaking sounds. His left hand clutched weakly at the curb. His eyes were wide, panic-stricken.

Light laid his weapon down gently, placed his left hand across the man's mouth, and with his right, pinched the driver's nostrils closed.

It didn't take long.

# CHAPTER 28

*38 hours*

**F**allon had been watching the other woman's eyes as they spoke. She'd seen their slight narrowing when she'd offered to exchange what she knew for what the other woman knew. So she was already lunging for her own gun when the Latina fired. Fallon felt the bullet whizz by her ear. She tried not to think about the fact that if she'd moved any slower, her brain would be too fragmented for even an Infected to find useful.

Fallon snatched the gun up, but she was neither an athlete nor an action hero, and as she tried to straighten awkwardly, she saw the Latina pointing the gun at her again, her smile feral. She knew in that moment that she was going to die.

*I'm so sorry, Jason.*

And then the door burst open and Warga rushed in, guns blazing.

Or at least that's what it seemed like to Fallon, half-crouched, still fumbling with her own weapon. She watched as the rapist fired two shots into the Latina's head before the other woman could turn and get a shot off herself.

As the curvaceous femme fatale collapsed on the floor, her head coming to rest in a pool of crimson blood and raven hair, Warga clucked his tongue.

"Damned waste," he said, shaking his head. "She was hot." He took a longer look. "Still is."

Straightening, Fallon looked at the other psycho, freshly stitched up and bandaged. Some of his color was coming back, but that might also have been from arousal at the sight of a female corpse.

"What the hell are you doing up here?" she demanded. "And where are the others?"

"I might ask you the same thing, Doc. And I think you know what I'm doing up here, and it's not something we need the others for."

Fallon scoffed, though inwardly she felt a flutter of fear.

*You have a gun, dummy.*

She pointed it at Warga.

"Even getting shot isn't enough to stifle your urges?"

Warga laughed, ignoring her gun as he moved closer, his own weapon held loosely in his hand.

"You've read my jacket, Doc. Hell, you *wrote* most of it. 'Hypersexualized, equates sex with violence,' the whole nine yards. All this shooting and blood is getting me hard, and I intend to do something about it."

Fallon's finger tightened on the trigger. Not enough to engage the firing mechanism, but enough that Warga could see she wasn't joking.

"You're going to have to keep it in your pants, Randy. Maybe after we bring the meteor back, we can set you up with a hooker or two, but—"

"Or four?"

"Okay," Fallon said, as surprised by the interruption as she was by his amused look. "Or four. But for now, we've got a job to do, with no time for extracurricular activities."

"What about your activities? What the hell was going on here?"

She ignored the question.

"I saved your life. You're telling me that doesn't warrant a little thanks?"

Fallon shrugged. "Thanks."

Warga looked at her for a moment, then laughed again. He lowered his own weapon and moved past her toward the dead woman. Fallon kept her gun trained on him.

"That doesn't mean you can go all necrophiliac on me, either."

He ignored her, knelt, and grabbed the woman's wrist.

"See these tats? And the ones on her neck? She's cartel."

"*What?*"

Warga stood, putting his gun back in his pants as he walked over to the bed where the woman's purse was. He dumped it on the bedspread, and thick rolls of cash tumbled out, as well as a .22.

"With this much cash, a case full of toys, and no bodyguards? Probably a hit woman. So what are you doing playing cops and robbers with the cartel, Doc?"

"You said it yourself. She's hot."

Warga's eyebrows tried to climb onto the top of his head.

"Wow, Doc, I had no idea you swung that way."

"There's a lot you don't know about me, Randy," Fallon replied quietly, but Warga wasn't listening.

"Gotta say, I'm impressed. And you've got good taste in women—brunette, busty, and dangerous."

Fallon had had enough. She fired a shot past Warga's head—one that came far closer to taking off his ear than she'd intended.

"Hey!" Warga yelped. "What the hell didya do *that* for?"

"It's time to go, Randy."

"Sheesh. You could have just said something." He pocketed a couple of the smaller rolls. At Fallon's look, he shrugged. "Might come in handy at some point. Not everyone in the zone is Infected, and people everywhere want the same basic things, especially at a time like this: sex, food, and security."

The observation was surprisingly astute, and Fallon realized she might need to revise her assessment of Warga. It wasn't a comforting thought.

He walked over to the case on the desk and started pulling weapons out of it—a Glock like the one Fallon had, a couple of other pistols she didn't recognize, several knives, and another pair of pliers. He started putting them in whatever pocket or through whatever loop they would fit in. As he did, he tossed the Glock to Fallon, who surprised herself by catching it one-handed. Following his lead, she placed the sleek weapon in a pocket on her left hip and replaced the other in the pocket on her right. When she was done, she looked back up at Warga, who was decked out like Rambo and grinning like an idiot.

"Locked and loaded, Doc. Let's go. The sooner we find that damned meteor, the sooner I get my hookers. And maybe a new light bulb," he added. And then laughed uproariously at Fallon's perplexed look.

Fallon sent Warga down ahead of her since she didn't want to deal with whatever the others might think about where they'd been, or worse, speculating about why they'd been there together.

Once he was in the elevator, Fallon stepped back into the room and went over to the bed. She ignored the cash Warga had left behind, instead looking inside the purse. As she expected, credit cards and a driver's license nestled in little slots in the leather lining. She pulled out the license.

The dead woman stared back at her from a blue square in the lower right-hand corner of a miniature

Grand Canyon. Not Jessica Conejo, but Carmen Gamez of Scottsdale, though Fallon suspected the woman's true address was probably quite a bit south of that.

She blinked to turn the camera and two-way radio back on.

"Book, you there?"

There were a few moments of silence, then Book came online.

"I'm here, Fallon. Sorry, I was trying to finish a mouthful of pizza."

At his mention of food, Fallon's stomach grumbled in complaint. She ignored it.

"I need you to find out who this woman is and what connection she has to Elliott Jameson." She held up the license so Book could get a clear view of it through her camera implant, deliberately looking toward the door and away from the dead woman.

"Your partner at the lab? Why?" She would have to answer carefully. She had turned her camera and radio off—or at least had signaled that she wanted them off—but Book would want to know what she was up to, not just why she wanted to track Elliott's cartel connection down.

The fact that someone could almost always keep track of her was simultaneously comforting and worrying. She didn't really like the idea of Big Brother Book seeing and hearing everything she did and said in real time. But knowing that she could check in with Book or someone else at almost any moment had made her feel safer, less like the psychos were out here on their own. Even though, for all intents and purposes, they were.

"Yes. Just find out, okay, Book? I've got to go."

She was starting to blink the command to terminate the connection—to keep him from asking more questions—when Book stopped her.

"Wait! Fallon!"

"What is it? I really need to rejoin the others." Preferably before Warga started regaling them with tales of her eagerly yielding to his sexual prowess.

"It's Briggs."

Fallon put two and two together—Book's serious tone and the specialist's circumstances when last she'd seen him, in quarantine with three other soldiers, waiting to see who'd been infected by Crazy 8s.

"Is he . . . one of them now?" She couldn't quite bring herself to say the word when she was talking about someone she knew. Someone she considered a friend—or at least friendly, which was rare enough itself these days.

"No. That's the problem."

"How could it be a problem?" Fallon asked before the answer dawned on her. "Oh, no."

"Oh, yes. The other soldiers became infected and started attacking him. He killed one before anyone could get in there and take out the other two. But he knows, Fallon. Knows he's immune, and knows what it means." Book paused for a minute, Fallon thought perhaps to swallow down his empathetic grief. She found herself hoping the young analyst was never exposed to the virus because he'd succumb in a matter of minutes. "He's having trouble processing it all, and he wants to talk to you."

"I'm a neuroscientist, not a psychiatrist," she protested.

"A neuroscientist who's immune to the virus for the same reason he is. But you knew sooner and had more time to come to terms with it." Another pause. "Please, Fallon. He needs you."

She relented, mostly because Book was one of the only other people on that side of the microphone that she considered a friend.

"Okay, I will, but not now. I'll call you back when I have time."

"I'll be waiting," he replied. "We both will."

# CHAPTER 29

*37 hours*

**B**ack in the lobby, Lilith told Fallon that Light and Sansome had taken off. She could ask Book to find them, but she had just given him a task and didn't want to interrupt him with another. Besides, if he was busy trying to find out who the cartel woman was, maybe he wouldn't bug her about talking to Briggs. Or notice that she had misplaced two members of her team.

Lilith, Pybus, and Antonetti sat together at the end of one of the long tables in the makeshift cafeteria. Coffee sounded good, as did food, but they'd have to wait until she found the runaways. "Did either of them say where they were going?" she asked.

Pybus spoke up. "Hank said he was going to check the perimeter. A little while after that, Joe got up and said he was going to bring Hank back. We tried to persuade him to stay put, but he wouldn't."

"Sansome isn't a guy you want to argue with," Antonetti added.

"Maybe not," Fallon admitted. "But we need him. We need—"

She broke off her sentence when a ratcheting sound that could only be automatic-weapons fire echoed down the quiet urban canyon outside. "That's people," she said. "Infecteds don't use guns. Come on."

The others hurriedly gobbled up the remains of their food and headed for the valet station. On the way, Fallon thanked Quinn and Parker for their help and wished them luck. Parker tried to get them to stay, but she just shook her head. She couldn't, even if she wanted to. There were two of her people out there, and their mission still wasn't anywhere near complete.

But the truth was that Fallon was glad to leave the hotel behind. The encounter with Elliott's torturer, followed by Warga's would-be rape, had shaken her more than she wanted to admit. She didn't regret what he had done to the woman, or what she would have done to *him* if he hadn't backed off. But it was still two close calls; a lot to deal with for someone who spent most of her time in sterile labs full of emotionless machines.

The others had grabbed their weapons and followed her outside. They ran to the south side of the hotel, which is where the sound had seemed to emanate from. When they didn't see anything there, they went to the end of the block and saw Light walking their way. Behind him was a UPS truck with bodies strewn around it.

"What happened?" Fallon asked when she was close enough.

Light nodded at the carnage and started back toward the truck. Fallon joined him. "Infecteds found these people in the back. Sensed them, somehow. Smell maybe, I don't know. They broke in, and the people tried to get away. One of them did—last I saw him, he was still running. But they caught these other three. I blew them away, but I wasn't in time to save the people."

Fallon walked around the truck, eyeing the dead UPS driver on the sidewalk and the other two bodies behind the truck, along with the ravaged corpses of the Infecteds. She didn't entirely buy Light's version of events, but the humans didn't have bullet wounds and the Infecteds did, so she couldn't call him on it.

"We heard the shooting inside the hotel, so I'm sure we're not the only ones who did," she said. "Have you seen Joe?"

"He's not with you?"

"Apparently he went out shortly after you did, looking for you."

"Haven't seen him," Light said. "He's not easy to miss, either."

"Let's scour the neighborhood, then," she directed. "Everybody watch for Sansome."

"We don't have to do it on foot," Light said.

Fallon wasn't sure she'd heard him right. "What?"

He held up a set of keys. "I found the keys to the truck, in the driver's pocket. We have wheels again."

"Can you drive that thing?"

"When you've taken an ambulance through Friday afternoon rush-hour traffic on the interstate, you start to think you can handle anything on four wheels."

"That truck has six."

"Close enough."

"Okay, then," Fallon said. "Climb aboard, everyone. Hank, cruise the streets around here. If Joe's around, we'll find him." *With any luck, before Book realizes he's missing.*

They'd barely covered a block when two Infecteds came out of a parking garage, running toward the truck. Antonetti and Warga cut them down before they got close. The next group they saw was larger, seven of them, and Fallon joined in. If her survival was going to come down to being able to shoot somebody, she needed all the practice she could get.

When they found Sansome, emerging from a driveway about six blocks to the west, she almost fired at him. She was holding the Glock up, steadying her right hand with her left and getting a bead on him when she realized who it was. "Joe!" she shouted. "Hank, stop!"

Light braked, and the truck shuddered as if trying to shake them all off it. It was no wonder her packages so often came looking like they'd been run over, Fallon decided. She jumped down while the truck was still rocking back and forth. "We've been looking all over for you," she said. Then she noticed his huge hands, which looked like he had dipped them in a bucket of red paint. "What happened?"

"I found a couple of 'em," he said. "Infecteds. I killed 'em."

"With your bare hands?"

"Yeah?" He said it like a question, as if unsure what her reaction might be.

"Are you okay?"

"Sure." He saw where her gaze was directed, and raised his hands, fingers spread. "Oh, this isn't all from that," he said. "Want to see?"

If it was just more Infected bodies, Fallon was sure she wouldn't mind skipping it. But Lilith, Warga, and Antonetti had already climbed down from the truck, and Pybus stood at the doorway. "Sure," Antonetti said. "Got me curious, anyway."

"This way," Sansome said. He wore a goofy grin, reminding Fallon of how Jason looked when he had built something with Duplo blocks that he was especially proud of.

They all followed, even Light after he'd killed the engine and pocketed the dead driver's keys. The driveway led to a small parking area behind the building. The corpses were there. One looked badly beaten. The other one was worse, nearly decapitated, except all Sansome had to work with were his hands, so it was a ragged, bloody mess.

But that wasn't what he wanted them to see. Like some mutated Vanna White, he stood beside the parking lot's back wall, right arm extended, open hand pointing to words written there in what Fallon wished was paint: THE SYKOS ARE HERE. The blood was still fresh, shiny and bright.

"What's that mean?" Fallon asked, confused. "You mean 'sickos?'"

"Psychos," Sansome corrected. "Us. Seven psychos."

Everyone laughed at that, but Lilith found it hysterical, almost doubling over in whoops of laughter. "That's fuckin' sick!" she said when she could breathe again. "I love it!"

"That means it's good, right?" Fallon asked softly.

Warga nodded. "To her generation, yeah."

"You really don't know how to spell 'psychos?'" Lilith asked.

"That's not right?" Sansome replied, surprised and maybe even a little hurt.

"Oh, it is now," the girl said. "Nothing else will ever be right again. The Seven Sykos."

"Like the *Seven Samurai*," Pybus offered. "Hopefully with a better ending."

"How does it end?" Antonetti asked. "They all die?"

"Not all," Pybus said. "Just most."

"Everybody dies," Light said. "It's just a matter of when and how. I don't know about the rest of you, but I'd rather die here, a free man—more or less—than rotting in a cell somewhere."

"Not me," Lilith said. "I'm never dying. Living's too much fun."

"That's not always a call you get to make," Warga pointed out.

"I know that. I've picked the time for enough other people. But I'm not dying. None of us are. The Seven Sykos are indestructible!"

She broke into another fit of laughter. Watching her, Fallon couldn't help smiling. Inside, she was wishing Lilith was right. They'd been lucky so far, and perhaps that luck would hold.

Counting on that would be stupid, though, and she was not a stupid person—her presence here in the zone notwithstanding. They would have to be wary as well as lucky. Even then, they might lose some people. They might lose the whole thing, and their lifeless, brain-eaten corpses would be obliterated by nuclear bombs.

But that was defeatist thinking, and she had to shake it loose and let it go. She looked again at Sansome's scrawled message.

THE SYKOS ARE HERE.

That they were. If the fates were willing and the ammunition held out, they would make it out of here, too.

**F**allon's detour had cost valuable time and had yet to bear fruit other than patching up Warga. Once they'd collected Sansome—and found a sink where he could wash some of the blood from his hands—they piled back into the UPS truck. Fallon trusted Light's knowledge of the city streets, so told him to head for Mesa. He took Jefferson past Chase Field, then 7th Street to Interstate 17, heading east. Behind them, the sun was lowering in the sky. Fallon saw the shadows lengthening and wondered if they should have stayed at the Hyatt overnight. It was nearly summer, though, so it would be light for a few hours, yet, and she wanted as many miles behind them as possible before they had to stop.

"Look at that," Antonetti said. Fallon sat on the pull-down passenger seat, and he was crouched in the space between her and Light.

"At what?" she asked.

"That, probably," Light said, pointing to the southeast. A massive fire raged there, probably a whole neighborhood in flames, or an industrial park. "Phoenix will never be the same."

"I don't see how it could be," Fallon agreed.

"Probably be like New Orleans after Katrina," Antonetti said. "Lots of government money for redevelopment, so grifters and con men will move in to skim off as much as they can."

"Isn't 'grifters and con men' redundant when you're talking about government?" Light asked.

"Hey," Fallon said. "Remember who sent us here. They're trying to fix this mess."

"I remember. That's why I'm expecting some colossal fuck-up along the way. The word SNAFU didn't originate in the private sector. Neither did FUBAR. Doesn't that tell you something?"

"My cousin Paolo was in the Marines," Antonetti said. "He said FUBAR all the time, but he never told me what it meant."

"'Fucked up beyond all repair,'" Light said. "And SNAFU is 'situation normal, all fucked up.'"

"He was a Marine, but he made you do all the killing for him?"

"He didn't *make* me." Antonetti was clearly hurt by the implication. "He *let* me. I wanted to. He'd killed plenty of people, in the Gulf, but I never got a chance to."

"It's not exactly something most people aspire to," Fallon said.

"We're not like most people, Doctor."

"No, Gino. No, you're certainly not."

By extension, then, neither was Fallon. And she realized she was actually perfectly fine with that.

# CHAPTER 30

*32 hours*

The freeway was jammed. It looked like the kind of rush hour Light had been talking about earlier, except it could more accurately have worn the "parking lot" tag that so many people used when talking about heavy traffic. These vehicles were abandoned. From her spot in the UPS truck, Fallon could see cars, trucks, SUVs, semis, a Greyhound bus, and a tour bus from Mexico. And that was just the nearest quarter mile or so. They drove with the passenger door open, having discovered that UPS drivers did it because the trucks weren't air-conditioned, and they sucked in the heat like rolling solar panels.

"Can we get through?" she asked.

"I think so," Light said. "Especially since we don't care if the fenders get a little dented."

"I just don't want to get stuck somewhere far from an exit. We'd be the proverbial sitting ducks. Only more like fighting-for-our-lives ducks."

"Breathe, Fallon," Light said. "I've got this."

He eased the truck into a narrow gap. Its sides squealed as they scraped against cars; the racket made Fallon's teeth ache. If she had any privacy, she could ask Book to send over a drone in order to see whether the freeway was open all the way to U.S. Route 60. But Light was right beside her, and being able to talk to Book was a secret she wanted to keep for the time being. She had no illusions about the danger of traveling with six murderous psychopaths, and her link to Book was an edge she wanted to preserve, just in case.

Light did an admirable job of picking out a path although sometimes it involved shoving vehicles out of the way with the truck's front end, which would never recover from the indignities heaped upon it.

Many of the vehicles were empty, but some still had drivers slumped over the wheels, their skulls opened. Fallon saw an entire family inside an SUV that sat with all its doors open. Dad, Mom, and three kids in back had all become victims of the Infecteds. Blood stained the interior, the doorway, and the pavement outside. She wondered if there was a law of diminishing returns at work. The more Infecteds there were, the more uninfected brains they needed. The Crazy 8s virus wanted to replicate itself, which was what made it so contagious, but after a certain point, if it kept replicating, it would eliminate its own food supply. The problem, of course, was that when that point came, it would mean everybody in the Valley—more than 4 million souls—would be either dead victim or hungry Infected.

Or a psychopath.

They had to get to that meteor, and soon. If they lost everybody, then preventing the nuclear option would be essentially meaningless. She had to believe there were still plenty of unaffected humans around, but hiding out, afraid to show themselves because they never knew who might be infected.

Given that urgency, they were moving too slowly for Fallon's liking, but they were moving, and that was the main thing. They crossed the Salt River and merged with Interstate 10, but when they reached the Route 60 interchange, the way forward was completely blocked.

"Can you stay on 10 to Baseline?" Fallon asked.

"That's my plan," Light said. His jaw was tight, his lips clamped together except when he was speaking. His knuckles were white. He pretended that negotiating the freeway graveyard was no big deal, but Fallon could tell that it was taking a toll. The sun was sinking ever lower, twilight now, and soon it would be full dark. She didn't want to be so exposed when that happened.

**T**he Baseline exit was the next one after the Route 60 interchange. Baseline was a major thoroughfare, running parallel to the 60 for miles and miles. It was clearer, and the truck could almost reach the posted speed limit. Fallon felt better as the miles slipped past, and they got ever closer to Mesa.

But night had fallen in the interim. They passed a few small groups of Infecteds, seemingly drawn by their headlights or the engine noise breaking the quiet. At Arizona State Route 87—also called Country Club Drive here—Light headed toward Route 60 again, to check its condition. Unfortunately, it was still too backed up to travel, so Light turned around on the on-ramp and headed back toward Country Club.

"Let's find someplace to stop for the night," Fallon suggested.

"We just passed a few motels," Light said.

"Those were too exposed," she said. "A motel's good, but something off the main roads."

Light shrugged and turned north on Country Club, away from the freeway and Baseline. At Hampton, Fallon saw a Motel 6, well away from the road. "There," she said, pointing. "Let's check that out."

The building was a long, two-story job, white with green doors, with strategically placed staircases at each end and each side of two wings jutting out from the main structure. Light pulled into the parking lot, past towering palm trees, and drove slowly toward the office. A few cars were pulled up close to rooms, and lights blazed in the lobby area, but nothing moved.

"We're going to see if we can get some rooms for the night," Fallon told those riding in back. "The place looks deserted, but be ready just in case."

Everybody piled out, guns at the ready. Fallon passed through glass doors into the lobby, followed closely by Sansome, then the rest. It looked empty at first glance, but when she went behind the counter, she found a pool of drying blood. Streaks emanated from it and through an open doorway, into what she assumed was the motel office.

She followed them and found two corpses on the floor, both female. Skulls split open, brainpans picked clean. She was beginning to get used to it. The carnage still got to her, the way their faces were distorted by the head wounds, but that was almost more on an aesthetic level than anything else—nothing was quite as ugly as someone whose face has been partly pushed down to make skull access easier.

"God, that reeks," Lilith said.

"What?" Pybus asked.

"Those dead skanks."

Fallon could smell them, but to her, it wasn't much different than the smell in the residential neighborhood they'd passed through. The smell of death. Unpleasant, but not overwhelming. She was surprised at the intensity of Lilith's reaction.

The girl had been that way earlier, too.

Psychopaths tended to have poor senses of smell, she remembered. Of the five senses, only smell was routed through the limbic system. It wasn't universal—almost nothing was, when you were talking about human beings, psycho or not—but it was common.

*What does that say about Lilith?* she wondered. *Maybe*

*nothing, but it's worth keeping an eye on her. Maybe she's not all that psychopathic, despite sharing the general brain structure.*

*And what might that mean about her immunity?*

One of the dead women wore a black cloth lanyard with various cards on it, including one bearing the motel's name. Fallon hoped it was a master key. Although it meant getting closer to the corpse than she wanted to, she knelt and worked the lanyard up over the woman's neck and head. One side got snagged in a shard of the shattered skull; Fallon had to work it free, which meant touching the skull itself.

It wasn't as bad as she'd expected. Just bone. The woman who had inhabited this body was long gone. Fallon felt pity, in an abstract way, but was otherwise unmoved. When she had it off, she held it up to the Sykos clogging the doorway. "Let's check this place out," she said. "They left a light on for us."

Some of the rooms were occupied by corpses, but they didn't find any Infecteds. After a quick look around, they settled on two adjoining ground-floor rooms with two double beds each, facing onto the parking lot behind the building. They left the door between them open and parked the UPS truck far enough from the front doors that it wouldn't signal their presence inside. The setup wasn't ideal, but it would have to do.

Fallon volunteered to take first watch. She was hungry and wired; sleep wouldn't come easy, anyway.

But she would have to sleep, at some point. She would be most vulnerable then. The others could slip away and leave her behind, or one or more of them could decide to kill her. It was bad to be as afraid of your own side as you were of the enemy, but it was the reality she faced.

Which meant she needed an ally.

She ran through her companions, one by one, and disqualified each almost immediately. Antonetti was too easy to manipulate. Light was too anxious to get away. Sansome was too dumb. Pybus and Lilith were too physically weak. And Warga was—just *no*.

Which meant she had to start over, to consider them more dispassionately. When she did, only one survived the cut: Joe Sansome.

He hadn't wanted to share a bed with anyone—probably he knew that if he did, that person would be rolling toward him all night long—so he was sleeping on the floor. Hoping he wouldn't startle upon being awakened, she crouched beside him and gently touched his shoulder.

His eyes snapped open.

"You're not asleep?" Fallon asked.

"No. I don't sleep good. I have nightmares a lot."

"Can you come outside for a few minutes? I'd like to ask you some questions."

"Sure, I guess." He pushed aside the light blanket that had been attempting to cover him and rose to his feet. Fallon opened the room door, held it for him, then closed it as quietly as she could.

"What do you wanna know?" he asked when they were outside. They strolled around the parking lot as they talked, Fallon always keeping her senses attuned for any sign of Infecteds.

"I just wanted to talk, Joe," she said. "It's been three years since I saw you."

"Saw inside my head," Sansome said. "With your machine."

She had to chuckle at his description. It was accurate, in its way, even if not phrased in very scientific terms. "Yes. That. How've you been? How are they treating you in prison?"

"Pretty good, I guess. Most of the guys leave me alone. You know, 'cause I'm big, I guess. It's lonely there, though."

"I'm not surprised. Sometimes it feels like it's lonely everywhere."

Surprise registered on his face, his eyes widening, his mouth dropping open more than usual. He rarely seemed to close it all the way; in her younger, more callous days, Fallon would have called him a mouth-breather. He had never finished eighth grade, and his IQ was in the double digits. Some people like that—especially psychopaths—compensated with a certain animal cunning, but not Sansome. She would have judged him, back in college or grad school, and dismissed him as beneath notice. Those days were, she hoped, well behind her.

"You get lonely, too?" he asked.

"Of course." Then, realizing it probably wasn't as

self-evident to him, she added, "Yes. All the time, in fact."

"But you're a big-time scientist. You have a family, right? And people you work with. Friends."

Not so many of those, she'd come to realize. The only person she had wanted to talk to before entering the zone—the only one she thought would really care—was Jason, and he wasn't much of a conversationalist. She had acquaintances, sure. And she occasionally socialized with employees at the lab, but there was a strain on those relationships from the start. Only Elliott was truly her equal there; everybody else worked for her as much as with her. "Not as many as you might think, Joe. I work a lot. That doesn't leave much time for anything else."

"You should take more vacations. You're the boss, right? Nobody can tell you no."

Fallon laughed again. "You'd think so, wouldn't you?"

"Yeah, you would," Sansome said.

"I guess you've had plenty of time to reflect on your murders, huh? To think about them?"

"I do all the time. That's why I have bad dreams."

"What do you think about them?"

"I wish I never did them. It was so stupid. I was just mad all the time, but . . ." He swallowed hard; fighting back tears, Fallon thought. " . . . but those girls didn't deserve that. They didn't do nothing to me. I was so stupid."

Fallon put a soothing hand on his upper arm. It was

like touching a cinder-block wall. "You were young and troubled. You didn't know any better. And yeah, it was stupid. But given who you were, given your genes and your upbringing, it's not a surprise."

"It's not?" he asked.

"I'm not saying you had to do it. It was wrong, and I think you know that now. And people always have the option of deciding not to do the wrong thing. But it's harder for some than for others. For you, it was just a little too hard, then. You wouldn't do it now, would you?"

"I don't really even like killing these sick people. The Infecteds."

"We'll be done with that soon, I hope."

"Me, too."

She gave his arm a gentle rub, then released it. "You should get some rest, Joe," she said. "I'm glad you're here with us."

"You are?"

"Of course," she said again. "You've always been one of my favorite Sykos."

She went back inside with him. He was beaming. She watched him settle into his spot on the floor, pull the blanket back over as much as it would cover, and she stayed there until his breathing was steady and slow. He would have her back, she thought. He wouldn't let any harm come to her if he had anything to say about it.

She did have an ally here, after all. One she could count on.

The best part was, she had been telling the truth. There had always been something likable about him, an innocence that she found refreshing in a serial killer. He wasn't constantly trying to play her. He was direct about his feelings, and he said what he meant.

She really was glad he was here.

Not being here at all would have been better still, but that didn't seem to be an option at this point.

# CHAPTER 31

*31 hours*

**A**fter Sansome closed his eyes, Fallon got up and stepped outside. The temperature was finally down in the low eighties, though it felt chilly to her in comparison to the day's earlier heat. At least that's what she attributed her sudden shiver to, and not to the eerie silence so close to a major highway.

But as she listened, straining in the darkness to hear something, anything normal—kids playing, couples arguing, horns honking, TVs blaring—she did begin to hear noises that represented a different sort of normal.

Cicadas chirping, birds singing and squabbling, wind chimes dancing in the slight breeze, the tinkling sound of a water feature somewhere close by that had kept running even after there was no one around to enjoy it. It was surprisingly peaceful, and Fallon found herself thinking that there might just be some advantages to Crazy 8s, after all.

Just then, a mosquito buzzed by her ear, and she slapped at it, her hand coming away bloody. It made her pause. What if they were wrong, and the vector wasn't the meteor, but something ubiquitous, like an insect, or pollen, or even the ever-present desert dust? She dwelled on that for a moment but eventually shook her head. No point in worrying about that now. Find the meteor, get it back to PIR, and pray for a vaccine. If that didn't work, they could look into other sources of the virus.

After they watched from the minimum safe distance as Phoenix got nuked out of existence.

But the mosquito reminded her that she needed to talk to Book, so she tried to raise him on the two-way, hoping the young analyst wasn't yet asleep.

"Hey, Book," she said softly. "You up?"

"I'm here," he replied quickly.

"Any luck with Carmen or Elliott?"

"Haven't had a chance to look into it yet; sorry. Robbins has me doing nonessential stuff like following your progress, monitoring hundreds of security cameras across the valley, and following the video feed from a dozen drones." If Fallon had been talking to him face-to-face, the sarcasm would have splashed her, it dripped so heavily off his words.

"Down boy," she said dryly. "I get the picture. But, please, if you have a spare moment—it really is important."

"Is that all you called about?"

Book's tone was faintly scolding, as if Fallon were a child in need of reprimand. She tried not to bristle, knowing what prompted it.

"No, it's not," she answered calmly. "I called to see if I could talk to Timothy. Everyone else is asleep, it's quiet here, seemed like a good time. And I may not get another, so . . ."

"Hold on. I'll see if I can get him up here."

While she waited for Briggs, Fallon found an overturned patio chair and righted it, easing herself into it with a sigh. It seemed like it had been forever since she'd relaxed. Which was probably because it *had* been forever—even before Crazy 8s turned her lab and her life upside down, she was prone to stress headaches, and her shoulders were one giant knot of tension. One of the few luxuries she allowed herself was a monthly visit to Massage Envy, but even those trips had come further and further apart as they got the prototype in working order.

And then, of course, Elliott had stolen it, and Fallon hadn't relaxed since.

She wasn't feeling so great, either. She hoped it wasn't a summer cold—those were the worst. Touching a hand to her forehead, it felt hot, as did her cheeks. A fever, or maybe a hot flash? She was a little young for menopause, but common wisdom said it happened for daughters at the same age as it had happened for their mothers. Not that that information was particularly useful, since that wasn't the sort of thing she and her mother had ever discussed, or were ever likely to. If Fallon came off as cold, her mother was the iceberg that sank the *Titanic*.

Then another thought struck her, and Fallon's chill returned.

What if it wasn't anything so mundane? She'd gotten scratched on the cheek by an Infected earlier, so what if they were all wrong, and she wasn't really immune? Would she get redder and redder, eventually turning on her companions and trying to eat their brains?

No. She'd put a bullet in her own head before that happened.

Which, she supposed, was her ultimate assessment of the likelihood of their mission succeeding or of a cure being found even if they did. But what else could any of them do? They had to try.

Fallon tried to remember that quote by Byron. What was it, again? Oh, yeah: "They never fail who die in a great cause." Funny how it was only people who weren't in any danger of dying who thought that.

Well, either way—by her own hand or that of an Infected—she'd keep going as long as she could, and when she couldn't, she'd take as many of them as possible with her.

But even that resolution wasn't enough to keep her from touching her cheek, then looking down at her gun, wondering.

**B**ook followed Briggs into his ersatz control room. The specialist stopped inside the doorway, looked at all the monitors and computer equipment, and let out a low whistle.

"This is some setup!"

"Yup. Spared no expense." Book's lips twisted as he moved up next to Briggs. "Well, you know, in Army terms."

Briggs laughed, a short, unpleasant sound. "I'm familiar," he said, then pointed at one of the monitors. "That Fallon?"

He was indicating Fallon's monitor, which showed a view of the Mesa night sky, full of stars that could actually be seen now that there were fewer people turning on fewer lights.

"That's her. She's got first watch."

"Can I talk to her?"

"Sure," Book said. He gestured to his seat. "Go ahead and sit there. You can talk into the microphone and she'll hear you, and her voice will come through the speakers so you can hear her."

"Yeah, I understand the general concept, thanks," Briggs said as he brushed past Book and took his seat. Book was taken aback by the specialist's attitude. He'd never seen Briggs in such a foul mood. He supposed he couldn't blame the soldier, though—if he'd had to kill brothers-in-arms who'd turned into brothers-wanting-brains, all the while knowing the fact that he hadn't developed a hunger for grey matter meant there was something seriously wrong with him . . . well, Book imagined he'd be kind of an asshole at first, too. It was a lot of information to process, very little of it good.

"Okay, then," he said, walking up behind Briggs and leaning past him to hit a couple of keys on the keyboard. He didn't miss how the specialist stiffened, one hand going instinctively to the holster on his hip. He straightened quickly. "You're good to go."

"Are you there, Dr. O'Meara?" Briggs asked into the microphone, his tone quite a bit more respectful now than it had been a moment ago.

"I am, Timothy. Book told me what happened. I'm so sorry for your loss."

Normally, when Book spoke to Fallon, he was wearing a headset so no one else could hear her, but he needed to be able to hear—and record—what was said between her and Briggs. He recorded all his own conversations with her, and everything he heard and saw through her implant, under direct orders from Billings. It was all a matter of national security, so it all had to be studied, dissected, and analyzed by a contingent of other nerds like himself who were safe in their various non-virus-threatened cubicles around the country and to whom the situation in Phoenix was all academic.

"Thank you."

"Of course. Book said you had some questions for me?"

"Yes, ma'am. About . . . about being a psychopath." Briggs's voice broke on the last syllable. Book couldn't see his face, but he thought the other man might be crying. And once again, Book couldn't blame him. Who knew how he'd respond in a similar situation?

Well, he knew. He'd either be dead or Infected, because he wouldn't have been able to fight off three virus-crazed soldiers, especially friends. He didn't have the stomach for it, or the skill, and he thought maybe he might be blubbering the entire time. Briggs's stoicism was a testament to his Army training. And probably to residual shock.

"Timothy, what you've been through—what all soldiers who see combat go through, particularly those who live it, day in and day out for months—is sometimes enough to rewire the circuits in your brain, especially when you're young. Unlike most of our bodies, our brains aren't really fully developed until we're well into our twenties—which goes a long way toward explaining why teenagers make such stupid decisions. And even when we're older, the things we experience can create new neural pathways and destroy others. Alzheimer's is a good example. Genetics, lifestyle, experiences—all those things contribute to our brain structure over the course of our entire lives. Sometimes it means you start to forget who you are when you get older. And sometimes it means you become immune to a space-borne virus that's ravaging the country's sixth largest city. Me, I'd rather have the immunity."

"But being immune means you're a psychopath. A cold-blooded killer. Or that you'll become one, anyway." Timothy's voice was so full of distress and despair, it was all Book could do to keep from laying a comforting hand on the other man's shoulder. But he was also so on edge that he'd probably shoot Book before he realized who was touching him.

"No! No, it doesn't, Timothy. Haven't you been listening? It takes more than structural changes or rewiring to make someone a psychopath. *I* have that brain structure, but I've never killed anyone." There was an uncomfortable pause. "Well, not a human, anyway. And not in cold blood."

"But that's *you*, Dr. O'Meara. You know how to fix yourself. I don't. There's nothing to stop me from becoming just like that human waste you're traveling with, from preying on the very people I joined the Army to protect."

"Timothy, part of my job is researching a cure, and—"

"There's no cure for evil, Doctor."

Book wondered why Fallon hadn't mentioned the prototype she'd been working on. If it worked, she could use it on Briggs when she got back with the meteor, and he'd be back to his old, cheerful self. But then he didn't have time to wonder about anything because he saw Briggs's arm moving toward his hip. Heard the specialist tell Fallon goodbye and good luck. Started toward him, trying to stop him, but too late.

He was two steps away when a loud *boom* echoed through the room, and the back of Briggs's head exploded outward, covering Book in hot red goop, pelting him with pieces of skull and chunks of brain. He'd had his mouth open, screaming "No!" Now he closed it, but not before blood splattered his tongue and he breathed a fine pink mist into his lungs.

"Briggs? Book? What the hell *was* that? Are you guys okay?" Fallon's voice seemed distant, distorted, and Book didn't know if it was because the report had left him momentarily deaf or because he was in shock, or both.

"He . . . he . . . oh my God, Fallon, he *killed* himself. Right here in my chair. Stuck the barrel of his gun in his mouth and pulled the trigger. I'm covered in his blood. God, I don't know what to do."

"Jesus. It's all right Book—it's not your fault. You couldn't have known, and you couldn't have stopped him." She paused, then spoke again so softly he wasn't sure he was actually hearing her or if he was just imagining he could. "I could have, maybe, if I'd told him."

Then the door opened and people were pointing guns at him and yelling at him to lie on the floor. And as he complied, the tears he'd only thought he might shed began coursing down his cheeks, disappearing one by one into the bright red pool of Briggs's blood.

**F**allon was glad she was already sitting down. She couldn't believe what she's just heard.

*He killed himself . . . stuck the barrel of his gun in his mouth and pulled the trigger. . .*

Jesus. Poor Briggs.

*I don't know what to do.*

Poor Book.

And it was probably all her fault. If she'd told Briggs about the prototype, how close they were to being able to "cure" psychopathy—or at least some of the brain issues that helped cause it—maybe that knowledge would have given him the hope he needed to keep from eating his gun.

Or maybe not. A lot of soldiers suffered from depression and other mental illnesses, usually brought on or exacerbated by the things they saw and had to do in service to their country. Briggs had no doubt been depressed after having had to kill his friends and discovering he had the potential to turn into something he loathed. And the main hallmark of depression wasn't necessarily overt sadness or apathy but rather that the sufferer's brain lied to them, told them things that in a different state of mind they would realize were untrue.

*You're fat, ugly, friendless, a failure. You're never going to amount to anything. You're worthless—a waste of space and oxygen.*

*Your son doesn't need you.*

Fallon shook the thought away, but the tears and guilt weren't so easily dismissed.

*I'm so sorry,* she thought, though she wasn't entirely sure whom she was apologizing to anymore.

A distant, bloodcurdling scream split the night open like a chestburster, bringing Fallon out of her reverie.

*One more life lost to this damned virus,* she thought. She was determined to make sure there weren't any more on her watch.

Speaking of which, it was Sansome's turn to stare out into the darkness and contemplate his mortality. She gave the night sky one last, searching look, then turned and went inside to get him.

## CHAPTER 32

*24 hours*

**A**fter Antonetti had come out, grumbling, to relieve him and start the fourth and final night shift, Light headed toward the front office.

"Where're you going?" the smaller man said suspiciously. "Not to go shoot up more Infecteds, I hope."

"Not unless I have to," Light replied, laughing at Antonetti's fear. It was an emotion he wasn't all that familiar with, and it amused him to see its expression in others. Especially when they were craven to begin with. "I'm actually headed for the kitchen, to see if I can rustle up some breakfast for us. I don't know about you, but some of us haven't eaten in close to twenty-four hours. Even your scrawny ass is starting to look good, especially with enough ketchup."

Antonetti scowled.

"Fine. Go. But if Fallon asks where you went, I'm not covering for you."

"Never for a moment imagined you would."

Light walked back to the lobby, its lights still blazing. He didn't really like the idea of being so exposed, but there didn't appear to be another way in to where the kitchen was except through those big glass doors.

He peered into the night, made darker and more ominous in contrast to the brightly lit lobby. Nothing moved.

So why was the hair on the back of his neck standing up, then?

A sudden stiff breeze that tasted of rain ruffled his bangs. That's what it must be—a biological response to air-pressure changes. Not anything as blatantly human as simple nerves.

With a shrug, he purposefully turned his back on the darkness and went into the lobby. Before, they'd only ventured far enough for Fallon to find the keys, but this time, Light went the other way, into the breakfast nook, which was lit only by the glow from the fluorescent lobby lights. A dozen square wooden tables, each surrounded by four chairs, had been placed in a precise three-by-four grid pattern that told Light either the hotel manager or one of the janitorial staff likely suffered from OCD.

Well, *had* suffered. It was doubtful anyone with an uncontrollable need for neatness would survive long in this new, chaotic world.

One wall was all windows; on the opposite side, a counter held a toaster, waffle iron, pastry case, a juice dispenser that offered orange, apple, and cranberry, and a built-in trough where warm things could be kept warm and cold things cold. And next to that, a metal swinging door—the exact thing Light had been looking for.

He listened at the door for a few moments, trying to ascertain if there might be some Infecteds inside looking for a midnight snack, but once again, he heard nothing. He pushed through the door into a smallish kitchen with an industrial-sized grill, a large fridge/freezer combination, a double sink and racks for drying dishes, and a walk-in pantry.

Light saw no one, so he walked cautiously into the room, making his way around the grill. No Infecteds and no bodies, but there was blood. A trail of it led to the pantry, but bloody footprints told him he wasn't the first to follow it.

He drew his gun, grabbed the door handle, and pulled.

A body lay on the floor inside, its head bashed in—a nearby dented and bloody can of corn the likely weapon—its brain, predictably missing. Face down and wearing a baggy white chef's uniform, the body could belong to a woman or a man, with no way to tell but by turning it over. Light was going to take a pass on that, but he did step over one sprawled leg to grab a six-pack of cartons holding dehydrated hash browns. As he was surveying the other nonperishable items, wondering what else he could use to make breakfast, he heard a noise behind him. He whirled, gun up, finger on the trigger.

There was no one there.

Light frowned.

He heard the noise again, this time at his feet. Looking down, he saw a rather fat rat chewing on the chef's calf. Chuckling to himself in relief, he raised his foot and brought it down on the rodent's back as hard as he could. The rat's spine broke with an audible *snap*, and it shuddered once, then lay still.

"Sorry, little guy," he said, though he really wasn't. While he held no belief in an afterlife, and the dead held very little interest for him except when he was helping people to achieve that state, he nevertheless felt like the rat's flagrant feasting on someone who'd been human was a desecration. And even if he hadn't, he was one of those psychopaths for whom the largely discredited "homicidal triad" was actually true. He had wet his bed well into his grade-school years, earning himself a beating by his father every time. He'd liked to set fires, though he'd never progressed to arson, and he'd eventually outgrown it, as he had the nocturnal enuresis. But he still derived pleasure from snuffing out the lives of small animals whenever the opportunity presented itself.

Which he supposed gave the lie to his putting patients out of their misery for their benefit as opposed to his own. But that was a secret that didn't need sharing with his fellow Sykos, who he was sure all had secrets of their own. Especially Fallon. In fact, he suspected she had more than the rest of them combined, and he intended to find out what a few of them were before this was all over. But for now, breakfast.

He added some hot water to the hash browns to soften them up, then went searching for other morning fare, like bacon and eggs, or maybe cinnamon rolls. Just the thought of them made his mouth water.

There were eggs in the fridge, and a quick float test proved most of them edible. The fruit was a wash, and he was hesitant about the milk even though it was only a few days past its expiration date. He did find some precooked bacon that just needed heating in a microwave, which he spied over on a counter he'd missed in his initial perusal.

After setting the grill to warm for the eggs and hash browns, and starting some coffee brewing, Light began ferrying rashers of bacon to and from the microwave. The juggling act of preparing large quantities of foods with three different cooking times and two different methods reminded Light a little of the adrenaline rush he got from being the first on scene to help a victim he knew was not going to make it, and he found himself smiling and humming "Vegetables" by The Beach Boys.

When everything was done, he dished the food up on plates and brought them out to the breakfast nook. He put out a squirt bottle of ketchup, salt, pepper, cream, and sugar on each of the two tables. Then he got silverware and napkins out, and set them around the tables in the order one of his strict stepmothers had virtually engraved in his skin with her belt.

"The knife protects the spoon from the fork," he murmured, no longer humming, or smiling.

Finally, he poured seven cups of coffee, set them on saucers, and placed them above the plates of food just so, then went to go get the others.

There was some grumbling and cursing at first; the sun wasn't even above the horizon yet, though the outside temperature was already climbing. But it hadn't taken much convincing to get the rest of them to come to the breakfast nook once they smelled the tantalizing aromas drifting from the lobby. And if those smells came with an undertone of decomp, no one was rude enough to point it out.

The Sykos set to and devoured their meal in record time. Even so, Light—who was sitting with Fallon and Pybus at the "big kids' table"—finished first. He watched the others eat for a few moments, then his eyes wandered around the room, coming to rest on the wall of windows. He looked down on the leftover ketchup on his plate and an idea struck him. As the others finished up, he took the squirt bottle, walked over to the window, and began writing.

The others had been talking quietly among themselves as they ate, sharing idle chitchat, but they fell silent as Light worked. When one bottle of ketchup ran out, Pybus stood and brought him another, then another. And then Light was finished and he stepped back to reveal his handiwork.

.EREH ERA SOKYS

"It's not blood, but you can't tell that from a distance."

"What is that, Russian?" Sansome asked.

Lilith let out a piercing laugh. Light couldn't blame her, but he held his amusement closer to his chest, allowing himself a sly smile.

"Seriously?" she said. "You can't read that?"

"If it was in English, I—"

"It *is* English."

"See?" Antonetti said. "I said he was a Dumbo!"

Fallon slammed a butter knife down on the tabletop, hard. "That's enough! God, you people are all *children*. *Worse* than! None of you are exactly rocket scientists, and let's not even start on your moral and ethical standards."

"I was just having some fun," Antonetti said, pouting.

"I didn't think it was so fun," Sansome countered.

"We're all in this together," Fallon said. "Wouldn't it be nice if we could all get along?"

Light was about to reply when Warga's voice came from the lobby. "That might be nice, but this ain't."

Light and the others looked out to see a group of Infecteds coming out from behind the hotel. They were going room to room, checking the hotel for squatters who'd moved in since the last round of "Where's Waldo's Brain?" Their usual animalistic grunts and growls were quiet, and almost sounded like the murmur of conversation from here.

"They're going to be between us and the truck soon," Warga said.

"Should we try for it?" Antonetti asked.

"We'll never make it," Fallon replied.

"Then what?" Light asked.

"What about over there?" Lilith asked, gesturing across the street to the south. They all looked. She was pointing at a castle, guarded by a pirate ship and a lance-toting dragon. "It's so cool; I dreamt about it all night.

"What the hell is *that*?"

"Golfland," Light said, just as Fallon said, "Sunsplash."

Fallon laughed. "In the dark, I guess didn't realize where we were," she continued with a small smile. "It's a water park with a miniature golf course and games and food inside. Mark and I came here before I had Jason."

"You actually went somewhere and had fun?" Light asked, surprised.

Fallon's smile disappeared.

"I didn't say that."

"While you're strollin' down Memory Lane, Doc, the Infecteds are strollin' closer and closer to us."

Warga was right.

"I say we make a break for it," Light said.

Fallon looked unsure for a moment. "Why not just

head the other way? They're coming from the east—we go west. And north."

"I don't think that's going to work, Dr. O'Meara."

While the others had gathered in the lobby, Pybus had stayed behind, finishing his meal in a slow, stately manner rather than slurping it up hungrily as the rest of them had. He was standing now, pointing out the windows Light had defaced. Peering through the big, backward red letters, Light could just make out a second crowd of Infecteds across Country Club Drive. Coming this way and not using the crosswalk.

"West is no longer an option, Doctor," Pybus said. "Or north."

Fallon looked resigned, then nodded.

"Golfland it is, then. There's fencing all around it, thick wrought iron with pointed tips in some places. I don't *think* they know how to climb, but that's just a guess."

"They're still behind the truck, but not for much longer," Warga said. "If we're gonna go, we need to go *now*."

"Count of three?" Fallon asked.

"Fuck that shit," Light said as he pushed the lobby doors open and started running quietly across the parking lot. The others followed suit, Pybus and Sansome bringing up the rear.

They made it to the pirate ship without being seen, though the western group of Infecteds had now crossed the street, and the eastern group was swarming around the UPS truck.

Light started to run for the fence line, but Fallon stopped him.

"Wait until the two groups meet up. There'll be some confusion then, and they'll be less likely to notice us."

"And that much closer if they do."

"You want to vote on it?"

Light surveyed the others quickly. Sansome had moved protectively toward Fallon when she asked the question, and Pybus was staring him down. They'd vote with her. Warga would probably vote with him, and Antonetti, but Lilith was a wild card. Even if she agreed with him, she was just as likely to vote with Fallon as she was with Light, for the sheer pleasure of spiting him. If the Greek Goddess of Discord had a human avatar, it would be Lily June Ogden.

"Not this time," he said.

Fallon nodded, and they waited until the two groups came together and started to merge.

"Now!"

They ran for it and reached the gate . . . only to find it chained shut. Lilith scrambled over while Fallon turned to Sansome.

"You need to get it open, Joe, and fast."

Sansome moved forward without replying, grabbing the gate's frame with one hand and the fence post it was chained to with the other. With a mighty heave that popped out the veins in his neck and created an instant sheen of sweat on his broad forehead, he pulled the gate away from the post, straining the chain so much the links started to deform.

"Go . . . now!" he said through clenched teeth, and the others needed no further encouragement. Antonetti went first, then Fallon, then Light. Pybus got stuck partway through, and it took the three of them to yank him inside, popping a link on the chain as they did. The additional stress had forced the gate open a little wider, so Sansome was just able to squeeze through.

Fallon told the others to scatter, but she stayed by Sansome.

"Get it closed again," she said to him. "Quickly!"

She said something else, but Light was already heading into the course's interior and didn't hear what it was. He watched from a distance as Sansome bent the gate back into some semblance of its former shape, then turned and ran with Fallon just as the first Infecteds started streaming into the parking lot.

Against all odds, they'd made it in without being seen. Light hoped that was a harbinger of things to come.

Somehow, he doubted it.

## CHAPTER 33

*22 hours*

The Sunsplash side of the park smelled like a cocktail of chlorine and mildew, with a urine chaser. It looked like it had been vacated in a hurry. Water still ran on some of the rides Fallon could see, and no one had bothered to clean up the messes that must have been made on its last day in operation. Fallon remembered it as being clean and bright, and guessed that it took a lot of regular maintenance to keep it looking fresh when it was open, what with children peeing where they shouldn't, dropping ice cream, and spilling soda, combined with the natural effects of water that didn't always stay where it was put.

Mosquitoes were everywhere, and she saw ants swarming something that might have been half of a hot dog. She considered stepping on them for a brief moment before deciding against it.

They had entered the park near the Buccaneer Bend Activity Pool, according to the signs. Big waterslides sloped from a platform surrounded by fake rocks and into the pool. After crossing a man-made river, which Fallon had a vague memory of floating down in faux inner tubes, they circled around the end of the activity pool, wanting to get out of sight of the fences.

As they rounded the end of the waterslide, Lilith let out a whoop. "Look at that waterslide!" she cried. "That looks fuckin' amazing!"

Fallon had to agree. On their left, there were actually four separate tunnel slides, two that dropped from seven stories up, one from five stories, and another from four. To the right was another set of slides, with names like the Hurricane, the Tornado, and the Cyclone. She and Mark had gone down a couple of them, at her insistence—he wasn't a fan of fast-moving, twisty-turny rides of any kind, so whenever she wanted to ride on a roller coaster, or rides like the Kamikaze or the Reverse Bungee, she had to manipulate him into joining her. Or shame him. She didn't mind doing either one, as long as she got what she wanted.

*Some people would feel bad about that. Guilty,* she thought, unable to suppress a small smile.

"That blue and yellow one's pretty intense," Fallon said. "It's 'sick.'"

"I want to slide," Lilith said. "How often do you get to play in a place like this when you don't have to pay out the ass for everything?" Lilith spun around to face Fallon. "Can we? Please? Just for a little while?"

Fallon was torn. It would eat up valuable time, and they were down to almost twenty-four hours. But if they were trapped in here anyway, until the Infecteds outside moved on, what was the harm? She remembered how hard she had worked to get Mark to agree and how much fun it had been once he had. The day was getting hot, too. And maybe playing together would be a team-building activity.

But then she imagined Lilith, and maybe some of the others, whooping and shouting as they careened down the slides. Some of them were seven stories tall, high enough to be seen from outside the park. "We're trying not to attract attention," she said.

The girl gave her an exaggerated frown. "Come on, Fallon," she said. "It's not like we aren't stuck here for a while, anyway."

"I get that," Fallon said. "But when we have a chance to go, we need to be ready to take it. If you're up on top of some slide—"

"—then I'll be at the bottom in twenty seconds."

"I'm sorry, Lilith," Fallon said, shaking her head. "When we get the meteor and get back, I'll see to it that you get a water park trip out of it. But not here, not now."

Lilith held her gaze for long moments. Fallon tensed, half expecting the girl to attack. Maybe she was every bit the psychopath her scans suggested because her look was simultaneously glacial and fierce, as if she could tear Fallon apart piece by piece without the slightest hesitation or remorse. Finally, Lilith broke the stare-down, muttering, "Tight-assed bitch."

Hot fury rushed through Fallon—she was tempted to grab Lilith and remind the girl who was in charge here—but she decided a little rebellion from psychopaths was probably to be expected. So far, they'd been surprisingly cooperative. Each for his or her own reason, no doubt; certainly not for the good of the city, or each other.

But that was okay. She'd expected as much and had deliberately kept the potential rewards vague, in part because she wasn't sure what she was allowed to promise but also because that way, each of them could imagine the payoff being whatever they wanted most.

"I'm going to see what the south side of the park looks like," she said. "Maybe we can get out that way."

"What good would that do? We still couldn't get to the truck," Antonetti reminded her.

"We'll find wheels of some kind," Fallon countered. "Joe's been wanting to hotwire something since we got here." She eyeballed her team—her Sykos—all seemingly distracted by their surroundings, at least for the moment. "I'll be back in a couple of minutes, Gino," she said. "Keep an eye on everybody for me, okay?"

"You got it," Antonetti said. He almost sounded proud that she had singled him out. He had been the junior partner, someone to whom the affirmation of others was important. More commonly, psychopaths were narcissists, but as with everything else, one size didn't fit all.

She started walking toward the south, trying to find a way through or around the attractions stacked up in that direction. She was barely out of sight when she heard Antonetti's voice.

"Dr. O'Meara said not to do that!"

"She's not here, is she?"

"You're supposed to go down the slides in those tube things," Pybus said.

"Fuck that. I like riding bareback!"

Fallon backtracked until she could see Lilith rapidly ascending the long staircase in undershirt and panties. She caught her instinctive shout before she released it in the girl's direction, remembering her own injunction to stay quiet and not attract the Infecteds' attention. "Dammit!" she said, but almost under her breath.

"Nobody said herding psychos would be a picnic, did they?"

She turned to find Warga standing just behind her shoulder, arms folded over his chest, watching Lilith with a kind of spaced-out but beatific grin.

"No, I pretty much knew it wouldn't be," she said.

He touched his bandaged shoulder. "I can't really blame her. I was just wishing I could do that . . . slide. Looks like a good time."

"I'm not sure it would be safe." Her tone made it clear that she wasn't just talking about the ride.

Watching Lilith climb, Fallon almost forgot, for a moment, why they were here. This was almost like real life, normal life, which had been eradicated so suddenly from the Valley.

Then again, had she ever known "normal life" at all? Did anybody? Or was everyone's life just as fucked up as hers, each in its own way?

"Definitely looks like fun," Warga said.

Again, Fallon wasn't sure if he meant the slide or the half-dressed, youthful Lilith.

"Don't worry, Doc," he said, as if reading her thoughts. "I won't hit that. Young meat's not my style."

" 'Meat'?"

"I just call it like I see it."

She supposed that was true. If Randy Wayne Warga had thought of his victims as human beings, rather than dehumanizing them in his mind to the point that they were nothing but meat, his for the taking, he wouldn't have been able to rape and murder the way he did, without apparent remorse.

She remembered reading through his case files. Even when he had attacked people he'd known, which his first few victims were, he had a hard time remembering their names. He could recite details about their bodies and what he'd done to them, but letting them have identities of their own didn't fit with his particular pathology. He was categorized as an "anger-excitation rapist," which meant he got his sexual thrills not from the rape itself, but from the anguish of his victims as he raped and tortured them.

After his arrest, he had readily confessed to his crimes, seemingly unable to grasp that to other people, human beings had value. He'd been subjected to the usual battery of tests, including the controversial Abel Assessment for Sexual Interest, the standard polygraph, and the penile plethysmograph. The latter was a device attached directly to the penis, so levels of arousal at being shown different photographs could be measured. Warga hadn't responded to the young ones, but when viewing middle-aged women, he was off the charts.

Lilith's voice cut through her thoughts. "Fallon!" the girl cried. Fallon looked up, into the sun. Lilith was at the top of the platform, pointing toward the southwest. "Infected!"

Fallon couldn't see anything from where she was. She ran down the path to where she had a view of the Golfland miniature golf course. Sure enough, there was a lone Infected, ambling through the Old West course. She drew her Glock, raised it, steadied her hand.

But before she fired, she saw another one, coming around the windmill in the park's northwest corner.

Then another.

They had breached the fence, somehow. Or been inside all the time. Either way, they didn't seem to know where the Sykos were yet. She clambered up the end of a red-and-white tube slide, high enough to get a better view looking toward the golf course.

There were more. A lot more. They were coming toward the park from the buildings across the street, including the hotel. And they were approaching the park from every direction. Many were pressed up against the fence, trying to squeeze through. Some were climbing although they weren't very good at it. Still others had found the gap in the northwest corner and were squeezing through that.

If in fact they didn't know where the Sykos were, she sure didn't want to tip them off. Instead of firing, she lowered the pistol and raced back to the others. Lilith was already down the slide and headed toward the others—probably with friction burns, since she had refused to slide down on an inner tube.

They gathered around Fallon when she got back. "Infecteds," Fallon said. "Tons of them." She pointed toward the west. "They have a way in, over there somewhere, and more are coming over the fence between us and the motel. We should have checked the perimeter before we started playing." She shot Lilith a steely look and held it until she knew the girl had seen it. There wasn't anything she could do to punish the Sykos; they had been removed from punishment and given a mission, and she had to try to hold them together until it was done. Disapproval was, at this point, her strongest weapon. And these were people who spent their lives engaging in acts that others disapproved of, so you could guess where that got her.

"What do we do?" Antonetti asked. "Shoot our way through?"

"They're between us and the truck," Fallon said. "We could try that, but there are an awful lot of them, and we're not exactly ammo-rich here. I'd rather save that until we absolutely need it if we can."

"What, then?" Lilith asked. "We can't just wait here."

"No. We can't wait here, and there's nowhere safe to run. The fence around us isn't keeping them out, but it might make it hard to get away."

"Hide in the slides?" Sansome offered.

"I'm thinking!" Fallon snapped. "I'm sorry, just let me—"

Pybus cleared his throat, loudly enough to signal that it wasn't an accident. Everybody looked at him. "I might," he said, "have a viable solution. We're in a water park, so . . ."

"So what?" Fallon asked impatiently.

"So let's use what we have in most abundance." They all looked at him, perplexed. He sighed.

"Water."

**CHAPTER 34**

*22 hours*

**S**ansome, who had worked as a carny on a few occasions—or, as he said, been "with the show"—took the lead and managed to find steps leading down into the park's control center. Warga, Antonetti, Sansome, and Fallon took some tools, mostly at Sansome's suggestion, wrenches of various sizes, and went back up into the day. Light, Lilith, and Pybus stayed underground.

Fortunately, the Master Blaster water coaster was near the park's northeast corner and in the back, where there were fewer Infecteds to worry about. Then again, there were still the ones ringing the rest of the park—and coming inside—so Fallon pretty much worried constantly anyway.

Once Light's group shut off the water, Fallon's

went to work. The water coaster didn't rely only on gravity to propel riders from top to bottom. Instead, it contained multiple high-pressure water jets, pushing them over a course that included uphills as well as downs. All the coaster's high-pressure jets were fed by the same pair of master pipes, reaching up from underground, with branches to the actual jets along the way. The water pressure had to be such that the highest jets had as much force as the lower ones, which were gauged down to limit their outflow.

Fallon and Antonetti went to work on one of the master pipes while Sansome and Warga tackled the other. Sansome would put in the most effort, Fallon was sure; there were times she wondered whether Warga had intentionally goaded Antonetti into shooting him, just so he could get out of chores. They used their wrenches to remove the bolts at the lowest pipe joints, which Sansome said were flanged connections. There seemed to be no sort of manual labor he hadn't done at some point, and she was glad that included pipefitting.

The bolts were tight, some rusted in place. Fallon tugged on the wrench until her palms ached. A couple of times, it slipped out of place, and she rammed her own knee, drawing blood. She was already putting sweat into it, and after the second such incident, she wasn't far from tears, so she figured spilling blood was only natural. She touched her cheek, where her scratch from yesterday was scabbing over nicely. *So far we've been lucky*, she thought. *We're all still here. Our worst injury was caused by one of our own. I hope it can hold . . . but I have my doubts.*

As if reading her mind, Book's voice sounded in her head. Fallon started. She'd forgotten that she hadn't terminated their connection after Briggs's suicide.

"You've got to hurry, Fallon. We just got a look at your location via satellite. You're in the clear so far, but they're getting closer all the time."

"Working on it," she muttered.

"Work faster. I'm not kidding."

"I'm really not used to this kind of labor. Randy's hurt, and—"

"Fallon, I'm on your side. I'm just telling you, you don't have a lot of time. In a few minutes, you'll have to start shooting them. When you do, that'll tell the rest where you are."

"Okay!" Frustrated, exasperated, and scared, she said it louder than she'd intended. Sansome and Antonetti looked up.

"What?" Antonetti asked.

"Nothing, Gino." She started leaning on the wrench, cranking it with everything she had. Sweat dripped into her eyes, slicked her sides. "Just hurry!"

When they had disconnected the master pipes from the vertical plastic ones feeding the jets, they capped one with a fitting from the tool room and started pulling down the plastic. Sansome bolted on an elbow section, then connected the plastic to that, removing the jet branches as he went. When one side's plastic piping ended, they hooked up the pipe from the other side, giving them almost two hundred feet of fairly flexible piping.

They were admiring their handiwork—Fallon wondering if it would actually function as intended—when Antonetti snatched up his machine gun and opened fire. Fallon whirled around to see seven or eight Infecteds who had somehow gotten to within twenty feet of them without being detected. She yanked out her Glock and joined Antonetti. In less than a minute, all the Infecteds were down.

But that didn't mean the others hadn't heard. This was what Book had warned her about. They could be overrun any minute now. She wondered how the Sykos in the pump room were doing because so far, nothing was even trickling from the pipe. She was about to step away and ask Book for an update when Lilith came racing toward them. "He says cap it!"

Sansome drew on a cap, closing off the pipe, and secured it with a couple of screws that he tightened by hand.

"Should be any second now," Lilith said. "They gave me ninety seconds to get here before they started it up. We heard shooting."

"Just a few Infecteds," Fallon said. "But I'm sure the rest heard. Help us with this thing."

Everybody got a grip on the long pipe, and they carried the capped end back toward where they'd come in, near the activity pool. They were almost there—could see Infecteds against the fence, massing between them and the UPS truck. The pipe bucked in their arms, and started wriggling like the world's biggest snake, trying to break their grips. Fallon felt it and held on tighter, but she knew Sansome's presence was the only thing keeping it under control. At the long pipe's end, he had the hardest job of all.

Light came dashing up from the pump room and grabbed onto the pipe, helping to steady it. Pybus was a little behind him, not moving as fast as the fit EMT.

"It's time!" Sansome shouted. *Past time,* Fallon thought—the thing wanted to knock her over. The big man pulled one of the screws and swiveled the cap out of the way, and water shot out the end like it was a cannon.

And with Sansome controlling the aim, miraculously, it worked.

The Infecteds around the fence were blown off their feet. Some went skidding a dozen feet or more back into the parking lot. Sansome shifted the stream and blasted some more, opening a pathway. Infecteds tried to regain their footing, but the pavement was so slippery now, they fell more often than not.

"Now for the hard part!" Sansome called over the deafening blast of water. He had scouted a place in the ticket booth where he thought he could wedge it, but that was before he knew just how powerfully it wanted to break free. Light released his section and ran up to help him, and Warga—to Fallon's surprise— did the same. Between the three of them, they got it in place—shooting a heavy stream of water at full force right into the Infecteds gathered near the gap Sansome had made.

When they were satisfied it would hold, they released it, and so did the others.

Then the shooting started.

The water couldn't blast directly at the gap, or across the path the Sykos would have to take to the truck. It would be hard enough to keep their footing on the wet pavement as it was; add shooting at moving targets into the mix, and it'd be downright treacherous. Light, Warga, and Antonetti went first, using their machine guns to part the sea of Infecteds, slipping and sliding as they went. The others came behind, Sansome bringing up the rear.

Fallon reached the truck and spun around to see where the rest were. Just as she did, Sansome's feet lost their grip on the pavement. They flew back and he hit the ground, hard.

As soon as he was down, Infecteds swarmed him.

"Joe!" she cried. She opened fire on the Infecteds tearing at him. Antonetti was still holding the machine gun, and he used it to keep more Infecteds from joining the first batch. He seemed reluctant to fire at the ones on Sansome. *Afraid of hitting him,* Fallon figured.

She saw blood. Flesh. Sansome was fighting back, and he was strong, but he was facedown on wet pavement now, which didn't give him much leverage.

"Come on!" she said, wading back into the current. "We've got to get him out of there!"

"Let him go, Fallon," Book said. "Get out of there."

"Not a chance."

"Fallon . . ."

She ejected a magazine from her gun, slammed in a new one, and tried to blink "Off" at the same moment. She was pretty sure she screwed that up, but Book got the message anyway. She heard a heavy sigh, then silence.

But only on the inside.

On the outside, where her attention was, the sound of gunfire, the scuff of hundreds of feet on wet pavement, the shouts of humans, and the guttural, near-animal noises of the Infecteds all battered her ears. The odors of gun smoke and water bringing out the oils on streets that hadn't seen a serious rain in months filled her nostrils.

She felt like she had been almost blinded by fear and rage. When she blinked, she saw that she had charged all the way to Sansome's position. He was trying to get to his knees, but he had the weight of three Infecteds on his back and legs, and more clawing at his head, tearing the flesh.

Looking for uninfected brains.

Fallon held her gun against the skull of the nearest one and squeezed the trigger. The gun bucked in her hands, the Infected's head blew apart, and blood and diseased brain splattered her. She ignored it and turned to the next one. It—she—must have been pretty, once. She had long blond hair and a big green eye—the other one had been torn from her head, probably when she'd become infected—and plump lips, twisted into a ferocious scowl.

Fallon put a round in the remaining eye.

She was starting to get pretty good at that part.

Around her, the guys with machine guns were carving a swath. She and Pybus, who still handled a gun with an air of distaste, finished off the Infecteds on Sansome and helped the big man to his feet. Together, holding Sansome between them—his head drooping, blood splashing into the water on the road—they ran to the waiting truck.

The truck had been splashed but not a lot. Light jumped into the driver's seat. Fallon helped Sansome onto the floor in back, then flopped down in the jump seat, firing through the open door. The rest lined up in the gap between the shelving units, Antonetti and Warga laying down fire out the back doors until the Infecteds stopped chasing them.

Pybus's idea had worked. They'd reached the truck, and though it had cost ammunition, it wasn't as much as it might have been. Still, Fallon was starting to be concerned about how much they were going through and how much more they might yet need. *One more thing to worry about,* she thought as she glanced back at Sansome.

Of those, there never seemed to be a shortage.

## CHAPTER 35

*21 hours*

Light sped north up Country Club Drive, then took a right on Southern, ignoring the traffic signal and the camera that snapped a picture of what was left of his back license plate for running a red. He didn't get far down Southern, though, because just past the Fiesta Village Mobile Home Park, a red Dodge Charger, an Xterra, and a couple of landscaping trucks were blocking the road.

But it wasn't like on the freeway, where the cars had been abandoned where they were—crashed or parked—as drivers fled, or tried to. These vehicles didn't look like they'd just randomly stopped. They looked like they'd been pushed into place to form an impassable wall.

"It's a trap!" Antonetti muttered. When Fallon looked at him, he shrugged. "Sorry. *Star Wars* fan. Couldn't resist."

"Geek or not, he's right," Light said. "Something's off. I'm turning around."

He slowed, then braked. He cranked the wheel hard to the left and moved his foot from the brake to the gas pedal. The truck made a clumsy U-turn, and they were facing back the way they'd come, looking at what should have been an empty street.

Except it wasn't.

*Of course it isn't,* he thought.

Infecteds filled the road in front of them, more than they'd ever seen in one place before. Light tried to do a quick count and gave up at forty. There were easily three times that number of Infecteds, pouring in from the trailer park to the south and the residential area to the north.

"This isn't good," Fallon said in her new role as Captain Obvious. "First the building-to-building searches, now a serious ambush." She shook her head. "This is much more elaborate than the one with a handful of burning cars. They're getting smarter."

"Well, last I checked, being smart didn't make you invulnerable to Detroit steel. Hold on!"

He threw the truck in reverse and backed up toward the blockade, where even more Infecteds were gathering. When he'd gone as far back as he could without running into the rapidly advancing wall of virus-tainted flesh, he put the truck back in drive and gunned it.

The UPS truck lurched forward, gaining speed. It wasn't a brown bullet—it was too beat-up for that— but it was as fast as the ambulance he'd used to plow down Infected a bare handful of days ago. Remembering that drive, Light couldn't suppress a grin.

"That's right, you bastards. Come to papa."

Spurred on by Light's lead foot, the truck slammed into the wave of Infecteds, a rectangular metal-and-rubber cutter trying to climb to the crest before being swamped. Light shot out of his window with one hand and steered with the other. Fallon and Antonetti fired out the other side, and the others waited anxiously in the back for their turn to shoot, holding on for dear life.

They almost made it.

The problem was, the Infecteds were ten deep. And even as they plowed a path through the first three rows with little resistance, there were just too many. By the fourth row, bodies were starting to pile up under the wheels, and the truck was beginning to slow. By the fifth, the Infecteds were reaching in to the front of the truck, hands grasping air, but sometimes hair or clothing or skin that was subsequently ripped away with a curse. By the sixth, the truck was so bogged down that the Infecteds were starting to climb on the roof. By the seventh, the Sykos knew it was time to bail.

"We have to get out of here!" Fallon shouted. Light could barely hear her over the sound of gunfire ringing in his ears, but he was pretty sure it was yet again something blatantly apparent. Warga and a still-bleeding Sansome were crowding up behind them now, also shooting. Light was momentarily amazed at the man's ability to keep going despite his injuries; it was almost like Sansome was an Infected himself, except he preferred heads over their contents. Still, it was an unsettling thought, and Light quickly pushed it away, replacing it with another equally amazing one—somehow none of the Sykos had been a victim of friendly fire yet—Warga's little through-and-through notwithstanding.

"My door or yours?"

"Mine!" Fallon yelled, elbowing an Infected that had gotten through their barrage of bullets square in the face.

"Count of three?"

"Okay!"

"One, two . . ."

"Three!"

Fallon and Antonetti jumped out into the buffer zone created by their suppressing fire, parting so Warga and Sansome could come out next, then Lilith and Pybus. Light was the last to leave. With no one else shooting out his side of the truck now, the buffer zone on that side was much smaller, and Infecteds were encroaching closer by the second. He didn't want to turn his back on them, so he eased himself backward out of the truck, still firing at the Infecteds as they started to crawl in from the other side.

The nearest one was a red-haired woman in a low-cut blouse, breasts straining against the thin material as she reached for him. Under other circumstances, Light might have found her sexy. Then again, under other circumstances, her face wouldn't be as red as her hair, her breath wouldn't stink of brains, and her crimson eyes wouldn't be weeping blood.

Light aimed his barrel right in the middle of that sanguine gaze and pulled the trigger. Her face exploded in a shower of blood and bone. Light closed his eyes briefly against the barrage, and when he opened them, another Infected was about to take her place.

Time to go.

He blew this one's head off, too, then turned and hopped out of the truck.

"Let's move!"

They had three more rows to fight through until they were in the clear, and the Infecteds near the roadblock were almost on them. The Sykos formed up in a circle, backs to its interior, a moving ring of death. They pushed unevenly toward the west, back toward Country Club Drive, gaining a few feet at a time, until finally Lilith and Pybus broke through.

As they turned and started picking off the Infecteds still plaguing the others, Sansome and Warga made it out. Light was next, leaving only Fallon and Antonetti still surrounded.

But the Infecteds coming from the east had arrived, and the two Sykos were quickly cut off from the rest. Without a word that Light could hear, they moved together so they were back-to-back. They were still making progress toward the open road and freedom, but it was halting and slow and becoming ever slower.

"I'm going back," Light said before he could think too closely about it. "Cover me."

Trusting the others to do as he said, Light started blazing a trail of gunfire toward the trapped duo. He was coming in at an angle, so that his shots and those of the other Sykos wouldn't inadvertently hit Fallon or Antonetti. The suppressing fire created a little bubble around him as he moved, and soon his small circle of safety merged with Fallon and Antonetti's slightly larger one.

"This way! Come on!"

Fallon shook her head.

"We'll never make it! You go, take the others and get out of here. Gino and I will hold them off as long as we can."

"They won't follow me," Light said, knowing it was true. "It's you or no one, Fallon."

"He's right," Antonetti yelled, his voice hoarse with the effort to be heard over the cacophony of gunfire and the subvocal moaning and animal sounds of the Infecteds. The gunpowder and smoke were so thick that he sneezed before continuing, allowing an Infected to dart inside his reach and leave a Wolverine-style claw mark down his arm. The young Italian grabbed the Infected, pulled her close, rammed his pistol against her head, and fired. He shoved her corpse back into the crowd of Infecteds before continuing.

"Get out of here, Doc. Without you, the mission fails."

"Then we all need to get out!"

Antonetti shook his head even though she couldn't see him.

"Not happening, Doc. You and Light go. I'll keep these fuckers busy. Show 'em how shootin's really done."

The good doctor looked like she was about to argue, but Light grabbed her arm.

"*Now*, Fallon."

After a moment of hesitation, she nodded.

"Good luck, Gino. And thank you."

The Syko handed her something Light couldn't see but didn't reply. He moved forward into the fray, toward the truck, yelling something in Italian that Light was pretty sure was a particularly vile insult.

Fallon slipped whatever he had given her into one of the many pockets their uniforms sported, then Light and Fallon went in the other direction, working their way back to where the other Sykos' gunfire gave them a wide enough berth to run out of the crowd and into the open street.

They continued to fire into the swarm of Infecteds as they backed away, but fewer and fewer paid attention as Antonetti's screams drew them like moths to a Roman candle.

Light had no idea how accurate that simile was as Antonetti somehow got a final burst of shots off. The next thing the Sykos knew, a concussive wave threw them all to the ground as the UPS truck exploded in a ball of fire.

"Damn," Warga muttered, as they all scrambled back to their feet.

They watched the fire in silence for a moment, each of them, perhaps, saying goodbye in their own way to the first Syko to fall.

Then Fallon spoke.

"Let's not waste his sacrifice. We need to go."

They needed no further urging to turn and follow her north into a copse of trees separating the residential neighborhood from the commercial area.

Light was the last to disappear into the foliage, and he couldn't resist a look back.

The Infecteds seemed to have forgotten their existence—those that hadn't been killed in the blast or weren't stumbling around like living torches just milled aimlessly, as if the destruction of the truck and the loss of their prey left them without purpose.

As he watched the truck burning, Light's eyes narrowed.

"Fucking copycat," he said with grudging admiration, and spat on the ground, the only benediction he was willing to give the other man. Then he turned his back on Antonetti's pyre and slipped into the green.

**CHAPTER 36**

*21 hours*

They ran from copse to copse, making sure at each that there were no Infecteds following them before sprinting to the next. By the time they ran out of trees, they were all physically and emotionally exhausted. Add thirsty, hungry, and hurting to that, and Fallon knew tempers would be flaring soon—hers among them.

She at least knew the cause of her anger, beyond the physical stress.

She shouldn't have let Antonetti sacrifice himself. It should have been her.

Fallon suspected that he and Light had been correct when they said the mission would fail without her, but that knowledge wasn't what had deterred her. At the last moment, contemplating going to her death, she imagined Jason growing up without her. With only Mark to raise him.

The thought was enough to make her turn tail and run. She'd have run back to PIR if she could have, mission be damned. She'd let the whole Valley be nuked rather than let her son grow up with only Mark's influence. He'd wind up as one of those kids who lived in his parents' basement until he was thirty, playing video games and subsisting entirely off Mountain Dew and pizza. And given his genetics, that could lead to places she never wanted her child to go.

So she'd let Antonetti go to his death even though that was arguably her job as the leader of this merry band of Sykos. All because she didn't want her son to turn out to be like him.

Or like her.

But she couldn't run back to the racetrack; she'd never make it. So the only other option to get back to Jason was to make sure she survived this mission, with as many of her Sykos as it took to get her home in one piece. Well, her and the meteor.

Fallon's bitter reverie was interrupted by a woman's scream. It wasn't Lilith—too far away for that.

She hadn't been in the lead; Lilith and Light were stopped in front of her, and she pushed her way between them to see what had caused them to halt.

In front of them was a large greenbelt, bounded by evenly spaced poles painted sunshine yellow, with chains of the same hue strung between them that would keep no one out except perhaps faeries with a distaste for cold iron. A pavilion with several picnic tables took up the west end. To the north, a large, squat Mormon church shaded by immense palm trees held court over a vast, empty parking lot.

That was where the scream had come from.

A man and woman were fleeing across the parking lot, followed by a small herd of Infecteds—five, so far. Fallon couldn't tell if the couple had come from inside the church or from behind it; she supposed it didn't matter, unless there were supplies her people could use inside.

As the Sykos watched, more Infecteds began to converge on the couple—three from the pavilion, four from between two houses across the street. Soon the two were surrounded, the woman—still screaming—armed with only a butcher knife; the man, with a shovel.

"We have to help them," Fallon said decisively. She'd just watched one human fall to the Infecteds. She wasn't about to watch two more without doing something about it.

"Why?" Light asked. "Why not sneak past while they keep the Infecteds busy? We've already wasted enough time fighting them."

"Sometimes running *is* the more noble option," Pybus agreed, surprising her. Of all of them, she'd come to think of him as a calm and logical presence, but also one who—paradoxically, after the crimes he'd committed—would do the right thing, given the choice. But she supposed that sometimes practicality had to supersede morality, especially when two lives were weighed against millions.

Fallon knew that, understood the rationale behind it. In any other situation, she'd probably have been the one making that argument. But not this time. Now, she didn't care about reason or common sense. She couldn't just walk away and leave the couple to die. Not so soon after Antonetti—Gino. She felt like she owed it to him, to give his sacrifice meaning. Anything less cheapened what was, at its core, the act of a hero.

"Fuck nobility," she said, loading a fresh clip into her Glock. "I'm going to help them. You can come along, or you can watch, I don't care." Warga and Sansome had moved up while she spoke, so the Sykos were all in a ragged line as they stood in the shadow of the last trees. "I'm going."

"Then so am I," Sansome said simply, pulling his own pistol out. His face was still bleeding in spots. Much of it was hamburger, and there were worse wounds—a ragged flap of skin under his left eye had been clawed almost off, hanging on only by its bottom edge; the far right side of his forehead sparkled with bits of glass smashed into it from being ground into the street.

Fallon looked at the others. None of them seem ready to man up and join her and Joe.

*Okay, then.*

"Let's go," she said to him, and set out running from the cover of the trees into the greenbelt, the grievously damaged Sansome her unlikely partner.

"Well, shit," she heard Light say behind her, then they were all around her, sprinting toward the Infecteds.

The man was swinging his shovel in a wide arc, while the woman darted forward and back, stabbing and slicing rather ineffectually at the circle of Infecteds. Fallon noted how the Infecteds appeared to be holding back a little now, not quite as hunger-mad as they had been before. Almost as if—as they'd seemed to become smarter and more organized the farther the Sykos traveled—they'd also rediscovered the idea of self-preservation. She'd noticed it in the Sykos' own most recent encounter, but hadn't had time to process it, being busy running for her life. Now she did, and she wondered what it meant.

And how the Sykos could use it to their advantage.

As they ran, her team picked the Infecteds off one by one, selecting their shots carefully in order to preserve their ever-more-precious ammo. Head shots, because not even Infecteds who had the strength of The Rock in a 'roid rage could keep coming after their skulls had become airborne jigsaw puzzles.

The gunfire drew Infecteds in a way the woman's screams had not, and soon more began trickling into the greenbelt, heading for the Sykos. Which sort of discredited Fallon's self-preservation theory, since a shovel and a knife were a lot easier to defend against than a gun.

The Sykos took them out, too, with a few more well-placed shots. And then there were no more targets. The couple stood, staring at them with slack jaws, inside a circle of corpses.

The woman recovered first.

"What the fuck did you do *that* for?"

Fallon's own jaw dropped, but before she could find words for an appropriate response—one that was likely to include the words "ungrateful bitch"—she heard the sudden sound of engines roaring to life. Two groups of pickups and ATVs rounded the church, one on either side, racing toward the Sykos and across the browning grass like twin bats out of hell.

As the lead vehicles stopped a few feet away from them, Fallon could see that the riders were seemingly uninfected and armed with serious firepower—M4s, M240B SAWs, RPGs, the works—most of which they were pointing straight at the Sykos. They were an odd mix—tattooed biker types, men and women who could have been suburban soccer moms and dads, young black and Hispanic men. Each vehicle had RR painted crudely on the hood.

"What happened, Kayleigh?" The driver of the nearest ATV stood, a Hispanic man wearing a dress shirt with the sleeves torn off to reveal a Ranger tattoo.

"*They* happened," she said, gesturing toward Fallon and her people. "Danny and I had a small group around us and were just starting to attract more when they showed up, guns blazing, like some sort of freaking cavalry riding to our rescue." She directed her next comments toward Fallon. "Except we didn't *need* rescuing. We were trying to lure more in—the more we attract, the more we can kill." She looked at the bodies on the ground. "A lousy fifteen, thanks to you guys. Not even a drop in the blood bucket."

The former Ranger looked over at Fallon.

"Looks like you guys acquitted yourselves pretty well. Reedley's always looking for more survivors who know how to handle themselves in a fight. We've fortified the Bass Pro Shop up by the Red Mountain Freeway, northwest of here. You come with us, Reedley might agree to make you all Raiders. Interested?"

Just then, a woman in the back of one of the pickups let out a sharp whistle. She was pointing behind the Sykos, to the south. Turning, Fallon saw the Infecteds who'd survived Antonetti's swan song start streaming out of the trees into the greenbelt. They seemed to have gathered reinforcements along the way, because where before they'd faced somewhere north of a hundred, there were easily three times that many now.

"Well, we lured some more in for you," she said to Kayleigh, who just glared. "Feel free to start killing them. We won't get in your way this time."

"Yeah, we're not prepared to deal with that many," the Ranger said, shaking his head. "No point in wasting the ammo." He gestured to the other vehicles. "Move out!"

Then he looked back at Fallon.

"You coming, or what?"

**CHAPTER 37**

*20 hours*

**F**rom the outside, Bass Pro Shops—every sign Fallon saw was plural, as if the building contained multitudes, and it might well have—could have been a hunting lodge somewhere in Montana, if giants lived in Montana and had built themselves log cabin-style dwellings. Everything about it was oversized, from the acres of parking lot to the massive timbers decorating its heights. She was sure they weren't structural because the other descriptor that came to mind was "artificial." Mesa, Arizona, wasn't in the mountains, despite the implication of its name, and this looked as out of place as an undertaker at a wedding.

She had hesitated only a moment when the Ranger invited them to get in a couple of the pickups. He ordered the other Raiders to redistribute themselves among the vehicles and had one of them take the ATV he'd been riding, so he could sit in the open truck bed with Fallon, Warga, and Sansome. His name was Alberto Cuaron, though everybody called him Al, and they obeyed him with a discipline that was less rigid than what Fallon had seen at PIR, but no less responsive. Al was a natural leader, and the others, ragtag though they were, treated him as such.

Fallon had only provided her first name, and Light seemed to catch on immediately and did the same. The rest followed suit.

It wasn't worth the possibility that someone might recognize a full name and wonder why a convicted murderer was here in the Valley instead of in prison.

The decision to go along with the Raiders had been made easier by imminent death at the hands of a few hundred Infecteds. But even without that incentive, she would have wanted to know more about this Reedley. She hadn't heard about anyone mounting an organized, military-style defense within the zone, but if such a thing existed—and evidence pointed to "yes"—then they might know something about the cartel's presence in the city. Maybe even something about Elliott. And if she could persuade them to help, they could make finding the meteor and getting it out much easier.

It was a long shot, but her very presence in this ravaged city was a gamble. Survival was even less certain. She should probably stop somewhere and pick up a couple of lottery tickets, because if she made it out alive, then luck was *definitely* on her side.

"You sure about this, Fallon?" Book's disembodied voice asked. He had been quiet for long enough that she'd begun to wonder whether he'd been called to deal with some other situation. Surely, he had other responsibilities and had to be replaced at the monitor sometimes. No one else other than Briggs had ever talked to her, though. The idea that some silent observer was looking out through her eyes was more than a little disconcerting.

"Not at all," she said, almost at a subvocal level. If she had dared add more, it would have been something like, *It isn't like we had a whole lot of options. Let the Raiders drive us away, or stay for dinner—by which I mean our brains would have been dinner.*

"Just be careful," he said.

She nodded. He couldn't hear that, but if he was watching through her camera, he'd see it. The way the truck was bouncing, she hoped he wasn't prone to motion sickness.

As soon as they exited Route 60 onto Dobson, she saw the first of the sentries. They were positioned in spots they could hold in the event of trouble, but from which they could see the road, and be seen. Al raised a hand to a couple sitting in the shade thrown by the street-side monument sign for the Mesa Riverview shopping center: CINEMARK, CHILI'S, FAMOUS DAVE'S, HOWIE'S GAME SHACK ("WHERE GAMERS COME TO PLAY!"). They had what looked like RPG launchers in their hands and a tripod-mounted machine gun standing between them. Fallon wouldn't have wanted to come down that off-ramp unannounced.

After that, she saw more, all heavily armed, all watching the road and the surrounding environs. They weren't hiding; they wanted to be seen, as long as they could also see.

"How many people does this Reedley have?" she asked.

Al shrugged. He was handsome, with lively brown eyes, high cheekbones, and a strong, clean-shaven chin. And he was built. Not her type, necessarily; she was into more cerebral guys. But she imagined he would be lots of people's type. And the closer to the end of the world they got, the less picky people would be. "Lots. Three hundred, maybe."

"Not a lot compared to how many Infecteds there are."

He chewed on the inside of his cheek for a moment. He was sitting up against the side wall, legs bent, muscular arms stretched out over his knees. "Infecteds? That what you call 'em?"

"Yes. I mean, that's what we think they are. Infected by a virus, some kind of pathogen."

"I guess. We call 'em Red-eyes. That's what they are, too, right?"

"I can't argue with that."

"Anyway, yeah, there are lots more of them than there are of us. But we're organized. Smart. Well-armed. In most encounters, they don't have a chance against us unless they have a big numerical advantage, like back there by the Mormon church. That's why Ben wants to get as many good people—real people, live ones—on his side as he can."

"Ben?"

"Ben Reedley. *El Jefe*. We don't have a lot of brass—we're all warriors first. Ben especially. But everyone knows he's the boss. Some guys just have it, right? That air of command. Dude's got it in spades. He was MARSOC. Marine Corps Special Ops Command. He was a Raider, so now we all are. You don't fuck with Ben."

While they talked, the convoy approached the gigantic fake lodge. The road had been narrowed to one lane, so the ATVs and trucks had to advance in single file. Guards with automatic weapons scanned every face as they passed through, and Fallon couldn't help thinking their eyes narrowed as they caught sight of the Sykos.

Her feelings were confirmed when the pickup bearing the Sykos stopped, and one of the guards eyed them with suspicion, checking to make sure they weren't holding a gun on Al or the driver. "They're with you?" he asked Al.

"Roger that," Al said. "I saw them in combat. They'll be a big help."

"We can use every gun we can get." He shot them a toothy smile. "Welcome."

"Thanks," Fallon said. "Glad to know there's a resistance movement."

"To the last ounce."

"To the last ounce," Al returned.

The truck moved through the checkpoint, toward the huge store. "Last ounce of what?" Light asked.

Al shrugged again. "Blood. Grey matter. Take your pick."

*If that's a motto,* Fallon thought, *it's not a very optimistic one.*

*Then again, there's not much cause for optimism, is there?*

"How much territory do you actually control?" she asked him. "Seems like a lot."

"Bass Pro is headquarters and armory," Al said. He waved an arm at the store's surroundings. "But we hold the entire commercial area, including the Walmart and a bunch of restaurants. For now, those are sources of food provisions, while the Walmart also provides tools, vehicle parts, and more guns and ammo. Those locations are closely guarded to make sure nobody decides to help himself to supplies that the Raiders need. Not that we don't trust our own people, but you know, when society collapses, some folks are bound to put themselves first."

"Sure. What about intelligence? Do you have eyes on the rest of the city?"

"You ask a lot of questions."

"Can't make informed decisions any other way," Fallon replied, undeterred, hoping her nonchalance would be enough to keep the Ranger talking. She didn't want to seem too eager, though she was chafing to know if they could tell her where the cartel was holed up.

"Fair enough. To answer your last one, we're gradually expanding that capability. Cell signals and radio frequencies are jammed, as you probably know, but we've got troops positioned with walkie-talkies on a frequency that still works. They don't have much range, so we network them together—if somebody five miles out has a report, maybe that'll take six or seven troops in between to get that report to us here. We're still optimizing that, but we're getting there. We've also got personnel out on motorcycles and ATVs, so they can get around the worst traffic snarls and get word to us as needed."

Fallon looked at the big store's immediate vicinity. Instead of high walls and bulwarks, there were acres of open space all around; the store's vast parking lot, then cleared dirt or gravel areas surrounded by wide, empty streets. Defenders in the Bass Pro Shops building would be able to see anybody coming a long way off, and there would be nothing to shield attackers from the Raiders' weaponry. Closer to the structure, vehicles had been positioned nose to tail, forming a wall that looked to stretch all the way around it, with the only visible gap the one they had driven through. Inside the ring were dozens of SUVs, trucks, motorcycles, and ATVs. A few big tanker trucks, Al pointed out, stored water pumped from the nearby canal. Fallon was still learning the ins and outs of combat strategy, but the layout made sense to her.

"I have to say, it's impressive," Fallon admitted. Noticing numerous gas cans standing around, she added, "What's with the cans?"

"They're in case Red-eyes need to be burned, to keep their disease from spreading. You all look healthy," he said, though his eyes lingered on Sansome. "Are you?"

"So far," Fallon replied.

"That's good. One of our missions is to seek out and execute the sick *before* they have a chance to turn completely. Where'd the uniforms come from?"

Fallon had been anticipating the question. "We hit a surplus store. There were only a few of us, so we figured urban camo would be a good idea."

"Gotcha," Al said.

The truck came to a halt outside the store's truly enormous front entrance. The Ranger grinned at her. "Last stop." He stood and vaulted over the side, in one smooth motion, landing on the balls of his feet. Fallon climbed down more cautiously. Two trucks back, Light, Lilith, and Pybus were getting off theirs, too.

If the outside of the building was striking in an overblown, artificial fashion, the inside took those qualities as a starting point and multiplied them. Taxidermy animals were everywhere—bears, wolves, deer, eagles, and more. A waterfall tumbled down rocks near the center of the store, feeding a little creek stocked with live fish. The décor tried to bring the outdoors in—or at least, an imaginary version of the outdoors, with all the good parts, but no stinging insects, no burning sun, no buffeting wind or punishing rains. It was all climate-controlled and just a little too perfect.

"This," Light said as they entered, "is awesome."

"Fuckin' A," Warga added.

Lilith, for once, was struck speechless. She regarded her surroundings with eyes wide, jaw hanging open. Even Pybus was grinning.

"Kind of fake," Sansome said.

"Yes, Joe," Fallon replied. "Real fake. But in a fun way. It's like an amusement park for hunters and fishers."

"Like Disneyland?"

"Sure, that works."

"I went to Disneyland once. It didn't look nothing like this."

Fallon opened her mouth to respond, then realized she didn't know what to say to that. Instead, she just let it lie there, and Sansome nodded his ravaged head, a self-satisfied smile turning up the corners of his mouth and narrowing his eyes. She caught herself wondering if that was the last thing his victims saw right before he started in on their necks with his bow saw.

Al's people filed inside, skirting the Sykos as if they were boulders in a river that the Raiders flowed around. The Ranger and a couple of others had stepped to one side for a quick, hushed conversation with people at what had once been a customer-service stand of some kind. Now he returned. "Fallon," he said. "Reedley wants to meet you."

"Already?"

"Somebody reported in about how you guys took on the Red-eyes. He's been waiting for you."

"Shouldn't we . . . I don't know, freshen up, or something?"

Al snorted a laugh. "The new world order is a little short on showers. He doesn't give a flying fuck how you smell or look, he just wants to know if he can count on you to kick Red-eye ass."

She shrugged. "Okay, then. Where is he?"

"Follow me," Al said, and he started toward the waterfall.

Ben Reedley waited in what had been a classroom, upstairs near the firearms department. Rows of tables had been shoved to the side, some with their legs folded under and stacked on top of one another. At the back of the room, enormous elephant tusks flanked a big, stone fireplace, curving inward like the blades of twin scimitars.

Reedley himself was hardly less impressive. He stood well over six feet tall and ramrod straight, and his shoulders looked broad enough to carry the rest of the elephant. The arms hanging at his sides were long, roped with muscle and vein and leather straps he wore from his wrists to just below his elbows. Since leaving the Marines, he had let his hair grow past his shoulders and grown out a thick, brushy black beard. The hair softened his face a little, but nothing could disguise those eyes; narrow, with crinkles at the corners, as blue as a springtime sky, and so piercing Fallon felt punctured when he turned his gaze on her, like there was no point in trying to keep secrets because he could see more than an MRI. He was wearing a black leather vest over a brown tank-top style shirt, cut low enough to display the tops of his massive pectorals. His gut was probably more prominent than it had been in his MARSOC days, but that didn't lessen the sense of danger surrounding him. His booted feet were spaced well apart, his jeans worn and tight against bulging thigh muscles.

He tried on a smile when Al ushered the Sykos in. He shouldn't have. It looked like something he did maybe once or twice a year, then discovered he was no good at it and hid it away until the next time he was forced to use it.

"Welcome to Raider Country," he said. His voice was thin, almost shrill. Fallon suspected that when he was shouting orders or facing enemies, it took on a more menacing aspect. "I'm Ben." Three other men were in the room, sitting in chairs, but compared to Reedley, they seemed almost invisible. Afterthoughts. Nobody introduced them, and Fallon didn't ask.

Instead, she strode up to Reedley, radiating confidence of her own. Some people would have been anxious, even intimidated, she knew. Even she might have been a few days ago, although meeting new people had never been a problem for her. Now, her gaze was steady, and the handshake she gave was as firm as the one she got. "Fallon," she said. She cocked her head to the side. "My crew."

"You're the boss lady?"

"That's right.

"You must be badass."

"I do okay."

"I heard what you did against the Red-eyes. I was impressed."

"Not our first rodeo."

"You Army? National Guard?"

"We're civilians," Fallon said. She repeated her lie about the uniforms. He seemed to buy it, nodding. Those eyes never cut away from her.

"You just out killing Red-eyes, or you got something else going on?"

"Is there anything else? If you don't kill, you get killed."

"Way it is," he agreed. "It's not boring."

"Hardly that."

"There must be something else to it, though. You all in uniforms. Those guns. That hard-line attitude against the Red-eyes. Most people go into hiding. Not you."

Fallon could stall him all day long, but he wasn't going to give up. She saw that now, in his relaxed posture, hands big enough to palm a basketball hanging loosely at his sides. He could wait her out. She had to give him something that would satisfy, while still keeping the nature of their mission private.

"It's not just killing them. That's a good fringe benefit, but I'm looking for someone who stole something from me. Something important." She felt the others shift behind her and knew she'd have some 'splaining to do.

"That's vague," Reedley said.

"It's the best I can do."

"You might have to give it up," he said. "It's hard to find anybody these days. And survival is a hell of a lot of work. It has to take priority over revenge or anything resembling justice."

"Nothing says we can't hope for both."

"Hope? Sure, you can do that. It doesn't come cheap anymore, but you can try it. In the meantime, you're welcome to join the Raiders, if you want. The task before us is a big one, and we can use all the human beings we can get. Especially ones who know how to fight. I think we'll win—I'm talking straight here, so I hope you can see that. The Red-eyes have to live long enough to spread the disease. Finding them fast and killing them early is the best way to stop its transmission.

"But that requires constant forays. I've got multiple teams on patrol at all times. Law enforcement and medical professionals were among the first to go, so they're not an option. We can't rely on anyone but ourselves. As more civilians join us, we're getting stronger and stronger, but we need more personnel. If the people don't stand up, society's done for. And if it spreads outside of Phoenix, then we're all in the shit."

"We're here," Fallon said. She felt no hesitation about speaking for the team. "We're with you."

"Glad to hear it," Reedley said. "If you need new

weapons, ammo for what you've got, anything like that, just let us know, and we'll take care of it. We're pretty well stocked here. We hit all the gun dealers we could, while also taking over this shop and the ones nearby."

"Good plan."

"I do me—"

A loud Klaxon drowned out the rest of his sentence. "What's that?" Fallon shouted.

"Alarm!" Reedley replied. "Red-eyes have breached the perimeter! Let's get you guys outfitted! You ready to fight?"

"We were born ready!" Fallon called back. Mentally, she added, *Or not quite—but we were born predisposed, anyway.* She allowed herself a quick smile as she followed Reedley from the room and into the chaos outside.

# CHAPTER 38

*19 hours*

Light wasn't as sure about joining up with these Raiders as Fallon seemed to be, but he assumed it was only a temporary thing—mostly because it was T minus twenty hours until they nuked paradise and made it a parking lot. And he was sure about killing Infecteds. It wasn't the same as giving an old lady on her deathbed a little nudge to help her cross over, but they *were* sick, and he *was* putting them out of their misery. With the government's permission and their weapons, even. Being an angel of death was turning into a pretty plum gig.

So when he heard the alarm, he was as gung ho to man the place's defenses as any of the Raiders whose home it actually was. The Sykos hadn't been issued any gear yet, so once they were back downstairs, he grabbed a clip for his M249 off the long buffet table before the woman checking out weapons could do anything more than shout doubts about his paternity after him. Then he ran after Fallon and Lilith, who'd been "ladies first"ed and already had new ammo.

The Infecteds were attacking at the same entrance the Sykos had been brought in through. Even before he got there, though, Light could tell something was wrong. Instead of the calm confidence and efficiency that had marked the gate crew when the Sykos arrived, people were rushing around, seemingly aimlessly, their faces tight with worry.

"What's going on?" he asked a blond man who was running back toward the building, maybe to get reinforcements, maybe to tell Reedley something they didn't want broadcast over the regular channels.

"Red-eyes. With clubs, using cover. We need snipers."

Well, that left him out. None of the Sykos were that good with a rifle, except for Antonetti, and Light sincerely doubted hell would give the Italian a furlough just to come back up here and kick some Infected ass.

Still, if it was moving, he could shoot and kill it. Might take a few shots, but it almost always did with Infecteds, so lack of skill wasn't really a problem.

While Fallon and Lilith stopped to talk to one of Reedley's lieutenants, Light found an unmanned spot at the wall of vehicles. He loaded the new magazine into place, then surveyed the landscape.

There was a mob of Infecteds coming toward the

gate, but they weren't moving en masse. The larger force held back—out of the range of most of the guns the defenders had, hence the need for snipers—but small groups moved forward, using almost anything for cover. Parked and abandoned cars, trees, saguaros, even low bushes. The Infecteds didn't really seem to get the concept, though. They were like the kid who closes his eyes and thinks you can't see him, or stands behind a flagpole and thinks the fact that the pole is between you and him means he's hidden.

But they'd already demonstrated an ability to evolve, or learn, or something. They were loosely coordinated now, in a way they hadn't been that first day in the ER. Methodically searching buildings, executing pincer maneuvers, using cover and tools.

And now weapons. Crude ones, to be sure—heavy tree branches, broken broom handles, a baseball bat. One even had a short flagpole, the black POW/MIA flag still attached. He was the first one Light took aim at.

His first shot went wide—through the white head on the flag, nowhere near the head he'd actually been aiming for. He corrected, and the next shot hit the roof of the car the flag bearer's group of Infecteds was hiding behind. One more correction—and then another, because the Infected moved—and then he fired.

Neck shot. He fired again, took off the Infected's left ear. The third shot was a direct hit, and for an instant, the POW/MIA flag was black, white, and red. And then it and the Infected disappeared behind the car and didn't reappear.

"What are you doing?" one of the gate guards yelled at him.

"What you apparently won't," he replied without bothering to look at his questioner.

"You're wasting ammunition! The snipers could have taken out five Red-eyes with as many shots as you took."

"Snipers aren't here, are they? And while you hold off, waiting for them, they"—he nodded toward the Infecteds—"are getting closer." He moved the barrel of his machine gun a few inches to the left, and fired. The side of another Infected's head exploded in a crimson shower. "Making sure they don't keep doing that is worth a couple of extra bullets in my book."

"He's right." Fallon's voice was a welcome intrusion. He'd let the doctor talk sense into the guard while he kept sending the sick to their much-deserved rest. But before she could, another Klaxon sounded, at a slightly less annoying pitch than the last one. "What's that?" Fallon asked.

"The east side. Infecteds are attacking there, too!"

This time Light did look at the gate guard, who'd gone white with fear. The gate guard looked back at him, seemed to take some strength from the Syko's continued calm, and took a deep breath.

"Waste all the ammo you need to. Just take those bastards out!"

He turned and started giving orders to the others assembled, which now included all the Sykos aside from Light and Fallon, who were already at the wall.

"Attacking on two fronts at once?" Fallon asked, shaking her head worriedly. "This isn't good."

"None of it is," Light replied with a shrug, "but it doesn't change anything. Smart or dumb, we kill 'em if they get in our way."

Fallon nodded.

"You're right. Again." Then she smiled. "Let's do what the man said and take some of those bastards out."

A third, different alarm sounded while the Sykos and the others at the gate played Shooting Gallery with the Infecteds, and Light glanced over at the gate guard, who'd taken up position next to him.

"Another front?"

The guard nodded, not taking his eyes off the scope of his rifle. On the other side of him, one of the much-vaunted snipers had arrived to bat cleanup. There were only a few Infecteds left now, at least at this gate, and it had become a matter of figuring out how to entice them out from behind their cover so fifty people could shoot at them at once. Light was surprised they hadn't yet learned the concept of "retreat" from this battle, but he suspected the next batch would probably have it down pat.

The last Infected shifted out of the cover of another car. Light had taken the guard's words to heart and shifted the weapon out of the single-shot mode. He fired a burst, and his rounds hit it first, followed by two dozen more. By the time the gunfire stopped, all that was left was what looked like dress blues, stuffed and flopped over the hood of the car. Everything else was shredded flesh and splattered blood. He turned to Fallon, whose own bullet had been one of the twenty-five, but who looked sick because of it. Whereas he felt nothing but satisfaction.

"You okay, Fallon?" he asked.

"Just thinking about Gino."

*Ah.* Light had finally figured out that the object the Italian had given her before throwing himself into the volcano had been Paolo's dog tags. The uniform had no doubt brought him to mind. He was the first Syko to be lost—though probably not the last—and Light figured Fallon must be taking it as a personal failure. She was the one who'd agreed to use him when she'd learned Paolo—her first choice—was dead. She probably felt guilty, and maybe sad, though seeing as the brain structure she shared with him tended to decrease—or obliterate—empathy, he wasn't sure of anything beyond the failure bit. Brains were tricky things, after all.

"Who's Gino?"

It was the gate guard. Fallon had been unconsciously touching the metal chain she wore around her neck—Paolo's dog tags—as she spoke, but now she pulled her hand away, maybe a little too quickly.

"One of our guys. We lost him just before we met Kayleigh and Danny."

The guard's eyes lingered on Fallon's neck so long,

Light began to wonder if he had some sort of vampire fetish. Then he spoke.

"Reedley gave you guys a pass because you stole those uniforms, but that guy out there?" He indicated the dead Infected, who Light was sure now had been a Marine, probably home on leave, glad to be somewhere safe, never realizing he was in far more danger here than he'd ever been in over in the sandbox. "Reedley would have shot him first. He hates the government—is convinced that they're the ones behind this apocalypse. So if he thought you guys were actually military—even just reservists—he'd wrap you all up and throw you out as bait for the Red-eyes."

"We're not," Fallon said—too quickly again, in Light's opinion. "What we said about the uniforms is the truth. We're no more government agents than you are."

The guard didn't look entirely convinced, but he also didn't look like he was about to tattle, so Light decided he could probably let the guy live. For now.

"For your sakes, I hope it *is* the truth. No skin off my back either way though I did have a sister in the Corps."

"Did?" Fallon asked. "What happened to her?"

"Reedley."

"Oh."

"So if you *were* actually grunts, you'd probably want to take care to hide that fact. Just saying."

"Understood," Fallon said. "And I'm sorry about your sister."

The guard shrugged, but Light noticed his eyes had gone hard, like frozen flint. "She pushed our grandmother down when we were running from some Red-eyes, before we got here. They stopped chasing us to eat her. Nana, I mean—the woman who gave up everything to raise us. So much for 'honor, courage, commitment.'" His lips twisted, and he laughed bitterly. "Selfish bitch got what she deserved even if she was my sister. I only wish it would have lasted longer."

One of Reedley's lieutenants called him away then, and he nodded to Light and Fallon before he left. Fallon turned to look at Light.

"Warning, or threat?"

Light laughed.

"Fallon, we're psychopaths. We face nothing *but* threats—you know that. They're just a little more likely to actually kill us in the zone."

**CHAPTER 39**

*17 hours*

**H**eading back inside after the shooting stopped, Fallon ran into Al. "Everything go okay?" he asked.

"We got to shoot some Infec—Red-eyes," she said. "So yeah, everything was fine."

"Good," he said. "Ben said you're gonna stay for a while."

"Looks that way. Thanks for putting in a good word."

"Thank *you* for deserving it."

She drew him aside, out of the main flow of people coming in, all of them smelling like gun smoke. On a shelf above her head was some kind of stuffed, dead animal, but all she caught was a glimpse of brown fur, so she didn't know what it was. "Have you ever seen that kind of behavior before, Al? Infecteds using weapons, hiding behind cover?"

"Or attacking on multiple fronts at once?" he added.

"Hell, no. I would have told you it was impossible."

"That's what I thought, too. So what do you think it is? They're getting smarter?"

"They used to be people," he said. "Maybe they're just getting less stupid. Or someone's training them, I don't know."

"I don't like it," she said.

"Neither do I."

Al excused himself, and Fallon stood there for another couple of minutes, trying to puzzle out what this change in tactics might mean. Before, there had been some degree of safety in the fact that although the Infecteds tended to mass together, at least they hadn't really displayed anything like complex planning or forethought. Shooting a mass of people who won't run or hide was pretty easy work, really. The Sykos were getting closer and closer to the meteor's probable location, but as they did, the Infecteds were getting harder to deal with.

Maybe the Raiders could help, though. If she could come up with a reason for them to stage a heavy assault on the neighborhood where the meteor was, maybe they could clear a path. Time was getting short, too, so finding it and getting out of the zone again was growing ever more important. And, unfortunately, the less time they had, the more difficult it would be to locate Elliott or to justify the effort.

The ground floor was crowded with Raiders, talking over their victory, sharing horror stories about the changes in Red-eye behavior, or generally shooting the shit the way Fallon imagined soldiers did after a win. In at least one case, literally—she walked past a youngish man who looked like he could have been a high school football coach, who was saying, " . . . came outta my ass like it was jet-propelled, man. You shoulda heard the splash . . ."

Fallon picked up her pace, not wanting to know the rest of that story.

She saw Sansome—almost always the tallest guy in any crowd, except that Reedley, though not as massive, was a little bit taller—leaning tiredly against a fake-rock outcropping on which a pair of elk or deer grazed. Behind him was the store's giant aquarium.

As she approached, she heard Warga's voice, then one she didn't recognize. She slowed her stride a little, hoping to hear some of the conversation. " . . . did you all meet up?" the other voice asked. "You friends before this all started?"

"Friends?" Warga sounded like the idea—maybe the whole concept of "friends"—was offensive to him. "Shit, no. We were—"

"Randy!" Fallon called, moving in fast. "Joe. I've been looking for you guys."

She rounded a store display that had been blocking her view of everyone but the towering Sansome. They were all there, to her surprise—Pybus, Warga, and Lilith sitting on collapsible camp chairs, Sansome standing, Light on the floor with his back against the aquarium glass. Two of the Raiders were crouched there. Everybody still had his or her long gun nearby.

"Oh, hi," she said, acting surprised to see the Raiders there. "Am I interrupting?

"Just gettin' to know your crew," one of the Raiders said. He had dark, greasy hair and a mustache that drooped over the corners of his mouth. If he'd waxed it and twirled it into points, he could have been a silent-movie villain, ready to tie poor Nell to the tracks. When he said "crew," Fallon remembered where she had seen him—he'd been one of the unremarkable men sitting in with Ben Reedley when Al had taken them in, and where she had introduced the Sykos as her crew. The other one might have been there, too, but there was nothing noteworthy about him, so she wasn't certain.

She still wasn't sure of the outfit's org chart, but if these guys were officers, or what passed for it in what Al had described as a pretty flexible command structure, she didn't want them asking a lot of questions. Or any questions. Psychopaths could be skilled liars, but they typically lied in their own self-interest. They might not know they needed to lie now.

Putting on the dog tags Gino had given her was a mistake. She should have left them in her pocket. Or tossed them altogether. She'd wanted to honor Gino in some way, but she'd come close to exposing their government ties. Now that she knew how antigovernment Reedley was, she didn't want to take any more such chances.

"They're a good bunch, aren't they?" she asked, forcing a smile. "Guys, I think we need a quick debriefing."

"You want to join ours?" the guy with the mustache asked. "After an engagement like that, Ben's going to want to have a command staff briefing up in the classroom."

"Okay if we get there in about ten minutes?" Fallon asked.

The other guy offered a noncommittal shrug. "Whenever you can, I guess." He and his comrade got to their feet and picked up their weapons. "Good meeting you all," he said.

Fallon waited until they were out of earshot, then looked around to make sure no one else could overhear. "What kind of questions did they ask?"

Lilith answered first. "Where we were from, if we lived inside the zone, what kind of jobs we had before. Shit like that."

"What did you tell them?"

"As little as possible, Doc," Warga said.

"Like he says," Light added. "I told them I was an EMT, which is true. But the rest of these folks didn't say they were in prison before this."

"We're not *stupid*," Lilith said.

Fallon chose not to address that. "Did they believe you?"

"I don't believe so," Pybus said.

"Why not, Caspar?"

"You don't get to be my age without knowing how to read people."

"Or people cookbooks," Light tossed out, drawing snickers from Warga and Lilith.

Pybus shot him a hurt look but didn't respond. "Anyway, I don't think they bought any of the lies they were told. They were trying to tease something out of us. Testing a hypothesis."

"Could you tell what the hypothesis was?"

"They can look at most of us and see that we're not really military, Fallon—they're not really worried about that," Light said. "But you *could* be. And you're obviously in charge. I think they believe you're with the Feds."

"Oh, yes," Pybus said. "That was unmistakably the impression I got."

Fallon hoped her expression didn't give away her concern. "We need to get out of here," she said. "Right now."

"How?" Warga asked. "The place is crawling with them. They're watching every approach—they'd see us leaving."

"Grab your things," she said. "We'll figure it out on the way."

They did as they were told. Either they were getting better at following orders, or she was getting better at giving them. She led them outside, not at all sure what she would do when they got there. Warga was right; running would probably get them shot. Detained, at the very least. Reedley had said they were welcome to join, but he hadn't said anything about letting them leave.

As soon as they cleared the doorway, the sounds of many revving engines reached her ears. "What's going on?" she asked a young Asian woman in a vest with the RR symbol painted on it in white. "Somebody going out?"

"Patrol," the woman said. "They're going out to see if they can mop up any Red-eyes that got away during the assault."

"We didn't see much action. You think it would be okay if we went along?"

"You'd have to ask Rodell—he's leading it." As she spoke, the woman gestured to the side of the building, out of sight from here.

"We'll find him, thanks."

As the Sykos hurried away, the young woman called out, "I'll let Ben know where you've gone, in case he's looking for you."

Fallon didn't answer, just kept walking as if she hadn't heard a thing.

**R**odell was wiry, with a long, sharp nose and sparse whiskers and bad teeth, with which he chewed on the plastic filter of an unlit cigarillo. If he wasn't nicknamed "Rodent," somebody wasn't doing their job. He was dressed in tight black leathers with the RR painted in white on front and back. That five-finger discount must have come in handy in Walmart's paint department.

He was sitting astride a trike, one wheel in front, two

in back, RR adorning the gas tank. Behind him, nine or ten other vehicles, mostly pickups, were moving into position. He looked questioningly at Fallon as she approached. "Reedley said we should go out with you," she said. "Get a feel for what patrol's like."

Rodent looked confused. "I'll have to ask him."

"He's got the command staff in with him," she said. "What's-his-name told us that Ben wanted us to go." She spread her thumb and forefinger apart, pantomimed the shape of the drooping mustache. "Guy with the 'stache. I can't remember his name."

"Oh, Fowler?" Rodent asked.

"Yeah, that's right. Fowler came down from the briefing and said Ben wants us out with the next patrol. I'd hate to still be standing here when the briefing's over."

"Okay, whatever. Hop in wherever you can find space."

Fallon had hoped they could all ride together, but getting out before Reedley came down or sent an emissary was more important. She told the Sykos to split up. She and Sansome found seats in the bed of an aging green Jeep Comanche pickup. Lilith sweet-talked someone into letting her ride behind him on his motorcycle, her arms wrapped tight around his midsection. Light wound up inside a primer-grey Suburban, and Pybus claimed a seat in the extended cab of a Ford F-350 Super Duty.

Once they were outside the territory controlled by Reedley's Raiders, they headed under the freeway. A few Infecteds were walking beside the road—whether late to the fight, early to retreat, or entirely unaware of it, Fallon couldn't tell. Rodent, out in front, had an Uzi attached to his handlebars. He swiveled the weapon as he passed the Infecteds and unleashed a long burst that ripped through them. They jerked like marionettes with their strings suddenly clipped and fell. Rodent gunned his trike and continued down the road.

By the time Fallon's truck drew up to where the Infecteds had fallen, they were already taking their feet again, torn and bloody but still hungry. That truck and the one behind it stopped. Two Raiders jumped out of the bed of the Jeep, and three from the Nissan following. The Raiders walked up to the Infecteds, pointed guns at their heads, and squeezed the triggers. Blood and bone chips and brain matter burst into a pink mist, and the Infecteds crumpled again, this time for good.

They turned around; the Salt River lay dead ahead. The patrol climbed the ramp onto the 202, headed west. The Raiders in Fallon's truck weren't interested in talking; they had divided up the view from the truck into near, far, and middle; north, south, east, and west, and each scanned his assigned block, looking for Infecteds, human survivors, or anyone who might be getting sick and need a bullet in the brain to shake it. Fallon didn't push it; the less conversation, the better, as far as she was concerned.

The patrol found small clutches of Infecteds: three, four, seven, up to ten once. By the time they drove away, all the Infecteds were usually dead, though a few times one or two got away. They were acting like the typical ones she had known all along—not taking cover, not using weapons. She saw no evidence of co-operation or advanced brain function.

Was the attack on Bass something else, then? How did they coordinate that? How did they know to use weapons—even if those weapons were meant for close-up work when they needed long-range firepower—or to seek cover from the hail of bullets the defenders sent their way?

At Scottsdale Road, they left the highway and drove south. The name changed to Rural Road. They continued, over the Salt again, then west on Rio Salado and south on Mill into Tempe. One of the guys in the truck—Fallon hadn't learned any names, and didn't want to—said that there had been a lot of Infecteds reported in the area. All the guys were still hyped-up from the battle and wanted to shed more Red-eye blood.

Fallon couldn't deny that she felt the same way. There was a camaraderie in the air despite her efforts to deny it. They were engaged in a struggle against a common foe. They'd won some fights, and those victories primed them for more.

Then, the walkie-talkies in the truck bed crackled to life all at once. A voice that Fallon recognized through static as Ben Reedley's came through the tiny speakers. "If anybody's got eyeballs on those uniformed fucks who came in with Al Cuaron earlier today, don't lose them. I want them back here, on the double. Alive, if possible, so I can talk to them before I administer the appropriate justice."

Fallon froze. Everybody in the truck was staring at her and Sansome. How to play it? She could run, but the other Sykos might not follow—and she'd probably be shot in the back for her efforts. She could try to convince them that he was talking about some other uniformed fucks. She could pull a gun and shoot everybody in the truck, but that would still leave her and the others outnumbered and outgunned.

Before she could even formulate a plan, as they were approaching 7th Street—Fallon could see the Steak & Shake sign—they ran into another ambush.

Once again, vehicles had been rolled across the road, and with the buildings hemming it in on either side, the way forward was closed. Rodent spun his trike around to go back the way they'd come. It was harder for the trucks, and the first ones had just started trying to back and fill their way into 180-degree turns when Infecteds swarmed from within and behind the storefronts on the north end of the block. The Raiders opened fire on what looked like a hundred or more of them.

Fallon had an uncomfortable feeling. She spun around, looking toward the roadblock to the south. Sure enough, Infecteds were flowing between those vehicles like water finding cracks in a dam.

"Behind us!" she shouted. She and Sansome started firing in that direction, and some of the Raiders joined in.

Then more Infecteds emerged from the buildings on either side. The block echoed with automatic-weapons fire, the shouts of the Raiders, the inhuman moaning and growling of the Infecteds. Smoke filled the air. Windows shattered, blood sprayed, the sidewalk turned crimson, and the gutters ran with red rivulets.

The Infecteds had numbers on their side, and they managed to drag a few Raiders from truck beds and off ATVs and motorcycles, but they couldn't stand up to guns and cases of ammunition. Gradually, their numbers were depleted. It was obvious how the battle would turn out.

Fallon spoke a few words to Sansome, then found Light and told him the same thing—firing all the while. Keeping up appearances. Light and Sansome did the same, respectively finding Warga and Lilith, while Fallon tracked down Pybus. He was alone in the big F-350 while the Raiders who'd been in it performed mop-up duties.

Within minutes, they were all in that truck, with Light at the wheel. "Go!" Fallon shouted as soon as Sansome slammed his door.

Light gunned it, up on the sidewalk, rolling over the bodies of Infecteds and a few fallen Raiders, glass crunching beneath tires, scraping trees. Raiders shouted at them. Rodent swiveled his Uzi in their direction, but Warga fired a couple of bursts from his M249, forcing the Raider to dive from his seat and take cover. Warga and Sansome leaned out the windows and fired at the other vehicles, taking out tires, puncturing engine blocks. Raiders fired back, but the way Light was weaving on and off the sidewalk, their rounds did little serious damage.

"I feel a little bad about leaving them there with the Infecteds," Fallon said when they were in the clear. "But not too bad."

"You're a Syko," Lilith reminded her. "Feeling sorry for other people is for chumps."

"They have walkie-talkies," Fallon continued. "They can call for help."

"I'm so relieved," Light said, sarcasm dripping from every syllable.

The truth was, Fallon should have felt worse than she did. What really bothered her wasn't the fate of these particular Raiders but the fact that the Raiders as a whole seemed to have a long reach.

And the Sykos had just made enemies of every one of them.

With luck, maybe the Infecteds would finish off the ones trapped in Tempe before they had a chance to tell anyone who'd stranded them there.

## CHAPTER 40

*15 hours*

"**W**hy were they even with that group? They've got less than seventeen hours to wrap this up," Robbins demanded, here on one of his increasingly frequent visits to check on the Sykos' progress.

"They didn't have a choice—it was that or get killed by a horde of Infecteds. And as you just saw, they got out of the situation as quickly as humanly possible." Book tried not to stress the word "humanly," but he was pretty sure Robbins thought the Sykos had some sort of superpowers because their brains allowed them to function with less empathy than most. Just like individuals with Williams syndrome were empathetic to the opposite extreme, the amount of empathy displayed was a result of genes—missing ones in their case. But whether they had too much or too little, they were all part of the human spectrum.

Of course, he couldn't say that to Robbins. Not because the general wouldn't understand—Book knew he was an intelligent man—but because it wouldn't matter to him. His only concern was the clock ticking down to Phoenix's destruction, not the mental condition of those he'd sent to jam its gears.

"Anyway, they're back on track now, and I'll get in contact with Fallon to make sure they stay that way."

Robbins snorted, but he knew by now that was the best he was going to get out of the analyst, so he just nodded, said, "See that you do," and left the room.

After the door closed, Book changed the view on one of the monitor screens back to the hit he'd gotten off the driver's license Fallon had shown him. He'd hacked into the FBI's facial-recognition database to get it, and boy, was it a doozy.

Carmen Gamez was the widow of Enrique Gamez, a recently deceased drug kingpin from Sinaloa. The FBI's operating theory was that she'd come to Phoenix to assure her U.S. connections that even with Enrique gone, business would go on as usual. The U.S. was her biggest market, after all, and Arizona was her gateway. What business she might have had with Elliott was the million-dollar question.

"Fallon? Can you talk now?"

There was a long enough pause that he started to wonder if there was something wrong with her transmitter, then he heard her mumble, "Not really, but I can listen."

*Good enough,* he thought.

"Your Latina torturer is—was—the wife of the head of the Gamez Cartel. Enrique, her husband, was killed a few weeks ago, leaving her nominally in charge. She's a long way from Sinaloa, which is probably safest for her right now. And she likely came to shore up her American counterparts."

"Warga was right, then. Cartel."

"Did you know Elliott was meeting with her?"

"Of *course* not. How would I?"

Her denial sounded genuine.

Of course, she *was* a psychopath, and they were damned good liars. But he believed her surprise and the anger behind it.

"He is your partner."

"Was," she murmured, the view from her implanted camera changing from the windshield of the crew cab and the road in front of her to the side window, presumably to keep the others from realizing she was talking. Book could barely hear her over the road noise, so he had to assume it was working.

"You don't have any idea why he might have been?"

"Not a fucking clue."

"Okay," Book said. "Since you won't tell me why you care, I don't know if it'll help—and I'll probably be thrown in prison for even telling you—but I have located other high-ranking members of the cartel, hiding out from the Infecteds at the Mesa Country Club, on West Fairway, off Country Club Drive. They've got a cutting-edge video surveillance system; I'm still trying to tap into it."

"Thanks, Book. That does help. Gives me somewhere to look, and it's on the way."

"Hey! Earth to Fallon. You in there?" It was Light's voice, angry and suspicious. Book saw Fallon's camera view change again as she turned to look at the EMT. From the expression on his face, it was clear the jig was up.

"Looks like you've got more pressing matters on your hands right now. I'll contact you when I have more information." Fallon didn't respond, but Book hardly expected her to, given the circumstances. "Be careful."

"Always," she said, but Book couldn't be sure if she was talking to him or to Light. "Did you want something?"

"Yeah, I want something," Light said, braking and pulling the truck over. "I want to know who the hell you've been talking to, and I want to know now."

**" . . . a**nd that's why I hid the two-way with Book from you, even though I shouldn't have. And why it's so important to get the prototype back," Fallon said. "To cure people like us."

Light scoffed, both at the excuse and the idea.

"What makes you think any of us *want* to be cured? I *like* what I do."

"I'm sure that's true, and you might not want to be cured, but there are others who would."

"You?" he asked. From the way her eyes flicked away from his for an instant, he knew it was true. "Why? You haven't killed anyone. As far as I can tell, your being a psychopath has had nothing but benefits for you—immune to Crazy 8s, your own lab, top in your field. Hell, you'll be able to parlay all of this"—he gestured toward the windshield, taking in the wrecked cars, dead bodies, and general chaos—"into a freaking bestseller. Why would you want to mess with that?"

"I have my reasons," she said, her lips compressed and her brow furrowed. She clearly didn't want to talk about it. Which only made Light want to talk about it more.

"Maybe you really did kill someone before all this, but were so good at it that it didn't come up in your background check." Her face didn't change. "Burn down a building? Kick a puppy?" Still no change. "Maybe it's not *you* that you want to cure?" Ah, there it was. He didn't think her lips could get any thinner, but they did. "Someone else, then. Husband? No, if you have one, he's a wuss—you'd never marry someone you couldn't control. None of us would. Oh, I know!" He smiled triumphantly. "You have a kid."

Her shoulders slumped infinitesimally, signaling defeat.

"I do," she admitted. "A son named Jason. He's three."

"And you're afraid he's inherited your brain abnormality," Pybus said quietly from the second row of seats. "If he has, you want to be able to fix him before he turns into one of us."

"Or you," Lilith, who was seated between her and Light, added with particular relish.

"Or me," Fallon agreed in a small voice, looking out the window again. Maybe blinking back tears.

Light was stunned to realize he actually felt sorry for her. Pity, anyway, if not actual compassion. He changed the subject, glaring into the rearview, daring the others to contradict him.

"Whatever. As long as you keep that thing away from me, it's all good," he said. "We've got more important things to talk about, anyway."

Fallon's gaze returned to his, sharper now, maybe even appreciative.

"Such as?"

"We've been talking, comparing notes. The attacks at Bass, the ambushes—that smacks of conscious planning. And unless they just set up the latest ambush in hopes that someone would come along eventually, like those earlier ones, it means there's some kind of communication between the ones who managed to escape from the first ambush and the ones laying the second one."

"Happenstance," Pybus opined, "Monkeys accidentally writing Shakespeare."

"Bullshit," Lilith said, and Warga shook his head, "I'm with the egghead on this one."

"Joe? What do you think?" Fallon asked, meeting his eyes in the rearview.

"I hope Caspar is right," Sansome said after a moment. "But I don't think he is."

Light figured that pretty much described all of them, Fallon included. They were all secretly hoping the Shakespeare faction was right, doubting it all the while.

After a few minutes, Sansome slapped the side of his ruined head. "Stop it!" he said.

"What the hell?" Warga asked him.

"I have this stupid song stuck in my head. It's all 'Sugar Sugar.' "

"The Archies," Pybus said. "The number one single of 1969, believe it or not. The ultimate bubblegum record. Wilson Pickett covered it in '70 and did it better."

"Jeez, will you both shut up with that oldies shit? Caspar, you can sing, right?" Lilith asked.

"So people tell me. Country-western music, mostly."

"Sing something that'll get the song out of his head. And keep you from giving musical-history lessons."

Fallon turned in her seat. Pybus sat back in the seat, crossed his arms over his chest, pressed his lips together. "I think I might have something," he said.

"What?" Fallon asked.

Pybus took a deep breath and started to sing. "By the time I get to Phoenix, she'll be . . ."

**A**fter that, conversation lagged. With the eastbound 202 and all its on- and off-ramps completely jammed,

Light was off-roading. He'd found a place where the K-rail placed during road widening had been knocked aside by an out-of-control semi, forced the truck through, and was now driving on the shoulder, between trees—over the smaller ones—and saguaros. As they approached Alma School Road, he brought the truck down into the staging area for the ongoing ADOT construction, zigzagging through belly dumps, water tanks, and other random oversized yellow equipment that Light didn't have names for beyond the bulldozer and the backhoe.

As they were bumping across the poorly graded ground, Fallon suddenly pointed off to the right.

"What's that?"

Light looked. He didn't see anything at first, and then he did.

Smoke.

"Let's try to get a little closer. If there's a new fire, it might mean some people are in trouble."

"Yeah, like 4 million of them," Lilith muttered, but both Light and Fallon ignored her. Abruptly, he was reminded of a family on a road trip, Mom and Dad in front with the troublemaker teen in between, the three older boys in back, each immersed in their own thoughts. Which made him "Dad" and Fallon "Mom" and, frighteningly, wasn't all that far off the mark.

Light slowed and brought the truck closer to the smoke, which was black now, easier to see. He could even smell it through the vents now—not the pure, clean scent of a wood fire but the acrid odor of industry in flames.

As they inched nearer, the story revealed itself, and it was firmly in the horror genre. The Infecteds were once more going from building to building, this time in a small industrial park on the corner of Alma School and McLellan. But where before they would enter the building to search for survivors, now they were setting fire to the buildings to flush those survivors out.

"I know where we are," Fallon said suddenly. "There's nothing but residential homes to the south and east. It's only a matter of time before they start in that direction and put entire neighborhoods to the torch. And with no firefighters able to respond . . ."

"Burn, baby, burn," Lilith breathed, almost reverently.

"That street across from us is Harvest," Fallon said. "If you take it, then your first left, you can get us back to McLellan without having to go past them. Then it's a straight shot down McLellan to Country Club."

"You're the boss," Light replied, preparing to step on the gas.

Just then, an Infected stepped out from behind a house on the corner, heading north—no doubt going to join the hundred or so of his brethren partying around the bonfire. He saw them just as they saw him.

Worse, a group of Infecteds at the fire turned and looked straight at them, too, as if the first one's seeing them somehow tipped off the rest. That group started south, toward them, as did the lone Infected on Harvest.

Light didn't need Fallon to tell him what to do next.

"Path of least resistance," he said, and gunned it. Light mowed the single Infected down like he was a stalk of wheat and the Ford F-350 Super Duty was a seven-ton scythe in Tuxedo Black Metallic, then tore down Harvest and made the left, leaving the group of Infecteds that had spotted them still heading south to where they had been, while they were now headed north.

He made it to McLellan, turned right, and drove slowly down the street, so as not to attract the attention of the remaining Infecteds burning down Deano's Custom Painting and the other businesses in the industrial park. He watched the rearview, but no swarm appeared. It looked like they had gotten away clean.

"Well, looks like we were wrong about the monkeys," he said then.

Fallon looked at him, her brow creasing in confusion.

"Wrong, how?"

"I think they skipped Shakespeare and went right to Stephen King."

## CHAPTER 41

*14 hours*

**"W**hat's the best way in, Book?" Fallon asked, glad she no longer had to hide her conversations with him from the others—or the Raiders. The Sykos hadn't been happy to learn she'd kept the information from them, of course, but psychopaths were inveterate secret-keepers, and none of them could honestly say they wouldn't have done the same thing in her position. She had known she'd have to tell them soon, anyway, even letting Book listen in while she did. If she hoped to get inside a cartel-infested country club, she would need their help, and another bullshit story about first-aid kits wouldn't fly.

Although every time she caught a glimpse of Sansome's face in the mirror, she wished they had one. And maybe a plastic surgeon.

"Looks like the Tempe Canal runs along the southern border of the golf course. There's an access road that follows the canal, though it's on the south side and ends at the tennis courts. But, wait, let me zoom in . . . yes, it looks like there's a bridge for golf carts to cross over the canal not far from there. There's a pool house you can use for cover if you approach from that direction, and a ton of cars still in the southern parking lot. The loading dock is there, close to the massed heat signatures in the clubhouse—which I'm assuming are near the kitchens, since humans like to be around their food source."

"Infecteds, too," Fallon muttered.

"Them, too. But they're like locusts—they devour all the resources a place has to offer, then move on. Since these signatures have pretty much stayed in this area for at least a few hours, I'm going to say they're human, and the people you're looking for are probably there."

Book's words prompted a question she hadn't even considered.

"Do Infecteds sleep? Maybe they have nests?"

Book didn't answer immediately, and she realized the question had probably never occurred to him, either.

"What the hell are you talking to that bookworm about, Fallon? Nests of Infecteds?"

She looked at Light, who had one eye on her and one on the road as he drove. Luckily, there were no other cars moving and no pedestrians they didn't *want* to run over, so his divided attention didn't pose as much of a danger as it might have otherwise.

"Book says there's a heat signature in the back of the clubhouse that hasn't moved much. He thinks that means they're human. I'm . . . not quite as sure, I guess."

"Well, we've seen them at all hours, so we don't have evidence that they need to sleep," Pybus interjected thoughtfully. "But we do know they started out as human, and are still alive in bodies that have basic human limitations, even with their rage-induced strength. I'd say that alone would require them to sleep. If not, they couldn't survive very long—weeks, at most."

"Too bad we don't have weeks to just let them burn out and extinguish themselves," Fallon said, thinking Pybus probably had the right of it—the virus kept them from sleeping and would eventually kill them because of it. Maybe they needed to eat other people's brains in order to keep their own synapses firing, so they could survive that much longer.

She wondered, suddenly, if Robbins or Thurman had acquired a few to study back at PIR, in order to answer questions just like this. But if they had, Book would know, wouldn't he?

"Book?"

"I don't think they sleep."

Something in his voice made her certain her hunch was right.

"Because the ones you're studying haven't yet?"

Book's silence was confirmation enough.

Fallon had used the basic human rights argument when they'd experimented on Warga, and it hadn't worked. She was pretty sure Robbins wouldn't buy basic used-to-be-human rights, either.

"Okay, we'll assume they're human and head in through the loading dock. Thanks for the help, Book."

"No problem," he said. "But, Fallon—do me a favor?"

His tone was anxious, and Fallon frowned.

"Of course, Book. Anything."

"Just hurry. The brass are breathing down my neck; I don't have to tell you how much is riding on a speedy end to this mission. And I've gone so far off the reservation now with this Jameson thing, there might be no getting back on. At some point, even if you succeed— and I still believe you can—there'll be an after-action review, and all the ways I broke the rules will come out. So . . . save the world, save my ass."

Fallon knew that was a pop culture reference of some sort—from a TV show, maybe, or a movie— but she didn't get it. What she *did* get was that helping her retrieve the prototype was probably going to cost Book his job.

She felt bad about it, but not bad enough to abandon the prototype, especially when she was so close to it. And it had to be there—Carmen's men couldn't take Elliott out of the city, so they'd hole up like rats someplace they thought was safe until the storm blew over. Except this storm wasn't going to blow over—it was going to blow down their back door.

"I'll do what I can, Book."

"I know," he said quietly, his confidence twisting her gut with guilt. "You always do."

She let the conversation lag after that. What more was there to say, really? He expected her to pull a miracle out of her ass. They all did. If she wasn't a psychopath, the stress of so much regard would drive her crazy. Instead, it was kind of pissing her off.

"We're at the canal," Light said. "Unless there's more than one around here."

"No, this is it," Fallon replied. "That's the golf course, there. Take a left on the service road. And find someplace to hide the truck."

"How about in plain sight?"

They were passing what looked like the back side of a hotel, complete with a parking lot half-filled with cars.

"Perfect."

Light drove over the xeriscaping separating the building from the access road, pulled into a parking spot, and they all piled out, weapons in hand. As they walked west along the service road, keeping to the trees as much as possible, Fallon noticed a residential area to the southwest of them, adjacent to the hotel. A cinder-block wall separated the two, but it ended where the property line intersected the road right-of-way, and was purely ornamental in nature since it didn't actually close either property off. The hotel property, residential neighborhood, and a larger, private residential lot all met in that corner, so there was a second cinder-block wall—this one actually functional, surrounding the private lot—six feet from the first one, forming a sort of corridor that led right from the neighborhood to the canal, a virtual river of death for any child who stumbled that far out of their parents' sight.

Fallon peered in that direction as they went, looking for signs of smoke. She was so focused on the sky and rooftops that it took her a moment to realize there was movement on the streets below—a lot of it.

"Infecteds!" Lilith hissed at the same time.

A mob of Infecteds moved along the part of the residential street they could see, with groups peeling off to do the by-now-familiar house-to-house search.

"Hurry! Behind the wall before they see us!"

Fallon didn't have to tell them which wall she meant; they all sprinted for the one that enclosed the private lot, then kept going.

And almost ran right into a lone Infected crossing the golf cart bridge.

Instead of stopping, Fallon ran right at him. The others trailed, not daring to shoot for fear of hitting her or alerting the horde just one street over.

She knew she was taking a risk. If there were more Infecteds on the golf course, this one would lead them right to the Sykos. But he'd already seen them, and they couldn't risk shooting him. So she did the next best thing.

She slammed into him with her shoulder, toppling him into the canal.

"Come on!" she said to the others, barely slowing

as she made for the tennis courts, which were screened off on the south and west and offered plenty of cover.

Once there, she stopped, grabbing the chain-link fence with one hand as she bent over and tried to catch her breath.

"Might want to vomit while you're down there," Light, who was barely panting, said.

Fallon straightened.

"Why?"

"Take a gander at the roof of the clubhouse."

She looked where he was pointing. There were sentries perched on the apexes of the dual-framed construction like gargoyles on Notre Dame, looking in all directions for approaching threats.

"Shit," she said, then her gaze fell on the pool near the courts, and she had an idea.

The patio of the pool house-slash-bar hid them from the sentries' view without hindering the Sykos', and the open counter provided easy access to its interior.

"Quick, you guys hide out in the pool house. I'll be back in a minute."

"What? Why?" Light demanded to know. "Where do you think you're going?"

"Just following the Raiders' example."

"That's comforting."

Fallon flashed him a smile before taking off at a dead run back in the direction they'd come. She hoped they'd follow her instructions; if not, they were probably going to regret it pretty quickly.

It only took a minute or two to get back to the

bridge. The Infected was still splashing in the canal, unable to get out.

"Hey, Red-eye!" she called, waving to get his attention. When he looked at her, his irises were brown disks in a sea of blood. It looked like the worst case of subjunctival hemorrhage she'd ever seen. She doubted the dirty canal water made it any better. "Tell your friends to catch me if they can!" Then she turned and jogged slowly away, so the Infected could clearly see she was headed toward the clubhouse by way of the pool and tennis courts.

Once she got to the pool house, she was hidden from the Infected's view, as well as from that of the sentries. There was no sign of the other Sykos. And the door was too far down the eastern wall; if she tried for it, she'd risk being seen from the clubhouse. Instead, she climbed over the open counter, only to step on Pybus, who was crouched behind it on the other side, along with the rest of them.

"Ow!" he said, and she immediately shushed him as she stepped unsteadily off his shoulder, onto the sticky bar floor, and into a yeasty miasma.

"Shh! They're coming!" She hoped, anyway.

The Sykos fell silent as they all listened for the shuffle of a multitude of footsteps. When Fallon figured they'd waited ten minutes without the larger group of Infecteds showing up, she decided her theory was wrong. However they were communicating, it wasn't telepathically, since the Infected in the canal knew right where she'd gone. She was about to stand up when Pybus grabbed her arm, shaking his head and pointing to his ear with his other hand.

She stopped and listened, straining to hear over the water lapping gently against the sides of the pool and the breeze rustling the leaves of the trees and the tennis-court screens.

There it was. They *were* coming.

Now she just had to hope they didn't decide to do a search of this place before heading up to the clubhouse. She cast about the small bar for another exit just in case, saw a door on the north wall that must lead outside, judging by the light coming through the small inset square of opaque glass that served as a window. She was just thinking they could go out that way when a shadow fell across it. And then another and another and another as the Infecteds split around the pool house, a beer-scented island in their sweat-scented stream.

They waited until the shadows and the sound of footsteps had passed before daring to peer over the counter at the pool deck and tennis courts.

Empty.

Then the gunfire started, and Fallon smiled. Not only had she confirmed her theory that the Infecteds could in fact communicate via some other means than technology, she'd also led them right into a trap. A trap that would keep the cartel sentries too busy to notice when the Sykos snuck in the back door.

## CHAPTER 42

*13 hours*

**T**he receiving area inside the loading dock was empty, probably because everyone who'd been guarding it had gone outside to fight the Infecteds. With the big loading door closed, it was dimly lit, but Fallon could see receiving tables, stacks of empty, flattened boxes, and another area set up with shipping materials. Beyond those were tall shelving units holding supplies that appeared to be separated into kitchen and bar, pro shop, and miscellaneous categories. The floor was smooth concrete, zigzagged by tire marks from the forklift sitting in a corner. The combined aromas of stale coffee sitting in a pot, exhaust, spoiling food, sweat, and the vanishing dreams of minimum-wage shipping and receiving workers made the whole place smell musty and grim.

Holding her M4 at the ready, Fallon led the others through the maze of shelves. An open doorway on the far side of the warehouse area hinted at a brightly lit hallway. Its pale yellow walls made her think of afternoon sunlight on sails in Tempe Town Lake, not far from where they'd escaped Reedley's Raiders.

Heading for that opening, she caught herself expecting to face Infecteds on the other side, then remembered they were all outdoors. She could still hear the crack of gunshots as the cartel thugs defended their hideout. It disturbed her that her theory had proved out—what one Infected saw could somehow be communicated to the rest. That explained how they could plan ambushes, which were growing ever more sophisticated. Some Infecteds had seen the patrol at various points along their route, so had probably communicated to others the general path the patrol was following. Once the patrol turned toward Tempe, it was probably clear that they would check out the neighborhood with the most reported Infected action.

Maybe that had all been part of the trap.

Fallon had a psychopathic brain structure, but she wasn't entirely fearless. The idea of intelligent Infecteds sent a chill from her neck to the bottom of her spine.

When the Sykos neared the doorway, Light and Warga moved ahead of her. Light flattened himself against the wall, then took a quick peek through the opening. He nodded, and Warga went to the other side, repeating Light's action. When both were satisfied that the coast was clear, they entered it simultaneously, guns ready, Warga looking high and Light low. Fallon went in behind them, then Litlith and Pybus. Sansome brought up the rear. They were in a long, well-lit corridor. Framed photographs of golfers who Fallon assumed were famous hung on the wall, but there was only one other opening, at the far end. The hallway seemed to exist only to provide a buffer between the sounds and smells of the receiving dock and the parts of the building enjoyed by members.

Warga and Light repeated their performance at the corridor's end. It connected with another hall, this one containing club offices and public restrooms. Fallon had just passed the men's room door when it opened with a squeak. A man emerged, looking down, right hand checking his zipper. Sensing the Sykos, he looked up, said, "Hey!" and reached for a gun in a hip holster. Fallon and Lilith both reacted at the same time, firing. The man jerked backward, slammed into the men's room door, and fell, half-in and half-out,

"Dammit!" Fallon said. "I guess they know we're here."

A momentary pang struck her. These were human beings they were killing—or about to kill, since she knew this man was probably only the first. *Uninfected.* It was different . . . or it should have been.

She looked at the corpse again, didn't feel much at all, and decided she was okay with that.

"Which way?" Light asked.

Fallon did a quick mental calculation, then pointed

to her right. "Down there," she said. The left seemed to head toward the public areas, whereas to the right, past the offices at the hallway's end, stood double doors that looked like they might open into a kitchen. It made sense that food deliveries wouldn't go past the areas frequented by guests.

They were halfway there when those double doors swung open and two guys carrying automatic weapons burst into the corridor. They were young and Hispanic, both lean, wearing designer jeans and fancy shirts that were immediately torn to shreds by rounds from the Sykos' guns. As they fell, the Sykos—Warga in the lead now—raced to the double doors. There were windows inset from about chest high on Fallon, and he peered through those for a few seconds before kicking the left-hand door open. The others went through right behind him.

They found themselves in a good-sized restaurant kitchen. There was a lot of stainless steel: worktables, sinks, drainboards, and more, some of it stained despite the name. The gigantic stove and the door to a walk-in freezer were also stainless steel. The Infected corpse and the guy in kitchen whites with his head smashed open—whom the Infected had been feeding on when she was found and shot to death—weren't stainless steel, though, and neither were the flies buzzing around them and the bloody tile floor on which they lay.

They checked the kitchen for living people and found none. Fallon was watching Lilith—who as far as

Fallon knew had just shot someone for the first time in her life—to determine whether the girl was in a state of shock. Nobody had spoken much since the guy from the restroom had been killed, but Fallon had noticed that Lilith seemed almost untethered from what was going on around her. She hadn't looked at the body of the man she'd shot, or those of the two guys who'd come out of the kitchen, or even at the kitchen worker and the Infected who'd made a Happy Meal of him. She hadn't looked at much at all, just kind of stared straight ahead and followed the other Sykos. When the group had split up in the kitchen, some to check the walk-in, others to look underneath the worktables to make sure no one was hiding there, Lilith had simply stalled out, as if pulled in so many directions, she didn't know where to go.

Another set of double doors, this one windowless, probably led into the restaurant itself. That was their next goal, Fallon decided. She would stay close to Lilith when they went in.

With the kitchen cleared, she motioned to Light, who nodded once, then crossed to the second set of doors. Gun ready, he pushed one of them out just enough to see through the gap.

Rounds from an automatic weapon perforated the door. Light threw himself back against the wall, but not before one of the bullets creased his side. He paled and put his hand there, and it came away bloody. He took a few seconds to catch his breath, then readied his M249 again and pointed toward the doors. The other

Sykos took positions in the kitchen where they were at least partially protected by the stainless steel fixtures and aimed their guns at the doorway. Except for Lilith. She just stood there until Fallon pulled the girl down beside her.

When everyone was ready, Light kicked the nearest door wide open, then drew back again, lowering his gun and opening fire. Everybody else followed suit, firing through the doorway as the door swung back and forth in ever-smaller arcs, and through the other door. They returned the shots coming their way by about ten to one, Fallon figured.

When she raised her fist, everybody stopped shooting. The place was quiet, except for the echoes of gunfire, which might just have been a ringing in her ears. There was no answering fire coming from the far side of the doors. Leaning against the wall, clearly in pain, Light used the barrel of his machine gun to nudge the near door open again.

Nothing.

Fallon caught his eye and mouthed, "Are you okay?"

Light nodded. "Flesh wound," he mouthed back. Again using his gun, he pushed the door open wider. Still no response. He dared to step in front of it, a little unsteady on his feet. This time, when he opened the door, he looked at what was on the other side. Satisfied, he caught the door before it closed, held it open, and stepped through.

A gunman was dead on the other side. He'd been sitting at a table, facing the door. When the volley of bullets hit, he'd been knocked backward, still in the chair—the crash no doubt drowned out by the roar of the guns—and riddled with bullets. Blood had pooled around him, and more was spattered on the wall behind him, along with a couple dozen bullet holes.

The restaurant angled toward the clubhouse's main lobby, and from here they couldn't see what might wait past the corner. Fallon took a last look at Lilith, who seemed to be coming out of her waking trance, and at Light, whose color was returning slowly, then went to the corner, peeked, then stepped into the open. She heard the others follow, but her gaze was fixed dead ahead.

On Elliott Jameson.

And the man holding a gun to Elliott's head.

"I would lower your guns," the man said. He had a slight lisp, so "guns" became "gunthh." He was Hispanic, and his English was spoken with an accent, but not much of one. Fallon thought he had probably grown up in the U.S. He wore an off-white Western-cut blazer, a black Western shirt with pearl snaps, black jeans, and white ostrich boots with toes that came to an extreme point. He had short, neatly trimmed black hair. There was a thatch of beard beneath his lower lip, less than an inch across but trailing all the way down his chin. He had to point the gun up to aim at Elliott's head because Elliott was hanging from a ceiling beam by his wrists.

He was naked, and covered with bruises, welts, and gashes. So much blood was smeared on his flesh that in some places Fallon couldn't tell whether he was bruised or not. One shoulder appeared to have been dislocated. His face was pulpy, his right eye closed almost completely and his left just a slit, his lips swollen to two or three times their normal size. Both cheeks were cut, and blood had caked at the corners of his mouth. He saw Fallon. She could tell that by the way his left eye fixed on her. But he didn't acknowledge her presence. She wondered how much of a beating his brain had taken.

Having absorbed both Elliott's condition and the man holding the gun on him, she took the rest of the scene in with a glance. Standing behind them was a huge man, slope-shouldered and barrel-chested, with a big, tight gut and powerful arms. He was shirtless, but his arms, torso, and neck were covered with so many tattoos, it was hard to tell at first. His fists were encased in tight leather gloves, and he was bloody up to his elbows. That blood, Fallon was certain, was Elliott's, not his own. Two other men, both younger, longer-haired, in skintight Western wear, stood behind the others, pointing their machine pistols at the Sykos.

"Please," the man with the gun on Elliott said. "Lower them."

Fallon lowered her M4. As she did, her gaze dropped to a table, slightly behind where Elliott hung. On the table, along with what she supposed were various implements of torture, was her prototype.

"Thank you," the man said. "Now the rest of you."

"I don't think so, pal," Warga said. "There are more

of us, and we have bigger guns. Tell your boys to put theirs down. I don't know who that side of beef is, and I don't care. I'll shoot him, too, if it means I get to shoot you and the big ugly there."

The man glanced at his companions. They held their guns steady. He looked back at the Sykos. Ditto. He smiled, showing two gold teeth along with the rest.

"It appears we have—although I am loath to use the term—a Mexican standoff. Some irony there, yes?"

"What have you done, Elliott?" Fallon asked, ignoring the man's lame joke. "What the *fuck* were you thinking?"

His left eye rolled back in his head, and for a she was afraid he was losing consciousness. But then it came back and his mouth opened. Blood beaded on his split, ruined lips. When he spoke, it was so softly that he was hard to hear, and the words were slurred, almost unintelligible.

"Gamez," she thought he said.

"Carmen Gamez?"

"Unh . . . 'rique."

"Enrique Gamez." Carmen's late husband. Head of the Gamez Cartel. Most drug kingpins were narcissists, but not many had the stones to name their cartels after themselves rather than adopting the name of the region they called home.

"Yuh."

"What about him?" She thought she had already figured it out, though, and she was too impatient to wait for him to stutter through it. "You were going to sell it to him, weren't you? Our prototype. The MEIADD."

"Yuh."

"Why? We were making decent money. And it would have been much, much more when we were able to develop it for commercial use."

"Not . . . enough. Not fast enough . . ."

Part of her wasn't at all surprised. Elliott was a genius, but the fact that he could walk down a city street without being recognized as one always grated on him. He wanted fame, but he would settle for money. "But . . . a criminal like that? A drug cartel? Why?"

"Had . . . plenty of . . . cash. Willing to spend."

"What would he want with MEIADD? Doesn't he know a psychopath when he hires one?"

"Does . . . more than you think."

"Like what?"

"Scans brains for . . . psychopathic structure."

"Well, yeah. That's its intended use."

"Tweak the programming . . . it can dial them down."

"Right. That was always the goal. Diagnosis and treatment in the same device."

"Yuh."

"Still, why would Gamez want that? Doesn't he want psychos on his payroll?"

"Tweak . . . another way . . . ramps them up. *Way* up."

It was almost as if he'd been talking to SAC

Ramirez. "We never intended for that capability to be built into it."

"You didn't. I did. Told . . . Gamez I could."

"This is all so interesting," the man with the gun on Elliott said. "Truly. But we're in the middle of something, here, and—"

"One more word from you, and I'll shoot you where you stand," Warga warned.

"Before he does, I'll shoot you where you fuck," Lilith added. "Guess which one will hurt more?"

The man lowered the gun and stepped away from Elliott. The torturer had become a statue, unmoving, barely breathing. The two guys in back looked at each other, confused, then lowered their guns. Fallon continued her questions.

"So Gamez agreed to buy it, and in return you bastardized our scientific work to create something that could provide him with an army of bloodthirsty psychopaths. Soldiers who would kill anyone or anything one minute, but whose murderous impulses could be tamped down the next. That about sum it up, Elliott?"

"Yuh."

"And after Enrique died, Carmen decided she still wanted it. So you made plans to meet her in the city with it, and you stole it from the lab."

"Fallon . . . I—"

"If you're thinking about apologizing, save it," she said. "If these guys hadn't already beat the crap out of you, I'd pay them to do it."

Elliott closed both eyes. When he opened the left

one again, there might have been a tear in it. Then again, it could have been a trick of the light.

"One thing I don't get," Fallon said. "They have it, now. Why are you still hanging there? Why haven't they killed you?"

"I . . . had a plane ticket. Argentina. But the . . . airport was closed. I needed . . . their help to get out of Phoenix . . . alive. Told Carmen . . . if they got me out . . . they could have the key. They already . . . had the MEIADD . . . so the key was my only . . . bargaining chip." He twitched his head in the direction of the guy in the white boots. "In . . . stead of helping me get out . . . Luis brought me here."

"Nobody's getting out, Elliott. There was nothing they could have done for you."

"They are professional smugglers," Pybus pointed out. "If anybody could do it, they could. There's probably a tunnel half-dug under the fence already."

Fallon shot him a warning glance, and he clammed up. She turned her gaze to Luis. "So you decided it would be easier to torture it out of him? Or was it just more fun?"

"Efficient," Luis said. "And right. He agreed to certain terms, then refused to follow through. When Carmen gets here, she will—"

Fallon cut him off. "Carmen won't do anything, and you won't be seeing her again. Not this side of hell."

She stepped forward. The two gunmen started to raise their weapons, but a rustling behind her let her know that all the Sykos had just trained their guns on the young thugs. They lowered their guns again.

Fallon kept going. Close enough to Elliott to smell blood and piss and despair, then between him and the torturer. On him, she smelled blood and rank sweat. On Luis, too much cologne, and maybe some tequila. She went to the table behind him, picked up the MEIADD prototype and the small, stylized gold cross and chain lying beside it. The MEIADD was a white plastic cylinder, slightly larger than a standard temporal scanning thermometer. Instead of a single point of focus, at the business end it branched out into three sections, each with a different type of scanner. By combining electro-encephalography, voxel-based morphometry, and near-infrared spectroscopy, the MEIADD could produce a brain image almost as accurate and detailed as an fMRI. The idea was that it would be paired with a smartphone app, so it could be a basic part of medical kits for combat medics and EMTs, and might one day be included in every home or business first-aid kit. Fallon and Elliott had decided to take it a step further and had arrived at a method of using the technology to boost the electrical activity of those brain cells within the paralimbic region, resulting in increased performance, which would at least temporarily dampen psychopathic tendencies.

Obviously, Elliott had other ideas.

"These belong to me," she said. "And I'll be leaving with them. Anybody have a problem with that?"

"He's going to need that crucifix," Luis said. "I'll shoot your friend as soon as you're out the door."

Fallon spent a moment searching for feelings of pity or empathy, even remorse, but she couldn't find any.

Maybe it was her inner psychopath emerging in the face of all the horror she had seen in the zone. Maybe proximity to the Sykos brought it out. It was possible that she was succumbing to Crazy 8s. She didn't care.

"Elliott," she said, "I used to like you. Now?" She stopped in front of him, gave him a little bit of a spin. He hung there, swaying back and forth. "Now I just hope it hurts." To Luis, she added, "He's never prayed a day in his life. And this isn't a crucifix."

His jaw dropped open as he realized what she meant. The key had been in his hands the whole time. His gun came up, as did those of his thugs, but they never had a chance. The Sykos opened fire and ripped them apart.

Fallon didn't flinch when the gunfire started, just watched dispassionately as three more humans fell to her team. When it finished, she gave a finger wave to Elliott and headed for the restaurant's main door. "You guys coming?" she asked as she went.

"What about him?" Light asked.

Fallon stopped, glanced back at Elliott. Holding her prototype in her right hand, she felt a surge of triumph. Swollen with it, she smiled and shrugged.

"Fuck him. Leave him to the Infecteds. He doesn't deserve any better."

She turned and went through the door, then held it for the others before she let it swing closed.

From inside, she thought she heard Elliott calling her name, maybe trying to beg for his life. She shook her head. He really should know better than to expect mercy from a psychopath.

# PART III

# THE HIVE

# CHAPTER 43

*12 hours*

There were still sentries on the roof picking off Infecteds, but fewer than before. Fallon imagined some had fled, others fallen. But the remaining cartel thugs were still a threat, so when the Sykos left the clubhouse, they retraced their route through the loading dock, around the parking lot, using the cars for cover, and back to the pool house.

There, the Sykos insisted on raiding the bar for whatever food hadn't rotted, and Fallon let them. Even as they'd been sneaking back around the cars, it had been easy to see the carpet of Infected bodies covering the putting green. She imagined some of the corpses were actually cartel members but hadn't been able to tell from that distance and hadn't really cared. As long as they weren't around to bother her Sykos, she was happy.

"I'm gonna take a leak," Warga said.

"Not in the pool!" Lilith exclaimed, her nose wrinkling in disgust at the thought. "That's gross!"

"They got bathrooms in the pool house, genius," Warga replied, turning on his heel before he could see Lilith giving him the finger.

Pybus found a big plastic jar of pretzels that weren't too stale and a similar one of cheese puffs. Someone had left the lid partially off the cheese puffs, though, and they were crawling with ants. Sansome found some small bags of salt and vinegar chips, and Lilith found a single unopened Coke in the back of the fridge and couldn't keep from crowing in delight.

The Sykos sat in a circle sharing the feast of carbs, each with a glass of flat club soda from the tap. Except for Lilith, who was lovingly savoring her caffeine fix.

And Light, who had treated his wound with bar rags and water, then spent the rest of his time going from the bar counter to the back door, keeping watch.

The chips were as advertised and the pretzels almost as salty, and Fallon found herself sharing Warga's urge to use the bathroom. She excused herself and went over the counter after Light declared it clear.

The pool house hadn't been used in days, but was still damp and smelled of chlorine and, faintly, of mildew. She went in the side marked with the figure in a dress, was pleasantly surprised to find the locker room and changing areas free of corpses. She ignored the open showers and went over to the stalls, which thankfully had doors. One thing it had been hard to maintain while traveling with the Sykos was any sense of personal privacy. She was glad to be able to use the bathroom without having at least Lilith tagging along.

She rose, pulled up her pants, and went to flush, then thought better of it—the noise might attract unwanted attention. After rebuttoning and zipping everything that needed it, she opened the door.

Warga grabbed her by the throat, yanked her out of the stall, and slammed her up against the wall, all while jamming a huge wad of toilet paper in her mouth, effectively gagging her.

"Should have left them down, bitch."

He spun her around and shoved her up against the wall again, only this time, something cold and sharp pricked at her neck. A knife.

*Shit.*

She'd been struggling, trying to get her hand on a Glock, but she was a scientist who spent all her time in the lab, whereas he'd had little to do in prison except work out and dream of a moment like this. And she knew he would cut her in an instant—he was probably so jacked up from all the blood and violence, he'd have no problem desecrating her corpse while it was still warm, or even raping her while she died.

Because that's what he intended to do, she knew. In the back of her mind, she'd been expecting this though she hadn't been entirely sure it would be her and not Lilith. Choosing Fallon made sense, though—she was the one who'd been riding herd on him since they entered the zone, and now he wanted his turn.

"Oh my God, Fallon! Shit! I don't know what to do!" Book's voice in her ear was horrified and frantic, but there was nothing the analyst *could* do—she had the only two-way, so he couldn't alert the rest of the Sykos. She was on her own, and all that was left was for him to bear testament to her shame.

Warga grabbed her Glocks and tossed them into the showers, then did the same with the rest of her weapons, patting her down slowly and with great relish. When he was sure she was defenseless, he pushed against her from behind, rubbing his warm crotch against her as he reached around to undo her pants. All the while, the knife remained steady at her throat. Warga hadn't forgotten his moves while in prison, and he'd perfected them long before that. His wound didn't seem to affect his upper-body strength.

He jerked her pants down and grabbed a handful of bare ass, squeezing hard enough to bruise, then started on his own pants.

"You should have let me do one of those Army bitches before we left, or even Goth Girl. But, no, you had to spoil my fun and just let me get more and more worked up by all the shootin' and dyin'. So since I can't have them, I'm just going to use you, Doc. And I'm going to enjoy every quick minute of it."

*Maybe it won't be that bad,* she thought, her heart hammering beneath his blade. Maybe her psychopathy would kick in full force and she'd go numb, not feel it beyond the physical aspects. Maybe it wouldn't affect her as much later. For now, though, she was terrified, and more pissed off than she'd ever been in her life.

He'd just gotten himself free and was rubbing up against the crack of her ass when there was a sound like a bear roaring and feet slapping across turquoise tiles. Then Warga was being pulled off her, his knife scoring her throat as his arm was jerked away.

When she turned, Sansome was punching Warga in the face, then in the gut. Warga's knife went flying, and after jerking her pants back up, Fallon scrambled for it as the blade got kicked away from her by someone's foot.

She snatched it off the cool tiles, then straightened to see Warga returning Sansome's assault blow for blow. He focused his attack on Sansome's battered face, and it was working. Sansome was losing ground.

She was behind Warga and to his left. Without thinking, she rushed forward and drove his knife into his back, just below the rib cage and angled upward.

Warga cried out in pain, and Sansome punched him again as warm blood rushed out over Fallon's hand. As it coated her skin, she twisted the blade in deep, imagining it piercing his ascending colon and tearing into his liver. She didn't think it was long enough to reach his lung, but she drove it in again, hoping. His accompanying scream was gratifying.

*Fuck with me, you bastard, and this is what you get.* Fallon had no idea where the thought had come from, but she welcomed it.

Finally noticing what she was doing, Sansome punched Warga again, this time in the gut, which pushed his organs back against the knife, causing even more damage. Then Fallon pulled the knife out, stepped back, and together they watched Warga fall.

"Thanks," she said to Sansome.

He shook his head. "Not done yet."

Sansome held his hand out for the knife, and Fallon didn't hesitate. Then the Syko knelt beside Warga and began hacking through his neck while he was still alive to enjoy every not-quick minute of it.

"Jesus, Fallon," Book breathed in her ear, and she realized that it would probably be better for all of them if the brass back at PIR didn't see this part. She blinked the Morse code.

"What was that, Fallon? That wasn't the 'Off' command."

"Stop the feed! I'm a little distracted here."

"What? I can't—"

"Just do it. You don't want to see this, anyway."

He was silent after that though she had no way of knowing whether he'd complied with her request or not. For his sake, more than her own, she hoped he had. For her part—assuming they had no video to contradict her story—she'd just claim Warga had died of the wounds she'd inflicted in self-defense, and they'd never be able to prove otherwise.

It was a slow, bloody business, and Fallon had time to adjust her clothing, wash her hands, and gather her weapons back up. While in the stall collecting her

Glocks, Fallon wished she had time to shower, to try and scrub the feel of Warga's skin off of hers, but she had a feeling even steel wool wouldn't work for that. Acid, maybe.

When she turned back to Sansome, he was holding up Warga's severed head by the hair, like some sort of barbarian out of a fantasy novel.

"What are you going to do with it?" she asked curiously. He offered it to her. "No, thank you. I don't need any more reminders of that piece of shit."

Sansome's expression brightened.

"That's perfect."

He walked over to the nearest stall and dropped Warga's head in the toilet, where it landed with a pink splash. He turned back to her, smiling.

"That's where shit belongs, right?"

"Yes, Joe. Yes, it definitely is."

# CHAPTER 44

*10 hours*

**T**he sun stroked the western horizon in a sky painted in rose and tangerine and watermelon pink and blood red by the smoke filling the Valley. The shadows lengthened lazily, and the strident buzz of crickets filled the air, just like when the world had been sane. Light saw it when he woke from a doze, deep enough that he had been dreaming that he had been back on a tree-lined street in northern Virginia, in a neighborhood that transitioned from urban to semi-suburban but where the only constant was poverty. He still thought of that street as *home* despite having been away from it three times as many years as he had lived there.

The street looked pleasant enough if you were just passing through, but to Henry Todd Light, it had been a pathway to pain and fear and humiliation because it led toward home, and home was the worst place. In the dream, he had been walking away from home, but with each step another bug landed on him—moths and spiders and flies and grasshoppers and deer ticks and more—and each one seemed to weigh ten pounds, so whenever another one lit on him, he was weighed down that much more. He was beginning to think he would never make it to the end of the first block, much less farther than that, because he just *could not* bear up under the burden.

Then his hand slipped off the stock of his M249, and he woke with a start. He blinked and looked around to see who had noticed and who might if he just quietly slipped away. Lilith was sound asleep, Fallon was staring off into some big nowhere. Sansome sat there looking like his brain had taken a vacation far away. Only Pybus might have seen him. He was sitting across from Light, his head and shoulders moving to music only he could hear, his fingers rubbing across each other in silent snaps, keeping the bass line, Light thought. There was a smile on his face. When Light caught his gaze, Pybus tossed him a smile and a nod before he went back to grooving to unheard tunes.

"How long has it been?" Light asked, speaking to no one in particular.

Fallon's head jerked a little. "How long for what?"

"Since we've heard gunfire or seen an Infected."

"Must be close to an hour," Fallon said.

"Ask your boyfriend. He'll know."

"My what?" she asked. Then she went quiet for a moment. "Book says it's been fifty-two minutes."

"Almost twilight, Fallon. I think the coast is plenty clear. Let's get back to the truck."

"I'll take a look." She started to stand, winced.

"Stiff muscles," Light said. "Stretch a little. I'll check."

He got up easily, went up on tiptoe, hands elevated, and popped his back. Then he walked out into the gloaming and listened to the crickets, who were neither Infecteds nor gunfire. He saw nothing moving except soft magenta clouds, drifting as if they had no cares, as if no one in the world had a care.

The only way that could happen, he knew, was if there were no one in the world.

He turned back to the bar. "It's clear," he said. "Let's motor."

Once everybody was conscious again, they made their way back over the bridge, past the walls, and to the hotel or whatever it was, where they had left the truck. Two new corpses decorated the parking lot; both had undergone the crude craniotomies that had become so familiar. Whoever had first called the skull a brainpan probably had no idea how right they would become.

They looked like a thirtysomething couple. They had probably been holed up inside, thought they'd seen an opportunity, and made a run for their car. They didn't make it. Which put Light a little more on his guard because he and his fellow Sykos were doing the exact same thing. Only difference was they had big guns and no compunctions about using them.

But it was genuinely clear. Nothing attacked; the only living thing Light saw was a raven that landed on a wall, cawed once, then hopped to a different spot on the same wall before taking flight. The truck was where they'd left it. Light climbed into his usual spot behind the wheel, waited for the others to settle, and cranked the big V8 diesel. He reversed quickly out of the parking space, shifted into DRIVE, and headed for the service road.

**E**n route to the meteor site, they saw a few more Infecteds across the canal, on the golf course. Some wandered aimlessly among the holes. Some looked up from snacks—cartel sentries, most likely. Others just stood and watched the Sykos go by. None of them made a move toward the truck, but every one of them stared at it.

"It's like they're expecting us," Fallon said. "Like they know where we are, when we're coming. Like they're keeping track."

"It's fucking creepy," Lilith opined.

Pybus cleared his throat. "I believe . . ." the old man started. "I believe that they *do* know where we are. If one can see us, they all can see us."

"I've been thinking that, too," Fallon said. "But how?"

"This is my theory, Doctor. I recognize how it sounds, but bear with me for a few moments."

"Just get to it!" Lilith snapped.

"Patience, young lady, is a virtue you will learn by the time you reach my age."

"If," Sansome said.

"Beg your pardon?"

"*If* she reaches your age. Or mine. We'll all be lucky to make it another day."

"Pessimism, Mr. Sansome, does not become you."

Light glanced in the rearview. "I think all our tempers are a little short," he said. "What's your theory?"

"A hive mind," Pybus said.

"A what?" Lilith asked.

"I believe they're part of a hive mind. It's sometimes called a group mind. A shared consciousness, a swarm intelligence. Think of it in whatever fashion makes sense to you, if any do. Basically, all their minds are linked. What one thinks, they all think. What one sees or hears, they all see or hear."

"That would be confusing as hell," Light said.

"Not if you were used to it. Not if it was all you'd ever known. It would be as natural as your solitary mind is to you. Perhaps more so. In a hive mind, the individual barely exists. Think of an ant colony, or a beehive. You don't imagine that an ant has much sense of itself, do you? No, it functions as part of the colony, performing whatever task is necessary for the good of the whole."

"But the Infecteds were people," Fallon said. "Just days ago. Less."

"They were, until Crazy 8s took control of their brains. It shut down consciousness of the self and linked each Infected to all the others."

"And that's why they're getting smarter?" Fallon asked. "Because there are getting to be more of them, so they can amass experience and intelligence?"

"Perhaps. Remember, I'm only speculating about all this."

"It makes sense," Fallon said. "The virus attacks the brain, and once it's there, it begins to consume it. But no organism wants to destroy its host. So the Infecteds are driven to eat more brains, healthy ones. That's not going to sustain the virus indefinitely, but the Infected doesn't know that. It's almost like a reflex at that point. The virus wants brain matter, the virus controls the Infected, so the Infected wants brain matter. There's a parasitic fungus that does the same thing with ants— they call them zombie ants because the fungus takes over their brains, then their bodies."

"So then why are we immune?" Light asked. "We have brains."

"Maybe it's even more narrowly focused. Maybe the virus attacks the paralimbic system. Psychopaths' are so underdeveloped that the virus can't get a foothold."

"Where does the hive mind come in, then?"

"I don't know. Maybe the virus communicates with itself, the same way ants or bees do."

"That reasoning seems sound," Pybus said. "As sound as anything does in a world gone mad."

"Wait a second. An ant colony or a bee colony or whatever—" Lilith began.

"Hive," Pybus said.

"—okay, hive. Anyway, they both have queens, right?"

"Yes," Pybus said. "I was only using those as examples, though. This isn't nece—"

The collision was loud and hard and for that instant, filled the world.

# CHAPTER 45

*9 hours*

Light had been paying attention to Pybus's insane theory, but in the moment after impact, he was snapped back into a very powerful reality.

The access road took them from the parking lot to AZ-87, or Country Club Drive. As he started across it, he vaguely noticed a car rolling toward them. Tired and distracted, it hadn't occurred to him in that moment that moving cars were exceedingly rare and that this one was coming fast but silently. Searching his memory, he saw what must have been a group of Infecteds teamed up to push it. Instinct had made him start to turn away from it and hit the gas, but too late.

Now the truck bolted toward an abandoned car-

carrier trailer loaded with Volvos. Light yanked at the wheel, trying to correct course.

He was too late. The Ford's bed glanced off the side of the trailer. The steering wheel spun out of his hand, and by the time he caught it, the pickup had gone up on two tires. For a second he thought it was falling back down onto four wheels, but then the tilt was more pronounced, and he knew they were going over.

The truck landed on the passenger side and skidded, spraying sparks. The din was hellish, the stink of superheated steel and the burned-powder smell of the air bags seared his nostrils.

Then it was still. There were sounds: the whirr of two wheels spinning, the creaking of the settling vehicle, the moans of those inside. The windshield was shattered.

Light hadn't been wearing a seat belt; he was crushing Fallon against her door. Sansome had been last into the backseat, so Lilith and Pybus had landed on him instead of the other way around. *Probably saved both their lives*, he thought with a grim smile.

The idea of going back to sleep was tempting. He shook that off. Infecteds had pushed the car. "Anybody hurt?" he called. At the same time, he tried to get off Fallon, but his leg was pinned behind her. His ribs hurt where the bullet had grazed him, and there was blood on his forehead.

"I'm okay," Lilith said.

"Aches and pains," Pybus said. "I don't think anything's broken."

"Fallon?"

Sansome spoke up first. "I'll be better when these guys get offa me."

"I'm—something's crushing my kidneys," Fallon said.

"That's me. Lean forward a little."

"Oka—ahhh!" she said. She gave a pained hiss, but shifted her weight, and Light jerked his leg free.

"We have to get out of here," he urged. "If you can reach your guns, grab 'em. We're about to have guests for dinner." He braced himself against the seat and kicked the rest of the glass from the edges of the windshield. Easier to go out that way than up through his door. "Come on, Fallon."

"Just . . . okay, I'm coming. God, it hurts."

Light squeezed through where the windshield had been. The passenger side had been crunched out of shape, making it narrower on that end. He reached in and took Fallon's hand, helped her slide out, and wondered how Sansome would ever make it through that space.

If they had to leave the big man here, maybe he'd distract the Infecteds long enough for them to get away.

Fallon stopped halfway out. With a whimper, she tugged away from Light and leaned back into the cab, feeling around for something. When she had it, she pulled herself out. Her precious prototype. *Lot of good it's going to do if some Infected chomps on your psychopathic paralimbic system.* Lilith scrambled out next, bleeding from the nose. She looked like she would have a black eye but would otherwise be fine. Pybus moved more slowly; he said that every muscle he had ached, including some he'd never known were there. Once they were out of the way, Sansome stood up, shoved open the driver's side back door, and hauled himself up and out. His already-brutalized face was cut in several new places; blood was everywhere, discoloring the top of his uniform.

Light pointed up the road at the oncoming Infecteds. "We need to move," he said. His M249 was somewhere in the wreckage. Fallon, Lilith, and Pybus had their M4s, and probably their handguns. All Light had was a knife, a Glock, and a pocketful of ammunition.

"There were boxes of ammo in the bed," he said. "Grab what you can and let's go."

Fallon still looked dazed, so Light had taken control. He didn't know how she would feel about that, but at the moment there wasn't time to discuss it. Light snatched up a couple of boxes of 5.56-mm rounds for the M4s and waited while Pybus and Lilith did the same. Sansome shoved box after box into his pockets. "Come on, come on!" Light said. "We gotta go!"

The Infecteds were getting too close. There were thirty or more; it was hard to judge in the dark. Not so many they couldn't fight, except that they were all a little woozy from the crash, and he had no idea what condition the guns were in. For the moment, running seemed like a good idea.

"People!" he cried. "Run! Now!"

Finally, the reality of their situation seemed to sink in. Lilith broke into a sprint. Sansome looked shaky but ready to go; he waited until Fallon took off, then followed, with Pybus after him. Light could have easily outpaced the older man but didn't want to let him fall too far behind.

Across the street was a cemetery, dotted with trees among the tombstones. A road cut through the center of it. "That's the way we need to go!" Fallon shouted. Light was glad to see her coming back to herself. "Through there!"

Light liked the idea. In the dark, between the trees and the headstones, maybe they could lose the Infecteds.

The air was cooler in the cemetery and smelled like earth and pine trees. Grass and dirt didn't hold in the heat like concrete and pavement did, and the trees helped shade the ground from the day's sunlight. The Sykos were making good time, racing past the markers set flush with the ground and into a section where there were taller stones, even some obelisks and a handful of aboveground crypts. Fallon had led the team off the main road—Light assumed because they were more visible there than they would be among the trees. They'd have to watch their step, though, or risk tripping over headstones and losing whatever advantage they gained.

Then he looked back and saw that Pybus had slowed down. The old man was running with one hand clutching his side. A cramp, Light guessed. They couldn't afford that. He stopped and started back toward Pybus, hoping he wouldn't have to use a fireman's carry to get them both to safety.

"You okay, Caspar?" he called.

Pybus nodded, but his face was twisted with pain. Before Light reached him, his legs gave out, and he tumbled to the grass.

Light hurried to his side, looped an arm beneath his, and pulled him to his feet. With his free hand, he picked up Pybus's M4. "We can't waste any time," he said. "They're almost on us."

"Just go," Pybus said. "I'm done."

"Don't talk crazy. It's just a cramp. You're fine." He started to run, helping Pybus, half carrying him. They were slower than Light by himself, by a wide margin. But it was progress, just the same.

He couldn't see the rest of the Sykos. Could they have gotten that far ahead? He kept plowing forward, scanning the darkness.

A low whistle caught his attention, and he spotted Fallon waving at him from behind a big double crypt. He altered course and joined her and the others.

"Is he okay?" Fallon asked.

"He had a cramp, that's all."

He released Pybus, and the man slumped to his knees. "No, I'm not. Guess I was hurt more in the crash than I thought."

Without the warmth of the man's body against his, Light realized his side was hot and sticky. Had his flesh wound started bleeding again? He touched his shirt.

No, way too much blood for that. He crouched beside Pybus, pulled the older man's shirt aside.

Blood bubbled from a gash at his ribs. He'd cut himself on something, maybe squeezing out of the truck. It was bad—even in the dim moonlight that filtered through the trees, Light could tell that. He thought he could see muscle, maybe bone.

"Oh, God!" Fallon said. "Can you do anything, Hank?"

"If I had any supplies, maybe. As it is, not much. I can apply pressure, try to slow the bleeding. But that'll take time we can't afford."

"I told you," Pybus said. He gritted his teeth, sucking air between them. "Should have left me back there."

"We're not leaving you," Fallon told him.

"You have to. I can't keep going. I'll only slow you down."

"Caspar—"

He cut her off. "I never did you any good anyway. I can't shoot straight. I can't fight. I don't know why you brought me in the first place."

"I didn't know then that I'd be coming along," Fallon said. "I wanted you to lead the team. I brought you for your head and your heart, Caspar. You reminded me that a psychopathic murderer was still a person, no matter what he'd done."

"Guys," Lilith said. She was looking over the top of the crypt. "This is supersweet and all, but those fucks are getting too close. We have to move or get ready to rumble."

"There's one last thing I can do for you, Fallon," Pybus said. He put his hands on the crypt's side, forced himself to his feet. "Let me do this."

"What?"

He drew in a deep breath, let it out with a wince. "Goodbye, all. It's been a pleasure."

Fallon started to reach for him, but he twisted out of her way and took off at a run, angling toward the Infecteds. As he ran, he shouted as loud as he could manage. "I'm the one you bastards want! Come and get me! My brain's delicious! I should know!"

When the Infecteds had locked onto him, he veered away. As he made the turn, his foot clipped one of the flat stones, and he went down. He made it to his hands and knees quicker than Light had thought he could, but then he stayed in that position. Light was afraid he'd already run out of steam.

"Come on," Fallon said. "If one's paying attention to him, they all are. Let's not waste the gift he's given us. I don't want to see this, anyway."

Light snatched up the M4 Pybus had left behind but hesitated for another moment, watching him. The old man turned his head their way, and there was a broad smile on his face. His glasses had fallen off, but he didn't seem to notice. "This is Waylon!" he shouted. "Waylon Jennings himself! Or whatever's left of him! I fell right on him! This was meant to be!"

Fallon yanked on Light's arm. "Hank!"

"Okay," Light said. Fallon was already sprinting toward the cemetery's other end. Light followed.

Behind him, he heard Pybus laughing as he started to run again. "You know what Waylon said! I ain't living long like this! Mammas, don't let your babies grow up to be zombies! Are you sure Hank done it this way? Come with me! What'll you do when I'm gone?"

Light wasn't a big country music fan, but he recognized some of those as song titles, and figured they all were, or variations on them. Pybus was still hollering them into the night when Light couldn't hear him anymore.

Or if not, Light wanted to believe that he was.

# CHAPTER 46

*7 hours*

The Sykos were quiet after the cemetery, as though the loss of Pybus had taken something vital from the group that Warga's and Antonetti's deaths had not. She supposed it was somehow fitting that he, at least, had perished in a graveyard. She imagined him and Waylon jamming on a fluffy white cloud somewhere, and the thought made her smile.

"Care to share with the class?" Light asked.

They'd come out of the Mesa Cemetery, across from Hohokam Stadium, and Book had told them to bear right until they got back to the canal. It would lead them east, straight to the basin.

There wasn't a lot of cover in the end-to-end soccer fields they had to cross, so instead of walking by the canal, they took the road that led to the back parking lot of the stadium, where at least a row of planted trees would mask their movements—to someone just glancing their way, not expecting to see people, they might just seem like slightly thicker trunks.

Fallon nodded at the last few trees ahead.

"Just glad we're almost there, at the end of the road. Book thinks he can follow the meteor's trail from where it landed in the basin, so we find it, evac out of here, and save the world. Seems worth smiling about to me."

The basin—shaped like an upside-down Arkansas—was where Book had told them it would be. They could see the small lake that covered half the detention-basin floor as water from various inlets trickled in, and the impact crater where the meteor had hit and burrowed partially into the ground.

"We're here, Book," she said. "Now what?" For a moment, Fallon despaired. What if he hadn't been able to locate it? They'd come this far, overcoming impossible odds, with enough time to stop Robbins from nuking the city. They'd lost three members of the team, two of whom she'd come to consider friends. She'd gotten her prototype back, but everything else seemed to have been for nothing.

"Hold on, let me cycle back through the satellite images. I meant to do it earlier, but things have been a little nuts."

"This is bullshit," Lilith stated, as Fallon relayed Book's words, and they waited for the analyst to tell them what had happened to their Holy Grail.

"Straight up," Sansome agreed.

"I've got it," Book said. "I switched to infrared and traced it through images from just after it crashed into the basin."

"That's wonderful," Fallon said. "But just tell me where it is!"

"Right—sorry. It looks like it was taken to a home belonging to the Sutter family, in that neighborhood to the northeast—1322 North Wilbur. Follow Glencove east—it's the street that bounds the basin on the north—make a left, and the Sutter place is just a few houses down. It's on the west side of the road, that nondescript color I think they call 'sand.' Pretty generic, really, but the address is right over the garage doors, so you can't miss it. You're close, so leave the feed on unless there's really an urgent reason why not. I want to be with you every step of the way."

"Got it. Any Infecteds around the neighborhood?" Fallon asked.

"There are . . . a lot."

"Really? Mister NSA Analyst can't give us any better estimate than 'a lot?'"

"A helluva lot?"

"Helluva lot. So much better."

"Just say a shit-ton and be done with it," Lilith interjected. "I'm ready for this to be finished. Even my prison cell is an improvement over fighting these things all the time, and running from them when we're not fighting them. Let's get it over with already."

"Couldn't have said it better myself," Light replied,

and Fallon couldn't quite tell if he was mocking Lilith or not.

"Okay, then. Let's lock and load." The words didn't sound nearly as alien coming out of her mouth now as they would have at the start of this mission. Maybe she was taking to the role of military leader a little too well. Fallon was pretty sure that if she uttered the phrase "assholes and elbows," she'd have to shoot herself.

The other three Sykos complied. Fallon holstered her Glock and pulled the M4 off her shoulder. Lilith and Sansome did likewise, while Light hadn't bothered to sling Pybus's over his shoulder since he'd picked it up. He had it out and ready. They all made sure they had fresh clips, then looked at Fallon.

"Once more into the breach?"

Light nodded.

"It's a good day to die," he said. "Well, for *them* to die, anyway." His smile was feral.

Fallon smiled back.

*Killing zombies makes strange bedfellows, I suppose.*

"Let's go," she said.

They headed around the edge of the basin, none of them wanting to walk through the brackish water. They were immune to transmission via infected humans, but who knew about the source? Better to stay away from anything that might have touched it until they had no choice but to touch it themselves.

They walked down the center of East Glencove, headed toward Wilbur. They paid particular attention to the spaces between parked cars and landscaping that could hide anyone bigger than a toddler. Fallon was sick and tired of being ambushed by these things. She was going to be ready for them this time.

And then they rounded the corner and froze in their tracks.

A sound had been growing, slowly impinging on Fallon's consciousness, but once they stopped, it hit her full force. There was a mass of Infecteds in front of them, halfway down the street, in front of what she assumed was the Sutter place. Though "mass" didn't begin to describe them. There were hundreds, packed around the house like red-eyed sardines, far more than they'd seen in any one place before. And they seemed to be . . . chanting? Moaning? Like Tibetan monks with a bad stomachache. When had they learned to vocalize, to try to speak? Before or after they learned how to wield the guns some of them were carrying?

" . . . aye . . . aye . . . aye-nnn . . . aye-nnn . . ."

"What the actual fuck?" Lilith exclaimed, and one of them heard. He turned, saw them.

Then they all did.

"Great job, Lilith," Light muttered.

"Shit. We can't face that," Fallon said, as the mob surged toward them, like one giant, amorphous creature with several hundred heads and twice that many legs. "Run!"

They spun and retreated around the corner, laying down suppressing fire that took out several Infecteds on the leading edge of the tidal wave, then turning and hauling ass back toward the basin the minute they were out of the sight of the Infecteds.

"Fallon, wait!"

It was Book.

"Are you kidding me?" she panted. "For what?"

"You need to stop. I can't get a fix with you moving like that."

"What are you talking about?"

"I can even the odds, maybe tilt them in your favor, but I need you to stand still and let them get close to you."

*He needed* what?

She couldn't do it. Stand there and let certain death creep up on her? No. She'd faced a lot of things in the course of this mission, but this was too much. She was too scared. She didn't want to die.

And then she remembered the device in her pocket. Elliott had said he'd tweaked it so it could ramp up psychopathic tendencies in addition to dampening them. Decrease empathy even further. Increase aggression.

Increase fearlessness.

Stopping short, she turned back toward Wilbur, just as the horde of Infected rounded the corner, still moaning, " . . . ainn . . . ainnnn . . ."

She pulled the MEIADD from her pocket, looked at it, intuited the changes Elliott must have made, and recalibrated it for superpsychopathy. Then she held it against her scalp, making sure all three contact points were touching, and pressed the button.

It was like the electrical shock you might get from

accidentally touching the metal prong of an appliance while it was still partially plugged in. And she could feel it working immediately, feel herself getting angrier, bloodthirstier, wanting to wipe every last one of those bastard Infecteds off the face of the earth, not caring if they might be able to be cured. She zapped herself again and felt all her fear melt away, replaced with a sense of invulnerability.

As she did, she heard the sound of an approaching aircraft, instantly identifiable in the quiet sky. Smiling wildly, knowing Book's reinforcements were on the way, she started back toward the Infecteds, firing her M4 into their leading edge. Light, who'd never needed his sense of fearlessness amplified, joined her. Then Sansome, on her other side, and finally, Lilith—which surprised Fallon—taking up a position on Light's flank. Together, the Sykos advanced, tearing into the Infecteds with a deadly spray of lead.

Then Book was yelling in her ear.

"That's good! Now, run! *Run!*"

She responded to the urgency in his voice, repeating the command to the others even as she turned to follow it. The Sykos were a scant thirty feet away when the predator drone unleashed a hail of Hellfire missiles into the crowd behind them.

## CHAPTER 47

*7 hours*

**L**ight's ears were still ringing from the multiple blasts as he picked himself up off the pavement. Bits of flaming cloth and paper floated down through the air like a rain of fireflies. He grabbed the M4 that had skidded across the pavement when the concussive force of the Hellfire missiles striking their targets had lifted him and the other Sykos off the ground and thrown them a good ten feet.

He turned to look at those targets. Several gaping holes in the asphalt looked back at him, filled with what remained of a hundred or more Infecteds. Some of the body parts there and on the street were still aflame, adding to the surreal hellishness of the scene, and the stench was nearly overpowering. Other Infecteds, no longer whole but not quite dead, writhed around on the pavement, still moaning their eerie syllables.

" . . . ane-j . . . ane-ja . . ."

God, were they calling for some sort of angel? What sort of post-Rapture apocalypse had he wandered into, anyway?

Then he smiled. If they were calling for him, a government-sponsored angel of death, he'd be more than happy to answer.

Houses on either side of the street were starting to burn, as were a few of the cars. Landscaping was catching fire, and the burning foliage only added to the dreamlike quality of the situation, as though he'd wandered into the nightmare of some unrepentant atheist on his deathbed, whose worst fear was that he'd been wrong the whole time.

The other Sykos were standing now, too, observing the aftermath of Book's missile strike.

"Not bad shooting for a bookworm," Light said, and Fallon chuckled.

Then the Infecteds who were still standing noticed them and started in their direction. More poured into the street behind those, too far back to have been injured by the missiles. Not the hundreds the Sykos were facing before, but still more than the four of them could handle.

"Here we go again," Fallon said, looking around. They were almost back to the basin. She pointed at the house to the north. "We're never going to get there using the street. Let's see if they're as good at chasing us when there are more obstacles in their way."

"Parkour!" Lilith exclaimed excitedly, a little girl getting that coveted dollhouse at Christmas. Only in her case, Light decided, it had probably been a toy gun.

"Whatever it takes," Fallon replied. "Let's go!"

She sprinted toward the house she'd indicated—its roof was starting to smolder—and Light was right on her heels, with Lilith and Sansome on his. They darted in between the house and its neighbor, shoving through a gate to the backyard. As they ran through, he and Sansome paused to pull the black trash and blue recycling bins over to block the gate. It wouldn't hold the Infecteds back for long, but every little bit helped.

They skirted the pool and reached the back wall, the ubiquitous cinder-block property divider that could be found everywhere in the Valley, like some sort of uniting force. Different races, different socioeconomic statuses, same walls. Light thought there was probably something profound about that, but right now all he cared about was scaling the damned thing.

Fallon bent and made a basket with her hands that Lilith stepped into. The girl scrambled up the wall, where she waited, grasping on to the overhanging branches of the neighbor's orange tree. Sansome boosted Fallon up the same way, then did the same for Light, with the two women helping to pull him up.

Then it was Sansome's turn. But even with the three other Sykos pulling from the top of the wall, they couldn't get him up. As they were trying to figure out some way to lift him, a crash across the yard made them all look.

The Infecteds were at the gate, pushing their way through the bins.

"Shit!" Fallon said.

Light agreed, looking down into the next yard. Then he let go of Sansome's arm and jumped down.

"What the hell are you doing?" Fallon's voice was surprised and suspicious. She probably thought he was going to cut and run. She was partially right, though that running wouldn't occur until a more auspicious opportunity presented itself.

He pulled out his knife and crossed over to a large sycamore tree that boasted a tire swing. He climbed up into the tree—a feat made easy by the board ladder nailed into its trunk, leading to a wooden platform from which a small hand dangled—and shimmied out onto the branch the swing was tied to. He cut the rope, put the knife in his teeth, and grabbed the branch, lowering himself until his arms were fully extended and he was hanging there like a piece of ripe fruit ready to be plucked. Then he let go of the branch, landing badly on his left ankle.

*Dammit!*

He could immediately tell it was a sprain, not a break, but it couldn't have come at a worse time. Still, he powered through the pain, slicing the other end of the rope where it was attached to the tire, sticking the knife through a loop on his pants, then hurrying back to the tree where the others waited as fast as his injured ankle would allow.

"Here!"

He threw one end of the rope up, and Fallon caught it, immediately understanding his intent. She leaned over and tied it to the trunk of the orange tree, then pulled the other end up and flipped it over the wall so Sansome could use it to climb.

Light could hear the other man grunting and the women urging him on. He heard a small cry of pain, then Sansome was on top of the wall, and Fallon was pulling the rope up and over to their side. Sansome went down first, stepping away from the rope gingerly. Light saw a gash along the back of his right calf and realized one of the Infecteds must have tried to stab the big man.

*Damn but those fuckers are getting smart,* he thought as he moved over to examine Sansome's wound. Lilith was on the ground now, and Fallon was just starting down the rope when a sharp crack echoed between the houses. Light looked up, expecting one of his companions to have fired on an Infected in this yard. Instead, Fallon climbed awkwardly down the rope, one hand clutched to the opposite forearm. She looked at the others grimly, showing her own wound.

"They have guns, and these ones know how to use them."

"We're fucked up the—" Lilith began, but Fallon cut her off.

"We are if we don't keep moving. Come on."

Light had determined that Sansome's cut was mostly superficial and didn't need treatment, but Fallon waved him away when he tried to examine her.

"Through-and-through. I'll be fine."

Light shrugged. No skin off his nose.

She started off toward the front of the house, dodging small cactuses and other overgrown pokey things Light couldn't identify.

"The next house over backs up to the Sutter place," she said, pointing to the left. She was headed to the right of the house, though, because that's where the gate was. "If we can come in from the back, maybe we'll have a better chance of getting close to the meteor."

"Or getting killed faster," Lilith said, but everyone ignored her this time.

As Fallon unlatched the gate and started to pull it open, several bloody hands reached through.

"Shit! Help me get this closed!"

Sansome and Light shoved their shoulders up against the gate so she could relatch it. Then Sansome boosted Lilith up so she could tell them how many were over there. A shot rang out, narrowly missing her head. When Sansome lowered her back to the ground, she was pale.

"That gate's not going to hold. There's easily a hundred of them, and more coming."

"Climb the wall into the yard by the Sutter place?" Light asked.

Fallon nodded. "Let's go."

But when they turned back, they saw that the Infecteds on the other side of the wall they'd scaled had figured out how to get over it—from watching the Sykos do it?—and were starting to pour over the cinder-block divider.

"Plan B?" Light asked.

Fallon looked around, saw a door.

"The garage! If we can get in, maybe we can get a vehicle started and get out that way."

She hurried over to it, tried the door.

Locked.

"*Dammit!*"

"Here, let me."

It was the first thing Sansome had said in a while, and everyone looked at him questioningly. He motioned for Fallon to step aside.

"Give me a jolt with that 'My-Ad' thing."

"What? I—"

Whatever Fallon had been going to say was drowned out by the sound of wood cracking. The gate was about to give.

Without another word, she pulled the device out, adjusted some setting or other, and zapped Sansome with it. He face got red, and he bared his teeth like a rabid honey badger. Then he turned to the door and rammed it as hard as he could with his shoulder.

Nothing.

Again, with a growl this time, denting the door.

A third time, with a primal scream, and the door flew off its hinges, striking the vehicle in the garage and bouncing off it to land at Sansome's feet. Then he stepped aside and waved them in, a strained smile on his face. Light recognized that look—it was the expression you made when you really wanted to kill someone but couldn't.

The vehicle was a white Cadillac Escalade, backed into the garage and big enough to hold all of them.

And to act as an Infected bulldozer.

"Keys?"

They look around for a key rack, but saw nothing.

Fallon looked at Sansome.

"Can you hotwire it?"

Sansome's hands trembled uncontrollably, like a Parkinson's patient's. "I could've before, but not now. Your thing has me too juiced up." *Not just that,* Light speculated. *Multiple serious injuries to his face, then the accident, that slash in his calf—it's a wonder the guy can still function at all.*

Light walked over to the driver's side door, intending to try to hotwire it himself. How hard could it be? And what other option did they have? He didn't want to make his last stand with a rake and trowel.

The windows were tinted, so he was as surprised as anyone when he opened the door and a body and a gun tumbled out. A woman, dressed in an upscale business suit and wearing enough bling on her fingers to finance a small Central American country. With a hole in the center of her forehead.

"Well, that's one way to go," Light commented, reaching over her and quickly rummaging through the purse sitting on the passenger seat. He found the keys, turned around to display them triumphantly to the others. "Lilith! Behind you!"

An Infected was standing in the doorway—an old man with a long white beard, bad teeth, and an ancient revolver pointed straight at the girl.

Lilith reacted first, squeezing the trigger of her M4 and filling the old-timer full of holes. When he fell, another appeared behind him, and Lilith shot that one, too. Then they all piled into the Escalade, shutting and locking the doors as more Infecteds appeared in the doorway.

Light looked at Fallon, and she nodded. He started the SUV, put it in gear, and hit the gas—heading straight for the garage door.

# CHAPTER 48

*6 hours*

The door exploded in a shower of splinters.

Most Infecteds still had slow reaction times; the Caddy plowed through them like a bowling ball scoring a strike. Its wheels humped over bodies in the driveway, and then it was in the street, running smooth.

Fallon was glad to have a vehicle again, even though the Escalade smelled like death. To be fair, outside, the odor was nearly omnipresent now; on every block, there were bodies, and the stink from each one rose and joined the others in an invisible, choking cloud. She wished there was an air freshener in the Caddy, maybe one of those paper pine trees hanging from the mirror, like her father had always kept in his Grand Prix.

*Another advantage of the MEIADD—I can tell the reek is there, but it's not nearly as strong as it might be.*

On foot, she felt more vulnerable to the Infecteds. Even the ones who could use guns now didn't seem to know how to drive, so with a working vehicle, the Sykos could always outrun them if they needed to. Unless, of course, they ran into another ambush. The Infecteds were getting good at that.

The other thing she liked about it was the cushy leather seat that held her like a lover's hug. She remembered those, from early days with Mark. She had liked them then, and loved him. Did she still? She couldn't say for sure, and with an amped-up psycho brain, it was no time to make such calculations.

Still, with her thoughts traveling down such avenues, she remembered something else from those days. Not at home, though—at the lab. She had never loved Elliott, not that way, but they'd been close. Mostly, what they had shared was awe. They were exploring the human brain and doing so in ways no one else ever had. It was the ultimate inner space. Even the universe had boundaries, or so the astrophysicists said. She couldn't quite grasp how that was possible—didn't a boundary mean there was something on the other side?—but the brain was genuinely infinite territory. A dedicated neuroscientist could be many things, but bored was never one of them.

Still, when it came to adrenaline rushes, lab work paled compared to scrambling through a city of monsters with a license to kill. She didn't think discovering an anomaly in a brain scan would ever again carry the thrill it once had.

The trip was short. Gary to Pasadena to Glencove to Wilbur—a tight circle in this suburban hellscape. Light took the first couple of blocks fast, to leave behind the Infecteds who had massed around the house where they'd found the car. They saw a few stragglers on the way, but the closer they came to the Sutter house, the more there were. While they drove, Sansome slammed fresh magazines into each M4—the last of their hundred-round double-drum magazines. That reminded Fallon of her Glocks, so she reloaded those.

Then they were back.

The Sutter place was on fire, as were several of its neighbors, but the flames hadn't really taken a foothold yet. They danced around the roof, on the side opposite the two-car garage. Some shrubs flanking it on that side were ablaze, too, and possibly more problematic because they were pretty close to the wall. The house could have been any house on any street in the area, maybe any street in the Southwestern United States. It was well kept, the yard neatly landscaped and trimmed. A storybook house, if the story was set in middle-class middle America and was about a plague of brain-eaters.

Light stopped half a block away. No streetlights were working, but the glow from the flames and the Escalade's headlights shone onto the Sutter driveway. Infecteds standing there glared at the Escalade, as if sensing fresh brains inside. Pybus's hive-mind theory seemed sound—every Infected in sight had turned toward the Cadillac.

*And the rest of them—citywide—know where we are. Someplace important to them.*

"We have to get to that house," she said.

"It's going to be a fight," Light replied.

"I'm ready," Sansome said. "More than."

Lilith yawned, stretched, and said, "Let's get this done. I'm so tired."

Fallon looked at the Infecteds again. They were coming down Wilbur toward the Sutter house, emerging from the yards of nearby homes. She had been thinking of herself as a scientist again, when what she needed was the heart of a warrior. A killer. She pulled the MEIADD from her pocket, placed it so the probes surrounded her paralimbic region, and turned it on.

The charge flowed through her, and she felt the effect almost immediately. Her bullet wound seemed like an insignificant detail, no more than a paper cut.

The Infecteds wanted to get between her and her goal? *Let them try.*

"Let's go," she said, throwing open her door. "I'm ready to kick some ass."

Light stepped out of the SUV, favoring his left leg. The back passenger-side door opened, and Sansome extricated himself slowly, followed by Lilith. "I don't see a meteor anywhere," Light said.

"Where would you put a meteor if you had one?" Lilith asked.

Light shrugged. "Garage, maybe? Backyard?"

"Well, you can't see either of those from the street, can you? Sometimes you psychos are fucking retarded."

"Watch your step, girlie," Light snapped. "Don't think you're indispensable."

"We're *all* indispensable," Fallon said. The last thing she needed was for her Sykos to start in on each other. Everybody was exhausted, dispirited, and irritable. Herself included, and with her extra-psycho jolt, she could add impatient to the rest of it.

Lilith took Sansome's big arm in her two small hands. "Fuck with me, Hank, and Joe will demolish your ass. Won't you, Joe?"

"I don't—" Sansome started to say.

Fallon cut him off. "Ignore them, Joe. We have real things to worry about."

And they did.

The number of Infecteds they faced was nothing like it had been before the Hellfires. But there were more than twenty, maybe closer to thirty. They were milling around in the flickering firelight, so it was hard to get a solid count. More streamed toward the house from every direction, like ants drawn to a picnic lunch.

Like others they'd encountered in the neighborhood, some of these were armed. One woman in her late sixties carried a shovel that was almost her size and might have nearly matched her weight. A man wielded a chainsaw, but he hadn't started it, reducing its intimidation factor considerably. Others were genuine threats: a guy holding a shotgun in a way that suggested he knew how to use it; a woman in a Western shirt, jeans, and boots with a revolver in each hand; a muscular man in a blood-spattered butcher's apron slowly swinging a samurai sword to and fro.

Most of them were murmuring or snarling or outright chanting the now-familiar "ane-ja, ane-ja."

"Three-round bursts," Fallon said, rolling the safety to that position. "Conserve ammo."

As the others followed suit, the man with the shotgun raised it, pressed the butt into his shoulder. Fallon took aim and squeezed the trigger. Her rounds went low, catching him midchest. He staggered and jerked his trigger. The shot flew high, over their heads. Fallon corrected her aim and fired again, and this time, his head shattered like a ripe melon dropped from ten stories up.

An Infected six or eight feet behind him got a faceful of blood and brain matter. She ran a finger down her fouled cheek, touched it to her tongue, made a face.

Samurai butcher lowered his head and charged. His gait was uneven, and more so when Light fired a burst into the top of his skull. Momentum carried him one more step before he sprawled forward, his sword hitting the street and spinning like the metallic pointer in a children's game.

Annie Oakley fired her right-hand pistol, then lowered that and raised the other, arms swinging in rhythm like they were on a swivel. Her first shot *spang*ed off the Escalade. Before she got another off, Lilith—having ignored Fallon's order—opened up on her at full auto, stitching up the woman's body from jeans to brow.

"Bursts, Lilith!" Fallon shouted. She swung her attention back to the Infecteds but sensed the one-finger salute the girl directed her way just the same.

The Sykos started forward again. Each fired bursts into the crowd—even Lilith— thinning it with every pull of the trigger. With the most dangerous ones taken out early, the others posed little threat.

Or so it seemed.

Because before they could react, a scrawny guy in a Flaming Lips T-shirt snaked a small semiautomatic pistol from behind his back and opened fire. Sansome took a bullet in the fleshy part of his right thigh. He let out a moan, shook his leg, and put three rounds in Scrawny's left eye.

Light mopped up, putting down the last two Infecteds with carefully placed bursts, then there was no one alive—or impersonating that state—between them and the garage. After Light made a quick tourniquet above the wound with one of the Infected's belts, Sansome broke the lock on the double garage's doors. While he did that, Fallon checked in with Book. "I don't know how much time we'll have here," she said. "The place is on fire, and there are more Infecteds coming this way—it feels like every last one in the Valley is zeroing in on this place. Can you tell *where* the meteor is?"

"I wish I could, Fallon," he said. "That's the house.

It's there, somewhere. It went in, and it never came out. I can't narrow it down any more than that."

"I guess we'll have a look around." She was trying to sound more casual than she felt. She really wanted to get in there and kill some Infecteds. Some part of her mind rebelled against that idea—some part well away from the paralimbic cortex, no doubt—but it would lose the argument.

"Listen, Fallon," Book said. "I have a chopper en route to you. It'll lay down some covering fire, to keep the Infecteds away from the house while you're inside, then track you to the basin so it can drop the containment pod, then land. You stay safe in there, and we'll get you out."

"I'm counting on it," she said. "Watch if you want to. We're going in."

Sansome slid the door up in its tracks, and a light flickered on automatically. There was a car on the right side of the garage. A washer, dryer, and utility sink stood up against the back wall on the left. A workbench lined the side wall, tools mounted neatly on a pegboard above it. Underneath it were toys: a plastic tool set, a play kitchen with a pink plastic stove and refrigerator, a big bin full of Legos. Everything neat, everything in its place.

Except the chunks of rock on the floor. They were green, and seemed to almost shimmer in the dim glow. A grin spread across Lilith's face, and she started toward them.

"Don't, Lilith!" Fallon said. "If those are pieces of

the meteor, we shouldn't touch them. We don't know anything yet about its composition, or what else it might have brought with it."

"Dude, that's fuckin' Kryptonite!" Lilith said. "Don't scientists watch movies?"

Fallon sighed. "You getting this, Book? Are we done?"

"Those are crumbs," Book's disembodied voice replied. "We need the whole cookie. The biggest piece of it, anyway. Keep looking."

The scuff of shoes on the driveway alerted Fallon. She spun around. The drive had filled with Infecteds again, and there were more behind them, on the street, coming their way. Some of them started up with the "ain-ja" chant, and soon they were all repeating it.

"I don't think they like us being here," Fallon said, wondering just how far away that helicopter was.

"If they want us out," Light said with a grim smile, "then I think we need to get *in*. The meteor's got to be in there."

**B**ook was trying to keep up with so many screens, he wished he had more eyes. Two UAVs crisscrossed high over the city, sending back forward-looking infrared footage of the city streets. Fallon was right; the Infecteds were on the move. Every group he saw was headed east, toward her and the others.

He was also trying to watch what she saw, and to monitor the Apache's gun camera. It was still a few miles from her location, but closing fast. The radio chatter from the chopper was nonstop, but he was barely listening—a lot of "roger" this and "copy" that, all of it meant for other ears than his. While Fallon was in the house, there wasn't much it could do for her, but if Infecteds tried to surround the place, the chopper could strafe them, maybe unleash a couple more air-to-ground missiles if it came to that.

*Her,* he thought. *I'm not even pretending to care about the others anymore. Is it the forced intimacy of watching essentially through her eyes, hearing her every utterance, her breathing, even, in rare moments of quiet, the rush of blood through her veins?*

*Whatever. I'm not analyzing anything I'm not paid to. All I know is that I desperately want her to come out of there in one piece. Whatever happens then happens.*

The video coming in from the Apache was infrared, like that of the drones. Until the sun came up, it was the only way to get decent images. People—regular uninfected human beings—came through as bright white objects moving through what seemed like a photographic negative landscape. But Infecteds burned even hotter—where enough of them were massed closely together, no detail could be seen beyond a big, white mass against a dark background.

Fallon was looking at Infecteds gathering around the driveway, just outside the garage. Then she snapped her head around so suddenly, peering into the garage, that he felt a wave of vertigo. She was saying something, but the radio chatter from the Apache had turned loud and anxious, so he swiveled to that screen just in time to see a . . . something . . . arcing out of the night, carrying enough heat of its own to show up as a very light grey on the screen.

He realized what it had to be at the same time one of the guys on the radio said it.

"RPG! Shit! We're taking—"

A blinding flash, then the screen went black, the radio silent.

*Where the hell did that come from?* Book checked the locations of the UAVs, but they were too far out to help—one over downtown Phoenix and one farther northwest, toward Glendale.

Who would have rocket-propelled grenades in the city? His thoughts immediately ran to the Raiders. They'd had all kinds of military-style weapons and a profound hatred of government.

But hell, this was Phoenix. Hatred of government was practically the local pastime. Amassing weapons ran a close second. It could have been a drug cartel or a right-wing "Patriot" group or some kids who'd ransacked an abandoned armory for laughs.

All he knew for sure was that he'd have to interrupt whatever report Robbins was getting and make sure there was another bird on the way to Fallon, and fast.

"We're coming for you," he mouthed into the microphone.

He couldn't tell if she heard, or not. It didn't really matter.

She had other things on her mind at the moment.

# CHAPTER 49

*5 hours*

"Inside, then," Fallon said, and Light nodded. He turned and shot an Infected who'd stepped into the garage. He hadn't been much of a marksman when they'd first started out, but now he blew the top of the Infected's head off with one shot.

*Hell of a thing to be proud of,* he thought. *But I'll take it.* "After you."

The interior garage door led directly to the kitchen. It was free of Infecteds though there were a dozen of them pressed up against the sliding glass doors, trying to get in. Light watched as one in back shoved against one in front, smooshing that Infected's face into the glass so hard that her bloody eyes burst like red grapes. Light had no desire to drink that wine, though.

The kitchen fed into two rooms—a large family room with a big-screen TV and a great room. As they passed the archway leading to the great room, a wall of "ain-ja"-chanting Infecteds poured through it as though an invisible dam had broken. They slammed into the Sykos, rendering rifles ineffective. Lilith was borne to the floor beneath the wave, while Fallon was forced up against a wall, struggling to get her Glocks out but eventually succeeding, with one in each hand. Sansome withstood the onslaught like the rock he was, using his rifle as a hammer in a game of Whack-An-Infected. He looked pale, and Light wondered just how much blood he'd lost.

Light got off easy; he'd been behind the others, guarding their six, and so missed the initial wave, only to be caught up in a second, smaller one. Three Infecteds surrounded him, one holding a kitchen knife and another wielding a bat. The third had a pistol, but the close quarters rendered it mostly useless. The butt of Light's M4 across the back of the Infected's hand made the gun completely useless; she dropped the weapon, and one of her fellow attackers kicked it into the kitchen. Light brought his rifle stock up under her chin with all the force he could muster, snapping her head back so hard a piece of her tongue fell from her bloody lips. His follow-through jammed the barrel of his rifle into the Infected's abdomen, and so he did what was now coming naturally—pulled the trigger and kept his finger on it. The bullets ripped into her, spraying him and the other two Infecteds with blood and viscera.

Then the one with the bat struck at Light's gun, knocking it from his hands just as he'd done to the first Infected.

*Fuckers learn fast,* he thought, going for his knife.

He plunged it into the bat-man's neck, listening to the thing's unintelligible vocalizations become unintelligible gurgling. He tried to pull the knife back out to go after the third Infected, but the tip was wedged in this one's vertebrae, so he twisted, hoping to sever the Infected's spine. It must have worked because the Infected dropped the bat and collapsed, still trying to gurgle out . . . whatever it was the lot of them were saying.

As Light bent to retrieve the bat, he felt a sharp, burning pain in the back of his left thigh. Whirling, he saw the last Infected crouched behind him, her blade bloody. The bitch had tried to stab him in the ass!

Angered by that in a way none of the other attacks had affected him, Light continued to spin, bringing the bat up. The tip of the bat caught her jaw, and the force of the blow—of his singular, directed rage—ripped it half off her face. The dangling bone and flesh didn't seem to bother her, other than turning her "ain-ja" into a pitiful and slightly ironic "aye . . . aye." She swung at his ribs as he twisted, trying to reverse the momentum of the bat. He sucked his gut in at the last moment, and she missed scoring his middle by a hairs breadth, maybe two.

But he had his own swing under control now, and he caught the barrel of the bat in one hand while he gripped the handle in the other. Then he took a page from Sansome's book and decided he'd play a game, too—pool.

Pretending the Infected's head was a cue ball, he brought the bat up horizontally, level with her head, loosened his grip, pulled the length of aluminum back, then popped it forward, driving the knob straight in the Infected's nose, crushing it up into her brain. She staggered forward, made one last swipe at him with the knife, then fell forward onto her knees. Light delivered the coup de grace, bringing the bat down on the back of her skull once, twice, three times. When he was satisfied she wouldn't be rising again, he looked up, ready for the next wave . . .

. . . just as Fallon put one of her Glocks to the head of the last Infected and blew it back to the angels the things seemed to want to be with so badly.

From his position, he could see the front door, through which more Infecteds poured into the great room. He couldn't see the meteor. Fallon stuck her head into the family room, then shook it.

"Not here."

"There."

It was Sansome, pointing down the wide hallway between the great room and the kitchen. It was full of Infecteds who made no move to attack them, instead massing in front of a door.

"Good call," Fallon said, "but how do we get to it?"

Sansome looked at Light.

"Hand me your bat," he said, and Light did so

without question, then bent to retrieve his—no, Pybus's—M4. When he straightened, he saw that Sansome was smiling. It was a gruesome sight, considering the condition of his face. "Follow me."

Sansome waded into the hallway, swinging the bat back and forth like the Grim Reaper harvesting souls. Infecteds fell before him, smashed up against both walls and trampled under his feet. Improbably, he opened a path, and Fallon followed behind, dispatching the Infecteds Sansome didn't kill outright. Light went behind her, limping, his ankle and thigh both in agony.

And then they were at the door. Sansome wrenched it open and stood aside. The others looked in and saw stairs leading down.

"The basement," Light said. "Of *course* it's in the basement." Then he looked at Fallon. "Ladies first."

She side-eyed him but started down the stairs, the others following. Surprisingly, none of the Infecteds pursued them.

The stench of death was stronger here. Light had noticed it when they entered the house, but as an EMT—and especially after all the killing he'd done since leaving the PIR—the odor had barely impinged on his consciousness.

The farther down the stairs they went, the stronger the smell became. Soon, Light could see limbs, torsos, and even decapitated heads strewn all over the basement's unfinished floor, illuminated by a strange green glow.

At the foot of the stairs, they discovered the source of the glow. Across the room, nestled among more body parts in the bed of a little red wagon, sat the meteor.

And beside it sat a little girl, maybe six years old, wearing a dirty, shredded pink dress and knee socks, the remnants of a satin ribbon still clinging to her disheveled blond hair.

*Is she immune?* Light wondered. *A psycho like us?* He could barely imagine being trapped in this basement that even he, a bona fide serial killer, found horrific.

But then the girl turned, and Light realized he hadn't really understood the meaning of that word until this moment. She wasn't a girl at all, not anymore. Her skin was green and scaly, covered in open sores, her eyes bleeding and bright red, blood all over her mouth and chin. She finished chewing on a handful of something slimy and grey, then wiped her mouth with the back of her hand.

"Hello," she said. "I'm Jane."

## CHAPTER 50

*5 hours*

**F**allon stared at the girl, momentarily dumbfounded, when she suddenly put two and two together. The Infected weren't moaning "ain-ja" over and over again, a sound Light had said he thought might be their attempt at the word "angel."

They were saying *"Jane."*

"So, that's a meteor in your wagon, isn't?" Fallon asked. "Where did you get it?"

"From the basin," Jane said matter-of-factly. "I was playing ball in the front yard with my brother and my little sister when we saw it shooting through the air. We went and got it with the wagon. It was hot. So . . . hot . . ." Her voice had taken on a dreamy quality, and her mouth had curved into a smile of pleasure that was far too adult for the face making it.

"Then what happened?" Fallon prompted, sure she didn't really want to hear it. Jane had obviously been Patient Zero, and the more they knew about her symptoms and how she'd come to be exposed, the better they would understand the virus and the better they'd be able to fight it.

But Jane wasn't finished.

" . . . so hot. And it made me angry for a minute, but happy, too. Like when Dory said that mean thing about me at school and I shoved her down and she got hurt and cried. It made me feel strong, like a superhero. And like I didn't want anybody else touching it. But I needed my brother's help to get it into the wagon and downstairs to the playroom."

So far—except for her not wanting anyone to touch the meteor—Jane was describing being infected, only without the cold- and flu-like symptoms that appeared during the incubation period. So why hadn't she succumbed to the virus?

Taking another look at the girl's lizard-like, weeping skin and the insanity that hovered just behind her eyes, Fallon realized she had.

"And where are your brother and sister now?" Fallon asked, wondering if they showed the same symptoms. Especially the brother, who, like Jane, had actually handled the meteor.

Jane shrugged again. "My brother ran away. My sister stayed." Jane's eyes flicked over to a pile of pink rags in the corner, back to Fallon. "For a little while."

Looking closer, Fallon saw that it wasn't a pile at all

but the remains of a toddler wearing a pink dress like Jane's. For the first time since this whole thing started, Fallon thought she might vomit.

A creaking noise above her pulled Fallon's attention away from the girl. She looked up, saw dust floating down from the ceiling, then looked over her shoulder at Light, who'd gone back up to the top of the stairs, just out of reach of the Infecteds who wouldn't—or perhaps couldn't—cross the threshold.

"Getting pretty crowded up here," he said.

Their moaning chant, "Ja-ane . . . Ja-ane . . ." could be heard more clearly now. It was getting louder as more voices joined in.

Fallon realized that the chances of the Sykos getting out alive were slim, and getting slimmer with every new Infected who joined the party upstairs. For a moment, she despaired, wondered if a bullet to the head wouldn't be kinder to her and all of her fellow Sykos than what surely awaited when they tried to take the meteor out of here. The nuke deadline was only a couple of hours off, so they'd probably miss it anyway.

But then her gaze passed over the corpse of Jane's little sister—a toddler, like Jason, her life snuffed out horribly, and much too young—and her resolve strengthened. She *had* to make it out of here. For him.

"She's the Queen," Lilith said abruptly.

Fallon looked at her, then at Jane, then back again, not following.

"What?"

"Of the hive," Lilith explained, having put it together before Fallon and the others. "The hive mind. She's the one controlling the Infecteds. You can hear them calling to her. They know we're trapped here, so why aren't they coming down to finish us off?"

"Because *she's* here," Fallon answered, finally understanding. She looked at the body parts littering the basement floor. "They're not worthy to be in her presence or do more than fetch her food."

"No, that's not true," Jane piped up, as Fallon was hoping she would.

"Oh? Which part?"

"I am their . . . Queen. But they do more than bring me food. They spread my kingdom, and soon it will cover your whole planet. And then I'll be Queen . . . of everything."

Fallon was not going to let that happen. She knew a little about bees and ants and termites—kill the queen, make sure there was no replacement, and the hive or colony collapsed. She didn't think a replacement was going to be an issue, so kill the queen it was.

She raised her Glock and leveled it at Jane's head, finger on the trigger.

And then Jane's form wavered, became Jason's.

"Please, Mommy, don't shoot me!"

A part of Fallon's brain knew it was some sort of illusion, that this close, Jane didn't need the hive mind to project her will—she could do it directly. But that part had no power in the face of her son pleading with her not to kill him.

Fallon lowered her gun.

"Jason?"

The other Sykos shifted behind her, and the part of Fallon's mind that was still rational wondered if they could see Jason, too, or if Jane was showing them other people they'd never be able to kill.

"I'm not a sie-koe-paf like you, Mommy," Jason said, his little toddler mouth struggling with the big word, his blue eyes earnest. "My brain isn't like yours. Mine is normal. You should protect me, Mommy, not hurt me."

He was right. *She* was the danger here, not him. *She* was the psychopath. How could she ever hope to be a good mother when every day she'd have to fight all the violent urges awakened by this mission? She might hurt him without even meaning to, in a fit of rage. Or worse, she might do it intentionally, just because.

No. If anyone needed to die, it was her, not her precious towheaded son.

Fallon raised the gun again, this time pointing it at herself.

"That's right, Mommy. The best thing you can do for me is let Daddy raise me."

The gun wavered. Jason's face dissolved, became her husband Mark's.

"It is, Fallon. You know it. The best thing for him is not to have a psychopath like you in his life. You need to do right by our son in death in a way you've failed to do in life."

Fallon knew she was supposed to feel guilty, but instead, all she felt was fury. She turned the gun toward him.

"*Fuck* you, Mark," she said, and pulled the trigger.

And then the world collapsed on top of her.

**CHAPTER 51**

*4 hours*

"**F**allon? Fallon! Talk to me!"

She heard the voice, but it was so far away. She reached out her left hand, felt only emptiness. She tried to speak, but the air she drew in was thick with dust and smoke, and she choked on it. Coughing hurt, more than she expected, eliciting a sharp, stabbing pain in her midsection.

"Fallon! Is that you? Are you okay?"

She coughed again, tried to spit, but couldn't. "M . . . Mark?" she managed. "Is that—?"

"No, Fallon. It's me! I mean—dammit! It's Book! Booker Eisenstadt." He sounded frantic.

"Book? Are you here?"

"No, Fallon. I'm at the—what the hell do they call

it, again? The tactical operations center. The TOC. You're at the Sutter house. I think the ceiling collapsed on you. The others are close to you, according to their GPS coordinates. Sansome's closest. Are you okay?"

"I—everything hurts, Book. I can't see. I can't move." Panic welled in her chest. "Book, I can't move!"

"Breathe, Fallon. Take in a deep breath."

"The air's full of crap. I can't breathe."

"You're breathing now, Fallon. Shallow breaths, then. In and out. In and out. Don't panic. You've got to keep your cool. I can't lose y—can't lose any more of you. You're so close!"

Fallon tried to fix on his voice in her ear. She remembered that now, remembered where he was. Where she was. In the basement of the Sutter house. That horrible, tragic little girl. And something else . . . all those Infecteds upstairs. And the house was on fire. "The ceiling collapsed?" she asked.

"I think so. I couldn't tell for sure—I could only see what the camera showed, and it was obscured pretty fast."

"What do you see now?"

"I see—move your head a little to the right, Fallon. Can you do that?"

"I . . . think." She tried. It hurt, but she was able to tilt her neck that way. "Like that?"

"Just a little bit more."

She did. It hurt like hell. She bit back a yelp.

"That's good," Book said. "That's really good, Fallon. Hold it there."

"I can't see a thing. God, Book, am I blind? Am I paralyzed and blind?"

"Easy, Fallon. Breathe. Breathe with me. In, out. In, out. In, out. You okay?"

"I'm scared to death."

"I know, Fallon. It'll be okay. There's—I think there's a ceiling beam across your chest. And something over your head, or at least part of your head. It's like I'm looking under a shelf or something. Can you sweep that area with your hand? Move whatever it is? It's probably carpeting, or a floorboard or something. It's not so heavy that you can feel it, right?"

"If I broke my neck, I wouldn't feel it anyway, would I?"

"If you broke your neck, you wouldn't have been able to move your head for me."

"I guess."

"Just try."

Moving her arm hurt even more than moving her head. Panic was millimeters away—she couldn't think about that, or she would give in to it, start screaming and never stop. She could hear things now, besides Book's voice in her ear. She heard people moving around, shuffling feet. Moans and bangs and crashes and something else, a crackling noise she couldn't place.

Then her own wail of pain as she moved her arm again, toward her face. He was right, there was something on her, but she couldn't tell what. She tried to do what he'd said, just sweep it away. It was too heavy, though. It wouldn't go. It was soft, and it gave when she pushed. But it was on top of her head and her head was on something else and it was heavy. She pushed it again.

It pushed back.

She heard it murmur something. "Ain . . . ja?"

God, it was an Infected! There was an *Infected* lying on top of her. It moved again, and she felt fingers on her scalp, reaching through her hair, and she screamed, and screamed, and screamed.

"Fallon! Fallon!"

"Book?" she asked. "Book, it's on me! It's on top of me!"

"No, no, Fallon! It's me. It's Joe! Just hold on!"

"Joe?"

"It's Sansome!" Book's voice said. "He's right there, Fallon. Let him help you."

"I got it, Fallon," Sansome said.

As he spoke, a weight was lifted from her, and she could see again. She saw Sansome's huge bulk, illuminated by some uneven glow. He was holding an Infected off the ground. A teenage boy, it looked like. He was on the chunky side, his belly showing beneath a black T-shirt, and he was struggling in Sansome's arms. The big man had the kid's neck in the crook of his elbow, and he was twisting it, then twisting it more. There was an audible *snap*, and the boy went limp. Sansome dropped him on the ground.

He wasn't dead, though. Fallon could still hear him shifting around on the floor, muttering, trying to stand up even though his limbs wouldn't obey his commands. "Joe," she said. She cut her eyes toward the floor.

"Sorry," Sansome said. He raised his foot high—Fallon saw his knee almost reach his stomach, saw the blood streaking his pants from the bullet he'd taken—and brought it down hard and fast. There was a stomping sound and a squishing sound, and then the kid was quiet.

Now that she could see, she was even more frightened than she had been. Book was right, there was a beam lying across her chest. She wasn't on the floor, she had fallen on something bumpy, uneven. Then she remembered the room before the collapse and knew what it had to be.

Jane's unwanted leftovers.

She wanted to scream again, but she fought the urge. There were Infecteds all over the room. Many had died in the collapse, crushed by debris or by each other. But some were still alive, and they looked hungry.

And there were flames climbing the far wall. Some of the Infecteds were on fire, too. They didn't look particularly concerned about it, yet, but they would be soon.

"Joe, can you . . . ?"'"

"Hold still, Fallon," he said. The strength had gone from his voice, sapped by his wounds. "It's wedged under this other one."

"Hurry, Joe."

"Fallon?" Book again. "Listen to my voice. Let Joe do what he has to do."

"Where are the others? Hank and Lilith?"

"They're somewhere close by, that's all I can tell."

"Are they . . ."

"They're moving. They're alive."

Fallon heard Sansome grunt, then a massive creaking of wood and something else, followed by a crash. Then he swept back into her field of view and lifted the beam off her. It was a strain—veins popped in his neck and at his temples—but he got it done. He was reaching for Fallon's hand, to lift her off her bed of body parts, when she heard a piercing shriek.

"Get offa me, you mealy-ass motherfuckers!" The shout was followed by a long burst of automatic-weapons fire.

Apparently, Lilith was okay.

Fallon took Sansome's hand. He helped her to her feet. She was dizzy, still a little disoriented, but when he released her, she found she could stand on her own. "Thank you, Joe," she said. Remembering Jane, she turned too quickly to look for her and almost keeled over again. Sansome caught her arms and held her up.

Jane was nowhere to be seen. A pile of rubble topped by a thick cloud of dust occupied the place where she had been. "What happened to Jane?"

"I don't know. You shot at her at the same time the ceiling caved in. I don't know if you hit her or not—you might just have hit falling wood or Infecteds. I think she's dead. Haven't seen her move, anyhow."

Now that Fallon was upright, she took in the scene. Infecteds had come crashing down on other Infecteds. Many had survived and were either finding their footing or already up. Unlike before, though, they seemed to have lost their bearings, wandering around in the wreckage as if looking for the mental connection they had lost with their Queen's demise. Light was upstairs shooting them in single-shot mode—he had been on the staircase the last time Fallon saw him, and most of that had miraculously survived when the overloaded floor fell through. Lilith was across the big basement room, in a corner, swinging her M4 like a club at the Infecteds trying to get to her.

Several were gathering in the vicinity of Fallon and Sansome. She reflexively patted her hips, looking for her guns. Sansome recognized the motion; he reached into the rubble surrounding his feet, and came up holding an M4. "Here. I don't know where yours is, so take mine."

"Thanks," she said. Reaching for it, she saw, behind Sansome—mostly blocked from her view by his bulk—a muscular Infected swinging a chunk of two-by-four in a vicious arc. "Joe!" Fallon managed.

Before she could get any more out, the club had struck Sansome's head, tearing a chunk of scalp loose. He went down on his knees, and the Infected hit him twice more. The third one broke through his skull. He pitched forward, and Infecteds swarmed over him, all of them grabbing for brains.

Fallon whipped the M4 into position and opened

fire. When the Infecteds piling on Sansome were dead, she released the trigger briefly, then took aim at the ones Lilith was trying to hold off. She fired until the gun was empty, then dropped to her knees beside Sansome and pawed through his pockets. She would mourn him later; for now there were still Infecteds to deal with. He had two unused magazines—*just like Joe, protecting me even in death*—so she rammed one into her gun and tossed the other to Lilith. "Last ones!" she called. "Conserve ammo!"

"Got it!" Lilith shouted back.

With both of them shooting, it didn't take long to clear the basement of Infecteds. The sounds of Light's battle against those upstairs were encouraging, too, as the gunshots came farther and farther apart.

"Do you think we've killed them all?" Lilith asked, stepping gingerly among the Infected corpses to join Fallon.

Fallon did a quick mental calculation, thinking about the millions of people living in the Valley. "Maybe all of them in the house," she said. "But not all, by a long shot."

"But without their Queen—"

"We don't know what will happen. Maybe they'll get a new Queen. Maybe they'll just be like they were at the start: slow-thinking and disorganized. No way to tell except to wait and see."

"I guess."

Lilith had reminded Fallon of Jane. She went to the mound of debris that had fallen on top of the girl. It came up to Fallon's chest, and much of it looked heavy. She shoved some of it aside, then worked with Lilith to get a few of the bigger pieces out of the way. They didn't stop until they saw one of Jane's lifeless hands. Fallon poked it with a long stick a couple of times, but it didn't budge.

"Looks like she really is dead," Lilith said.

"So it seems."

"What now?"

"Now," Fallon replied, "we find that damn meteor in this mess."

# CHAPTER 52

*3 hours*

They needed Light's help to dig out the meteor and its wagon and to carry them up the fragile staircase. As they did that, Fallon filled Book in on their progress. "Just get it back to that basin," Book said. "I'm dispatching another chopper now."

"*Another?*"

"Somebody shot down the first one. It was pretty close to you, which means there's someone in the neighborhood with an RPG. Watch yourself."

"I will, Book, thanks." She turned to Light, whose limp was becoming ever more pronounced. "How are you doing on ammo?" she asked him.

"One magazine left, after this one," Light said. "And it's mostly gone."

"Us, too," Fallon said. "We've each used some of our last one."

"I guess we'd better hope we don't have to do much more shooting."

"With the helicopter coming, we shouldn't have to," Lilith said.

"Your lips, God's ear," Light said.

They hauled the wagon through the garage and put it down in the street. She looked toward the Escalade.

The fire had spread through most of the houses on the block, sending ribbons of black, oily smoke infused with the scent of death into the sky. And the Escalade was engulfed, too.

"Fuck," Lilith said. "Our wheels."

"I see," Fallon said. "We've got to hurry. The wagon will have to do."

"You sure that's any better than just rolling the damn meteor down the street?"

The meteor chunk wasn't round enough to roll well, but Fallon didn't see the point in arguing. "No," she said. "Let's go."

One wheel was wobbly, and the handle was short—it was made for a kid to pull, not an adult. But they traded off as they worked down Wilbur to Glencove and west to the grassy expanse of the basin. The wagon gave them more trouble on the grass, which should have been mowed a week ago, but they got it into a flat stretch, away from any trees.

"We're here, Book," she said. "At the basin."

"They had some trouble loading the backup containment pod, but the 'copter's en route. Sit tight, Fallon. You're almost out of there."

Fallon didn't respond. She heard something like far-away thunder, and she paused to listen. "I don't think that's good," she said.

"What?" Light asked.

She held a hand to her ear, indicating that he should listen. He and Lilith both did. "What is that?" Lilith asked.

"I think it's just what we don't need," Fallon said.

Within minutes, her hunch was confirmed. Pale moonlight revealed that the sound was really the tread of many feet on pavement. Hundreds of Infecteds came from Glencove, and more from Pasadena, from Sirine, from the canal service road. A thousand, she guessed, or more, converging on the basin. They weren't chanting some mixed-up version of Jane's name, or vocalizing at all, just walking.

Toward them.

"Don't they know Jane's dead?" Lilith asked.

"She is, but whatever's in the meteor isn't. Maybe it's somehow aware and feels like it's under assault. Or maybe this has been the goal of the Infecteds all along—to make it to the meteor."

"What do we do?"

"Hope they don't attack."

"What if they do?"

Fallon shrugged, feeling resigned. They'd come so far. "Go down fighting," she said.

*What else is there?*

The Infecteds spread out around the perimeter of the basin, surrounding the Sykos, ranked six or eight deep in places. Fallon, Lilith, and Light readied their guns. Their ammunition wouldn't last long against such a crowd. The best they could hope for was that shooting some of the ones in front would make the rest think twice about approaching.

That would call for thinking, though; not an Infected's strong suit, especially now that their precious "ain-ja" was just a pile of limp limbs like her little sister.

Fallon's fear was that when something happened to open the floodgates, they would all charge at once. In that event, there would be nothing the Sykos could do to save themselves.

Finally, one Infected—a hipster with long hair in dreadlocks, a knit cap, and pants that looked like they were made of carpet remnants—broke from the ranks and started toward them.

"No!" Fallon called, raising her palm toward him. She put every ounce of command she could into her voice. "Stop right there!"

The Infected hesitated for just an instant, then continued forward. Fallon started to raise her M4, but Light said, "Oh, let me. Please."

"Be my guest," she said.

Light shouldered the rifle, sighted in on the hipster Infected, and fired. Brains and skull fragments chased the bullet through the back of the knit cap.

Another Infected started from the south. It took

Lilith three shots to put her down. "Let them get closer," Fallon said. "So you're more accurate."

"I *suck* at this," Lilith said, frustration evident in her tone.

"Better at sweet-talking men into doing your killing?" Light asked.

"Whatever works," Lilith snapped. "Got a problem with it?"

"Enough, you two," Fallon said.

Three more Infecteds broke away from the line on the east side of the basin, splashing through standing water. At the same time, one came at them from the north side and another from the south. If the dam wasn't shattering, it was at least springing leaks.

Then, above the eerie silence from the Infecteds, Fallon heard the roar of engines, growing nearer every second.

The helicopter!

"Not a second too soon, Book," she said.

"What do you mean?"

"Your chopper. The Infecteds are starting to be a problem."

"Fallon, I told you, the second chopper's been delayed."

"Then what—"

"I don't know!"

Headlights sliced through the gloom, and she knew that the engine sounds weren't from a helicopter at all. She remembered what he'd said about RPGs.

"Oh, shit," she said.

# CHAPTER 53

*2 hours*

"**W**hat?" Book asked.

"Just a hunch." She counted headlights as they rolled down the street toward the basin. Six in pairs, and two more single ones. Five vehicles, then.

"What, Fallon?" Book asked again.

"I think it's Reedley's Raiders."

"I was afraid of that."

"Not sure yet, but it's looking that way."

"Oh, shit."

"That's what I said."

"Well, you were right."

"I'll talk to you later, Book. I'm about to be a little busy."

"Please be careful, Fallon. The 'copter's on the way. You're almost home."

"Might just be a bridge out between here and home," she replied. "Over and out, Book."

He said something else, but she was no longer listening. The vehicles drew up behind the Infecteds—herding some of them onto the grass and down the gentle slope toward the three Sykos.

Instead of stopping, the people in the vehicles opened fire with high-powered automatic weapons. They scythed through Infecteds, who danced at the impact of multiple rounds, fell, and in some cases got up again, grievously wounded but still ambulatory.

"Sounds like they've got plenty of ammo," Light said.

"No surprise there," Fallon answered. "Don't let them near the meteor, no matter what, or it'll be Jane all over again."

"We're fucked," Lilith said.

"Not yet. Help's coming."

"Soon enough?"

"Soon as they can, Lily."

"I hate that name, Fallon."

Fallon was going to reply—she wasn't sure how, maybe snap at the girl, maybe apologize—but it was too late. Infecteds were rolling into the basin likes waves onto the shore. Cutting through them, bumping up over the curb and down over the grass, were the Raider vehicles. Two pickup trucks, a Jeep, and two trikes. Rodell—Rodent—was on one of them, and a Raider Fallon didn't recognize on the other. Al was in the back of one of the pickup trucks, a machine gun hanging from his shoulder on a strap. Reedley himself, in the bed of another truck, held an RPG launcher.

The vehicles stopped about thirty feet from the Sykos. Infecteds continued flowing around them. "I figured we'd find something if we followed the Redeye migration," Reedley said. The smile on his face could have been put there with a hatchet. Fallon had seen happier-looking rattlesnakes. "Didn't think it would be you, though. It's a pleasant surprise. We have things to talk about."

"I'm afraid we can't stay," Fallon said. "We have a thing."

"I didn't say you had a choice," Reedley replied. "Anyway, I can do the talking. You don't have to be alive for it."

"I thought your gig was *saving* people," Lilith said.

"People who deserve saving," Rodent put in. "Which don't include you."

Infecteds swarmed between the vehicles and the Sykos, seemingly undecided about which brains to go for. Fallon was critically low on ammunition; she gripped the M4 by its barrel instead, lifting it to her shoulder like a baseball bat, ready to swing.

Lilith was close by her side, ready to shoot if any came too near. There were still hundreds of Infecteds around them, as well as the Raiders, so going out shooting made as much sense as anything else, Fallon figured.

It was at that moment she realized she couldn't find Light. He'd been right there with them, but she swiveled her head painfully in both directions and didn't see him. *Figures he would take off when things look the worst.*

And they did. The scene was chaos: Infecteds passing between her and the Raiders, breaking the burning headlights into shards alternately blinding her and then vanishing; Raiders occasionally firing into the crowd of Infecteds, their muzzle flashes adding to the strobe-light effect. An Infected charged her, hands out to grab or claw. She swung the stock of the M4 into the woman's skull. Teeth flew, blood splattered, the woman fell. Another Infected tripped over the first. Fallon brought her weapon's stock down hard and fast into the man's head.

Beside her, Lilith fired a three-round burst at a couple of Infecteds who ventured too close. Fallon turned her head, saw them fall, then saw, through the mass of bodies, Light. He had left the Sykos behind and was working his way toward the Raiders. He kept Infecteds between himself and them, crouching low when he had to, or moving with one, then changing course behind another that brought him a little nearer. She caught a glimpse of his rifle in his hands, then lost him altogether in the mob.

An Infected grabbed her from behind. When crooked fingers caught her shoulders, Fallon lunged forward and bent down at the same time, drawing the Infected off-balance. She was still holding her gun by the barrel, but she whipped it around, upside down, so it was pointing behind her, and squeezed the trigger.

The Infected lost his grip. Fallon straightened, whirled around, jammed the barrel into the thing's face, and fired again. Only when he was falling backward did Fallon see that it was a boy who could have been president of his high school chess club. It took another few seconds for his identity to sink in. His sister had babysat for her and Mark, on some of the rare occasions that they went out without Jason. The boy had dropped his sister off and picked her up a few times, often enough that Fallon knew him by sight. They lived in Maricopa, but had family here in Mesa, if she recalled correctly. His name was Weldon, she thought. Something like that.

She closed her eyes, shivered, and decided having her eyes closed was the worst of all possible ideas.

For the moment, she was free of Infecteds. She scanned the basin for Light, found him again. He had almost reached Rodent's trike. He glanced back once. She thought his gaze found hers, but his eyes were in shadow. She couldn't see anything in them, or any hint in the traitorous bastard's body language that he had any doubts or regrets about abandoning her and Lilith.

Then he turned away again, dropped to a crouch, and aimed his M4 at Rodent, waiting, Fallon assumed for a clear shot. The Infecteds parted for a moment, and he took it. The gun barked, the muzzle flared, and Rodent crumpled, sliding from the trike's seat. One leg remained wrapped around it, and Rodent twitched uncontrollably as the life ebbed from him.

Raiders in Al's truck reacted. Fallon couldn't hear

what they were saying, but one of them jumped down and started toward the trike. Light leapt from behind some Infecteds and sprayed a long burst. The man went down, and another fell from the back of the truck. One headlight blinked out.

In the midst of that, Light darted to the trike and shoved the wounded Rodent off. Then he threw his leg over it and parked himself in the seat. He gunned the engine, jerked into motion. Light swiveled the handlebar-mounted machine gun toward the Raiders and squeezed the trigger. Fifty-caliber rounds slammed into the trucks and the Jeep, shredding tires, shattering glass, and punching through steel. Light bolted forward, into the crowd of Infecteds. Some scattered before him, others stood, motionless, as he ran into them.

For a brief moment, Fallon thought he was angling toward her and Lilith—that he had stolen the trike because all three of them could ride on it, and escape the Raiders and the Infecteds. That he meant to rescue them. It would mean leaving the meteor behind, but—

But no. He looked her way again, his shoulders square, his gaze steady, and he turned the trike away from them, headed toward the canal.

In the pickup truck, Al spun a tripod-mounted gun around and opened fire, cutting through Infecteds, churning up grass, then tearing apart the trike's rear tires. Light urged it on, but Al shifted his aim just a little. Fallon could see when the rounds hit Light; he released the handlebars and threw his hands out to his sides, his back arched, and he fell off the trike, which continued forward another few feet without him before coming to a halt.

Al kept shooting for a long time. Light's body jerked with every round, even long after he was dead.

"We're done for, aren't we?" Lilith whispered.

"I . . . maybe."

"I need to tell you something."

"Later," Fallon said.

"No, now. I just need to say, I only ever killed one person. You know, before. All this."

"Lilith, you don't have to—"

"Shut the fuck up, okay? Yes, I do. It was Uncle Phil. He and Aunt Bess mostly raised me, after my folks died. But I was just a toy for them, a fuck toy. When I was fifteen, Aunt Bess was giving me some money, to run away on. I guess she felt bad, or I'd gotten too old for her, or something. Anyway, Uncle Phil caught us, and he shot her. Then he started crying like a baby, and he begged me to shoot him. I was so pissed—a lifetime of pissed. So I did. I shot his ass with his own shotgun, then I reloaded and shot him twice more.

"So I just wanted you to know that. You know, in case we don't make it out of here."

"We will, Lilith."

"Yeah, right. You probably hate me now, huh?"

"No!" Fallon said. "Not at all. I appreciate you sticking by me through all this. You shot a bastard who abused you. Nothing wrong with that. Even if there was, you're more than that. Every one of you—even

Hank—is more than the bad things they've done. More than—"

She broke off the sentence. More Infecteds were closing in. "Get ready," she said.

"Fallon!" Book's voice, in her ear. "Fallon, it's almost there. You should be able to see it. Do you see it? Hear it?"

"Hear what?" she asked, distracted. "Never mind."

She looked at the western sky. There it was. The brilliant light in front, beaming down ahead of it, like the headlight on a train, the distinctive *whir* of its propellers slapping the sky. "I see it, Book. Tell them to fire at will, or whatever the phrase is. There are only two of us left, and everybody else here is trying to kill us. Smoke them."

"Is that safe?"

"It's the only thing that *is* safe. If they don't mop up this place, somebody's going to kill us. And it's not gonna take long, so let's get it done."

For a long moment, she thought the command hadn't been relayed. The chopper came closer, the circle of light skimming the ground just ahead of it. It dropped lower. Its light circle settled on the basin, and the helicopter hovered just behind it. The Raiders were looking up, and some started to lift their guns to shoot. The Infecteds, if they noticed it at all, glanced up and looked away.

Reedley raised the RPG launcher to his shoulder and balanced it there, trying to gauge his shot.

"Give me your gun," Fallon said. In the same instant, she snatched away Lilith's M4.

"Hey!" Lilith complained.

Fallon ignored her, put the gun's stock against her shoulder, aimed quickly, and fired.

Her aim wasn't what it should have been, or maybe it was the distance. Her rounds hit the truck's cab, blew out the windshield, and tore through two other Raiders before hitting Reedley. Even then, she only got him in the left shoulder. The RPG was on the right. She squeezed the trigger again, but she had emptied the magazine.

She had distracted him, though, slowed him down. Just enough. When a missile darted out of the sky, the entire truck he was in bounced into the air, spun once, and came down again in flaming shards. The shock wave hit Fallon seconds later, passing through her while she was still trying to process the brilliance of the explosion.

Then a machine gun started firing into the crowd. Its ratcheting noise was louder than the 'copter's engines, and its muzzle flashes were almost sunlight-bright. It started by shooting randomly into the mob of Infecteds, but soon corrected and pounded into the Raiders. Al got off a couple of shots before heavy rounds jellied his head. Another Raider shot a handgun at the 'copter, to no avail. He reached for a long gun, but bullets perforated his arm just below the elbow, and it hung there, connected by threads, until more churned into his chest, and he fell.

Fallon watched it fire, and fire, and fire some more.

"The pilot wants to make sure you're the people standing by the glowing wagon," Book said.

"That's us. Me and Lilith. We're all that's left."

"I'll let him know."

She had almost come to know when he was there and when he wasn't. When he was, he was like a presence. Like the way a house with somebody else in it feels different from an empty one. He was reassuring even when he didn't say a word.

He came back. "Okay for the chopper to move into position?"

Fallon surveyed the scene. Bodies everywhere. In the stark light it looked like a photograph of Gettysburg after the battle. They were Infecteds, mostly—a few Raiders, and Light—but still, it stung. In the rest of the country, people would get up tomorrow, go to work or school or stay home and clean and watch the little ones. People would love and sing and cry. Ideas would be born that would change the world.

These people—these who had been people, before they got sick—would never have those things. No more weddings for them, no more first days of school, no more promotions, no more vacations in France or Las Vegas or New York. No more sitting down to dinner with family and friends. No more rolling over in bed and caressing a partner's leg.

And the Valley? Phoenix might one day rise from the ashes, like its namesake. But not soon, not while the memory of contagion and slaughter lived on.

At least with Reedley and most of his lieutenants dead, his fiefdom would probably collapse of its own weight. That would help the healing, she hoped.

"Fallon?"

"Yes, Book?"

"You okay?"

"I'm fine."

"I've dated enough women to know what that means. You did it, Fallon, with almost two hours to spare. They're recalling the bombers."

"Yay," she said, too tired to summon genuine enthusiasm.

"What about the chopper? Is it safe to move in?"

A few scattered Infecteds still moved among the bodies. Some had started feasting on Raider brains, and a couple of them were near where Light had fallen, though she could no longer see his corpse. "Yeah, I think so."

A few moments later, the helicopter left its hovering position and seemed to nudge the sky out of the way until it was hovering again, directly over them. Fallon shielded her eyes with her hand but still couldn't look straight up at it. Wind from above blew her hair around, flapped her clothing, and when it hit the ground and kicked up again, it brought soil and loose grass with it.

"They're going to lower the containment unit, Fallon."

"Tell them to lower away. We're ready."

A momentary pause, then: "Here it comes."

Fallon shielded her eyes again, looked up, and saw what looked like a huge steel ball descending from the helicopter. She supposed she ought to feel something like triumph, or pride, or relief.

Instead, all she felt was numb.

## EPILOGUE

**G**etting the meteor into the lead unit was easier than Fallon had expected. The contraption was heavy but well designed, with hinges and catches right where they should be, and it opened smoothly on what she guessed were hydraulics. When she threw the final catch, there was a hiss as the unit was pressurized to keep whatever was inside it in.

Once it was sealed, the chopper landed so the unit could be hauled aboard, and Fallon and Lilith could climb in. Fallon was almost too tired to be airsick. In the east, the sun was rising into a clear sky, and she watched the light slide across the landscape, like the helicopter's, only much, much bigger. Lilith sat in her seat, hanging onto the straps that buckled her in, weeping quietly. Fallon couldn't tell if her tears were happy ones or sad, and guessed it didn't really matter. She would be evaluated, and she might receive a full pardon, or be released for time served, or at least be moved to a more comfortable facility. Part of that depended on her psychological condition. Now that Fallon knew the prototype worked, she figured she could help with that.

Which gave her an idea. She fished the MEIADD from her uniform pocket, reset it, and used it on herself again. Lilith watched, openmouthed. "Shit," she said, "are you going to go all Incredible Hulk or something?"

Fallon was quiet until she had finished dosing herself. Then she lowered the device to her lap. "I was going the other way this time," she said. "Tamping it down."

"You can really do that?"

"That was the original concept. Diagnose and treat."

Lilith looked at the thing as if it had just performed a miracle.

In a way, maybe it had.

"You want to try?" Fallon asked.

"Not . . . not now," Lilith said. "I gotta think about it. I'm all empty inside. Worn out."

"I understand. It's okay. Whenever you're ready, Lilith. Just say the word."

Lilith shot her a smile. Even with the filth and ash and the bruises she'd taken, when she smiled, she looked her age. Not so psycho at all. There was hope for her, Fallon thought.

Then they were landing on the helipad marked on

the raceway's infield, and a welcoming committee was waiting for them. General Robbins, Soledad Ramirez, Jack Thurman—most of the assembled brass stood at attention in the morning sunlight, along with a contingent of soldiers and equipment to cart the containment pod into a sterile facility, where the meteor could be safely examined. They were optimistic of being able to create a vaccine, Thurman said, based on work they'd done with captured Infecteds. Having the actual source would make the research go much faster.

Book waited there, too. He looked like he hadn't slept since they'd left. He probably hadn't, and Fallon knew she more than likely looked worse. Just the same, he broke into a huge smile when he saw her step off the helicopter, and she felt her own face doing the same. He walked toward her, fast but managing not to run. When he was close, he said, "Fallon," and she only heard it coming from his mouth, not that disembodied voice in her ear. She wanted to say something back, even if it was just his name, but she couldn't. Instead, she opened her arms and he came into them, and his hug was fierce and warm and real, and she liked it.

Finally, she was able to say, "Thank you."

"For what?"

"For being here. For being there. I don't think I could have done it without you."

"Oh, hell no," Book said. "You wouldn't have had a chance."

They both laughed at that, but then a sad look washed away Book's jubilation.

"What?" Fallon asked.

"Somebody's waiting to see you."

"Robbins, Thurman and those guys? They can wait a few minutes."

"No, not them. Over there." He nodded over her shoulder, past the helicopter. She turned but had to step around the helicopter to see anyone.

When she did, Jason spotted her. He tore his little hand from Mark's, and his face lit up as though the morning sun had brightened just for him, and he ran to her, arms out, laughing by the time he reached her. She dropped to a crouch and swept him up, held him, felt his arms around her, and she was laughing and crying at the same time, once more unable to speak.

Mark came next, moving more slowly than Jason's sprint. Reluctantly, she put Jason down so she could hug him. "Welcome home, honey," he said. He kissed her, but her lips barely responded, and he felt stiff in her arms. That was her, she realized, not him. He was trying, but all she could see when she embraced him was the past. Like an artifact from a lost civilization, he was something from before.

And this was after.

She wasn't the same woman he had known, had married. And he wasn't part of her tomorrow.

She looked at Jason again, standing, hands at his sides, watching her, still smiling. She wanted to raise her son, but not with Mark. She wanted to take care of him.

She wanted to make sure he was not a psychopath and never would be.

Then he coughed. Fallon knelt beside him. "Are you okay, baby?" she asked. She looked up at Mark, then back at Jason. "His face is flushed."

"It's just a little cold he picked up somewhere," Mark said. "Maybe a flu, I don't know. It's nothing."

"Nothing," she said. She wrapped her arms around her son again and held him, tighter and tighter, until he started to wriggle and writhe, struggling against her grip.

Until she had to let go.

## ACKNOWLEDGMENTS

The authors offer great thanks and appreciation to some of the people who helped bring this book to fruition: agent Howard Morhaim and Kim-Mei Kirtland, for finding it a home; editor David Pomerico and Rebecca Lucash for inviting it in and making it comfortable; Erica Wilson and Autumn Chartier, for service above and beyond; Catherine, for inspiration; James Fallon, author of *The Psychopath Inside* and Dr. Kent Kiehl, author of *The Psychopath Whisperer*, for information, and our family, for putting up with us.

## ABOUT THE AUTHORS

**MARSHEILA (MARCY) ROCKWELL** and **JEFFREY J. MARIOTTE** have written more than sixty novels between them, the most recent of which include *The Shard Axe* series and a trilogy based on Neil Gaiman's *Lady Justice* comic books (Rockwell) and *Empty Rooms* and *Season of the Wolf* (Mariotte). They've also written dozens of short stories and comic books/graphic novels, separately and together. Some of their solo stories are collected in *Nine Frights* (Mariotte) and *Bridges of Longing* (Rockwell). Mariotte is also editor-in-chief of Visionary Comics.

You can learn more about upcoming projects, both collaborative and solo, at marsheilarockwell.com and jeffmariotte.com.

www.harpervoyagerbooks.com

Discover great authors, exclusive offers, and more at hc.com.